Around the Way
Girls 11

Around the Way Girls 11

by

Treasure Hernandez,
Clifford "Spud" Johnson,
and *India Johnson-Williams*

URBAN
BOOKS

www.urbanbooks.net

Urban Books, LLC
300 Farmingdale Road, NY-Route 109
Farmingdale, NY 11735

ISBN 13: 978-1-60162-092-7
ISBN 10: 1-60162-092-6

First Mass Market Printing February 2019
First Trade Paperback Printing March 2018
Printed in the United States of America

10 9 8 7 6 5 4 3 2 1

Distributed by Kensington Publishing Corp.
Submit Orders to:
Customer Service
400 Hahn Road
Westminster, MD 21157-4627
Phone: 1-800-733-3000
Fax: 1-800-659-2436

Around the Way Girls 11

by

Treasure Hernandez,
Clifford "Spud" Johnson,
and *India Johnson-Williams*

Meal Ticket

Treasure Hernandez

CHAPTER ONE

"How in the fuck could this shit have happened? My son really never did anything to anyone and this done popped off. I can't believe it. That fool who shot him is gonna pay. If he and his mother think I'm just gonna sit here and not give a shit about this, they wrong. I swear on my life, the streets gonna run red with their blood when I get done!"

En route to the hospital, Yanna Patrice Banks was enraged. She was trembling with every deliberate word she spoke. Her lip quivered, and her heart was pounding. The Hennessy buzz the mother of two had no less than twenty minutes before was now completely gone. Keeping one hand firmly placed on the steering wheel, she used the other to search the contents of her purse. After removing a knife she kept just in case someone needed some act right, she tossed it on the dashboard. "I mean it. My baby is a good boy. He didn't deserve this. Motherfuckers gonna pay. I swear I'ma cut me a bitch tonight."

"Yanna, please stop all that cussing and drive like you got some sense. You gonna mess around and get us both killed. And, for God's sake, stop talking about who you wanna cut."

"Auntie, right about now I don't give a fuck." Yanna swerved around several cars that she felt were moving too slow. Repeatedly she honked her horn and flashed her high beams at a few more.

"Well, you should. What good are you or, for that matter, am I gonna be to that boy if we both dead and gone? Now, like I said, slow down."

Refusing to take her auntie's cautionary advice, Yanna did the complete opposite, in fact, speeding up. She had run every red light as soon as she got the frantic call from her neighbor. Her maternal mindset was reckless.

With the hospital finally in sight, she roared up toward the entrance in her truck. Just a few hours ago, she would have never been so hard on her brand-new truck, but right now she couldn't care less if somebody hit, scratched, or towed it. Not caring about the uniformed security guard pointing to the NO STANDING sign, she barely slowed down. Defiant, she blocked the emergency trauma room entrance of the hospital anyway.

Yanna turned the engine off and illegally parked. Hysterical, she abandoned her auntie, jumping down from the vehicle and bolting through the door, just as her injured son was being unloaded from the back of an ambulance. She couldn't stop her tears from falling, and she felt her heart racing as she strained to catch a glimpse of her son. When she finally saw him, it was as if the wind had been knocked out of her. His shirt was drenched with blood, and an oxygen mask covered his face. Yanna wanted to see his eyes. The streetwise mother wanted him to know she was here and everything was going to be all right. However, things were moving at a swift pace, much too fast for affirmations or emotions.

"Quick, hurry, bring him into trauma room four." The emergency unit nurse motioned to the paramedics. With a stethoscope around her neck, she ran alongside the stretcher. Yanna was, of course, trailing close behind as the nurse took charge. "A team of doctors is already waiting. Hurry for the patient! He appears to be going into shock."

"His pulse is dropping rapidly, and we can't get a heartbeat," one of the paramedics responded with extreme urgency. As he struggled to get the heartbeat, he realized the boy was bleeding heavier than before. He immediately knew there was something seriously wrong. Though he'd worked at the high-anxiety job for years, seeing these types of serious wounds still made him extremely nervous. Knowing their young gunshot victim was clinging to life, he started to sweat. "It's getting worse! This isn't looking too good. He's bleeding out. He's bleeding out! We need to hurry and get the bleeding under control. I need some help over here!"

JoJo had regained consciousness. He was moaning out in sheer pain. The pit of his stomach was burning, and the teen couldn't open his eyes. He couldn't seem to breathe. He couldn't move his legs. He tried, but he just couldn't. Suddenly his arm went limp and fell to the side of the stretcher, causing everyone to panic even more, especially Yanna.

"Oh, naw! Oh my God." Yanna's diamond tennis bracelet, which JoJo had just blessed her with a few days before, sparkled underneath the bright emergency room lights. It was as if this were an awful nightmare she was having, as she screamed out in painful denial. "Oh my God! Why, God? Why me?" It was almost more than she could take, watching her teenage son seem to be losing his battle to see another sunrise. "Please help him! Please! Please! He's just a baby! Come on, y'all, help him! Help him! Do something," she demanded in an ear-splitting voice, with tears pouring out of her eyes.

"Wait a minute, miss. I'm sorry, but you can't go back there." Though her tone was sympathetic, the gray-haired nurse held up both hands.

"But that's my son. I need to be back there. I need to let him know I'm here."

The nurse stopped the anguished Yanna dead in her tracks at the swinging metal double doors that led to the triage area. "Don't worry, miss. He's in good hands. The team back there is the best in the city. And I promise you, just as soon as we know something, one of the doctors will be right out to speak with you," she assured the boy's mother.

"Aw, fuck. Why did this bullshit happen in the first damn place?" Yanna hyperventilated as her sobs echoed loudly throughout the walls of the crowded hospital. Holding her chest, Yanna panted in an attempt to catch her breath. It felt as if someone had their hands wrapped around her throat, pressing on her windpipe. The bright overhead lights started to make her swollen eyes sting. The mild, temperature-controlled waiting area suddenly felt as if the heat were on "hell."

Yanna was emotionally drained. JoJo was her only son, her heartbeat, her rock. Now her child was on the other side of the door fighting to stay alive. The thought of that was almost too much to endure.

The frenzied mother collapsed into the arms of her auntie who, out of nowhere, had just come inside the building. Dressed in tight jeans and stiletto pumps, Yanna was close to blacking out entirely. "Why? Why is this happening to my baby? It wasn't supposed to be like this. It wasn't part of the plan," Yanna cried repeatedly, wishing she'd never let JoJo sell drugs to pay the bills and help feed the family.

"Yanna, stop it. Hush! You're making a scene."

"You think I give a fuck about any of these niggas in here? My baby is back there with blood coming from every-damn-where. I'ma say what I wanna say."

"Yanna, I understand that, but you still can't carry on like this. Now, come over here with me and let's sit down. Let's allow the doctors to help my great nephew."

As she snatched away from her auntie's grip, the anguish Yanna was feeling was apparent to everyone within earshot. "Naw, Auntie, I swear, if I could turn back the hands of time, I would. I'd trade in all the shopping sprees, the trips to the casino, and this jewelry I'm rocking." She snatched her gold chain off her neck, throwing it to the ground in desperation. "And that new Range Rover I'm driving; that too. I'd give all that bullshit back if I could only have my baby boy in one piece, not lying back there with two big bullet holes in his body!"

"Listen, Yanna, stop this. Keep your voice down, child." Auntie Grace sat in the dreary and drably decorated hospital waiting room, clutching her Bible. After opening her purse, she wiped away her distraught niece's tears with an old, tattered handkerchief she kept tucked in the side pocket. After somewhat calming her, she suggested she try taking it down a notch or two. "Everyone's looking at you over here performing. I know you worried, but please!"

"What?" Yanna shouted. She poked out her lips and sucked her teeth. "I don't care if they look at me 'til their eyes fall out their head. I'ma shut up when I want to, point blank and period! That's my son back there all shot up fighting for his life, not theirs." She gave real fever mean-mugging everyone sitting near her, including her auntie. Judging by her tone and facial expression, no one wanted to risk tangling with the agitated mother bear.

The longer her impromptu rant continued, the more she cried out in regret. Yanna resembled a raccoon as her eyeliner dripped down her face along with her tears. Normally she would never be out in public looking such a hot mess, but this night was definitely not normal. "JoJo ain't deserve none of what he's going through, not none of it. I wish I could see that no-good bitch and her son. It's both they fault my baby back there fighting for his life."

"You know what, niece? I'm going to, as you young people like to say, keep it real. Even at my age," Auntie Grace quietly reflected, handing Yanna her Bible, "it's simply amazing to me how things can go plum berserk so quickly. I mean, one minute you're riding sky-high on top of your game; and then, within a momentary blink of the eye, your soul is practically scraping the ungodly rock bottom of this wretched earth."

"Dang, will you please stop with all that church talk?" The weeping Yanna shoved the black leather book back into her aunt's hands. As she anxiously awaited any news about her oldest child, who was just yards away with two gunshot holes the size of golf balls in his chest, she was not in the mood for any lectures. "JoJo might die back there and you out here trying to take me to church! Old woman, bye! Kick rocks!" Yanna stopped crying long enough to give her auntie the hand.

"Now stop all that hand mess y'all young folk be doing and all that noise! Just stop it. And you can't really be sitting here blaming what happened to that boy on them." Auntie Grace hated that she was getting so frustrated with her niece's showing out. She couldn't believe that Yanna was in such denial about the role she played in her son's current predicament. It was no big secret that JoJo had gotten caught up in the streets just so he could help his mom. It was obvious to all what had played out over the past year or so. Plain and simple, Auntie Grace blamed her niece, and so would everyone else in the family. "You can't be serious right now. I love you and the kids, but come on, Yanna."

"'Come on, Yanna,' what?" Without shame, she turned her head to face her auntie.

"Now tell me, sweetie, was all that rotten, blood-soiled drug money your firstborn showered you with worth it? You running around town buying this and that, acting like a ghetto princess. Was it all worth it? That truck, that jewelry, those expensive purses and clothes?"

Yanna wanted to lash out at her auntie for what she had just said. She wanted to deny the insinuation that was made. After a few brief seconds, the red-faced mother sniffed, reaching for some tissue from her bag. Wiping her face,

Yanna didn't hesitate to respond, as others in the waiting room area ear-hustled on the low. "No, of course not. Why in the hell would I think any of those things were worth my son's life? Are you trying to be funny or some shit like that? Because this ain't the time. JoJo is back there messed the fuck up, and that nigga who shot him is alive and breathing out running in them streets."

Auntie Grace shook her head, realizing that Yanna was still missing the point. "First of all, that other boy has been arrested. Secondly, you need to take some responsibility for what you had to do with this, and have a long talk with God."

"Talk to God. That's some real bullshit. If God gave two fucks about me and mines why in the world did he let this happen to my baby? Making him be back there suffering?" Yanna questioned, looking up at the ceiling, arms folded as she rocked back and forth. "I know I was wrong to keep letting him sling those pills, but the money he was making day after day was so good, so he did what he had to do."

"Did what he had to do? Is that what you call making that innocent child your meal ticket?"

Yanna wiped her face yet again. She was not moved by her auntie's speech. "Look, the family needed it when your so-called God you love so much took my kid's daddy away from us. So, while you busy talking that shit about a Higher Power, we was in full struggle mode and JoJo stepped up." Yanna's tone was cynical as she moved her long blond-streaked sew-in weave out of her face, twisting it into a ponytail.

"God let all that happen, did He?" Auntie Grace sarcastically questioned.

"Here the hell we go. Yeah, He did. If you wanna keep it a hundred and wanna blame someone so bad for what my boy and me done suffered through the last few years, you can blame God. Or, better yet, maybe that no-good Tyrus and his crackhead mother, Dawn! JoJo's daddy got murdered messing around with them lowlifes so, yeah, that's about right." She focused on the entrance to the room where they were working on JoJo. "I should have known better than to let that troublemaking hooligan in my house! This shit is so fucked up. Fuck them and fuck God!"

"Yanna! You best hush up that mouth of yours, questioning the Lord and speaking ill of His name! Don't you dare blame Him for this awful tragedy." Auntie Grace jumped to her feet shaking her finger at her disrespectful niece. "This is entirely your fault, Yanna Banks, not the Man

Upstairs or those folk JoJo was running these Detroit streets dealing drugs with! Now, what you need to do, instead of flapping that smart mouth of yours, is think back to the role you done played in JoJo turning out the way he is." The old woman let her have it raw and uncut as the other people in the waiting room listened, shaking their heads. "Truth be told, you might as well have pulled the trigger of that gun yourself! Now, Miss I'm The Stuff, how's about that for keeping it real and, as you say, a hundred?"

Pissed, wanting nothing more than to curse out her old, sassy-talking auntie, Yanna sat speechless at her hurtful words and accusations. Yet, as her mind wondered back over the past couple of years, she couldn't help but question whether her auntie's words might hold some truth. Maybe she did put too much pressure on JoJo to step up to the plate after his daddy got killed.

Closing her eyes tightly and scratching her head, Yanna got chills as she thought back to where she might've gone wrong raising JoJo. Things were once so perfect in her life. She and her children used to be an entirely different family before drugs became the apparent head of their household. When JoJo started selling, things changed for the better so fast that it was hard to tell him to stop. Yanna had been struggling for so long. Easy street was a much-needed break. *Was I that selfish? Did I make my son sell drugs so I could live good? Dang, what did I do? Maybe it was my fault he got shot. What did I do?*

CHAPTER TWO

Five Short Years Earlier

"JoJo, call your father. Tell him dinner will be ready in about twenty minutes or so," Yanna ordered her son while wiping her hands on a dish towel. "Oh, and tell him I cooked his favorite: fried chicken, sweet corn, collards, biscuits, and gravy."

"Okay, Ma, I will," the elder of Yanna Banks's two children answered, and sighed. As he stood over his little sister, Jania, making sure she washed her face and hands before sitting down at the dinner table, he frowned.

"Oh, and please tell him to try to not be too late, either."

Joseph Lamar Banks Jr. was only twelve years old, but he shouldered a great deal of responsibility for a boy his age. Being the namesake of a stern but fair father was sometimes more than the rambunctious youngster could handle. Yet, he never wanted to disappoint the man he deemed as his time-to-time hero. Unlike most of his classmates, JoJo's parents were still married and living under the same roof. Even with the arguments and disagreements about anything and everything, they stuck it out. Although, truth be told, making the usual shameful call night after night was terrible. Summoning his dad home for his mother, supposedly from his "boy's house," was fast becoming a habit that was growing old with the youth.

"Hello, Daddy?"

"Hey, now, JoJo. Is your mom's dinner ready yet?"

"Yes, Daddy, and she said don't be late."

"Okay, I'll be there in a few. Tell her I said to keep the food hot."

"Okay, but she said don't be late," JoJo smartly repeated much to his father's dislike.

"Look, boy, I don't know who in the hell you talking to in that tone. But I said tell her to keep my damn food hot no matter what time I get there. Now go run and tell her that."

"Yes, sir." JoJo knew it was in his best interest to shut up and stop while he was ahead.

Each evening before JoJo went to sleep, he prayed his mother would get the courage to stand up for herself. He wanted her to stop being his father's constant doormat. He knew she deserved much better than how his overbearing father was playing her. However, if she didn't speak up, he knew he sure as hell couldn't. *God, please give my momma strength to stop Daddy from going over to that nasty, stank-looking lady's house all the time. I hate her and her dumb-dumb son Tyrus who gets to see him as much as me and Jania do. Amen!*

The man of the house, Joseph Sr., worked the early morning shift at General Motors on the line. He was a tall, muscular man in stature. Everyone on his close-knit block on the west side of Detroit knew him. Highly regarded wherever he went, whether it was out of fear of his quick-fire temper or just plain respect, the father of two was a force to be reckoned with.

Migrating from Alabama in the early eighties, Joseph Sr. had true swagger. He had Southern charm that made him the perfect gentleman to most. For those strangers who didn't know any better, from the outside looking in, Yanna was indeed blessed with a perfect man. It was true, and common knowledge to those living near the couple, that he was involved in an ongoing affair with Dawn Jackson. Ms. Jackson, a single mother of one, had recently moved into the area. Quickly known as the neighborhood good-time girl who slept with just about anyone who hopped, skipped, or jumped as long as they paid her, she currently had her claws in Yanna's husband.

Taking that one negative and outrageous factor out of the equation, Joseph Sr., head of the household, rarely missed a meal with his own family. A good paymaster, never late on one bill that crossed the modest threshold of their brick-framed bungalow home, he was a good provider. Since he didn't cause his wife to worry about the high mortgage, or about food in the cabinets or clothes on the kids' backs, he felt his shit didn't stink. Arrogantly, he felt his blatant indiscretions and the sideway glances of pity his spouse endured from neighbors were somehow allowable. Whenever his wife came in the house embarrassed and ashamed of what people would say out loud, as well as whisper, about his cheating ways, Joseph Sr. shrugged his shoulders. He would buy her a dozen roses or maybe treat Yanna to a brand-new dress to soothe her mental pain.

"Did you call him?" Yanna asked her son a few minutes later.

"Yes, Ma, I called." JoJo secretly rolled his eyes at her stupidity of dealing with his daddy and all his madness.

"And is he on his way?" Yanna wondered. She'd set the table and now rinsed out a few glasses. "I don't want his dinner to get cold."

"Instead of asking me all these questions, do you want me to go and get him from around the corner? I can." Receiving a cold, hard stare from his mother, JoJo instantly regretted asking her that million-dollar question. However, he couldn't help himself as he headed toward the front door. "I know what house she stays in. It's not a problem. I can go right now."

"What did you just say to me?" Yanna, with wet hands, slowly approached her son with a look of venom in her eyes. Jania watched like she was scared that her brother was seconds away from getting popped right in the mouth.

"Nothing, Ma." He wisely backed down, treading on dangerous ground, wanting to avoid trouble. "I didn't say nothing."

"I thought not." She angrily wiped her hands down her apron. In just those few seconds, her blood had boiled just enough to form a bead of sweat on her forehead. Embarrassed that now even her own children were mocking what she was putting up with, she fought back tears. "You ain't so big that you can't get a whooping. Now, go sit your wannabe-grown behind on that front porch and let me know the minute that man pulls up. You understand me?"

"Yes, Ma. I understand." JoJo twisted his lip up as he thought about how his father was disrespecting his mom every single day. *I wish he'd go away and never come back! I used to think he was everything. How could he do this to her?* JoJo looked at his mother and admired how pretty she was.

Yanna stood five foot three, with a sugar brown skin tone and shoulder-length, naturally curly hair. She had piercing brown eyes and a smile that could melt an iceberg. She took pride in being a good person. The thirty-four-year-old mother stayed immersed in helping the kids with their homework, keeping the house clean, and spending time with her kids every chance she had. For Yanna, her family was her life. She knew her husband was unfaithful, but she didn't want to be the one to rock the boat and break her family apart. Keeping busy, she hid from the reality that her husband was having an affair.

What didn't help the situation were the nosey women in her neighborhood, who always offered up their opinions about her husband's extra-marital dealings. It was like they had a personal vendetta, and made it their purpose to give Yanna daily updates on her husband's actions. Although most claimed they were just trying to help her or put her up on game, Yanna was by no means a fool. The loyal wife knew they were just trying to be all up in her business, and she refused to give them the satisfaction of knowing how hurt she truly was.

Yanna was determined to stay strong. She had convinced herself that this was just a bad season in her marriage and things would get better. She had come too far from her rough upbringing, and she refused to let anyone see her beak. She'd grown up in the projects and had no problem letting any female know, but she had long since outgrown street brawling.

Night after night it was getting harder and harder for her keep ignoring the truth, though. It took everything in her power not to march around the block and knock on Dawn's door. There had been countless times that Yanna had to stop herself from taking her good butcher knife out of the kitchen drawer and running up on Dawn. She'd thought about how great it would feel to shove the shiny and sharp blade directly into Dawn's black heart. The only thing that stopped her was the thought of going to jail if she got caught. She knew her children needed her. "For better or worse, richer or poorer," was Yanna's constant response to the women, while trying to hold her head up and keep her dignity intact. *One day, Dawn Jackson gonna get hers, y'all will see! That bitch can't just keep sleeping with the next woman's man and it be all good.*

Unfortunately, Yanna Banks wasn't the only one who suffered shame from her husband's constant cheating. JoJo would catch it going to the corner store, or at the playground, or even in the lunchroom line. Ridiculed by his classmates for having a "play stepbrother," Tyrus Jackson, JoJo tried his best to ignore the taunts. As much as he tried, though, the jokes and slick comments would eventually get to him, and he stayed in detention as a result of physical retaliation, disappointing his parents. His mother knew he was only taking up for her. And his father couldn't say much because JoJo's reason for fighting was something he refused to acknowledge. JoJo couldn't help but try to beat down the other kids for talking smack about how dumb his mother was for staying married to his no-good daddy. JoJo didn't want to fight, but he had to on principle even though deep down inside he knew his classmates were right: his mother was a fool.

JoJo did as he was told by his clearly agitated mother. Sitting silently on the wood steps looking back and forth up the block for more than twenty minutes, he grew inpatient awaiting any sign of his father. Just when he thought he'd die from hunger, Joseph Sr.'s two-tone pickup truck turned the corner and roared into the driveway.

"Hey, Pops. You know you're late," JoJo sarcastically pointed out to his father as he hopped out of the truck and made his way to the porch.

"What did I tell you about that mouth of yours?"

"I know, Pops. I was just saying." JoJo hoped he wouldn't receive a smack to his lips as he devilishly grinned.

"Yeah, okay, so just come on and let's eat," Joseph Sr. stated nonchalantly as he rested his hand on his son's shoulder and they entered the house.

They both walked into the dining room at the same time. "I'm starving, Yanna. I could eat a damn horse." Joseph Sr. smiled as the smell of the delicious foods assaulted his nose.

"I thought I told you to tell me when he pulled up." Yanna tugged her son's earlobe.

"Sorry, Ma. I forgot." JoJo quickly slid into his spot at the table across from Jania.

"What's the big deal, Yanna?" Joseph Sr. quizzed after witnessing his son's upbeat demeanor take a dismal change. "Just relax. Chill out."

"He's always forgetting something lately." Yanna judgmentally raised her eyebrow. It was obvious that she was more disappointed in her husband's tardiness than in her son's forgetfulness. Caught in her emotions, her eyes dared her husband to call her on it as she turned to retrieve the pan of homemade biscuits from the warm oven.

"Listen here, Yanna. I'm not in the mood to hear all that nerve-racking complaining you always doing day in and day out," Joseph Sr. scolded his wife as if she were a child. "That's why I stay away most of the time: that fly mouth of yours! I swear to God, you stay on your fucking period!"

She angrily turned with the platter of hot biscuits in her hands. "Joseph, have you completely lost your mind? Don't say that in front of my kids! Matter of fact, don't talk to me like that in front of my kids."

"Your kids? The last time I checked, they were my kids too, unless there's something you want to tell me. Moreover, I know damn well you not telling me what to say in my own house, are you?"

"No, but I—"

"But nothing," he insisted with his chest stuck out as he sat down at the head of the table. "Just bring me my plate so I can eat, take a hot shower, and go to bed. I'm tired."

Yanna, always one to back down to her bossy husband, decided to let him win this time. She knew if she kept at him his verbal insults would only get worse. In full submission mode, she prepared her family's plates and sat down, joining her husband, son, and daughter at the dinner table. As the family lowered their heads, Joseph Sr., who was the biggest hypocrite in the room, led them in a prayer before the family dug in. The family of four ate quietly as they devoured everything on their plates. First, the fried chicken disappeared, then all the greens, followed by the corn and mashed potatoes. Inhaling the aroma of a fresh, hot apple pie warming in the oven, the troubled husband and wife went through the normal ritual of idle chit-chat as they finished their dinner.

"So, how was your day?" Yanna asked Joseph Sr., trying to stay on his good side.

"Same as it always is, baby," he huffed while pouring honey on the last piece of bread, "long and drawn-out. I swear if I didn't have you and these kids who always need something or other I'd quit that factory and let some other fool have that headache-ass job."

"Babe, just be blessed you have steady work, as bad as the economy is."

"What you know about the economy? You ain't got no worries." He barely looked over to acknowledge her. "You living real good around here as far as I can see. You don't do shit but wake up in the house I pay for, cook the food I put on the table, and look after these kids I blessed you with. As far as I can see, you living the American Dream."

Yanna felt her spirits drop yet again. It was becoming harder by the day to endure her husband's verbal attacks and constant put-downs. Every time he left that home-wrecking whore's house he would come home acting as if he were a god without fault or sin. "I thank you for all you do, but you act as if I don't do anything at all and that's not necessarily true. It's not easy to do everything I do every day. And it's getting harder and harder to stretch the food budget you give me for these two here," she said matter-of-factly, watching her son and daughter drink their glasses of grape Kool-Aid. "And they say times are about to get much harder. So, um . . ."

Joseph Sr., fingers sticky and crumbs around his mouth, glanced upward from his plate. "Yanna, are you saying I don't give you enough to provide for my children? Are you saying I don't work hard enough in that sweatbox day after day?" He was now on the defensive as his voice got louder.

"No, dear. I was just saying the prices at the grocery store are going up." She once again backed down, fearing her man's harsh verbal tongue-lashing would increase in tone. "That's all I was attempting to say."

JoJo and Jania were used to the mental abuse their mother was forced to undergo, and they knew to just be quiet. It was best to stay out of grown folks' business, as they were reminded constantly.

"Can you tell me why you always find something to get on my back about?" Joseph Sr. barked at his wife with a slight pound on the dinner table, causing the pitcher of Kool-Aid to rattle. "I'm out there every day busting my butt, and all you do is sit around and constantly complain. If you don't appreciate me then—"

"Then what? Well, I guess that sleazy Dawn Jackson you keep chasing behind every day without any shame is perfect, huh?" Yanna mumbled under her breath as if she was second-guessing even making the comment in the first place.

You could've heard a pin drop around the table as Joseph Sr. let his fork fall onto the plate. He gave Yanna a wicked, crooked grin. "What did you just say, woman?"

Yanna took a deep breath before speaking. "You heard me correctly." She raised her usually timid voice, getting up out of her chair and showing she wasn't in the mood for any more of his bully routine. As she stood, she felt overwhelmed with confidence. She didn't know where this sudden burst of courage—or holy boldness, as the women in the church would have called it—came from, but she was going to use it up while it lasted. "I do my best to make you and this family happy, and all I get in return is grief. I'm tired of being second best. You gonna get rid of that home-wrecker Dawn once and for all, and I mean it. I'm done playing games with you and this marriage."

Joseph Sr. sat dumbfounded, at a loss for words. His wife had never called him out on his behavior before. And now, after seeing the hurt in her eyes and hearing the pain in her voice, he almost felt bad for messing around behind her back. He finally conjured up some words to speak. Yet, before he could respond or reassure his wife of his devotion to her, his cell phone rang, interrupting the spontaneous argument.

After taking his BlackBerry off his thick leather belt, Joseph Sr. looked at the screen. To his surprise, he saw Dawn's number flash repeatedly. Confused about the reason his side piece was calling him at this time of the evening, knowing good and well he was having dinner with Yanna and the kids, Joseph Sr. disrespectfully pushed the talk button. Sitting motionless at the table, his family listened in on his side of the conversation.

"Yeah! What? He did what? Oh, hell naw! Why is he even over there? Is he touching you? I'm on my way!" Joseph Sr. leaped to his feet. Grabbing his truck keys and almost knocking his small daughter out of her seat, he bolted toward the front door.

"Have you lost your damn mind, Joseph? Where do you think you are going right in the middle of dinner?" Yanna couldn't believe her eyes and ears as she and her two children followed her irate husband onto the front porch. In dismay she watched him jump in his truck. "Joseph Banks," Yanna irately called out, "you get back in here with your family right now! This is ridiculous! Enough is enough! I swear to God I done had it with this bullshit!"

"Yanna, y'all go back inside the house and finish eating," Joseph Sr. yelled as the nosey neighbors watched. "This doesn't concern you or my kids." He quickly backed out of the driveway and was on his way back down the street in the same direction he had come from less than a half hour prior.

Having no choice but to do as they were instructed, Yanna ushered JoJo and her young daughter off the porch and back into their home. Hours seemed to drag by as the evening sunlight disappeared, making way for the glow of the moon. The kids had long since gone to bed as Yanna, who sat on the couch furiously awaiting Joseph Sr.'s return, simmered.

I'm done! If he wants to be with that hood rat so bad, he can have her! I'm done! Yanna told herself, knowing deep in her heart, though, that she didn't want to lose her family just that easy. She closed her weary eyes for what seemed to be only a few seconds and fell into a deep sleep. Her subconscious took her back to her once "ra-ra, 'bout it, 'bout it" life in the projects before she was married with kids. It was a time when a bitch like Dawn Jackson would have been dragged out of her house by her hair for disrespecting Yanna.

"Yanna, why you keep having all these people knocking on my damn door all times of the day and night?"

"Dang, Momma, chill out. They're my friends."

"Your friends? Girl, them smart-mouth females ain't nothing but some troublemakers, and you turning out to be just like them. They out here selling drugs, setting niggas up, and just about begging to be killed or thrown in jail. You gonna mess around and get us all killed. Yanna, you need to straighten all the way up."

"Why you always tripping? Do I ask you for any money? Am I on your head about clothes or

sneakers or even buying this comb in my hand? Naw. I gets that shit how I live."

"Okay, smart ass. You wanna be so grown? One day that mouth is gonna get you in deep trouble and, when it does, don't come to me!"

Yanna ignored her mother's comments as she continued standing in the mirror fixing her hair. The wild-child teen teased her blond-streaked bangs. Then she sprayed spritz on heavy, making sure it stayed in place. After applying a huge amount of cherry-flavored lip gloss, Yanna was ready to hit the streets.

She and her so-called crew, the Cat Walk Posse, were headed to a party across town. They knew while there were going to be dudes posted in the basement who were getting money, there was rumored to be another all-female clique in the house. Simply Sleek were their rivals and were known for carrying blades. Yanna and her girls weren't scared. Matter of fact, they had sent word to the guy having the party that they were and would be ready for any female who wanted to pop off.

Arriving just before ten, it was all good. Piling out of the dark blue late-model Probe Yanna owned, they were already buzzed. Smoking a few joints and sipping on a case of coolers, the girls were in their zone. Time dragged by and the night seemed to be calm. There was no sign of Simply Sleek, which by all accounts was good. They were enjoying the party, the music was on point, and just about every one of the Cat Walk Posse had been chosen by the local drug dealers. Suddenly, as the clock struck midnight, all of that changed.

Seemingly out of nowhere, one, then two, then three, then four Simply Sleek girls appeared. Before Yanna and her homegirls knew what was happening, they were getting jumped. The same drug dealers who were just fawning all over them were leaning back on their expensive cars watching the show. Weave ponytails were being snatched out, acrylic nails were dug deep into faces, T-shirts were being ripped off, and breasts were exposed. Nothing was off-limits in this brawl.

Definitely holding their own, Yanna and her crew gave as good as they got. With each female almost out of steam, one of the Simply Sleek girls reached into her bra. When her hand came out, almost in one swift motion she opened a switchblade. Quickly searching around for something to use as a weapon, Yanna found a rake on the side of a house. The girl had blood running from her nose, and tears in her eyes. She held on to the blade and was swinging her arm wildly in an attempt to cut whoever got in her path. Watching the wounded bear like a hawk, Yanna and she locked eyes. In a mere matter of seconds, the girl charged at Yanna. It was back on as Yanna swung the rake, knocking the sharp blade to the ground. Before she knew what was happening next, her friend had picked up the knife and stuck it in the chest of a girl from the other crew. Blood was gushing from the wound, and everyone started to panic.

In the midst of the pandemonium, one of the neighbors announced that they had called the police. Everyone who'd come on foot ran. Each person who drove quickly pulled off the block. Even the dude having the party went into his house and shut the door. No one wanted to see the cops and answer questions. With the girl lying in the middle of the street bleeding out, she was surrounded by her crew.

Not wanting to risk going to jail over a fight they didn't start, Yanna yelled for the Cat Walk Posse to get in the car so they could bounce as well. Once in the car, Yanna tried over and over to start the ignition. However, as luck would have it, the vehicle wouldn't start. They were all yelling for Yanna to start the car, but it wouldn't turn over.

While they kept praying for the Probe to start, no one noticed that one of the Simply Sleek crew eased to the side of a house and went into a backyard. Seconds later, she returned with a small gas can in hand. Running up to the side of Yanna's car, she doused the doors and trunk. Just as she pulled a lighter from her pocket, God showed mercy on the Cat Walk Posse and allowed the car to start; but not before half the vehicle was engulfed. With screams of fear coming from the now-moving car, Yanna drove as fast as she could to a nearby alley where they all jumped out. They left it to burn as they ran as fast as they could. After they crossed a few vacant lots and were far enough from the burning wreck of a car, the girls caught two cabs back to the projects.

Back at home it was, of course, asked where Yanna's car was, but she lied and told her mother it had gotten stolen. Days later when the police knocked at the door, Yanna's mother kept the lie up, even stating that the car was no more than a piece of junk, and that was why they never reported it stolen. When asked about her daughter's reported involvement where another girl was stabbed and was fighting for her life, the mother lied once again.

After Yanna's mother covered up for her wayward child, Yanna was shipped out to the suburbs to live with her Auntie Grace. Luckily the injured female from Simply Sleek recovered and decided not to press charges on anyone, knowing her own homegirls would be in trouble as well.

Yanna knew she had dodged the bullet of bullshit and she was thankful. She decided to turn over a new leaf and leave the street life alone. Just like that, the bad girl from the projects had turned good. Right before her senior year, she met Joseph Banks, also a transfer student, and a football star. The two soon became inseparable. Yanna dedicated herself to making him happy. He was the love of her young life.

Yanna was startled by the loud sounds of the telephone. She sat straight up and wiped the cold out of the corners of her eyes. *Oh, now I guess he wants to call with some sort of an excuse before he pulls up. I wonder what lie he's gonna tell this time! I swear to God he can choke on a chicken bone and die before I listen to some bullshit excuse for dogging me and his kids out for some gutter trash.*

The angry wife recognized her husband's number on the caller ID, and she answered dryly, "Yes, Joseph. What is it? What do you want?"

"Hello, is this Yanna?" a strange voice replied.

A puzzled look instantly came across Yanna's face. Although she was certain it was her husband's phone number that appeared on the caller ID, the voice speaking on the other end of the line was clearly not Joseph Sr.'s.

"Yes, this is Yanna." She paused, momentarily shocked at not hearing his voice. "And just who is this?"

"This is Dawn." The woman's voice sounded meek.

"Dawn? Dawn Jackson? You have some fucking nerve," Yanna screamed into the receiver before she was abruptly cut off.

"Yanna, wait, please. It's an emergency! Please wait, it's important," Dawn begged.

"Oh, I bet it is. Well, you can take your emergency to nine-one-one, sweetheart, but don't call my house any damn more. It's bad enough—"

Once again, Dawn cut her off. "Yanna, wait. Just listen and don't hang up! Please!"

"How dare you! You've got some sort of nerve calling my house. Haven't you disrespected me and my children enough over this past year?"

"Please, Yanna, just listen to me!" This time, Dawn shouted with authority.

Yanna temporarily paused her crazed rant. She could tell at that point something strange was going on. "Look, what is it?"

"There's been an accident."

"What? Why are you calling me on my husband's phone? Where is he? Put him on the line." As she became nervous by the seriousness of the female caller's voice, Yanna fired question after question out to her husband's mistress.

"That's what I'm trying to tell you." Dawn started crying uncontrollably. "Joseph's been badly hurt. The paramedics are putting him in the ambulance as we speak. He's on his way to the hospital. He's asking for you. You'd better hurry. It doesn't look good."

"What?" Yanna loudly yelled, waking JoJo up out of a deep sleep. "Oh my God, what kind of accident was my husband in? Where are they taking him? To what hospital?"

"I don't know! I don't know! But it looks really bad." Dawn's tears increased. "There's so much blood everywhere!" She made the last statement sound as if she was looking at the blood as she spoke.

The fact that Yanna hadn't appreciated Dawn calling her one little bit now had to be put on the back burner as she dropped the phone to the floor and ran to get her purse. "Baby, I'll be back! Watch your sister and lock the door. Your father is hurt and at the hospital!"

JoJo was now out of bed. Standing in the doorway, he wiped the sleep out of his eyes watching his mother leave, rushing off to the hospital. Fighting the tears back, somehow he knew he'd never see his father alive again, and his young life would be forever changed.

CHAPTER THREE

The funeral was long and grueling for the many grieving relatives. Person after person got up to praise the deceased Joseph Banks Sr. for his past various deeds and work throughout the community. The way he was being honored definitely didn't fit the shameful way he had left this earth. Finding no comfort in becoming a widow with two young children to bring up in the wicked streets of Detroit, Yanna was emotionally drained over the entire thing. Thanks to one of Dawn Jackson's many boyfriends—who had shot her husband four times in cold blood, murdering him in a jealous rage—the distraught wife buried her face in her hands. As the service concluded and they rolled her man's silver and gray-trimmed casket out of the same church they exchanged vows in years earlier, Yanna sobbed.

Right before climbing into the back of the family car, JoJo, dressed in a dark blue suit, stopped dead in his tracks. He, like many others, couldn't help but notice the infamous Dawn Jackson and her son, Tyrus, aka his play stepbrother, standing amid the multitude of tearful mourners. It was rumored throughout the neighborhood and school that Tyrus, the same age as JoJo, unfortunately, had witnessed the entire murder take place, and he was the one to place the initial call to 911. JoJo wanted to ask his classmate right out what exactly took place the night his father was killed, but he knew he wasn't truly ready to hear the truth.

When Yanna became aware of the duo's uninvited presence, she removed her dark sunglasses and wiped her red, puffy eyes. After taking several deep breaths, she got in her zone. Confidently, the scorned wife-in-mourning marched over to Dawn while holding her Bible pressed close to her breast. With the stunned crowd of family members and friends looking on, the young widow was ready to give them a show. Yanna looked down at Tyrus, giving the little boy a faint grin, and then directed her full attention to his mother. Raising her hand, Yanna didn't hold back her rage and contempt for who she felt was the source of her pain. With all the force she could muster, she landed a well-placed smack across Dawn's face. Yanna, beyond furious, shook with every word she began to speak to the woman through her clenched teeth.

"How fucking dare you show up here of all places? Not even on this one day can you respect the union of our marriage. Haven't you done enough, said enough, and caused enough grief in my household? You got some nerve showing up, standing here like you give a fuck about anyone but yourself! It's because of you that my husband is lying up in that casket!"

Dawn was embarrassed. She was humiliated. The truth was a hard pill to swallow as it would be for anyone. The single mother of one just stood there silently, holding her stinging face with one hand and Tyrus's hand with the other. She wanted to speak out and defend herself. Dawn wanted to let the world know that what was being said was not who she really was, but she couldn't. At this point, it would be a battle she had no chance of winning, so she remained mute and took it all in.

Yanna continued her rant. Night after night, she had sat there and never spoken up about what was going on. For months she had been suffering the anguish from being looked upon as a second-class citizen since her husband first start running around behind her back. Yanna's husband was no longer around to hear what she had to say, but right now, in the land of the living, Dawn would endure the double wrath of Yanna's fury.

"You don't belong here, not at all. I don't care how you felt about my husband. How dare you even show up? You need to know that he never loved you! Never! I was his wife, not you." With malice, Yanna held up her hand, showing her wedding band. "Turn around, you no-good bitch, and take a good damn look at what in the hell you did!" Yanna pointed to JoJo and a crying Jania, who were off to the side holding hands, together mourning the loss of their father. "Do you see my kids standing over there?" She angrily waved her finger. "Thanks to you, they don't have a father anymore. Thanks to you, my husband is gone! Thanks to you, our family will never, ever be the same! You did that. You! Are you fucking happy? You're nothing but a home-wrecking slut! I hope all the wives standing around here watch their husbands whenever you around! You don't care who you open your legs to, you filthy whore! You lucky I don't do more than just slap you!"

Yanna shot her husband's side chick one last long glare before casting one last declaration. "You's a snake and ain't gonna bring shit but misery to whoever and whatever you come in contact with. I halfway feel sorry for your little boy even being cursed with having a mother like you. Trust, one day you gonna catch it! God don't like ugly, and He don't like tramps even more!"

When she was finished with Dawn, she walked over to her husband's casket. Since Yanna couldn't verbally give him a real piece of her mind, she had stayed up the night before and written him a letter. In the handwritten note, she made sure to inform her husband of how much she hated what he'd done to her and who he'd made her become. Yanna made sure to tuck it in Joseph's suit pocket. She wanted to have the final word with her spouse before he went to heaven or hell.

When the casket was closed for good, Yanna's family members ushered her to the long, dark-colored sedan. It was time to start the lengthy procession to the cemetery, which was located across town. Each of the married women in attendance whispered among themselves. Thinking that they could have easily been in Yanna's shoes, they thanked God they weren't. Tightly, they held on to their husbands' arms as they snarled, walking by Dawn Jackson, who was still subconsciously holding the side of her face and her young son's hand.

CHAPTER FOUR

After Joseph Sr. was buried and all was said and done, the reality of living as a single mom with two children set in. Yanna came to find out exactly where she and her children basically stood as far as finances were concerned. Her cheating husband had left his wife with several high credit card balances, one huge water bill and, of course, the mortgage. Even though she cashed in a $9,500 insurance policy, it mostly went to cover burial expenses, and she was almost flat broke. Having no other choice to provide for JoJo and Jania, Yanna took a job at a small factory. She knew that if they all didn't pull together, they'd be out in the streets or living with one of her relatives, which for her was definitely not an option.

"JoJo, fix the eggs while I get your sister dressed to go to Auntie Grace's. I'm running kinda late," Yanna ordered her son, who was now looked upon as the man of the house. "Thanks. I appreciate it."

"Not a problem, Ma. I got you!"

"Oh, yeah, I left that seven dollars you needed for a new gas container over there on the table." Yanna rushed through the house, getting ready for her shift.

"Okay, I'll get it as soon as I get finished with this," JoJo said as he began to prepare a skillet of scrambled eggs with cheese. After putting plenty of eggs on two plates for his sister and mother, JoJo scraped the last bit out of the black cast-iron skillet onto his own plate. "I've got three yards to do today," he shouted to his mom as he walked over to the kitchen table and sat down.

"That's good, baby," Yanna yelled back into the kitchen to her hardworking son. For the past four years since her husband's untimely death, JoJo had assumed the role of man of the house. He took on odd jobs in order to contribute to the household bills.

Those years had been harder than Yanna could have ever imagined. At some points, she grew so weary that she would lose hope. Each day in the single mother's life caused her to change for the worse as the bill collectors kept calling, demanding payments, and the shutoff notices piled up.

As the days dragged by, Yanna Banks, who'd easily gained thirty pounds over the course of the last four years, began sipping on more than just a small glass of wine with dinner. She had become spiteful and judgmental, still blaming Dawn Jackson and her son for taking away her husband. For Yanna, time stood still and the pain she felt after losing her spouse under those circumstances was weighing on her. Year after year, her anger increased and so did her bitter attitude. Yanna needed a crutch to lean on, and it was second nature for her to depend on the only man in her life, JoJo, whether or not he was ready for that responsibility.

JoJo was a good kid and just wanted to help his mother in any way he could. He hated having to see his mother work so hard. He also hated that she spent her downtime drinking. He missed the days when his mom would dedicate her time to him and his sister. Since his father's passing, his mother had become a different person. Being the only man in the house, JoJo stepped up and did everything he could for his mom and sister.

In between JoJo cutting grass, shoveling snow in the winter months, and staying on the honor roll in high school, he took care of Jania. The always-busy teen was faced with obstacle after obstacle. He was forced to grow up faster than the rest of his peers. When the new Air Jordans came out, of course he couldn't get a pair. Spending money on a fitted cap every week like some of his classmates did was also out of the question. Designer track suits, expensive jeans, or new games for a used Xbox that he and his sister shared, JoJo knew better than to even dream of. They weren't in the family's strict budget.

Things with his household's financial situation were looking more than dismal on one sunny afternoon when he walked up to his loyal customer's two-story home. Anytime he would cut Byron's lawn or trim the hedges, he never needed to bring his own equipment. Byron, a local drug dealer, had everything JoJo required in a shed located in the rear of the huge fenced-in backyard.

Byron wasn't like the average dope dealer in the movies, callous and demented with no use for anyone other than himself. He sat on the back deck reading books to his small son as JoJo cut the grass. Byron also coached football for the Police Athletic League. Even though JoJo didn't necessarily condone his over-the-top lifestyle and the way he made his living, he still understood the hustle and the grind. Life was hard in

Detroit and whatever someone felt they were forced to do to survive and feed their families was understandable, even if it was illegal.

Noticeably, this day was different from most as JoJo neared the front porch as he did every two weeks. Outside of all the strange cars parked in the driveway, something else seemed out of the ordinary to JoJo. Even though Byron knew a lot of people in and around the city, he never had this much company at his house at one time. The few occasions when he did see any of Byron's cronies, they were all pushing hotter whips than the ones that were now parked on the premises. It was like a used car parade.

"Um, yes, can I help you?" JoJo was rudely met by a middle-aged woman with a pile of men's clothes gathered in her arms. "What do you want?" the woman firmly asked as if she was getting impatient with him for taking too long to reply.

"I'm here to do the yard work. Is Byron home?"

"Naw, he ain't here, so don't be expecting no money for nothing or no handouts," she barked with her face twisted.

"Oh, he already took care of me, so it's all good." Byron always paid him for the entire month up front so even if, by chance, he wasn't at home, the job would still be taken care of without JoJo wondering when he'd get his money. Hearing loud voices, JoJo tried to inconspicuously play it off and look over the woman's shoulder. He was more than curious about all the noise and commotion coming from inside Byron's usually quiet home. "I come every two weeks," he added, still trying to investigate low-key.

Looking down at the growing grass then back over at the people inside, who were getting more boisterous as the seconds passed, the woman finally told JoJo to go ahead, cut the yard, and leave her alone. "Look, I tell you what, this is my house now anyway, and I don't want it looking a hot mess. So, yeah, go ahead and do your thing. And hurry up."

"Your house? Over my dead body," one man holding a small box of what appeared to be DVDs yelled out the doorway.

"Mine too," a female added her two cents. "He would've wanted me to have this house and that flat screen. I was his favorite cousin and y'all all know that."

What are they talking about, their house? When Byron shows up, he's gonna trip out on all these loud, crazy people up in his crib. Slowly heading to the rear of the house, a confused JoJo saw Byron's baby momma, Jasmine, and their five-year-old son pull up. Jumping out of the car, Jasmine appeared to be infuriated. *Good, here comes Jasmine!* JoJo knew Byron's son's mother was no joke. Everyone had heard the stories of her practically beating down any females from around the way who even considered trying to get with "her man."

"Hey! How y'all gonna be all up in the house like it belongs to y'all?" Jasmine huffed as she made her way up to the door, dragging her son by the hand the entire way.

"Girl, bye." The woman who had been so rude to JoJo was being just as rude to Jasmine. "This here is family business and don't concern you at all. You acting like you were his wife and not just another jump off after his money."

"Well, this is his son, his blood, so that makes it my business," Jasmine, with tears forming in her eyes, screamed back at the woman as she held on to her child.

By now, several people had come out of the house and had begun to congregate in the front yard. One by one, like tiny ants, they started loading clothes, shoes, televisions, and just about anything else they could carry from Byron's home into their hoopties.

"Listen here, Ms. Thang, with ya uppity behind," one other person spoke up, "real talk: unless you got papers to this or that"—she pointed around then planted her hands firmly on her hips—"then you need to step. Byron was our relative, so that gives us first grabs at everything in and around here!"

"Y'all so disrespectful it don't make no sense." Jasmine, now crying, shook her head in disgust. "He hasn't even been dead twenty-four hours and y'all over here behaving like a pack of wild vultures!" Byron's son started to cry as his mother shouted at his cousins, aunts, and uncles. "He couldn't stand none of y'all when he was alive, so what makes y'all think he'd want y'all to have anything of his?"

"Oh, well, he ain't here to answer that himself now, is he?" a cousin smartly replied as she carried three leather jackets in tow even though it was the beginning of summer. She then laughed, placing them inside of her open trunk. "Stop being a hater, Jasmine. You done got yours from my big cousin when he was alive; now we getting ours!"

"Yeah," another supposed relative concurred, holding a microwave. "And, anyway, what in the hell is you doing here anyway? You and that illegitimate baby of yours live clean across town and not here with Byron. Obviously you just mad we beat you to the punch." There was more laughter among several of Byron's family members at Jasmine's expense.

"Unlike all of you desperate bums," Jasmine said in grief, with puffy, red eyes, "I've got keys to this house, and the property inside belongs to me! Y'all assholes over here stealing from a dead man instead of mourning his loss! Y'all off the fucking hook!"

Frozen in his tracks, JoJo realized that Byron was not just away for the time being, but that he was dead. Getting a hard knot in the pit of his stomach, he leaned against the concrete wall in denial. Since his father's death, Byron was the closest person to the youth who had passed away. Even though they weren't homeboys or running partners, JoJo and Byron had a mutual respect for one another, and he would definitely miss their semimonthly chats. *Dang, I wonder what happened. Damn!* JoJo let his emotions take over as he closed his eyes thinking about why people had to die, especially so young. *Life ain't fair.*

Finally, after regaining his composure, JoJo went into the medium-sized shed and pulled out the lawn mower. Byron had paid him to do a job, and even though he wasn't gonna be there on the back porch making him laugh, he still knew that he wanted to cut the grass one more time to fulfill his obligation.

As the loud sounds of the mower ripped through the yard, JoJo couldn't help but overhear the shouts, screams, and apparent smashing up of items inside the house. While trimming the hedges, JoJo sadly noticed Byron's small son who'd somehow wandered out of the house and was standing near the curb.

"What's going on, li'l man?" he questioned the child.

"Nuttin'." The boy shrugged his small shoulders.

"Tired of all the big people making noise, huh?"

"Yes." He covered his ears, which were big just like his now-deceased father's. "And I want my daddy!"

Before JoJo could console the small boy any further, remembering exactly how he felt the day his own father passed, Jasmine barreled out the front door with arms full of her and her son's belongings that thankfully weren't snatched up by Byron's ill-mannered kin. After tossing the stuff in the rear of the car, Jasmine looked over at her son, who stared down toward the pavement to keep from crying.

"Come on, baby, let's go before Mommy messes around and catches a murder case!" She snatched the distraught boy up by the arm, practically throwing him into the passenger seat, not even bothering to safely strap him in.

"You best get on," one cousin yelled from the porch, watching Jasmine roar off the block, which was now crowded with onlookers from the neighborhood who'd gotten the word Byron had been killed the night before.

JoJo was pissed off to the eighth degree as he marched in the backyard and grabbed a broom to clean up before he left the premises for what he knew would certainly be the last time. When the teen was almost ready to leave, the same woman he'd first encountered when he'd arrived came out onto the back deck. With an apparent attitude, she walked out into the middle of the freshly cut grass. After seeming to survey his work, she called him over.

"Listen here." She frowned. "I want you to take that lawnmower and all the rest of that stuff out of that shed and off my property! Do you understand?"

"Excuse me, miss?" JoJo wanted to honestly smack the cow mess outta the rude woman, but he was always taught to respect his elders, so he held his composure. "I don't understand what you mean."

"Everything ain't always meant for you to understand." She placed her hands on her wide, oversized hips. "That ugly shack is blocking the place where my new gazebo gonna go! Now, is you gonna clean it out and take all that junk with you, or do you want me to flag down one of these guys out here scraping? Which one is it gonna be?"

After only a brief moment of hesitation, JoJo happily headed over to the shed to gather as much of the newly acquired lawn equipment as he could onto a steel pushcart. *Thanks, Byron. I know this is a blessing from you.* Snatching off the ground a royal blue tarp that was thrown in the corner, he noticed something strange. Leaning over to inspect what seemed to be hidden in a cardboard box, he couldn't believe his eyes as he crouched down.

Even though he was raised in a two-parent household before his father died, and he avoided the street life that tempted him on a daily basis, JoJo recognized what most would call a gift from the street gods. *What in the* . . . JoJo puzzled himself as he glanced over his shoulder to see if anyone was watching or paying attention to what he was doing. *I must be dreaming. I gotta be!*

As he peeked into the small duffle bag, which had a broken zipper, he pulled out a manila envelope. Opening it, he saw it was stuffed with twenty-dollar bills, neatly arranged with all the faces to the front, and wrapped in red rubber bands. Under the envelope were several thick gallon-sized Ziploc bags with huge amounts of pills in each. Digging deeper, JoJo discovered another brown paper bag with a couple of plastic tubes of weed and a digital scale. It took him all of five seconds to figure out his next couple of moves.

Instinctively, having been born and raised the hood, the teen tucked the bag inconspicuously under one of the hedge trimmers. After looking back over his shoulder, he tossed the worn tarp on the cart and used a few bungee cords and old clothesline to secure the items down.

"Hey, boy," the woman rudely shouted from the rear window, startling JoJo. "Hurry the fuck up and get off my damn property. And there ain't no need to come back around here, either. I'ma get a real company to do my landscaping from now on out, not some inexperienced little nigga looking for a handout!"

"Yes, ma'am!" Quick to grant her wish, JoJo began pushing the cart up the driveway with one hand and the lawnmower with the other. Sweat started to pour down his face and in his eyes as the summer sun beamed down. After turning back only once to see if anyone from Byron's house would change their minds about the belongings the woman just insisted he take,

JoJo nervously took the side streets to get to his house.

Preoccupied with what he'd just seen in the shed and now had hidden on the cart, the "lawn boy" had totally forgotten about the other yards he was scheduled to cut. For now, they would have to wait. He had other things on his plate to deal with.

CHAPTER FIVE

Rushing the pushcart into the empty two-car garage, he unfastened the cords to retrieve the duffle bag. Wasting no time, JoJo raced in the side door of his house and straight to his bedroom. After turning the lock with the skeleton key, he closed his blinds and took the envelope out. He was still pretty much messed up in the head about Byron's untimely demise, but this blessing that had fallen into his lap had him feeling anxious and excited. "This has got to be a dream or something. I can't believe it. Twenty, forty, sixty, eighty, a hundred." JoJo took his time counting all of the money in the folder.

By the time he finished counting, he realized he was $5,300 richer. That was the most money JoJo had ever seen at one time. It was way over the total amount his weary mother, who often volunteered to work double shifts and overtime, brought home in almost three months. Amazed with his sudden cash windfall he'd recounted repeatedly, JoJo didn't pay any attention to the bags of multicolored pills still in the duffle bag, or the weed.

"I'm gonna give half of this money to Ma," he proclaimed out loud, "then buy a new pair of sneakers for me and Jania and another lock and chain for the garage." He decided he'd take some time to figure out what he wanted to do with the rest of the money.

After spending all afternoon with a pen and paper, mapping out what to do with his half of the money, JoJo finally heard his mother come home with Jania trailing right behind. Before he could inform Yanna about his blessing, not to mention the tragedy of Byron's murder, he saw the look of despair plastered on her face.

"What's wrong, Ma?" He took two bags of groceries out of her hands and set them on the dining room table.

"My job at that tired factory just issued layoffs and, as you can see, your mother was one of the lucky ones who won't be getting a minimum-wage paycheck come next week."

Watching her ball up the pink slip and throw it into the trash, JoJo knew that it was his cue to save the day, so to speak. He dashed back to his bedroom, lifted his mattress, and grabbed the three stacks of money.

"Hey, Ma! Guess what," he asked, excited, returning to the kitchen. "I got good news and bad news."

"Please not now, JoJo baby." She sighed, fighting back tears from getting yet another disappointment from life. "I forgot the sauce for the spaghetti. Can you please run down to the store and get a jar?"

"Yes, Ma, but—"

"Please, baby. Tell me when you get back. Your sister has to eat, and I have a major headache."

"Not a problem, Ma. I got you!" Tucking the wad of cash in his front pocket, JoJo headed out the door and up the block to the corner store. The hardworking teenager never had that much money in his possession. He felt like a million dollars with every step he took.

Just when JoJo felt no one could rob him of his happiness, he bent the corner and ran smack into trouble. It was Dawn Jackson, the woman his mother blamed for all of their misfortune. Much to Yanna's delight, Dawn was now the proud owner of a few new rightfully earned titles. Instead of a being labeled a slut, tramp, and home-wrecking whore, she was now the neighborhood smoked-out crackhead always in desperate need of a fix.

Dawn's son, Tyrus, who detested the embarrassment of being birthed by such a female, was standing there as usual too. He was always trying relentlessly to get his mother off the streets. Every day he'd beg and plead with her to come home with him, but she never listened to her son. As fate would have it, she was not the slightest bit interested in Tyrus or any of his bright, life-altering ideas. Her life had gone from bad to worse ever since Joseph Banks Sr. had been murdered in her home years prior. The neighborhood's longstanding residents had heeded Yanna's warning. Dawn Jackson was ostracized and ridiculed by everyone who knew her now as well as back then. It was as if she actually wore the scarlet letter etched into her forehead. Ashamed and embarrassed by the way people viewed her, Dawn had turned to drugs to avoid facing her reality.

"Hey there, baby boy." Dawn sluggishly slurred her words, not immediately recognizing JoJo. "I know you want some of this good-good right here." She placed her boney hands on her hips and shook her body in a circular motion.

"Naw, I'm good." JoJo was five seconds short of throwing up in his mouth as he looked his dead father's ex-mistress up and down. He wondered what in the world his dad could've seen in this crackhead to make him cheat on his mother.

"You sure about that, baby boy?" Dawn squinted while trying to comb her dirty fingers through her tangled hair. "I don't need much to get me out the gate."

"Yo, Ma, what in the hell is wrong with you?" Tyrus snatched her up by the elbow, jerking her to the side of the doorway. "Is you all the way crazy or what? What is you doing? Stop it!"

"Get ya hands off me, nigga," she yelled at her son as JoJo disappeared into the corner store. "I could've got me a few dollars from him since you ain't giving me nothing to work with. And I know you got it with your selfish ass!" She rolled her bucked eyes with attitude. "You out here hating on me and that boy was buying. I know you seen him staring at me like he was."

"Shut the fuck up; damn." Tyrus shook his mother yet again while slamming her against the store's concrete wall. "Do you even know who the fuck that was you was out here trying to push up on? Do you? Huh? Do you?"

"What difference do it make to you if he got some money to give me? You always running behind me trying to act like you my daddy or something!" Dawn rubbed her shoulder as she snatched away from his strong grip. "I'm ya momma, nigga! You damn showl ain't mine!"

Tyrus shook his head with contempt. "Why are you always embarrassing me? Ever since I was a kid around this motherfucker, it's been the same damn thing! You need to get some help, maybe rehab!"

"I don't need no help, Tyrus. What I need is some damn money, and that straightlaced-looking boy seem like he got some to give, so fall back."

"Look," Tyrus demanded of his mother, "when he comes outside, leave him the fuck alone and don't say nothing else to him. You understand me? Nothing!"

"What's the big deal, Tyrus? Why you all up in my face about some fool?"

"You so high right about now, you don't even realize who that is."

"Whatever." Dawn posted up by the store's doorway still hoping to hit the teen up for his spare change. "Who is he supposed to be, the president or some shit like that? What in the hell makes him so damn special he can't be talked to?"

"Well, smart ass, that was JoJo. JoJo Banks! Now, does that name ring a bell in your dense mind?"

"Huh?" Dawn asked in a surprised tone, not sure of what her only child had just said.

"Oh, now you wanna pay attention and play the dumb role?" Tyrus, head lowered, turned around, walking off before his former classmate had the chance to come out of the store and clown him. "You make me sick. I swear to God I wish you were dead sometimes, like you caused that man to be. At least I'd be free! Ol' boy's mother was right in what she said all them years ago. Your black ass is a curse."

"That was little JoJo," Dawn whispered under her breath as she stared down at the pavement. She felt a bit of shame cloud her cracked-out brain. "Are you sure that was him? Are you positive?" she called out to her son, who was on the move.

Tyrus threw his hand up, dismissing his mother without even turning around as he walked out of sight. *I'm 'bout done with her crazy ass. That bitch getting all the way outta control.*

Standing over to the far side of the store's glass door, a jumpy Dawn waited as patiently as she could for the son of her murdered ex-lover to come out. She wanted nothing more than to apologize to him for her off-the-chain behavior. Even though the extremely addicted woman had a monkey on her back the size of Texas and was craving to get high, Dawn let potential sponsors pass by. Stunned by what her son had said as well, Dawn felt that she at least owed the young teenager an explanation why she'd come on to him the way she did.

Eventually, JoJo appeared from behind the store's doors.

"Hello, JoJo." Dawn tried unsuccessfully to rub her matted hair into a ponytail, straighten out her oil-stained blue jean skirt, and lick her dry lips.

Disgusted, he turned his head in disbelief that she even had the nerve to speak his name. "Please just leave me alone. Please."

"Listen, I don't mean any harm. Can I talk to you about something?"

"Talk to me? What could you possibly want to talk to me about?" JoJo twisted his face, shrugging his shoulder to the side in an attempt to avoid Dawn's filthy hands trying to touch him. He was in his feelings all the way around. "I already told ya crackhead ass I'm tight on anything like that bullshit you was talking, so you can kindly get the fuck out my face!"

"No, no. I just wanted to let you know I'm sorry for asking you what I did in the first place. If I'd known you was my Joseph's little son, I wouldn't—"

"Your Joseph? Did you just really say that? Are you fucking serious right now?" The youngster stopped in his tracks. Looking her up and down he laughed loudly. "Those drugs you on must really have your mind messed up or something, stepping to me like that. Your Joseph. Get on with all of that!"

"All I meant was that I was wrong and ain't mean to disrespect you." Dawn followed him halfway down the block. Still trying to plead her case, Dawn was relentless. Tyrus watched, ashamed, from the steps of the porch of one of his associates. "Your father was a good man, and I really did love him. How is your mother doing these days? Is she okay? How's your sister?"

JoJo was infuriated. He was trying his best to remain calm as Dawn continued to painstakingly trail behind him firing off question after question. Carrying the white plastic bag packed with his mother's spaghetti sauce as well as chips, pop, and a few candy bars he'd purchased for his little sister, JoJo finally lost control of his emotions. He proceeded to let his deceased father's ex-girlfriend on the side have it full throttle.

"Look, what in the fuck is wrong with your ass, besides the obvious? Stop talking about my father and asking about my mother, okay? Everybody in the hood knows if it weren't for you being such a selfish-minded hooker, he'd still be alive!" Though it wasn't in his usual character makeup, JoJo had no problem screaming at an adult, especially her. "So, for real, stop bringing up the past talking about how much you loved my father! Go somewhere and do what you've been doing for years: smoke crack and leave me and my family alone! We catching it bad enough these days without you stirring up ancient shit."

Momentarily standing on the corner, taking stock of what was said, Dawn felt remorse as JoJo angrily marched away. Like a true crack-head, though, the second she heard a car horn blow, her mind went right back to its original mission. As if that were a crackhead call to action, she walked over to the beat-up, old Ford Tempo that had honked at her.

"Hey, baby, you lookin' for me?" she asked as she leaned up against a stop sign pole.

"Yeah, I got a little bag with your name on it, Dawn. I'ma need you to come around the corner with me for a few, though." The driver signaled for the drug-addicted Dawn to come and ride with him around the block. He needed for her to go in the alley for a few minutes before he had to go home.

Dawn knew what time it was. Deep down she knew she had a problem. She knew her son was ashamed of her. But the monkey on her back and the guilt in her soul wouldn't let her walk away from that white snow. It was the only thing that made her feel good, and she was always willing to do anything to get her hands on some of it.

I don't know who she thinks she is talking to me like I care what she has to say, JoJo contemplated with each step he took. *I would tell Ma what she had the nerve to say, but things are already bad enough for her. And if she hears this, she liable to go back up there and beat the brakes off that bitch. So, naw, I'm just gonna let that stupid shit be. That ho ain't worth the trouble anyhow.*

"Yo, man, slow down!" Tyrus, with pants sagging, ran off the stairs. He caught up with his former classmate, who didn't even slow his pace. "Hey, JoJo, let me holler at you for a minute."

"Oh, my fucking God, what the fuck you want, man?" Still very much rattled with mixed emotions from his encounter with Dawn, JoJo was not in the mood to deal with her offspring. "If this is about what I just said to your mother, she straight had it coming. She was out of order from Jump Street, and you know that."

"Naw, guy, I know she be bugging out most of the time. That's what I wanted to say." Tyrus pulled up his sagging jeans enough to keep them from falling down to his ankles as he walked.

JoJo was relieved that's all he wanted. He didn't want or need any sort of trouble from Tyrus Jackson. At this point, all JoJo wanted to do was get back home and give his mom the good news about his day. "Oh. Okay, then, we good."

"Yeah, it's all that dope that got her acting the way she does, out here running with all these assholes who be taking advantage of her. You know what I'm saying." Tyrus hated talking about his mom's situation, but there was no use in trying to act like it didn't exist. The whole block knew what his mom was about.

Feeling a bit of sympathy for Tyrus, JoJo slowed his pace back to the house where his mother was, who was hardworking and would never think of doing the despicable things that Dawn did. "Dang, man, I'm sorry things are so messed up for you in your world, but—"

"It ain't nothing." Tyrus tried downplaying his pain, but unfortunately, he wore the grave appearance of sorrow written all across his face. "That's how it goes sometimes. We can't choose our family, 'cause if we could, I'd be out in the suburbs rocking out with some rich white family getting that serious bread."

"Yeah, I heard that." JoJo kinda laughed. Years ago, he hated Tyrus just for being Dawn's son. As time had gone on, though, JoJo had too many things going on in his life to have time to spend hating Tyrus. The more he thought about it, the more he realized Tyrus had nothing to do with what happened between Dawn and his father. They were all just kids caught up in their parents' mess. JoJo had decided a long time ago that his beef was not with Tyrus.

"But, shiddd, in reality, my black ass stuck here in the fucking hood," Tyrus said as he looked down at his sneakers.

"Hey, not to get into your business," JoJo said, continuing his strange, unexpected conversation with Dawn Jackson's son, of all people, "but how come you don't attend classes anymore? I haven't seen you around school since sometime before vacation started."

"Come on now, dude, you know it ain't no secret that them busters at that bitch was trying to hold me back another year. And a guy like me wasn't going for that. School just ain't for me," he reasoned with JoJo. "Besides, with a moms like mine, a brotha gotta get out here and grind if I wanna eat. You feel me? Shit ain't easy around my way."

Before the unlikely pair knew it, they were standing in front of JoJo's house, met by an impatient Yanna standing on the porch.

"Boy, get your behind in this house with that sauce. You know Jania gotta eat before she starts practicing for that recital of hers," she fussed, not recognizing who Tyrus was.

"Okay, Ma, I'll be right there." JoJo got an epiphany as he glanced downward at the bag in his hands that was stuffed with items he'd purchased with the extra dough that lined his pockets.

"All right, dawg, I see ya moms is calling you, so I'm gonna bounce. Good looking on understanding that ol' girl situation. I know she's fucked up in the head, but she still my blood."

If he'd been any other friend from school, JoJo would've invited Tyrus in to have dinner with his family. However, considering who Tyrus's mother was, JoJo knew that his mother would go off the deep end if he invited Tyrus to dinner. So, instead, he had an alternative idea. "Don't worry about it, man. It's all good," JoJo said as he leaned in to give Tyrus a pound. "Yo, you know I would invite you to stay at my crib for dinner, but with all that shit between your moms and mine—"

"I gotchu, man. Don't even worry about it. I know what it is," Tyrus interrupted him.

"Yeah, you know how it is. But, you know what? Are you busy tomorrow about noon? I've got a business proposition for you that might make us both some money."

The word "money" was all that Tyrus, who was always tangled up in some "get rich or die trying" scheme, needed to hear. "Nah, I ain't busy."

"A'ight, cool. Meet me in front of the store tomorrow at twelve o'clock then."

"Okay, see you tomorrow then."

The two parted ways. Tyrus decided to walk back to the store to see if he could convince his mom to go home with him, while JoJo ran up the steps eager to have dinner with his family.

As Yanna fixed the spaghetti, she asked JoJo, "Who was that boy you were out there talking to? I've never seen him around before."

JoJo didn't want to lie to his mother, but considering the anger and disappointment she was feeling about being laid off, he remained silent. In an attempt to change the subject, he brought up a subject that was always touchy with his mother. Her past life growing up in the projects had been deemed off-limits since he was a small child. The only thing Yanna ever spoke about was that Auntie Grace was probably the best thing that ever happened to her, and that if you run the streets with ill intentions, the outcome would always be the same: jail or death. "So, Mom, tell me again why you moved from the projects when you were younger. What happened?"

Yanna was shocked. Her son bringing up her life in the hood had thrown her off. "JoJo, why you wasting my time about that mess? I told you a long time ago, and I'm not about to rehash it. Just know that you better be out here doing the right thing. Trouble has a way of finding a person doing the correct things all the time, so doing the wrong things ups the ante."

JoJo knew this was the perfect time to bring up what happened to Byron. Although his mother had never met him, Yanna always appreciated the time the drug dealer would spend with her son, warning him about the ills of the street world. "So, you know earlier I was supposed to cut three yards."

"Yeah, and?" Yanna stood at the stove, pouring the spaghetti sauce into the pot.

"Well, when I got over to Byron's house, he wasn't there. But there were a lot of other cars parked there."

"Other cars? Okay, and so what's wrong with that? I don't get it."

JoJo had a lump in his throat. It was hard to swallow. "Well, like I said, Byron wasn't there. Some of his people were inside his house taking his things."

Yanna, who was now stirring the pot, stopped. Concerned, she then turned to face her son, who was now crying. The single parent had seen that look on plenty of people's faces throughout her years alive. It was easy to know what her son was going to say next. Saving him the trouble, Yanna beat him to the punch. "Byron is dead, isn't he? Somebody killed that boy, didn't they?"

JoJo broke all the way down. As Yanna held her child in her arms, she then decided to tell him all about her former life. For the first time ever, she left out no details. The two of them talked through dinner and cleanup and didn't stop talking until it was time for Jania's recital to start.

Before they left, the always incredibly loyal son blessed Yanna and his little sister with some money from the shed. At first, the proud mother refused the offer, but as the moments passed she changed her mind. She knew the bills were in shutoff status, and it was what it was. Byron couldn't use the money where he was, but her household definitely could benefit from it. Yanna had no idea whatsoever that would be the start of JoJo having an open pass to start slinging.

CHAPTER SIX

JoJo looked at the clock, which was hung on an old, rusty nail over the kitchen sink. Realizing that it was close to twelve, he got anxious. He was rushing his mother and sister out of the house. He had given his mom some more money this morning so she and Jania could go out shopping for some much-needed new clothes and sneakers. Jania was beyond excited to get to pick out some new outfits. She was used to having to pick things from the secondhand store because it was all Yanna could afford. Yanna had questioned JoJo about how much money he had stumbled upon, and JoJo gave her the partial truth about what he'd found in Byron's shed.

"Ma, you and Jania are gonna miss the bus if you don't hurry up." JoJo was doing his best to get them out of the house. He needed them out for the day because he planned on bringing Tyus back to the house for their business meeting.

He had stayed up all night thinking about what he was about to embark on. Still deep in thought today, he paced the floor with anticipation as well as hesitation as to whether he was about to do the right thing. His heart sank, and he cringed when he looked at the wastepaper basket that still had his mother's balled-up pink slip in it. Then he thought about the way Yanna's and Jania's faces lit up when he handed them the money and told them to go shopping. JoJo felt like he had to do what he had to do for his family. What he was about to embark on was a necessity. Even though the money he'd stumbled on was enough to keep them comfortable for a few months, he knew that blessing would eventually run out and then they would be back at square one. So, he had to start making moves from now so that they could stay ahead of the struggle and start living better lives.

The more he sat around thinking and waiting, the more he kept second-guessing himself, though. As soon as his mom and sister walked out the front door, JoJo bolted out not far behind them and up toward the corner store. At exactly twelve noon, Tyrus turned the corner wearing the same clothes he'd had on the evening before.

"What up, doe," Tyrus greeted him.

"Nothing much," JoJo replied, suspiciously looking around the store's parking lot. "For a minute, I thought you weren't going to come and meet up." He glanced down at his watch, impressed with the promptness Tyrus had shown. "But I'm glad you did. I need to show you something. Hold tight a second."

"Well, I sure hope it's some damn money, 'cause right about now that's the only thing a nigga like me wanna see." Tyrus had greed in his eyes as he watched JoJo dig deep into the pocket of his neatly ironed navy blue Dockers. Pulling out a folded-up piece of paper towel, JoJo looked around once more, praying no extra eyes were watching.

"Dang, dawg, you killing me acting all top-secret squirrel and shit," Tyrus mocked, growing slightly agitated. "What's the deal? What you got?"

JoJo paid no attention to his jokes while he carefully unwrapped the paper towel, still scoping out his surroundings the entire time. "Hey, dude, do you know what this is?"

Tyrus was confused as he took one of the small tablets out of the napkin JoJo held. He flipped it over to the side that was branded with a symbol. "I don't get it." He laughed, moving out of the way of some customers who were pulling up into the parking lot. "What fool don't know what these is? The question should be, what your Dudley Do-Right self doing with some Ecstasy pills? I know you not getting lifted, are you?"

"Ecstasy. I thought that's what they might've been, but I really wasn't too sure," JoJo said, confessing his naïve knowledge of drugs altogether. "And of course I'm not getting lifted. Imagine that!"

"Okay, well, if you not getting high, I don't get it. Where did you get them from? And, real talk, do you got some more you wanna get rid of?" Tyrus's eyes were still filled with greed, and now so was the sound of his voice. "'Cause we can bang the dog shit outta these bad boys!"

"Hey, do you feel like coming over to my house?" At this point, JoJo decided it would be better to just show Tyrus the real deal than to tell him.

"Yeah, all right. Just let me grab a juice and a bag of chips for lunch first," Tyrus insisted before they made their way to Yanna's house.

Immediately going inside the store, Tyrus bought his stuff as fast as he could so he and JoJo could get going. Tyrus didn't want to give JoJo any time to change his mind about inviting him over to the house. He really wanted to see what it was that JoJo had to show him he was working with.

Within minutes of arriving at JoJo's house, Tyrus felt a strange chill. He couldn't help but stare at the family pictures, school awards that hung on the wall, and the overall warm, homelike atmosphere he constantly yearned for growing up. He saw pictures of JoJo's father, the man he had seen get killed right in front of his eyes. As much as he was enjoying the warm atmosphere, seeing that man's picture killed his vibe, and it quickly reminded him why he was there in the first place.

"JoJo! Where you at, man?" he yelled out.

"I'm in my room. Second door down the hall."

Finally going inside of JoJo's bedroom, Tyrus saw the several big Baggies full of different-colored Ecstasy pills. JoJo gave him a brief explanation of how he came across the drugs and asked Tyrus to give him a crash course in pricing and selling the pills. Tyrus broke everything down to him and reassured JoJo that, no doubt, at twenty dollars a pop they were about to make some quick cash, even if they split the proceeds straight down the middle.

After carefully counting each pill one by one, the newly formed partners in crime determined they had over $40,000 in clear, 100 percent profit on JoJo's desk that was staring them dead in their faces.

"Forty thousand dollars. I can't believe it." JoJo shook his head at the value of what the evil, smart-mouth relative of Byron's had given him. *If she only knew what I'm sitting on thanks to her!*

"Yeah, JoJo, that's twenty stacks apiece, right? We gonna be partners in this, right?" Tyrus chimed in, making sure the cut was going to be fifty-fifty even though his first mind wanted him to snatch it all and run out the front door. However, twenty flat was more than good with him, especially considering he hadn't invested a dime.

After that was agreed, the only thing the two had to do was to organize their game plan and get to work on moving the pills as soon as possible. Knowing absolutely nothing about drugs or the world from which they came, JoJo relied solely on Tyrus, who was about that life. Dawn Jackson's son would use his street expertise to figure out the pros, cons, and logistics of them successfully converting bags of tiny pills into cold, hard revenue without getting shot, robbed, arrested or, even worse, killed.

"JoJo, let me ask you something."

"Yeah, what's up?"

"Why'd you come to me with all this shit? You ain't never said a word to me whenever you see me, and I know your mom hates me and my moms. So why are you bringing me on?"

"To be honest, man, I'm not sure myself. I know my mom hates you, and I can't front; what happened with your mom was messed up. But that shit had nothing to do with us. I decided a long time ago I ain't have no problems with you," JoJo explained. "And, besides, I figure you and I would make the best partners because nobody would ever think you and I are a team. Everybody in town automatically has you and me as enemies because of our moms, so it's the perfect way for us to stay under the radar!"

"Damn, JoJo, I hadn't even thought about it like that."

"Yup. So let's ride this out until the motherfucking wheels fall off, partner!" JoJo extended his hand toward Tyrus.

"Let's do this shit," Tyrus said as he shook his new partner's hand.

CHAPTER SEVEN

Over the next month and a half, life for both teenagers changed at a rapid pace. They had quickly established a long and loyal customer base, which gave them a heavy cash flow. They went from poor and struggling to ghetto super-stars quick. From day one—when Tyrus received a 911 call on his cell and set out to sling the first four pills of his share of the product to Tim-Tim and his boy, who were having a party with a couple of females, who soon also became customers themselves—each young man proved how differently they were raised and what was most important to them in their small corner of the world.

JoJo quickly got caught up in the money. He had promised himself he wasn't going to be like the rest of the dope hustlers and spend it on clothes and jewelry, but once his pockets started getting heavy, he couldn't wait to spend some of it. Trips to the mall for expensive outfits for his little sister were at the top of the list for JoJo, as well as a new Android and a solid gold chain with a huge diamond-encrusted cross for himself. Never having owned a pair of the latest Jordans, especially since he knew full well his mother could never afford such an extravagance on her meager salary, JoJo purchased three pairs the first chance he got. He just had to get brand-new outfits to go with each pair. Treating himself to fitted caps, a brand-new PlayStation along with every game he desired, and a pair of iced-out Cartier glasses, JoJo felt like a miniature kingpin. The once-wise kid, who now owned three designer watches, was spending money like it was going out of style.

"Yeah, let me get two pairs of those Balmain jeans in a thirty-four and them Hollister T-shirts. Let me get one in every color you got," JoJo instructed the salesman in the upscale store usually reserved for ballers.

"Yes, sir, not a problem." Although the salesman was old enough to be JoJo's father, he respected the ridiculous amount of money the teenager always spent at his store. There was no doubt in his mind that it was dope money the youth was throwing around, but oh well. His job was to move merchandise, not judge. After all, most of his clientele did something illegal for a living to afford what he was pushing.

Buying his sister every dress she wanted, and even her own clarinet, JoJo felt like a big man. He, of course, hooked Yanna up with lavish gifts, including money for a down payment on a new leased vehicle. The way his and Tyrus's unlawful product was moving, they'd be out soon, and with no available connect or any leads on getting any more, JoJo still felt he owed his mother some sort of temporary happiness. Though she'd not once questioned him on his out-of-the-blue windfall of finances, JoJo knew she had to know that his newly gained wealth wasn't the result of doing yard work.

When he came home riding a brand-new moped, she said nothing. When he got his ear pierced and started rocking a half-carat diamond stud, she stood mute. And even when JoJo showed up late one night having just gotten a huge cross with RIP and his father's name tattooed on his upper arm, Yanna didn't bat an eye. It was as if it were business as usual.

With the burden of being a grown man before he was truly ready, JoJo missed out on being a young boy: watching television, climbing trees, and hanging out with kids his own age. No sooner than his father's corpse had been lowered into the ground and the first pile of dirt was thrown on top had Yanna pressured him to fill the painful void in her miserable life. Every penny he'd make, every dime he found, and every free minute he had JoJo would spend in an effort to make his often-depressed mother happy once again. For that he would give almost anything, and selling Ecstasy pills was making that more possible. Even the risk of getting arrested didn't persuade him to stop.

Meanwhile, Yanna did manage to get another job after being laid off, but she unluckily lost that part-time gig after barely receiving her first minimum-wage paycheck. However, she didn't worry as much as she did the first time she got laid off, because she knew her son would certainly look out for the family. Matter of fact, she was counting on it.

JoJo was far from stupid, and he figured that this was why his once-strict mother neglectfully chose to disregard his obvious change in behavior and personal appearance. Once school had resumed, Yanna even took money from her son to let him sleep in and cut class for the day without having to hear her nagging. Anyone who paid attention knew JoJo's change in demeanor and his negative attitude toward school could point to only one conclusion: JoJo was now a true Detroit hood hustler.

As an unemployed single mother of two, Yanna needed the money for past-due bills. Not to mention that, for the first time since her husband's murder, the mentally anguished mom could now sit back and kick her feet up. Growing up in a huge family that was overly packed full of criminals, including backsliders, alcoholics, crackheads, murders, and other relatives who committed all types of mayhem, Yanna knew the dangers and risks that came with living the street life; but she chose to look the other way because she was really enjoying this new financial freedom. Despite having seen the ugly side of the so-called game by attending several family members' funerals, as well as making her fair share of trips to visit her kin in prisons scattered all across Michigan, Indiana, and Ohio, she was happy with their new lifestyle and didn't want to have to say goodbye to it.

Yanna herself had sadly fallen prey and was caught up enjoying fast money, ignoring the tangled strings that were always attached to it. It's true what is always said: money does change people. As Yanna, once simpleminded and easy to please, started dressing good, driving good, and eating good, how JoJo was making that happen was no more than an afterthought. Yanna was content allowing her son to take a chance with his life and freedom for her own selfish pleasures.

"Hey, JoJo, wake up. I need for you to get up and give me a few dollars. I've got some things I need to take care of, and I'm short."

With Yanna standing at his bedside, JoJo wished he were dreaming. He had been out late and wanted to get some much-needed rest. Acting as if he were ignoring what she'd asked, he turned over on his other side. With his face now at the wall JoJo hoped his mother would go away. Seconds later, when he heard the annoying sounds of her voice, he knew he wasn't that lucky. Yanna was not in the mood to be ignored.

"Dang, Ma, I'm sleeping."

"So damn what you sleeping? Get your punk ass up and give me a few dollars like I asked. I don't know what's wrong with you."

Even though JoJo loved all the nice, extravagant things he was able to bless himself and his family with, he was fed up with the crazy change in his mother's disposition. Once meek and hell-bent on doing the right thing no matter how hard it was, she now was on the nut, out for whatever was good at the moment. It was like she was the child and he was the adult.

Turning back over, JoJo reached down on the floor to get his jeans. Yanna watched him pull out a small knot in his front pocket. Peeling off a few twenties, the exhausted son just gave up any hope of sleep when his mother started cursing him out about being stingy with the drug money she allowed him to make while living underneath her roof. He wanted to ask her why she was tripping on his hustle and why she didn't just get a job and get her own bread, but he knew that conversation would only hype Yanna up more. Instead, JoJo tossed the cash on his dresser and told his greedy mom to take what she wanted.

Tyrus Jackson, Dawn's boy, however, was a horse of a much different color. While most would think he'd easily outshine JoJo when it came to letting go of the almighty dollar, Tyrus held on to it tightly. He behaved as if he'd lived through the Great Depression. Being a child of a crackhead, Tyrus knew that all good things come to an end. He understood the game and that their Ecstasy hustling run would ultimately be no different. Despite being labeled street savvy and surrounding himself with plenty of dime-piece females, Tyrus honestly didn't mind playing the background when it came to his and JoJo's venture. He was about the money and what it could do, not the fame. He was used to being invisible to most, and he wanted it to remain that way.

Wearing the same three pairs of pants he owned day in and day out was second nature to the only seed of a narcotic-addicted single parent. Tragically, Tyrus grew up having nothing to call his own, not even his mother's love, which ultimately belonged to the unfeeling streets of Detroit and whatever man could afford her cheap services. So now that he had come into some money, he wanted to be smart with it and not spend it on material things.

His number one priority was to take some of his money and get his mom off of the streets and into a rehabilitation facility. Tyrus had been trying persistently to get his mother off the streets for a while, but he couldn't afford to get her the proper treatment to keep her clean. Now that he had the money, he was willing to pay whatever it would cost to get her clean. The biggest obstacle was how he was going to convince his mother to agree to it. The heavily crack-addicted Dawn Jackson was having no part of it whenever he would try to talk to her about it.

Tyrus was so desperate to see his mother get clean that secretly at night, when he was sure no one was watching, wherever he was blessed enough to lay his head down, Tyrus would drop to his knees, lower his head, and pray to God to deliver his mother back to her right state of mind. *Dang, I'm tired of her being messed up and people dogging me about the foolishness she does. God, please help my mother be a better person.*

Sure, prior to the death of Joseph Sr., Dawn Jackson was considered the neighborhood tramp by most; but, in Tyrus's eyes, that insulting title was miles behind the one his mother held claim to now: a grimy, dirty crackhead who would do anything for a dollar. If there was one good thing that came out of Tyrus's ongoing tormented ordeal of being his mother's bastard son, it was that the life he lived had made him stronger. Now, in his opinion, everything was about to start paying off. If he just kept stacking his bread, he was gonna do what he had to do to get his mom clean, then go to school and make something of himself. Tyrus was focused and determined to be a success story.

CHAPTER EIGHT

"Hey, guy, everything seems like it's moving good, don't it?" Tyrus counted out his share of the day's profit. Smiling from ear to ear he stuffed the tiny knot of mostly twenties and tens deep down in his pocket for safe keeping until he got to the place he called home to put it in his ever-growing stash.

"Yeah, you're right." JoJo rubbed the side of his face in the mirror over his dresser. Eagerly checking to see if the beard he had started growing was getting any thicker, he smiled.

Tyrus handed him his share of the cash, and the two made their way toward the front door.

"I'm about to grab something to eat, hit the mall, and then go to the movies with my girl," JoJo bragged, counting his money before putting it in his pocket. "You wanna go hang or what? I can have her bring her homegirl."

"Naw, not me. I'm on my way in for the night." Tyrus shook his head as he walked onto the front porch of Yanna's house, where he was now regularly welcomed with open arms.

Greed along with selfishness was now the head of Yanna's twisted household. And if her dead husband's mistress's bastard son had anything to do with her new carefree lifestyle, then so be it. Tyrus Jackson would always have an open-door policy with her. Caught up in "getting hers," Yanna still tried avoiding as much contact with Tyrus as possible. But to keep the money flowing, she'd roll with the punches, letting bygones be bygones.

Yanna felt she'd paid her debt in full to the world in the way of her husband being suddenly and cruelly snatched out of her and her children's lives. So, if any of her holier-than-thou neighbors, like old Mr. Sims, or her nosey Auntie Grace had some smart remarks or opinions about how she was now raising Jania or JoJo, then they could just kick rocks as far as she was concerned. This was her life, and these were her kids, and she made that much perfectly clear whenever her parenting skills would come into question.

"Dang, Tyrus, you don't ever go out and have a good time, do you?" JoJo took his brush out of his back pocket.

"Yeah, man, but right about now I'm on a serious mission. I got real thangs to do and real moves to make. You feel me? This shit we doing ain't gonna keep us living good."

"I understand all that, guy, but honestly we's making nice money now." JoJo pulled back out the small knot of money he intended on blowing on clothes and females later. "So why won't you buy yourself a couple of outfits and maybe some new sneakers?" He brushed his waves repeatedly waiting for his friend's reply.

"All that high-priced bullshit just ain't for me right now. Maybe the bootleg versions, but not that official shit you be rocking. I'm tight on all that. Besides, every well runs dry and, if you haven't realized yet, we're starting to run low." Tyrus's mind thought about the small amount of pills they had left in the stash, and he swiftly figured out how much money they would translate to. "And, for real, it's not like we gonna re-up on the bullshit."

"Whatever, that's all good, but it still don't explain why you don't ever go out to the restaurant with me and eat good. In the past six or seven weeks, when I think about it, all I've ever seen you eat, outside of the meals my old girl might cook if she's at home, is Campbell's soup, Vienna sausage, ramen noodles, and Spam. Now, what's up on that? Dang, I know you got dough! Why you ain't spending that shit?"

"Listen, fam," Tyrus said to JoJo, "let me do me, and you do you, okay? I already done told you before, I'm on a serious mission, so let's just leave it like that."

JoJo let his curiosity of the past finally get the best of him. Ever since the afternoon he and Tyrus decided to go into this pill-selling venture, he'd avoided the other painful link they shared from years ago. But, at this moment, something strange came over JoJo, and he could no longer resist the temptation of bringing up the issue that drastically changed his and his family's lives.

"Dawg, before you go, let me holler at you about something else." He placed his hand on Tyrus's shoulder, letting him know it was all good. "I've wanted to ask you this for a nice while but, real rap, I don't really know if I want to hear the answer."

Both sitting down on the front stairs, Tyrus braced himself also for the inevitable conversation he'd dreaded having with his newfound friend, about the night Joseph Sr. was shot in cold blood in his mother's living room. "I already think I know what it is." Tyrus lowered his head, hesitating to speak out of turn and hoping to just let sleeping dogs lie. "But go ahead and ask just so I'll know we're on the same page. It ain't no thang."

"Well, it's about my father," JoJo said, confirming exactly what Tyrus speculated the topic would be. "I know it's been years, but I need to know what happened that night. You know, the night my pops got killed. My mother cries almost every time somebody brings up that evening, so it ain't no way I can go and ask her. You feel me? I been out here twisting in the wind on the shit. I want, naw, I need to know. You understand?"

"Yeah, I do." Tyrus bit down on the corner of his lower lip.

"My moms wouldn't even let me miss school to go to the murder trial so I could hear firsthand what had gone down. She felt like I was too young back then to understand, and she was probably right. But a nigga just wanted to know back then, like a nigga wanna know now."

Although the last thing Tyrus wanted to talk about was that tragic night that also haunted him, he obliged JoJo and did just that. Since his promiscuous mother was indeed truly to blame, he felt he owed him at least that much.

Only ten minutes or so deep off into the conversation down memory lane, JoJo felt himself grow more and more agitated at what he was hearing. His heart raced, and his blood boiled just as if the murder were taking place right now in front of his face. He could remember so vividly wishing that evening in his prayers that his father would go away and never come back home. He was consumed with emotions and guilt. Closing his eyes, JoJo could almost visualize his mother running out of the house that night, saying his dad had been hurt, and him being left standing there speechless and full of remorse that possibly his wish had come true.

The story Tyrus told of that dreadful nightmare unfolded from his end. He started at the very precise moment his mother, who was getting slapped around, placed that ill-fated, "Help me, help me," distress call to JoJo's pops. That was the phone call that led to the confrontation between Dawn's other man, who'd just been released from prison, and Joseph Sr. It was the confrontation that ended with the ambulance Tyrus ended up calling rushing the married man off to the hospital where he took his final breath. After calling his wife, Dawn Jackson had been right there clinging to Joseph Sr.'s side, much to the dislike of a hysterical Yanna who arrived at the hospital, bursting through the doors and jetting by security, just in time to see them pronounce the time of her husband's death.

Just listening to the details of how Dawn's other man had been beating on her and she had called his father over to the rescue, to be Superman, made JoJo's adrenalin rise. *Why didn't Dawn call the police? Why didn't Tyrus? Why did she have to call my father? Why did my father get up from the dinner table? Why was he thinking it was all right to cheat on my mother in the first place?* The more unanswerable questions he thought about sitting on the stairs, the angrier JoJo got. He could hardly contain his inner rage.

"You can stop," JoJo loudly ordered Tyrus. He held his head down buried in his hands. "I'm tight! I don't even wanna hear no more."

"Dude, I apologize for the role my mother played in your father's death." Tyrus tried consoling his new friend and business partner even though he knew it wouldn't soothe his pain. "That scandalous mess she did that night is what got her so jacked up now and out of her mind. They say God don't like ugly, so now I guess she paying for all that every day out in these Detroit streets strung out and pimping herself out. What's not fair is I got dragged out right along with her!" Tyrus felt the anger rising in his spirit.

JoJo lifted his head slightly, enough so Tyrus could see the redness of his eyes, and the complete look of disappointment on his face. "Yo, my bad, man. I ain't mean to get you upset too. You don't need to keep talking about it. I'm good. I just wanted to know what really jumped off that night."

Tyrus took that as his cue to get up and head to the crib. "There is one other thing, in case you wanna know," Tyrus added with compassion, looking JoJo in the eye. "When the ambulance was taking him away, I heard ya old man pleading with my mother to call your moms and tell her he loved her and his kids. Despite what you think, JoJo, ya pops was a real stand-up dude in the end, and he talked about you and your sister all the time."

"Oh, yeah, is that right?" JoJo, at that point, really didn't know how to take that last bit of information about his adulterous father, so he just nodded, lowering his face back down in his hands as Tyrus left.

CHAPTER NINE

I can't believe that! Why did I even let him tell me that garbage? Then he gonna lie and say my no-good, cheating-ass father said he loved us! Yeah, right! That's a joke. If he loved me, my sister, and my momma so much, he wouldn't have been messing around on her in the first place, especially with that boney crackhead! JoJo reflected on what he'd just heard, leaving himself numb to any type of respect for Joseph Sr. or his legacy.

His plans for having a good time later were halted as he sat on the porch infuriated, not knowing what to do next. As he simmered, shooting phone call after phone call to voice mail, he suddenly had the strange desire to not remember what Tyrus had put on his mind. There was only one way he could do that, and that was to buy something to drink. After all, it worked for his mother all the time. Whenever Yanna was depressed, which was often, facing the troubles of the world, that bottle hidden in the closet took the edge off and often seemed to put his mother in a much better and mellower mood.

I need to get drunk or good and buzzed for real. Slowly getting up and brushing off his designer blue jeans, JoJo headed down the block toward the corner liquor store where he was stopped by, of all people, Dawn. She'd darted out of the alleyway after trying to con some old man in a red Ford F-150 out of his money.

"Hey now, Little JoJo." Dawn smiled, showing her rotten teeth as she squinted. High as a kite, she had a flashback of the good old days before she'd begun worshiping the crack pipe. Tyrus's mother took notice of all the characteristics her boyfriend from once upon a time had in common with his son.

"Oh, hey, Ms. Jackson." JoJo, hard as it was, tried giving her a small amount of respect since he and Tyrus were now in business together, as well as friends. "How you doing this evening?"

"I'd be doing a whole lot better if you could just spare me a little bit of change so I can get something to eat."

"Come on now, Ms. Jackson, I know your son got your pockets straight enough to get a sandwich, so go pull that hungry routine with the next sucker. Besides, I'm not in the mood for listening to all those games you be trying to run, okay? Tonight is not the time."

Dawn, now feeling like she and JoJo were on good terms, placed her hand on his shoulder. "Listen, baby, Tyrus is stingy and don't be giving me no damn money. He think I'm gonna just blow it on getting high and whatnot."

"And is he wrong?" JoJo moved his shoulder backward so her filthy hand wouldn't dirty his expensive Pistons throwback jersey.

"Naw, he right, but so damn what? I'm a grown-ass woman. I'm the parent, not the other way around!" Dawn, already lifted beyond belief, clutched the five-dollar bill she'd just worked for in the alley. "He can't stop me from doing what I do, no matter how much he tries. Anyway, he ain't nothing but a hypocrite. I mean, look at him running around here playing big, bad dope man all week, and then trying to drag my behind to church with him on Sunday. He sounds like a fool! He can't change me talking about faith in God!"

"What?" JoJo paused, not believing what she'd just said. Shocked, as they continued to walk into the store's crowded parking lot, he finally responded, "Did you just say Tyrus be going to church? Tyrus? Are you serious?"

"Yeah, I said church. Every Sunday now for a month or so he keep waking me up or be out searching for me, thinking I'm going with him. He even claims he's getting baptized this week. Ain't that about nothing! Who do Tyrus think he is? He makes me sick sometimes! All I want is a few dollars to get high, and that cheap nigga won't even help his own momma out. JoJo, I know you ain't doing your mother like that. I see her driving by me in the new truck, still looking at me like I'm some trash."

"Wow, that's deep," JoJo replied, laughing to himself, trying to imagine big, bad, "I'm so cool, nobody can beat me" Tyrus posted in church like he used to be when he was younger. "And naw, I look out for my mother. Shitttt, she makes sure of that. But, hey, fuck all that. Right about now I need for you to do me a small favor. Can you hook me up or what?"

"Anything for you." Dawn was elated Joseph Sr.'s son was coming to her for assistance. Normally, in the world where she lived and in the seedy circles she traveled, it was common knowledge that when anybody wanted anything from her, they had to pay for it. But, of course, she would do anything to help out JoJo any way she could, free of charge. "What you need, angel face? Looking just like your daddy."

Letting her get away with even mentioning his father showed the black-hearted Detroit state of mind he was in. JoJo reached into his pocket, pulling out a crisp fifty-dollar bill. With hate in his heart, he handed it to Dawn. "Look, I need for you to go in the store and buy me a drink, some Rémy."

"You want a drink?" She couldn't believe what the once Goody Two-shoes had said. "Did you say you want some Rémy? Naw, not you, JoJo. What happened to that nice—"

"Yo, listen, Ms. Jackson, you can kill all that extra noise." Once again he was thrown back to disrespecting her and her drug-addict lifestyle. "You can spare me all them judgmental stares and trying to be all up in my business! Just do what I asked you! Besides, you the last one who needs to be around here acting like you anybody's mother! And oh, yeah, after you cop that bottle, you can keep the change so you can do what you do!"

"Good looking, sweetheart. Say no more. Momma Dawn got you!" Bobbing her head and scratching at her arms, Dawn happily went into the store so that she could cop JoJo's poison for comfort: a bottle of liquor. Soon after, with the change he so graciously was allowing her to keep, she would cop the poison of her choice as well: crack cocaine.

What seemed like hours slipped by as JoJo, who admittedly was not a drinker, attempted to drown his sorrows by nursing the fifth of Rémy Ms. Jackson had purchased on his behalf. Throwing rocks at his mother's empty flowerpots, which served as perfect targets, the young man sat posted on the third step from the top. Yelling out obscenities from time to time he cursed the name of everybody he felt was responsible for his father being snatched out of his life. That included Dawn, Tyrus, Yanna for nagging his pops like she used to, and his old man for being so dumb, selfish, and stupid to put the next woman and kid before his own.

JoJo was confused, and his emotions were running wild. *I hate my father! I hate him and everything about him!* echoed throughout his mind, consuming him with an intense fury and rage he had never felt before. *I'm glad that disrespectful bastard is dead! Good riddance! I hope he's burning in hell!*

Several of Yanna's longtime neighbors came onto their porches to see what all the commotion was about at the small-frame house that was normally quiet; that was, up until lately. Gossiping among themselves, they'd all taken notice of JoJo's now increasingly blatant and sometimes rude behavior. But they dared not bring up to Yanna the unexpected change pertaining to her precious baby boy's rotten demeanor, especially considering that she seemed to be suffering from the same wild, unpredictable transformation in her own lifestyle. The pair both kept late hours and had strange cars stopping by at all times of the night; not to mention, JoJo hadn't volunteered to cut their yards in months.

Yanna Banks used to speak to them every morning she went to work, or she would share a cup of coffee with them. But now, as the night-club-hopping single mother of two drove by in her new truck, she scarcely acknowledged her longtime neighbors. They were the same ones who stood by her when she and her kids were down and out. Maybe she was blinded by all the short dresses, tight jeans, and flashy jewelry she'd been rocking the last couple of months. It was the sentiment of most that those things were hindering her once-sensible judgment. Possibly that was also why they hadn't seen that much of Jania lately. And maybe that was why Yanna condoned the twisted reality of JoJo keeping company with the likes of Tyrus Jackson and that no-good, shady mother of his, Dawn.

Realizing that the young man was distraught and obviously troubled, old Mr. Sims, who was pushing seventy-one, decided to take action. Out of concern, he held on tightly to the black steel handrail, making his way off his porch and across the street to console the son of his former friend and Masonic Lodge brother, Joseph Sr. "Hey now, son." He smiled reassuringly like he had so many other times throughout the years. "Do you need to talk to someone?"

"Naw, Mr. Sims. I'm good." The teen's breath reeked of liquor as he stood, almost losing his balance. "I'm real, real, real good!"

"Well, you don't look good, son. Why don't you come on over to my house, put that bottle down, and let my wife fix you a plate of that good home cooking of hers you like so much?"

"I'll pass," he slurred as he burped.

Not ready to give up on JoJo, Mr. Sims tried insisting, hoping he'd change his mind. "Come on now, a hot meal will do you good. It's smothered pork chops and mashed potatoes."

"Naw. I done told you once, I'm okay." JoJo tried stashing the half-smashed bottle of Rémy behind one of the flowerpots as he wildly waved his arms, dismissing the elderly Mr. Sims. "You can go on and just leave me alone. I don't need nobody's help! I done told you, old man, I'm fucking good! Just leave me the hell alone!"

"All right, all right, all right." Mr. Sims reached in his back overalls pocket and got out a handkerchief to wipe the sweat from his brow. "I'm gonna do just that, son, because I see that you are intent on going down the road of self-destruction and defiance. But while you taking that hard, bumpy and, unfortunately, often-traveled journey, take these words of wisdom along with you for comfort: remember, son, it ain't never too late to turn back on that road and do the right thing."

The last thing JoJo wanted to hear about was doing the right thing. "Mr. Sims, please go on back to your house and leave me alone! And stop calling me son! You ain't my daddy," he demanded, falling back against the pillar and knocking one of the flowerpots to the pavement. "I ain't got no daddy! Matter of fact, my dad is dead! He ain't care about me or my momma! He left me! You act like you wasn't around back then! You know what he was doing." JoJo pointed around at all the other seemingly concerned longtime neighbors outside. "Y'all all knew what his no-good ass was up to!"

"Yes, son, that's true. I'm not your father, but remember this," Mr. Sims preached with a tone of certainty in his voice. "If you trust in the Lord, He'll never abandon you. And, as for Joseph Sr.,

I bet my last dollar he's up in heaven missing you every passing day. So, try to be the best you you can be and make him proud. You owe it to yourself."

"Heaven? Him? That cheating-ass nigga is burning in somebody's hell fire for how he played my momma and us! Fuck him!"

With his spontaneous sermon concluded, Mr. Sims went back to the security of his front porch. JoJo licked his lips and leaned back, reaching for his bottle, defiant of the advice he was just given. After twisting the cap off and raising the bottle to his lips, he glanced down at the bottom stair as he took another long swig. "Who do that old man think he talking to? Trying to tell me what I need to be doing! I'm gonna be a boss one day selling those pills! I'm the man, a way better man than my dead daddy ever was," he mumbled under his breath.

Mr. Sims watched the young, troubled teen from his porch and shook his head, wondering what was gonna become of JoJo if he kept on the path he was traveling. *One day that boy gonna learn. I just hope it don't be too late. And Yanna needs to be ashamed of herself for running around town like some unfit parent. It's like she taking Dawn Jackson's place.*

CHAPTER TEN

On his second trip to the store, a totally wasted JoJo tried and tried but couldn't find Dawn to do him the same solid she'd done earlier by buying him another bottle. Barely standing against the brick wall of the store's parking lot, he attempted coaxing person after person, no matter who they were. The teen hoped that one of them would be dishonest and dumb enough to break the law and risk getting ticketed to buy his underaged, already-drunk self some more liquor.

"Hey, you." JoJo belched out loud as his eyes darted around the crowded street. Cocky, he waved another fifty-dollar bill in the air. "Hey, man, can you grab something out the store for me? Can you look out for me?"

"Naw, young playa," responded one guy dressed in a suit and tie.

"Ain't that Yanna Banks's son?" another one commented to her friend as they walked past. "It's a shame how these kids behave when they raise themselves. Look at him, drunk as I don't know what. He ain't a thing like his daddy used to be."

"Girl, you right," the other woman replied. "I know that man turning over in his grave. His wife out here running the streets like she young again, and his son drunk as a skunk."

Hearing people ignore his demands had him heated. And they had the nerve to then talk about him and his mother like he wasn't standing there. Making matters worse, on top of that they were comparing him to his two-timing, cheating, womanizing father. JoJo grew more enraged than he was when he'd first walked down the block. His small frame shook, and his jaws grew tight.

"Y'all don't know shit about me or my mother," the youth shouted so the entire world could hear him. "I'm sick and tired of y'all hypocrites trying to judge me! I'm my own man! I make my own rules! Can't nobody tell me shit! I runs my own world and you bitches just around in it for nothing!"

As JoJo stood in the middle of the parking lot, jeans sagging, proclaiming his independence and manhood, two plainclothes police officers pulled up. After receiving a call from the store's owner who'd gotten complaints from several

older customers about a teenager outside disrespecting them, the duo was dispatched. They
observed the youth briefly before getting out
of their unmarked vehicle. They cautiously
approached him with their guns drawn, but
JoJo didn't care. He was spent, letting the liquor
take over his system, resulting in him cursing
the cops out without any regard whatsoever for
their authority.

"Y'all can beat it, ya feel me? Ain't nobody
scared of y'all 'cause y'all got a badge and a gun!
Everybody in the hood got a gun, even me! So,
get on with it and do what y'all gonna do!"

As if matters couldn't get any worse, one
last sign that JoJo shouldn't have been drinking jumped off as he violently vomited all his
stomach's contents on one of the officer's shoes.
The foul-smelling mixture slid down the front
of his expensive jersey as well when they body-
slammed him down against the concrete pavement, face first, checking the wild youth for any
weapons or drugs. Struggling with the police
officers for a good solid minute or so, JoJo was
easily outnumbered and overtaken by the two
cops. Finally, he was wise enough to stop resisting. Dizzy and out of breath, Yanna's son was
handcuffed and thrown head first into the back
of their maroon unmarked vehicle. Infuriated

that a struggle had to even take place, the cops quickly whisked JoJo off to the local precinct.

No sooner than they arrived at the station, the wild youth, still defiant, drunk, and pissed off, used his feet to repeatedly kick the car's rear window until it cracked. Fortunately for him, as luck would have it, the desk sergeant on duty recognized JoJo from cutting his yard in the past. That was the only thing that stopped his officers from any roughhouse retaliation that was sure to follow. JoJo was seconds away from really getting his ass handed to him, and he was much too drunk to realize it.

After logging in most of the young man's property that was on his person, the sergeant took notice of one particular item he wasn't used to seeing in JoJo's straight-laced possession: a few pills that seemed to be Ecstasy. Those pills were becoming increasingly popular with the youth the officers had encounter recently. It was damn near reaching an epidemic status in the city.

"And just what are these pills here?" he firmly inquired.

"Aspirin," JoJo wisely fired back, not so drunk he couldn't come up with a lie. "I have migraines real bad."

"Oh, yeah. Migraines, huh? Is that a fact?"

"Yeah, it is." With his lip split and his nose bleeding, JoJo stood his ground.

"Well, correct me if I'm wrong, but it sure looks like Ecstasy to me," the desk sergeant fired back as the youth he'd just given a break to tried playing with his intelligence.

"Wow," JoJo mocked as if it were a joke, "you must be CSI or something like that! I seen dudes like you on cable and whatnot."

Having had just about enough of the cat-and-mouse game he was playing with the arrogant teenager, the sergeant led a still-heavily ine-briated JoJo over toward the black desktop telephones. Making his one phone call, which was, of course, to his mother since he was legally still underage, a dizzy JoJo could hardly get the words out that he was arrested and being held at the tenth precinct.

Yanna was pissed. Immediately she started screaming at the top of her lungs. Holding the telephone receiver as far away from his ear as he possible could, JoJo closed his eyes, wondering how his life had gotten so far out of control in such a short time. Listening to Yanna's voice, which was filled with rage and contempt for her son interrupting her evening plans, made him want to throw up again. It seemed to JoJo that, between now being totally responsible for paying all the various household bills and giving his great-auntie Grace money to take care of his younger sister while his mom ran the streets trying hopelessly to recapture her youth, he was losing his mind.

Finally hanging up the phone, JoJo was glad to go to the holding cell where he dumbly believed he could lie back and hopefully sleep off the sickness in his stomach and massive headache he was suffering. He needed to get himself together before Yanna showed up and all hell broke loose.

Another police officer who escorted JoJo to his temporary home away from home was not as friendly or as reasonable as the desk sergeant. He, like the two cops who arrested him, had no problem whatsoever manhandling the teen. Practically dragging JoJo down the long, dark, mildew-infested hallway, it was business as usual with him. The officer didn't know or care about the reckless youth and his problems. To the Detroit Police Department, Joseph Lamar Banks Jr. was just another out-of-control juvenile throwing rocks at the penitentiary. They were there to administer a quick show of hardcore act right before a detainee moved on to the next step in their incarceration or bailed out.

Shoving JoJo into a small bullpen with several other men would normally have scared

Yanna's naïve-to-the-streets son to death. Up until recently, the only type of contact JoJo was used to having with the police or criminals was watching episodes of *Law & Order* on television. If it weren't for that bottle of Rémy still flowing through his system and him wanting to throw up again, the wannabe-tough teen would've been screaming for his mother. Instead, JoJo manned up and let more of that liquid courage kick in.

Taking a seat in the corner on a hardwood bench, he tried to shake off his awful case of nausea. As he sat there trying to keep his composure together, JoJo wrung his hands repeatedly. Paint peeled from the walls. To pass the time, JoJo read the various names that were scraped on the wall of the holding cell; but soon he was approached by a familiar face.

"Well, I'll be damned! What you doing in here, young blood?"

"Oh, hey." JoJo didn't know the older guy's name for sure, but he was used to seeing him all the time with Byron. "What up, doe? What's good?"

Smelling the youngster's breath made the man the streets had nicknamed Keys take a couple of steps back. "That's what I was about to ask you. The last time I saw you over my people's house you was looking like a schoolboy, all tight and whatnot. Cutting grass and drinking lemonade and shit."

"Yeah, school," JoJo slurred. "Forget school. I'm on to something else right now."

Confused, Keys shook his head. "Oh, really? You on to something else, huh? Well, dig this shit right here. I heard you got all that special lawn equipment and whatnot out the back shed at my people's crib."

"And what? I didn't do anything wrong." JoJo still felt a bit of liquid courage aggressiveness lingering that he needed to get off his chest. "A lady at the house said I could have it. I didn't steal it! I swear I didn't."

"Yo, fall back, killer." Keys laughed at the young teen who barely filled his jersey, which was torn and stained with blood and vomit. "My sister Jasmine told me what was jumping off over there that day after my manz got murdered. I ain't mad at you at all; believe that. All I'm saying is you looked like you done stepped your game way up. How that 'equipment' been working out for you in them streets? You good? You look like you been getting a lot of yard work in."

JoJo calmed down, knowing Byron's friend meant him no real harm. Far from being a fool, JoJo easily gathered that Keys had to know about the duffle bag and its contents he'd found that afternoon. "My bad. I'm just going through some stuff right now."

"What you doing in here anyhow? Why you get knocked? And who laced they shoes up on your young ass?"

"I ain't do shit. The police was bugging, trying to hold a black man down for nothing. All I was doing was trying to get somebody to buy me another bottle, and then the police showed up tripping."

"Oh, is that all?" Keys made two guys who were sitting on the bench ear-hustling move to the other side of the cell. "I thought it was that equipment that had you hemmed up. But naw, you straight gangsta now. Dig that!"

Realizing the kind of clout Keys had with the prisoners in there made JoJo relax. He started to feel as if he could spend the night, no problem, if his mother decided to teach him a lesson as she had threatened on the phone. "Yeah, that's all." He acted like he hadn't heard him mentioning the equipment once more. "My mother said she's coming to get me when she leaves the casino, so—"

"Your mother." Keys smiled. "I wish it were that easy for me to call my mother. Boy, you don't know how good you got it. My moms been dead ever since I was nine. I done got kicked out of three foster homes, spent a year in juvenile, and now I'm about to jail it this time for at least a twenty piece if not more."

"A twenty piece?" JoJo was lost on what Keys, obviously a seasoned criminal, meant.

"Twenty years. A twenty-year bid, fool," shouted out one guy who was obviously still listening to their conversation.

Keys mean-mugged the dude, daring him to say another word. "Listen up. I ain't nobody's daddy or nothing like that, but somebody needs to put you up on some game and kick some real knowledge to you. And since my manz Byron is gone and since you was his people, I'ma keep it a hundred with you."

JoJo leaned back, paying attention, seeing that Key was done playing.

"I know all about that duffel bag you found, kid. That bag you was blessed with was nothing. Me and my crew get down like that all the time; that's why we let you keep your little come up. Trust, we had other things on our plate to deal with after Byron got murdered." Keys grinned looking directly in the teenager's eyes, sensing fear. "We let you bang, schoolboy, because I thought you was trying to get college fare up or something; but you out here getting tangled up. You wanna run in our world, eat how we eat, bang how we bang."

"But—"

"But nothing. Your mother about to come get you; and, when she do, make sure you don't end up back in here with the rest of us clowns. Trust me, being locked up like an animal for that simple-ass bullshit you could easily avoid is the wrong move to make." Keys cracked his knuckles thinking about the various crimes he'd committed over the years. "Go to school and be a lawyer and come help me get up out of here. You still have a chance to change, young'un."

Tired of hearing all of the "you need to change" speeches, JoJo was relieved when an officer finally came, calling out his name.

"Yo, remember what I said." Keys walked him to the front of the cell. "And hold up. What size shoe you wear?"

"A ten," JoJo answered while wondering why.

"Oh, yeah, me too." Keys placed his hand on JoJo's shoulder. "Before you go, I'ma need those new Jordans you rocking. I was locked up fighting this case when they came out. So, run 'em. You don't mind, do you? You free. You can always get another pair."

JoJo wanted to tell Keys to kick rocks, but he knew he owed him at least that much for not letting the other guys in there beast him out, possibly taking more than his new sneakers.

Before stepping on the other side of the cell, JoJo turned back, facing Keys who was towering over him. "Hey, what you about to do twenty years for anyhow? I mean, a twenty piece?"

"For killing the dude who killed Byron. Not only was he my nephew's father, he was my best friend and, trust, good friends is hard to come by."

"What?"

"You heard me, li'l nigga. Now, remember what I said earlier! Don't let me see you back on this side of the wall again!"

Before another word could be spoken, the officer yanked JoJo by his shirt, leading him out the door.

CHAPTER ELEVEN

Less than an hour and a half later, a seemingly concerned Yanna Banks pulled up in the police station parking lot. With a designer purse on her arm, her neck full of gold jewelry, and her nails perfectly manicured, she stormed through the doors of the building, yelling out obscenities and cursing. "This don't make no kind of fucking sense! All the crime going on in this city! The police need to be out looking for murderers or these carjackers out here, not arresting kids who had something to drink!"

"Can I help you, miss?" one annoyed officer asked.

Approaching the main desk with a serious attitude, Yanna boldly demanded to see her son and the officers who arrested him. They had all caused her to leave the casino earlier than she'd planned and she was heated. "Yeah, I'ma need y'all to release my son, Joseph Banks Jr., and I wanna see the bored cops who ain't have jack shit better to do to earn that city paycheck my taxes go to!"

It was obvious to the officers on duty that Yanna Banks was the young boy's mother, because that apple definitely didn't fall far from the tree. He was rude, disrespectful, and obnoxious earlier, just like she was behaving now. How they saw it, she and the boy both needed some sort of counseling or family therapy in their lives. The desk sergeant shook his head. He was still amazed, after all his years on the job, how some so-called parents acted when their children broke the law. It was as if they were mad at the system for catching the little heathens rather than being mad at their child for being one.

"Yes, are you Josephs Banks Jr.'s mother or legal guardian?" the sergeant knowingly inquired.

"Yes, I am. Why else would I be down here asking about his dumb ass?" she loudly and bitterly stated. "Where's my son at, and what exactly did you pick him up for? 'Cause I know it couldn't be because the boy took a drink."

"Well, there are several charges pending against him: public intoxication, disorderly conduct, resisting arrest, destruction of police property, and drug possession."

"Oh, naw! All of that?" Yanna frowned as he went down the long list she knew her baby wasn't guilty of. "Not my son. I don't believe it!"

"Sorry, miss, but he is facing serious charges, and his bond is rather high. Do you often allow him to drink? You know he's underage!"

"First of all, I know how old my son is. I gave birth to him! And, secondly, a bond?" she quizzed, planting her hands firmly on her hips. "Can't you just release him to me and stay out of the way I raise mines?"

"I wish it were that easy, but unfortunately it's not." The desk sergeant looked over his wire-framed glasses. "He has to post bond or stay locked up; simple as that."

"Yeah, well, I ain't in the mood for any more speeches or impromptu parenting classes, so let's get on with it! How much is it then?" Yanna fumed as she opened her purse, ready to get out of there as soon as possible and hopefully back to the casino, where she'd been on a winning streak at the blackjack table.

When all was said and done, Yanna, infuriated to say the least, counted out $3,500. Of that, she had $2,000 in her purse. JoJo had $1,000 in small bills on his person, and she withdrew $500 from the ATM at the corner of the block. Waiting an additional forty-five minutes to an hour for the paperwork to be completed, her son, still sick to his stomach, was finally freed. Seeing that his shirt was ripped, he was barefoot, and he had red bruises on his face, not to mention a busted lip, Yanna was irate. Loudly she swore she was going to be pressing police brutality charges on both officers for their treatment of her innocent teenage son.

Settling into the passenger seat of the Range Rover, sympathy definitely was not on JoJo's side as Yanna read him the full-blown riot act. She informed her son that, by the time she got home from gambling at the casino, she wanted every single penny of the bond money she'd just put up on her dresser waiting, or there was gonna be pure hell to pay.

She's acting like I didn't give her that money in the first place or the dough for this truck. But I can't take hearing her mouth! I swear I can't! JoJo said to himself. Suffering from a pounding headache, he felt like throwing up again with each pothole Yanna seemed to be purposely riding over, and every corner of the Detroit streets she bent.

"How much was the bond anyway?" JoJo sheepishly asked his mother.

"You owe me twenty-five hundred," she spat, tossing the paperwork on his lap.

"Dang, Ma!"

"That's right. 'Dang, Ma,' my ass! Twenty-five hundred and trust, like I said, I want every penny back, asap!"

JoJo didn't even think he had that much money in his stash considering the way he had been blowing his money. *I knew I shouldn't have bought that dang chain two days ago or those new games,* he fussed at himself. *And especially the new bracelet for her ungrateful ass!* JoJo had to think long and hard about how he was gonna get his moms her money back and fast. Most of JoJo's customers were young kids from the high school, but he didn't have time to wait around for them to come to him. Although it wasn't something he particularly cared to do, he knew that tomorrow he would have to go up to the high school and push all the pills he could to keep his moms off his back. She didn't care if he sold the pills to a room full of pregnant females about to give birth. Yanna wasn't the same loving and nurturing mother she once was. She was a dragon lady, and she wanted hers by hook or by crook.

As he continued to think about where he could get the money, his mind kept flashing back to Keys and the advice or, rather, warning he'd given him.

CHAPTER TWELVE

Dawn was good and toasted. After purchasing the bottle of liquor for JoJo, she had well over thirty-five dollars left. Having bought a bottle of wine for herself, and having spent the rest on some crack, she was happy. Feeling like nothing could blow her high, she sat back quietly, letting her son tell her all the reasons she was an unfit parent.

"How many times do I have to tell you to stop using that garbage?" Tyrus frowned watching his dazed, underweight mother lie across an old couch. "You don't eat anymore, you don't bathe, and you ain't washed your hair in months. It's obvious you don't care about me, but at least you could try caring about yourself again."

"Whatever, Tyrus. Leave me fucking be."

After going into the kitchen of the sparsely furnished studio apartment they had moved into illegally, Tyrus came back into the room with a bowl of ramen noodles. "Here, Ma, at least eat some of this to soak up some of that cheap wine you got in your system."

"I ain't hungry. Now go on somewhere and leave me alone unless you talking about giving me some more money," she demanded, staggering to her feet.

"That crack got you gone enough." Trying to force the issue, Tyrus held the bowl of the chicken-flavored poor man's feast up to his mother's dry, split lips. "Here, just taste a little bit."

"Naw, Tyrus. I done told you I ain't interested."

Disappointed he couldn't get his mother to sober up so he could talk to her like she had some sense, Tyrus lost his temper altogether. "I'm done with you. Do whatever you want from this point on. Smoke crack, drink yourself stupid, run the streets 'til the sun comes up and goes down again. I'm tight on you!"

"I don't need you no more, nigga." Dawn got loud with her son. "JoJo got me. He the only one who look out for me."

"JoJo?" Tyrus set the bowl of noodles on the table. "What you mean he got you?"

"Don't worry about what I mean."

"I know he ain't give you none of that work!"

"I don't want none of them pills y'all boys got."

"Then how he got you? I'm confused, so put me up on some game."

"None of your damn business, boy, but just know JoJo and me is tight now. We got our secrets!" Dawn smiled, showing her yellow teeth; then she passed out cold.

"Okay, then, we'll see how tight y'all is." Tyrus stormed out the door.

Dang, I swear I don't wanna hear her mouth whenever she gets home! Why did I jack all that dough on stupid shit? JoJo paced the floor persistently in hopes of coming up with an immediate solution to ensure Yanna wouldn't be on his back about her money. His plan to go up to the school and push some pills failed miserably. Apparently, there was a bomb scare that morning, and extra security was called in to patrol the inside of the building and the outer perimeter. The high school was on total lockdown. There were a couple of suited-up security guards who had everybody annoyed, including JoJo. He felt it best not to push his luck. The last thing he wanted to do was end up in jail again and owe his moms even more money; that was, if she would take any more time out of her hectic "good time" schedule and even show up to bail him out. Plus, he didn't want to run the risk of running back into Keys before he got shipped upstate to the penitentiary. JoJo knew that dude wasn't playing.

Craving another drink to fight the demons that filled his head, JoJo retrieved a bottle of Absolut his mother kept on the top shelf of the kitchen cabinet behind her good set of dishes for so-called emergencies. *I need this right here so I can figure this madness out.* He twisted the top off and took it to the head for a quick swig, but then he was stopped by a series of hard knocks at his front door. The thunderous barrage of bangs increased. First came three hard-fisted knocks, then several more.

"Yeah, who the fuck is it?" JoJo was still hungover from the day before. That, combined with the swig he'd just taken to the head, had him feeling all messed up in the head. Not thinking clearly, he grabbed a pistol he kept tucked underneath a sofa cushion. Gripping the small, hair-trigger revolver he'd traded for a few pills to a desperate customer from the suburbs, he took a deep breath, asking again, "Yeah! Who that? I said who the fuck is it?"

"Yo, it's me, dude. Open the fuck up," Tyrus shouted as he pounded his fist against the wood door once more as if he were the Detroit Police Department. He hit it once more, causing the frame to rattle.

Hearing who it was, JoJo set the gun, which made him feel extra tough, on the mantle above the fireplace. He happened to put it right next to an old family portrait taken back when his father was still alive, and life was simple. After staggering toward the door, he turned the knob, letting his homeboy into the house. "What up, doe," he slurred to some extent, nodding upward.

"Hey, nigga, did you give my ol' girl some money before you bugged out last night getting yourself arrested?" Looking his friend directly in the face, Tyrus, visibly livid, wanted a straight answer. "Because she tripping all the way out. She fucking gone off the deep end this time. Claiming y'all two is in cahoots."

"What in the fuck? Naw, I didn't. Why you say that crazy-sounding bullshit?" JoJo, who was far from being in the mood or mindset to care about anything dealing with Dawn Jackson and her ghetto mess, took another swig of the bottle of liquor.

"Because she got enough bread from somewhere to get high as three kites and she keeps mumbling something about you and her and some big secret, acting like y'all buddies."

"Aww, damn, my nigga. Maybe before, when she copped me some Rémy and I let her keep the change," JoJo nonchalantly recalled as though it weren't a big deal.

"Yo, why you do that stupid shit?" Tyrus, out of nowhere, lunged at JoJo, yanking him by the collar and knocking the bottle out of his hand.

"Yo, nigga, is you crazy or something?"

"Naw, but that was foul." He tightened his grip.

"Bitch, get off me! Is you crazy or what?" JoJo shoved him back, then straightened out the shirt he'd just taken the price tag off of earlier. "Why you going all in like that? You acting like I strung her out or some shit like that. How in the hell did I know telling her to keep the change was gonna be such a big deal? Wouldn't you throw my old girl something if she asked or needed it? My bad."

Tyrus regained his composure. "Damn, JoJo, you right. I'm sorry, guy, but I've been trying to wean her off that poison and convince her to get some help, maybe go to rehab. So when she got to talking that secret shit, I just knew she must've hit you up for some loot or pills or something."

JoJo reached down, picking up the spilled bottle from the floor. Dazed, he took another sip of what was left. "You want some?" He extended the Absolut to Tyrus as sort of a peace offering.

"Naw. I gotta get back to the crib and make some phone calls about this house I'm trying to get. Besides, you need to put that garbage down before you end up fucking your kidneys up at

a young age. You already looking fucked up enough." He pointed, making reference to JoJo's
split lip and bruised face courtesy of the altercation with the cops. "The last thing I need is you
and my moms both lifted, getting high!"

"Oh, Tyrus, I get it. So, you my daddy now
too, huh?" JoJo started to zone out. His mind
thought back to old Mr. Sims from across the
street, trying to tell him what to do with his life
just yesterday, as well as Keys.

Tyrus was trying his best to remain calm, but
he was seconds from losing it again. "Look, man,
I'm just trying to be a good friend. I'm trying to
put you up on game, all right? I already done
been down that road of drinking all day, tripping
all night. You messing up big time. That's all I'm
saying. You need to get that shit under control."

"Well, so what, Tyrus, you been down that
road? You ain't me and I ain't you!"

"I know I ain't you, but—"

"Yeah, but I just been through hell on earth."
JoJo finally smiled, realizing a quick solution to
his money woes. "But you can help ya boy out
until next week. I got a problem only you can
help me with."

"Help you out?" Tyrus was puzzled, wondering where this was about to lead. "Help you out
with what?"

"Well, I'm gonna need to borrow some cash real quick to repay my moms for that bond she had to post. I got arrested yesterday, and she had to pay to get me out. Now she riding me about paying her back. You know how she be acting about her money! If I don't pay her back as soon as she get home she gonna straight be bugging on that ill shit."

Tyrus, who'd been on a mission of stacking dough since the day he and JoJo linked up, didn't waste any amount of time stopping that notion from growing. "Look, I wanna work with you, but I ain't gonna be able to do it. I got plans for all my bread. Now, I gotta bounce and make them calls. So I'm out! I'll get at you tomorrow sometime."

"Whoa! Hold up, home team. So it's like that?" JoJo took a huge gulp, giving him more courage than usual. Angry, he tossed the still-open bottle across the room, spilling the remaining liquor out onto Yanna's new, plush carpet. "Dawg, I know you got it! You ain't spent no money since day one, especially on clothes." Low-key, he was dissing Tyrus about his personal appearance.

"And so what's your point about what I do with mines?" Tyrus laughed as JoJo got deeper in his feelings.

JoJo, who was once intimidated by Tyrus and the rough street life he lived, had no problem whatsoever stepping to his supposed friend now. "My point is if it weren't for me hooking you up from jump, you'd probably still be up there on the corner with that tramp mother of yours, dead broke!"

Tyrus was not naïve. He knew all of this bullshit with JoJo was because he was still feeling some type of way after they talked about his pops's murder. That's probably why he had all of a sudden found a new friend in the form of alcohol. Tyrus was trying his best to be mindful of all that and was trying harder than he normally would to overlook JoJo's disrespectful statements.

"Look, guy," Tyrus attempted explaining, "I'm saving all my money so I can get my mom into a rehab center and so I can rent a crib out in the 'burbs and get my mother out this neighborhood. I want to get her away from all the horrible memories that haunt her and me every day. It's been hard for both of us over the years living around here." Tyrus continued to let JoJo know why he wouldn't and couldn't afford to loan him any money, especially with the way his boy let money slip through his fingers like water. "Now, I almost have enough money saved and you know we're almost out of product. So I can't risk it."

"So, it's been hard for y'all, huh?" JoJo interrupted and stepped back, not believing what his boy had just said. "For real, though, are you serious? It's been hard on y'all? If it weren't for your mother being so hot in the ass seducing my dad back in the day, he'd still be alive, and things wouldn't have been so hard on me. I've been the man around here since the night my ol' girl came home from the hospital with my father's belongings covered in blood! And, PS, no matter where you take your momma, she always gonna be nothing more than a slime-ball crackhead and a home-wrecking whore!"

"You know what? I'm gonna pray for you." Tyrus flipped the script, coming out of left field with his response. "Going to church helped me not be so angry, and it can help you too. It can help you change, because you need to get your act together."

"Look, dude. Been there, done that. The only thing that's gonna help me is that money I need to give back to my mother. So, I'ma need for you to run me that bread and not run your big mouth." He yanked forcefully on Tyrus's arm then swung on him, hitting his friend dead in the jaw.

Having no choice but to defend himself, Tyrus fired back, delivering a strong uppercut to JoJo's midsection, undoubtedly fracturing a rib. The harsh hit he suffered caused the inebriated teen to get weak and wobbly in the knees. Tyrus then followed the first punch up by a clenched fist in JoJo's left eye. As chaos and pandemonium broke out inside Yanna's house, the neighbors heard the loud commotion spill out into the street, and they called the police for assistance.

Consumed by a desire to not disappoint his mother, whom he'd die for, JoJo gathered his self-control and composure. Wasting no time, he charged like a bulldog at his friend once more, not wanting to take no for an answer. Enduring three additional swift socks in his face and landing on the floor near the fireplace, Yanna's son, physically worn out and beaten down, saw no other alternative. Out of options, he reached up to the mantle and grabbed his pistol.

"Real rap, I said run that money," JoJo repeated from the floor with fury in his tone. "I'm trying to keep it a hundred with you! My momma needs it, and I can't leave her hanging like that! Now, Tyrus, I ain't playing around with you no more. Run them pockets!"

"Run my pockets for what, JoJo? So ya moms can gamble it all away? Or so she can ride around in that new truck and stunt like she better than everybody else who live in the hood?"

"Well, if she does, it's sure as hell better than smoking crack and running behind every dude who got a dollar in his pocket. Not to mention sleeping with the next woman's husband 'cause she couldn't find one of her own!" JoJo held his injured side with one hand and the gun with the other. "Matter of fact, where is your father at anyway? Or do that ho even know who he is?" He stood, grinning as the alcohol kept his words slurring. "Now, give me all the fucking money you got on you, nigga, or else I'ma take it by force. My moms needs it and I ain't letting her down for shit!"

"Dawg, your mother ain't no better than mine despite what you think or say." Tyrus hyper-ventilated with resentment while staring down the barrel of the gun. "And my moms needs the money too!"

Tyrus took his chances bum-rushing JoJo, which resulted in both of the troubled teenagers crashing on the oak-framed coffee table. Then, rolling around in the sharp pieces of the shattered glass top didn't slow the pair down. Taking turns being on the bottom, both suffering from deep cuts, the inevitable finally happened.

The deafening sounds of the revolver being fired twice echoed throughout the house. Tyrus and JoJo both lay motionless on the floor, one in shock from shooting his friend, and one in shock from being shot. The neighbors gathered around outside wondering what had happened behind the closed doors. With multitudes of police sirens in the distance getting closer, neither teen moved a muscle.

Minutes later, but after what seemed like an eternity to the boys, Yanna's house was swarming with police, including the same cops who'd arrested JoJo the prior evening. After a short while, gawkers who'd gathered across the street watched the paramedics sadly bring out one of the teens on a stretcher, barely clinging to life.

Mr. Sims placed a call to his longtime neighbor, Yanna Banks, to give her the bad news. After informing her there had been some sort of altercation at her home involving her son as well as Dawn Jackson's son, with Bible in hand he quietly prayed for the injured youth as well as the shooter.

Tyrus, badly cut up from the glass he and JoJo had rolled in, was totally distraught in a zombielike trance. As he was being handcuffed and led toward the squad car, everyone shook their heads. Word spread quickly of the shooting up to the corner store where Dawn, as usual, was begging for money for her next rock. She rushed down the block to check things out with her only son and provider. Most of the folks standing around gave Dawn cold, hard stares of contempt like they had years ago after Joseph Sr.'s death. Now, they blamed her for the actions of her son.

"That boy didn't have a chance in life from the beginning," one woman hissed so Dawn could hear.

"I'd probably shoot someone then myself if I were cursed with a mother like her," another remarked.

A third person couldn't help but join in. "Yeah, look at her trying to act all concerned. She'll be getting high on that crack rock no sooner than they bend the corner with that bad seed of hers!"

Ignoring the cruel judgments the slew of nosey bystanders passed on her, as the squad car pulled off with Tyrus in the rear seat in tears, Dawn asked one of the policemen still on the scene exactly where they were taking her underage son.

"By the looks of the victim and the amount of blood he's lost, your son is probably on his way to prison for the rest of his life, that's where," the officer nonchalantly replied.

CHAPTER THIRTEEN

Here and Now. . .

Lying on the stretcher, drifting in and out of consciousness while the doctor assessed his condition, JoJo started to panic. Suddenly he started realizing how serious his gunshot wounds were.

"Oh, God! Oh, God." The numbness to reality caused by all the liquor he'd drunk was fast wearing off. The pain became excruciating and almost unbearable to the teenager. "Somebody get my momma! Get my momma! Call her." He squirmed from side to side as the nurses tried restraining him to put an IV in his arm.

"She's already here, son, so relax. If you relax, we'll help you," the doctor bargained with JoJo, who was just about his own child's age. "Just close your eyes and calm down while we do our job. Just relax."

How did things turn out like this? God, please help me make it! JoJo prayed, feeling the pinch of a needle in his arm and a hot burning in the pit of his stomach. *I don't wanna die like my father! I wanna live!*

For some strange reason, his thoughts stayed focused on Byron and the day he found out he'd died. JoJo relived the nonchalant manner in which his family behaved, as if his life didn't count for anything except for materialistic belongings. He most definitely didn't want to end up like that. He wanted to do something great with his life, something memorable besides selling pills on the streets.

He then remembered the words of Mr. Sims, about making his father proud, and Keys saying he should stay in school. JoJo knew for the past couple of months or so he'd been living straight-up foul, and all he could do now was pray that God was willing to give him a second chance. He couldn't change his past or what led up to him getting shot up and fighting for his life, but he could change what he did if God was willing to let him walk away from here. It was now in God's hands.

One thing JoJo knew for sure was that, if he lived to see another day, the first thing he was gonna do was to tell Tyrus he was sorry for his part in everything that jumped off, and he was 100 percent right. No matter what mistakes Dawn made, she was still his mom, and she should come first in his life, like Yanna was top priority in his. Both mothers had used them as a way to make ends meet, as their meal tickets, and that was wrong as hell.

JoJo, fighting to survive, was in the triage area and then surgery for what seemed like hours.

"It just don't make no kind of sense to me. I swear you might as well have been the one to pull the trigger on that gun. You knew what that boy was doing in the streets, and you didn't say or do anything to stop him. It's your fault that baby is lying on that stretcher fighting for his life," the old woman repeated once more, shaking her head at her niece's recent bad parenting skills and lack of concern for her children.

"Don't say that, Auntie Grace," Yanna shrieked, her voice echoing throughout the hospital. "I'm a good mother! I'd never do anything to harm one of my kids, so stop saying that!"

"You say that now, but you did harm him. Maybe not on purpose, but you still did. Forcing that boy to take his daddy's place and work every day after school. Then pressuring him all those times to keep his little sister every Saturday instead of allowing him to be a normal teenager. Thank God I stepped in and started looking after Jania while you ran around partying every night. I should have taken JoJo and Jania in like I took you in all those years ago. Although now it looks like it's all a little too late. But, still, it was all plain wrong, Yanna. There was no way that boy could fill a man's shoes, but you made him feel like he had to!"

Yanna thought for a moment, taking in her aunt's judgmental words as she remembered how she handled things after the death of her cheating husband. "I never thought about it like that. I love my baby and just want him to be all right." She continued to sob. She was overcome with emotion and grief, and her tears started to flow even more. She was almost hysterical when the unthinkable happened.

Wiping her face, she couldn't believe her eyes. "What in the fuck are you doing in here? Who let you in here?"

Not knowing what to do or say, Dawn, still heavily under the influence of drugs and alcohol, slowly walked toward Yanna and her aunt. "I don't mean to bother y'all, I promise, but—"

"But what, Dawn? What are you about to tell me?" Yanna jumped to her feet wanting an explanation but really not expecting one. "You about to tell me you didn't mean to sleep with my husband all those nights? Or you didn't mean to call him that night he got killed? Or is you about to tell me sorry for that animal you raised up shooting my baby? Which one is it?" Yanna didn't give a mentally unbalanced Dawn a chance to respond as Auntie Grace pulled her back by the forearm. Yanna looked like she was ready to attack. "Look at you, bitch! Joseph Sr. was nothing but a damn fool to put you over me and mines!"

"Look, I don't want any trouble. I swear I don't." Dawn was attempting to come down from her high. "But they brought Tyrus here to treat him for some deep cuts and wounds he got in the fight and—"

Yanna broke loose from her aunt's weak grip. "Cuts! Are you seriously fucking in here wanting some sort of sympathy because your boy got some damn punk-ass cuts? You best get on, bitch! I'm warning you it's about to get real hectic for you in about two seconds!"

Auntie Grace had had enough of the long-feuding mothers focusing on the wrong thing, and she tried telling them just that. "Are you both crazy? Each of your sons has been out here doing wrong, breaking the law, and y'all let them; and instead of trying to guide them in the right direction, leading by example, y'all in here fighting over something that happened years ago! That man y'all openly and knowingly shared is to blame for all this mess. And he dead and gone and y'all are still arguing like fools!"

Time and time again, Dawn wanted nothing more than to approach Yanna and just apologize for what her selfish actions had caused to happen, but she knew Joseph Sr.'s widow wasn't trying to hear it. And deep down inside she couldn't blame her for holding a grudge.

· "Naw, Auntie Grace." Yanna couldn't be controlled or reasoned with. "First she killed my husband, and now her boy tried to kill my son! She got me twisted! I want this bitch head!"

"Look at her, Yanna," Auntie Grace demanded repeatedly. "What else can you do to this poor creature that she hasn't already done to herself? And as for you, Ms. Jackson, you need some serious help. It's a sin and a shame how you are letting your son see you as you are."

Before the overly distraught Yanna could get an opportunity to swing on Dawn, two police detectives entered the hospital waiting room wanting to question both mothers with regard to their sons and their recent illegal pill-selling enterprise. After interviewing several residents on the block, they'd become aware of that activity as a possible motive for the shooting.

The finger-pointing and allegations had just started to fly when the doctor emerged through the double doors and into the hospital's waiting area. There he found his young patient's mother and great-aunt, who were arguing with a remorseful Dawn Jackson and the detectives about who did what to whom. As the doctor held a chart in his hands, Yanna bravely stood tall, preparing herself for whatever she'd have to face.

Dawn took a deep breath as she waited to hear the news too. She hoped, for Tyrus's sake, that Yanna's son would be okay.

"Hello, Mrs. Banks." The doctor took a deep breath as his patient's mother braced herself, holding on to her elderly aunt's arm. "It was touch and go for a good while, but fortunately we removed both bullets with a minimal amount of damage. It must've been divine intervention, because the bullets missed every vital organ. It might take a couple of months of your son being hospitalized to fully recover, but he's young and strong-willed. He'll make it."

Yanna dropped down to her knees and cried out, "Thank you, God, for giving me a second chance with my son to make things right!"

"Well, that's good news, Mrs. Banks, and we'll be back to talk to your son when he's up to it," one officer announced.

"And as for you, Ms. Jackson, when they finish up here with your son, Tyrus, he'll be transferred to the county jail. More than likely he'll be charged with attempted murder," the other detective advised her, handing her his card. "Be grateful. It could've been worse. He is still looking at quite a few years in prison so you might wanna get him a good lawyer, or pray for a miracle like that young man back there just got."

Six Months Later. . .

"All right, JoJo, promise me you're gonna take it easy out here."

Getting out of the used vehicle his mother was now driving, JoJo smiled while his sister climbed in the front seat. Yanna had traded in her brand-new Range Rover for an older car to save some money. After reaching back inside for his cane, JoJo kissed his mother on the cheek.

"Mom, don't worry. I'm gonna be fine, and I'm gonna take it easy; I swear. Since you started back working, you never have any fun. Maybe since I won't be home all weekend, you and Jania can have a girl's night together watching movies or something," JoJo said as he leaned in to look at his mother. JoJo had decided to get away from the hood and spend the weekend in the quiet suburbs with his friend.

"That's not a bad idea." Yanna smiled at her son. She was proud of the man he was becoming. He was growing up on his own terms and not because she was putting pressure on him. "Take it easy this weekend and don't push yourself too hard."

"I won't, Mom. I'll be fine," JoJo said as he slowly made his way down the brick pathway. His walking wasn't back to 100 percent but, with therapy three times a week, he was improving every day.

"Don't worry, Mrs. Banks. He'll be fine. I'll make sure of it." Tyrus met his best friend at the curb, helping him with his bag. "Besides going to church with me and my mother on Sunday, we gonna pretty much stay in the house so I can beat him on Xbox."

Yanna gave Tyrus a slight smile. "How is your mother doing anyway?"

"Great! Since moving out here, she's been off drugs for a hundred and ninety-seven days, and counting," Tyrus proudly announced. "Going to NA meetings and everything!"

Yanna looked on as the two friends let themselves into the house. She thanked God that things had turned out for the best for everyone.

When JoJo had woken up from surgery, he'd insisted on testifying on behalf of Tyrus. He explained to the judge that it had all been an accident. Being that Tyrus was still seventeen and had no prior arrests, the judge allowed him to be tried as a juvenile, and the charges were dropped against him. As for JoJo, he went to court for the night that he was arrested, and he paid all the fines with what was left of his drug money. The judge also charged him as a juvenile. JoJo was to remain on probation until his eighteenth birthday, at which point his juvenile record would be sealed.

Both boys had plans to graduate high school and were undecided about what career paths they wanted to take. Tyrus was considering going to college to be a rehab counselor. He saw what drugs did to his mom, and he really wanted to help people get clean and have better lives. JoJo, on the other hand, was leaning toward getting a business degree. He liked the feeling of being his own boss and running his own business. It was just a matter of deciding what kind of business he wanted to go into. Whatever it was, he knew he'd keep it on the legal side things.

As for Yanna, after seeing how Tyrus and JoJo were able to let go of the past and become friends, she decided to try to make peace with the entire ancient beef she and Dawn had. Although they ran in different circles and would most likely never be the best of friends, they could at least be cordial with each other. Their sons were becoming best friends, and Yanna had grown to respect that bond. She knew it wouldn't happen overnight, but she was working toward building a better life for herself and her kids. She no longer wanted to be an angry, bitter woman. She was determined to be the best she could be for herself and her family.

The End

Party Girls

Clifford "Spud" Johnson

CHAPTER ONE

The Honorable Judge Tammy Burdine was eager to get home so she and her best friend in the entire world could go on their weekend excursion to Dallas for some fun and games. She was getting moist just thinking about the kind of fun and games they were about to play. Tammy and Debbie were freaks of the highest order. When it came to their sexual exploits, nothing was off limits. They'd had orgies, female-on-female sex, and almost every sexual experience a woman could have. Sex was all they wanted other than their successful careers. They felt nothing else was needed, especially love or any kind of relationship.

They had it all and life was good, and that was so important for them both, being that they came from the notorious Prince Hall projects located on the east side of Oklahoma City. Life had thrown several curveballs at them both, yet they were able to prevail and come out scratched but not scarred. Tammy could smile now at that fateful night that changed the direction of her life, and Debbie's. Those Hoover Crips who attempted to rape her changed her in so many ways. To this very day, she thanked God for that night, not only for stopping her from being raped but for the eye-opening experience. She knew it had to be God, and she was ever so grateful.

Now here it was, twenty years later, and she was a prominent and well-respected federal judge in the state of Oklahoma. She couldn't help but stick her chest out at the accomplishments she'd achieved. The hard work had paid off, and she was good in every way. She owned a nice, spacious home in Edmond, and she was financially secure. She had seen most of the world with her girl Debbie, and they did it how they wanted to. Not bad for some girls from Prince Hall.

Now, she couldn't wait to get home and get ready for the short three-hour drive to Dallas to get her freak on. She wanted to touch herself as she drove toward her home. Yes, this weekend was going to be one to remember. She then laughed out loud. "Hell, every time me and Debbie's wild ass go out of town has been one to remember!"

***

Debbie Bell was smiling as she got into her new Lexus SUV and eased into traffic. Work was over, and now it was time to go have some fun and act a little cray cray, she thought as she grabbed her phone and made sure the suite she reserved for her and Tammy was on point. It was a suite at the Aloft near downtown Dallas so they could be close enough to all the action, yet stay in a respectable place to remain safe at all times. That was one of their rules, and they had several of them when it came to their playtime. They did it how they wanted; and, whether they got wicked and hood with it or classy and bougie with it, they had to remain safe.

One would never think Debbie and Tammy, with their careers and how they looked, were some cold hood rats at heart. Debbie was five feet five inches with light brown eyes and a body that made men want to beg just to touch her. Tammy was a slim goody with a pair of double D's that made men want to turn into babies just to be breastfed by her. Thanks to hard work in the gym three days a week their bodies were fit, and they had been blessed to have aged well. They were looking super fine at forty-five years of age, and there was nothing in this world that was holding them back.

Debbie knew that once they made it to Dallas, wild-ass Debbie Dick was going to come out. That was the nickname Tammy had given her years ago once she realized how much Debbie loved the dick. Tammy was just as wild as she was and craved young dick. She swore that the young ones fucked the best. Debbie didn't give a damn how old the man or woman was; as long as she came multiple times throughout the night, she was good.

Her life was so good. She owned her accounting firm as well as a condo in downtown Oklahoma City. She was blessed, and she knew it. "Oooh, wee! Dallas, here we fucking come! And I do mean cum!" she yelled as she raced home so she could change and go pick up Tammy for their ride to Dallas.

Though they knew better than to drink while driving, they were both quite tipsy from the Cîroc Apple and green-apple Gatorade they drank during the drive to Dallas from Oklahoma City. Once they checked into their suite, they took off their clothes and started getting their outfits ready for the evening's festivities.

First was dinner at their favorite seafood restaurant in Dallas, Pappadeaux. After drinks and some great seafood, they planned on hitting a few clubs to see if they could find some men who could feed their sexual hungers for the night. They intended to make sure all of their sexual desires would be fulfilled before heading back to Oklahoma City Sunday afternoon.

It took them over two hours before they both felt their outfits were perfect. Debbie had on a form-fitting wrap dress with some killer open-toed stilettos to show off her perfectly manicured toes. Tammy decided on some silk slacks and a low-cut blouse that left very little to the imagination. You could damn near see her areolae, but she didn't mind one bit. The ladies were on a mission to have a good time and find some good dick. They weren't like the rest of the hood rats out there just looking for any man to buy them dinner and pay for their drinks. They were classy, intelligent career woman who could pay for their own meals. They were not going to settle for anything less than grade A prime dick and plenty of it!

After enjoying lobster and Pappadeaux's lump crab and spinach dip topped off with the restaurant's signature drink, the Swamp Thing, the ladies were ready to hit the first club. They preferred the mixed crowd with both a younger and older scene, so they went uptown to a club called Side Bar. Once there, they stayed only long enough to have one drink because the pickings were slim, men-wise. Debbie did see some sexy women, but she just wasn't in the mood for that tonight.

They left and went to another club located in North Dallas called Park Ave. It was a bit better than Side Bar because the men were on point, so they stepped to the bar, ordered their drinks, and turned and let their eyes roam around the club.

Debbie spotted a man dressed in some nice jeans and fitted shirt, looking casually dapper. She winked at Tammy and off she went with a drink in hand. She and Debbie weren't the type to stand around and wait for men to approach them. "See what you want and go get it!" was their motto. They applied that to everything in life.

Tammy was smiling as she watched her bestie do her thing. Just as she was about to step away from the bar, she noticed a young man at the opposite end of the bar looking absolutely scrumptious. As she stepped his way, she saw he was a young tender. She smiled at his baby face and guessed he couldn't be over twenty-one, or maybe twenty-two. That thought alone made her wet. His body looked lean and toned. She could see his muscles through his fitted shirt, and she noticed he had a nice-sized bulge in his pants. *Oooh, you're about to get you some grown-woman pussy tonight!*

She eased next to him and gave him a sexy smile. "Hey, you. What you drinking?"

The young man looked at her, then looked over his shoulder to see if she was, in fact, speaking to him. When he realized she was talking to him, he was shocked. He didn't want to seem immature, so he smiled and said, "Hello. I'm drinking Crown Apple on the rocks."

Tammy ordered a round for both of them and then pounced with no preamble. "So, how can I get you to come to my suite after the club so I can blow your mind?"

The young man was sipping the last of his drink, and he almost spat it all over her expensive blouse, but he caught himself. "Damn, baby, you ain't playin', huh?" he managed to say after clearing his throat.

"No. I don't like to play like that. I like to play in the bedroom. So, what's your answer?" she said as she leaned in toward him and winked.

"Not trying to sound like a cornball or nothing, but you don't even know my name." She started to speak, but he raised his index finger, silencing her before she could say a word. "My name is Jerron, but I prefer J-Run. And yours?"

She smiled because she liked how he was taking control of the conversation, and that was a major turn-on for her. *Young man, but a strong young man. I love it*. She gave him the name she used whenever she and Debbie were on their freak trips. "I'm Tennelle."

He reached and grabbed her right hand and said, "Hi, Tennelle."

"Now that the proper greetings have been made, can you answer my question?"

"I'm not the type of man who just jumps at an offer like that from a female I know nothing about."

With a smirk on her cute face she said, "So, you're telling me that you've never left a club with a female you just met?"

"No, that's not what I'm saying. Shit, look at me; you don't think I get ass thrown at me on the daily? All I'm saying is I'm the cautious type. If I don't know you, I don't trust you. Simple as that. So, we got to get to know one another a li'l bit before I decide to go somewhere with you and let you do some freaky shit to me. With that said, tell me a little bit about yourself."

Slightly irked but still horny for this divine-looking young man, Tammy asked, "Like what?"

"I know you not from the D. So where you from?"

One of Tammy and Debbie's rules was to never give up too much information about their personal lives while out of town. So, instead of saying she was from Oklahoma City, she generalized it and said, "I'm from Oklahoma."

His eyes lit up for a second like he had just made a big discovery. He sipped the drink that Tammy bought him to try to cover up his reaction. Luckily, she hadn't noticed his reaction.

"Where in Oklahoma? I was out there in Oklahoma City some time ago, but I had to get up outta there. It was too damn slow for me. I've been in the D for a minute now."

"Oh, great. So now we're going to sit here and make small talk, pretending to be interested in getting to know each other? How long are we going to be doing this for?" she said as she slightly rolled her eyes.

"Oh, I see you got the slippery lips and attitude, huh? What you on, baby? I mean, for real what's the deal with you? Because for real for real, I'm not feeling this. If you think you can just walk up to me, offer your body, and then catch an attitude when I try to be respectful and learn a few things about you, then you got the wrong one." He scoffed at her before taking another sip of his drink.

"I'm a direct woman," Tammy responded nonchalantly. "When I see something I like or want, I go for it. I'm not interested in nor do I have time for small talk. I want what I want, and that's that. Period."

"And what you want right now is to fuck me?"

The smile was no longer on her face when she replied, "No. I not only want to fuck you; I want to blow your mind in ways you never imagined possible."

"Is that right?"

"Yes. That's right."

"And then what?"

"What do you mean, then what?"

"It's not a hard question, honey. You want to fuck me. You want to blow my mind. Okay, suppose we go back to your suite and we do all of that. What comes next?"

"Then we fall asleep, wake up, and part ways. Hopefully, we'll both walk away feeling real good. And if you can give it as well as I can maybe we can hook up again before I head back home."

"That simple, huh? Some 'NSA' shit, right?"

"That's right. No strings attached at all, baby. Now, are you with that or what? Because if you're not, I need to keep it moving while the night is still young."

"It sounds good, hon, but I'm gonna have to pass on this one. You be sweet, sexy." Jerron grabbed her hand, placed a soft kiss on it, and stepped away from her without a backward glance, saying to himself, *no fucking way!*

Tammy was not a woman who was used to rejection, but she was also not the type of woman to get discouraged just because a man turned down her offer. She felt she was too bad of a bitch to ever let a man think he got to her. Not a single fuck was given as she downed her drink and turned toward the dance floor.

She took her time scanning the area for the next fine man. She noticed Debbie still had her prey cornered; and, judging by the way the man had his arm around her friend's waist, the night was going to end well for her. She was happy for her friend, but she was starting to feel frustrated about her situation. The more she looked, the more she couldn't help looking over toward Jerron's direction.

Get yourself together, Tammy. Stop looking at him. There's no way you're going to let that youngster get to you. No way! She stepped up to a decent-looking man, grabbed his hand, and led him to the dance floor where they began to dance to a hot single by Drake. She was getting her groove on nicely, letting her dance partner get a few feels of her luscious body.

Every now and then she would glance around and catch Jerron watching her as she danced. She would dance a little more provocatively, showing the young man what he was missing. *Fuck you, youngster. You lose, not me,* she thought as she continued to dance. After three straight dances, she was thirsty, so she went to the bar and ordered a bottled water along with a shot of Cîroc Apple. She was sipping her water when she saw Debbie headed her way, pulling her man for the night along with her.

"What the hell you got going on, girl? I saw you with a cutie at the bar then you was on the dance floor with a so-so nigga. What's up with that?" Debbie asked. Then she ordered a drink. "This here gorgeous gift of a man is Mick."

"Hi, Mick."

"Hi."

"Mick and I are about to head out. He has to go to work early in the morning, so I'm going to his place, and then I'll catch an Uber to the room. You cool?"

"You know it! Go have fun and make sure you send me all of Mick's information. You know the rules."

"No question. I already dropped you a pin with his address and number." She gave her friend a quick hug and an air kiss on the cheek, then grabbed Mick's hand and said, "Let's go, baby. It's time for you to see how Dee Dee gets down!"

Tammy was laughing as she ordered another drink. Just as the bartender brought her drink, she felt a tap on her shoulder. She turned around and couldn't suppress her smile as she stared into Jerron's intense brown eyes.

"Finish that drink so we can roll out. And, no, we not going to get down on the freaky freaky. We going to another spot I know of to set the tone for later. You with that?"

She answered his question by downing her drink and grabbing her clutch bag. "Let's go."

Fifteen minutes later, Jerron pulled into the parking lot of DGZ Gentlemen's Club, and Tammy was all smiles as she pulled into the parking lot behind him. She got out of Debbie's SUV and watched as Jerron paid for both of the vehicles at the valet.

He grabbed her hand, led her into the club, and took her straight to a reserved table in VIP. Once they were seated, he ordered a bottle of Cîroc Apple for Tammy and a bottle of Moët for himself. If Jerron was trying to impress her, it was definitely working.

She took a look around the club at some of the fine young ladies dancing on the different stages. She smiled seductively at Jerron and asked, "Can I have a table dance, baby?"

He started laughing and said, "Freak. You are something else for real. Yeah, you can get that. Let me pick the dancer, though, cool?"

"No problem."

He looked around the club until he spotted the female he wanted. He waved her over, and she made her way to the table. He then introduced the dancer to Tammy. "Tennelle, this is Dynasty, and she is about to give you the best lap dance you've ever had."

"Hi, Dynasty. I'm ready if your fine ass is."

"Oh, I'm always ready, honey," the dancer said as she began to dance to the groove of the music playing. When she was on Tammy's lap, she bent forward, and Tammy took one of her nipples in her mouth and began to suck on it lightly. Jerron was laughing the entire lap dance because Tammy was showing no shame at all as she let her hands roam all over Dynasty.

When the dance was over, Dynasty smiled and gave Tammy a kiss on the cheek and said, "Girl, you are a frisky one, ain't ya? You worse than some of these niggas in here!"

"You better believe it. If I weren't here with him, I'd have your ass right now! But I got this cutie who's gon' get all of me tonight."

"I know that's right, girl. You got the right one. J-Run is something special. Y'all have fun."

As soon as Dynasty left, Jerron smiled at Tammy and said, "Okay, crazy lady, you wanna kick it some more or you ready to go do this?"

"Baby, I been ready. And, after that lap dance, I have a pool for you to dip in."

"All right. Let's head out to my place. I don't do hotels."

"Okay. Can you drop me a pin so I can call my girl and let her know where I'll be?"

"No problem. Let's see if you're really gonna blow my mind." He laughed as he pulled out his phone, asked her for her number, and dropped his pin with his information. They left the club hand in hand, and Tammy was so wet she knew without a doubt she was about to fuck the shit out of Jerron. She just hoped he wouldn't disappoint her.

After the first hour of sex with Jerron, Tammy's only thought was that Jerron had the stamina of a top athlete. She had cum so many times she had to roll off of him to catch her breath. He was relentless. As soon as she was on her back, he dove between her legs and started sucking her pussy some more. She moaned and screamed, "Yesssssss, baby, yessss!" When she came, she came so hard she knew that she had met her match. She was damn near delirious.

"I need to take a break before we do another round," she said as she tried to catch her breath. Suddenly there was a knock at Jerron's door. She turned toward him and asked, "Are you expecting someone this late?"

He got off the bed and went toward the door naked and answered, "Yep. I'll be right back." Jerron returned to the bedroom two minutes later, followed closely by the dancer from DGZ. Jerron had a smile on his face as he sat on the bed and stared at Tammy. "You remember Dynasty, right? You wanted to have an unforgettable night. Well, baby, it's about to go down. Now, come here while Dynasty gets herself fresh for us."

Before Tammy could respond, Jerron eased himself between her legs and started to lick and suck her pussy ever so softly, causing Tammy to tremble with pleasure. She had been with women on different occasions, so she wasn't offended by Jerron's move of adding Dynasty to their night of pleasure; actually, she was even more turned on!

Though it was well after two in the morning, the night was still young as far as she was concerned and she was going to enjoy every luscious minute. She pushed his head away from her pussy and positioned her body so she was sitting backward on top of his head, and they then started having a hot sixty-nine. Tammy was holding nothing back with her head game, and she was pleased by the reaction she was receiving from Jerron. When she felt a soft hand on her ass, she moaned because she knew Dynasty had joined the party and that alone made her start to cum all over Jerron's face.

"Yes! Yes! Yes!" she screamed, and those types of screams continued well into the early morning.

CHAPTER TWO

Tammy woke up smiling. She got out of bed and went to the bathroom to get herself together. When she saw how she looked she frowned because she was looking a hot mess; her hair was all over the place. She thought about the night, and she couldn't help but smile again. Thoughts of how Dynasty and Jerron rocked her world were still vivid in her mind. Replaying the freaky sex they had sent chills all over her body, and she couldn't believe she was actually starting to get wet again.

Mmmm, I wonder if I should go wake Jerron up for some more of his dick before I leave. It was so good with Jerron and, when Dynasty joined them, it got even better. Licking and sucking on Dynasty while Jerron served her his huge man piece made her feel as if she had died and gone to heaven. *Mmmm,* she thought again as she went back into the bedroom to see Jerron sitting on the edge of the bed talking to someone on the phone. She waved good-bye to him as she grabbed her clothes and started to get dressed.

"Trust me, bro. When you see me, I'll make everything crystal clear for you. Look, let me go. I need to take care of something. Hit me back in an hour or so," Jerron said and then ended the call. He stood and stepped to Tammy and gave her a hug. "So, did you enjoy yourself?"

"Mmmmm, definitely," she purred in his arms.

"So, does that mean we'll have an encore tonight?"

"That depends."

"On what?"

"I need to check with my bestie to see what she has planned for us this evening. Be easy, baby. Last night was amazing, and if I can't see you again tonight, just know that I'll never forget all of the pleasures that you gave me last night."

"All right, hon. Listen, I gotta take a quick road trip, but I'll be back this evening, so if you want to hit me up later, I'll be around. If not, then I guess I'll see you when I see you. Just know that I want and intend to see you again," he said as he smiled confidently at her.

"Wow, so I guess I made a good impression on you then?"

He ran his hands all over her curvy body and whispered in her ear, "Fucking right, you did, and you better not think that I won't be inside of you again." He kissed her softly then turned and stared at Dynasty, who was sound asleep. "The next time we won't need her help. I have more in store for you, sexy."

Tammy went from being a little wet to soaking wet. She was clenching her pussy muscles tightly, trying to control the urge she had to jump onto that young man and fuck him one more time before she left. She couldn't do that though; it was time to go. She had to stick to the rules she and Debbie had. One was no relationships with men after they had gotten what they wanted and the night was over. They usually made it a habit to leave before the sun came out, so she was already breaking the rules since it was already morning time and she was still there. As tempted as she was to have a quickie with Jerron, she couldn't let that affect her next move. She had to go. The night they had spent together would be a great memory, but that was it.

After getting herself together, she grabbed her purse and let Jerron lead her out of his home. Once they were at her car, he gave her another hug and kiss.

"All right, then. I guess I'll talk to you later?" she said as she started the car.

"How are you going to do that when we haven't exchanged numbers? I know you ain't trying to shake me, Tennelle."

She kept her game face on and laughed as she grabbed her phone and said, "Did you forget I got your number last night when you sent me the pin to your place? Besides, there's no way I'll walk away from that good dick, sir." She laughed as she grabbed a handful of the package between his legs. "I'll give you a call later on after I know what my girl has planned for us tonight."

Shaking his head, he said, "Okay, call my phone now so I'll have your number just in case calling me later slips your mind. I deleted the text when I dropped you that pin. I'm not letting you get away that easily."

"One: I'm not trying to get away from you, and two: I said I will call you later. I have no reason not to. You proved to be a great choice last night."

"I hear you, but why you ain't dialing my number now like I told you to?"

"Told me to?"

"Yes, like I told you," he said staring directly at her.

Though she knew she was breaking a rule, she didn't care at that time because she picked her phone back up and did as she had been told. When his phone started ringing and he saw the

405 area code, he smiled and said, "That's my girl. I'll be waiting for your call. If I don't hear from you, best believe you will be hearing from me. Be safe." He turned and went back inside of his house smiling.

Tammy was smiling too as she pulled out of his driveway and headed toward the hotel. She had broken one of her and Debbie's rules, but she didn't give a damn because she was feeling Jerron. She wasn't planning on seeing him after they left Texas but she definitely wanted to make sure she got some more of that good dick before they headed back to Oklahoma City. After having such a great time with Jerron, she felt he should be the one who got to rock her pussy for the rest of the weekend and that's all there was to it, she thought with that smile still in place.

As soon as Tammy entered the hotel room, Debbie jumped off the bed and said, "It's about damn time, girl! I've been wondering where your ass was. That youngster must have really put it down since you just now got your ass in."

"Oh my God. Yaaas, girl, yaaas! That man laid down some good pipe!" She walked over to her friend and the girls high-fived each other. "Let me tell you how it all went down," Tammy said. She gave her friend the recap of her encounter with Jerron and Dynasty.

Once she finished, Debbie was laughing so hard tears were streaming down her face. "Damn, and I thought I had a hell of a night with little dick Mick!"

"Little dick Mick? Girl, don't you tell me that tall, handsome man wasn't packing."

"That's exactly what I'm telling you! But he made up for it in different areas. I still had a good time. That man sure knows how to eat some good pussy. You know I don't roll nowhere without some help just in case times like these arise. I brought one of my nice-sized dildos with me, and it came right in handy. While Mick let his oral skills go to work, I was working this pussy cat real deep and, let me tell you, the combo between his tongue and my toy was perfect. It got even better when I had him fuck me in the ass while I went deep in the pussy, so it was all good!"

"Girl, only you would do some shit like that."

"But, for real though, I'm hating on you for real right now. You don't even like to rock with pussy too often, and you got some last night. Shit, that's my lane right there. I should have been with y'all."

"I know, right? Let me tell you, Dynasty's sexy ass knows how to lick some pussy, too. Had me so wet that it was dripping down my leg. I had to go on and return the favor while Jerron worked me doggie style. All in all, it was a great night. So, my question to you is, what are we going to do tonight?"

"Same as last night, woman. We're gonna go out for dinner, get a nice buzz going, and go look for some different dick."

"I'm kinda in the mood for some more of Jerron, but I guess I can give it a go."

Debbie frowned and shook her head. "Now, you know we don't do the same dick twice when we go outta town. I don't know why you would even want to spend another night with that Jerron guy when there's so many sexy-ass men out here. Don't you go catching feelings and fucking up our get-down." The guilty look on Tammy's face made Debbie get mad. "Oh, shit. I overlooked you walking in so late today, but you done broke some more rules, haven't you?"

"Yeah, I have. I gave him my number and told him I might be able to hook up again with him this evening. But it's no big deal. Once we go home, I'll block his ass, and that will be that."

"Save that weak shit for someone who doesn't know you, girl. We made those rules for a reason, Tammy. But I'm not gonna trip. I just hope you can get enough of this guy and leave it all here in Texas. Last thing we want is for you to go putting that pussy on him super good and getting him hooked. Next thing you know he'll be all fucked up in the head and bring his behind to the city looking for your ass."

"He doesn't know where we live exactly and he damn sure doesn't know my real name, so I doubt it will get that far. It's all good. Now, let me lie down. I need some rest before we get into another night of fun and fucking!" They both started laughing as Tammy went into the bathroom to take a shower.

Debbie lay down on the bed and wondered if her friend had made a mistake giving her number to Jerron. *Time will tell,* she thought as she closed her eyes.

Jerron was lying on his bed relaxing after fucking Dynasty one more time for the road. She wanted to stay longer, but that was not happening. He gave her a couple hundred dollars for her time and made her leave. Now he was waiting for his big brother to call him back. When his cell rang he laughed out loud and answered the phone, and waited for the automated voice to finish so he could accept the call from the federal prison where his brother was serving a 210-month sentence.

Once he pressed the number five key on his phone, his brother said, "I got your email, bro, but you lost me. Who did you meet last night, and how in the hell will that get me out?"

"I told you I can't explain it all on that thing. Just know that all is good and you will be home way sooner than 2025. I got you."

"I hear you, but I sure wish you could put me up on everything. You got me in here fucked all the way up."

Jerron grabbed the remote and hit the play button for his flat screen and smiled as he saw Tammy's face while sucking him off. He pressed the forward button and watched as Tammy was getting her pussy sucked by Dynasty, and he finished watching the recording with him fucking Tammy hard from behind while she was eating Dynasty's pussy. The cute little butterfly tattoo on her right ass cheek made him laugh. *That's a good verifying mark, baby,* he said to himself.

To his brother, he said, "Don't trip. I'll be out there to see you in a week or so, and by then everything will be put into effect. Then you will see how your little brother gets down."

"Yeah, yeah, you just make sure you don't get into any trouble, man. I don't need nothing happening to you while I'm in here. I'd lose my fucking mind. I love you, bro. I'm about to go hit the yard and walk the track."

"Love you too. I'll see you soon and, don't worry, I got you."

Jerron ended the call and smiled as he Googled the name Tammy Burdine of Oklahoma City. When the search came back with the Honorable Judge Tammy Burdine, he clicked the name and saw a picture of the woman he had spent all night fucking like crazy. She looked so cute and innocent in that picture, wearing her black robe.

"Tennelle my ass. I knew that was you, bitch. Yeah, I got your ass, and you're about to make my brother a free man, you coldhearted bitch." He laughed out loud. He put his phone down and laid his head back and started forming the rest of his plan to free his brother.

He couldn't believe it when she approached him at the club last night and came on to him. He knew he had played it right by not jumping at her offer right out of the gate. Now, he had her ass right where he wanted her. He was about to blackmail her ass and make her overturn his brother's 210-month conviction by using the recording his security cameras made while they were fucking. This was a dream come true, and he loved it. He was gonna get to free his big brother and have some bomb-ass sex in the process. Just thinking about how he was going to fuck that sexy judge literally and figuratively made his revenge even sweeter.

He thought back to the day his brother was sentenced, and he felt his anger rise. He remembered the nasty attitude Judge Burdine had when she gave his brother the time for conspiracy. She told everyone in the courtroom that she wished she could give him more time because she felt he was a menace to society. That angered Jerron so much that day that he swore if he ever crossed paths with her he would get her back for doing that to his brother. She took his brother from him and, for that, she would pay dearly.

My time is coming. I'm gonna get you out, big brother, he thought as he closed his eyes and drifted to sleep.

Saturday night in Dallas, Texas was lit, and Tammy and Debbie were in full THOT mode. They both chose revealing outfits and made sure they were on point because it was time to find some men to give them pleasure for their last night in Texas.

After giving it deep thought, Tammy decided not to call Jerron, or answer if he called or texted her. She had to stick to the rules they had. She was feeling somewhat sad about that decision, but she knew it was best. Rules were made to be followed, and that was that. Debbie smiled when her friend informed her of her decision, but she didn't say anything else about it.

After checking a few clubs that were disappointing, they finally landed at Club Quill uptown, and it was definitely lit in there. The crowd was nice, and the men were nicer! Debbie and Tammy were licking their lips at all of the sexy men in there. They were so excited that neither knew which way to go first. They laughed as they made it to the bar and ordered some drinks.

"I think this is going to be a night to remember, Deb."

"I hear you, girl. Look at all these fine-ass niggas. I'm telling you there's something about these Texas niggas that turns me the fuck on."

"I know, right," Tammy said, and she sipped her drink. She turned to look around the place, and her eyes bulged when she saw a smiling Jerron looking handsome as ever in a pair of slacks and a white shirt. The shirt outlined his perfect physique making her become wet instantly as she thought about how she had run her hands all over him the night before. *Fuck,* she said to herself just as Jerron stopped in front of them.

"Hello, Tennelle. I see you did try to shake me. That's cold. But it's all good. You ladies have a good evening. Just wanted to come and say hello and good-bye." Without saying another word, Jerron walked away and didn't look back.

Debbie could read the hurt and disappointment on her friend's face, but it also gave her relief because she felt in her gut that nothing good could come from her friend catching feelings for that guy Jerron. She grabbed her glass and raised it in the air. "Toast with me, girl. The night is young, we looking good, and it's time to get lit!" They clinked their glasses, downed their drinks, and ordered another round.

After their third shot of Cîroc, the ladies were feeling good, and they went on the hunt. By the time the club was closing each woman had a man on her arm. They each went with their men to have another night of fucking and sucking.

Debbie found a stud who was packing, and she could've sworn she felt his dick inside of her rib cage. Tammy found a handsome man who made it feel as if he was making slow love to her and it felt good, so good that she made him get off of her so she could suck him off until he came. She sucked his dick as if her life depended on it and, when he came, she swallowed every drop of his nut.

"Mmmmm," she said as she lay back and watched as he put another condom on. He proceeded to make her feel like heaven on earth for the rest of the night. After they were done, although she'd had a great time with this guy, she couldn't help but think of Jerron. *Damn, I wish I could get with that fine-ass man one more time.*

the night. After they were gone, although she
had a great time with the guys, she couldn't help
but think of Deacon. Dang, I wish I could get over
that phony man on my mind.

CHAPTER THREE

Inside her judge's chambers, Judge Burdine
was sipping on bottled water as she went over
the appeal motion she was about to rule on. She
loved her job, but at times like this, she hated
it. Where she came from she saw and somewhat
understood why young black men chose the
street life, even though it was a dangerous path
with bad consequences. Nonetheless, it was
wrong, and they had to pay for their crimes
regardless of their reasons for committing them.

The war on drugs wasn't designed to entrap
the bottom workers; it was designed to get the
kingpins, the cartels, and the bigwigs to lower
the drug trafficking in the U.S. But, over the
years, it had all backfired. The poor were getting
caught up in the system while the bigwigs, cartels, and kingpins were getting off because they
could afford to pay top-notch lawyers.

She thought, *now, here we are again, sitting
back and watching as this so-called war on*

drugs starts over again, locking up even more people who come from poor areas in this crazy country. The president made a good effort to reduce certain federal drug laws, but that lasted only so long. He hasn't been out of office a year yet, and the powers-that-be are already planning to fill those overcrowded federal facilities right back up. Ridiculous. I'm bound by the law and the federal guidelines to do what I was sworn to do: uphold the law and rules of our country, whether I personally agree with them or not. It's a tough job, but someone has to do it.

After she finished reading the appeals motion, she started her response to deny the motion so that particular inmate would have to finish serving the rest of the sentence she imposed on him many years ago. Once she finished all of the paperwork, she stood and stretched. "Wow, I can't believe I'm still tired from Dallas. I sure could use me some more of that sexy-ass Jerron, though," she said aloud and wondered where the hell that thought came from. There was no way she would ever see that young man again, let alone have sex with him. She shook her head, grabbed her phone, and called Debbie.

"Hey, girl," Debbie answered on the second ring.

"Hi, love. How's your day going so far?"

"It's going." Debbie sighed into the phone. "How has your day been?"

"Mine has been long and stressful, girl. I need to do something to unwind."

"I'm definitely down for that. Honestly, I wish we would have stayed in Texas one more day for some more good dick." She laughed.

"I swear I was just thinking the exact same thing. But since that's not happening why don't we meet for dinner and some drinks?"

"I'm with that. What are you in the mood for?"

"Let's keep it simple. How about Pearl's?"

"Cool, I'm with some seafood. It may not be Pappadeaux, but it'll work."

"I know, right. All right, I'll be leaving here at four. I'll go get cleaned up and meet you there, say, by five-thirty."

"Okay, girl, see you there."

Debbie hung up the phone and turned off her laptop. She'd been working all day and hadn't even stopped to take a lunch break, so dinner and drinks were much needed. *No more work for me today. Time to go relax a little bit.*

Her phone rang again, interrupting her thoughts. She saw the number and smiled. "Hi, sexy man. What made you decide to bless me with a call?"

"I'm in the city for a few days on business and thought I'd see if I could take you out to dinner. Then after dinner, I'll feed you some of this chocolate dick for dessert. It's been way too long, Debbie."

Laughing, she said, "Now, what makes you think I want to give you some of my goodies after the way you just up and left a sister a few months back?"

"Come on, babe, I told you I had to catch an early flight back, and I couldn't stay the night. I sent you flowers the next day. Why can't you let that one slide off you and let's kick it while I'm back in town for a few days?"

"If that's another form of an apology, I want you to know that I still don't accept that weak shit. What I will do is accept your offer for dinner. Meet me at Pearl's at five thirty, and we can discuss this a little more. Maybe after some alcohol has been consumed, I may just consider letting you taste some of this kitty, Chris Tates. But don't you get extra with it. Let me make the decision. If you try to put too much pressure on me, you will find yourself playing with yourself and by yourself. Byeeeeee," she said, laughing as she ended the call.

She quickly sent a text to Tammy, informing her that the drinks and meal they would be having at Pearl's would be on her ex-lover, Chris Tates. She also added an LOL and told her friend to make sure she ordered the most expensive food on the menu! Tammy responded with the thumbs-up emoji and an LOL of her own.

"Okay, Chris, your wack ass wants another shot at the pussy? Be a good boy and you just might get some, but that's all you will get. You prick." As she finished getting herself together, Debbie couldn't help but think about Chris.

He was fine as hell with his athletic physique, bald head, and dark chocolate complexion. God, was that man hung, and the sex was out of this world. Chris was too damn pretty for himself; those perfect teeth along with the perfect body made him more prissy than a female, and that irked Debbie to no end. He was too high-maintenance.

When she met him some years back, she kept telling herself to dead him, but she continued to see him and was mad at herself and surprised when feelings for his ass started creeping into her heart. And, as soon as she opened her big mouth about trying to get serious with it, the bastard was in the wind informing her of his move to Atlanta to open up his own barber shop. She was hurt and even tried to offer to help him open up his own shop in OKC, but he wasn't trying to hear that, using the excuse that he wouldn't make any serious money here in the city like he would in the ATL.

When it was all said and done she was glad he had gotten the fuck on because she had no business dealing with a man like that. Despite the time that had passed, they had never lost contact. He would always make sure to call her when he was in town. Debbie's feelings for him were long gone, but the dick was too good to pass up, so she always took his calls.

It was that particular relationship that had changed her outlook on men and relationships, though. She had learned from that experience not to trust men because every man would let you down at some point. Men were good for one thing and one thing only. She loved that she and Tammy were both on the same page as far as that went. They both were very strict with each other about sticking to the rules of not ever catching feelings for a man. It was another reason why she was glad Tammy had stuck to her guns about not keeping in touch with that guy from Dallas.

There was no room for men in their lives other than to serve them some dick. *Fuck love. Fuck men for real.* Their lives were good just the way they were. They were successful black career women, and they would continue to handle their business and strive to be happy, living their lives carefree without ever having to worry about a man causing them any harm whatsoever.

As soon as Tammy got inside of her car her phone rang. She didn't look to see who was calling and answered it from her Bluetooth. When she heard Jerron's voice, she was surprised, shocked, and instantly horny. *Damn, I forgot to block his number.* She started to press END and hang up on him but decided to listen to what he had to say.

"You sure do know how to make a brother feel unwanted, Tennelle. Why you do me like that, ma?"

"It's not like that," she stammered. "I got caught up with my girl, and we just did us."

"Stop. You don't have to play me like that. You didn't want anything further from me; that's cool. I just don't respect how you got down with it. You gave me the impression you was one hundred with it, especially how you came at me in the first place. I guess I was wrong. No biggie, though. It's all good. I ain't gonna hold it against you. But a man does have an ego. You can't be just crushing a guy like that. It may be detrimental to my future get-down. Now, tell me you sorry so I can forgive you."

Tammy was driving now and waiting to hear him laugh or something, but the silence on the other end of the line told her he was dead serious. She loved how aggressive and straight the point he was. That turned her on, and she felt the moisture forming between her legs. *Damn.* Before she realized what she was saying she was already saying it and didn't regret it one bit.

"I'm sorry, Jerron, honestly I am. Yes, I should have kept it all the way real with you. I normally don't do things like that. It's just that—"

"That you're feeling me and are afraid things may get outta control. Like you may get gone for a young brother," he said, cutting her off. "I feel all of that, Tennelle, I really do, because for real for real I was thinking and feeling the exact same way."

"You were?"

"Yes. I'm feeling everything about you. You're smart, sexy, and can hold your own in the bedroom. I really liked how you weren't intimidated by Dynasty. Most mature women would have felt some kinda way with that situation. Instead, you rode with it, and we all enjoyed a great time because of it. That's another reason why I was so fucked up that you shook me like that. But, anyway, what's done is done. I just wanted to have some form of closure with this. I called you from a different line in hopes that you would pick up. You did, and I've said my piece, so you won't have to worry about me calling you again. I am no one's bugaboo, baby, believe that."

"I understand and, again, I apologize for not being upfront with you. If you want, we can keep in contact, Jerron. I'd like that."

Jerron smiled into his phone because he knew he had hooked Tammy right where he wanted her. *Bitch, you gon' regret the day you met me, and you gon' regret the day you fucked up my brother's life. I swear you will.*

"If you're for real about wanting to remain in contact with me, ma, first you have to be the one who initiates the next call. And, second, you have to stop ignoring me when I call!" They both laughed.

"I'll do both, baby, I promise."

"Baby, huh? It's like that?"

She laughed and said, "Yes, it's like that."

"Okay, cool. I gotta get into some thangs, so I'll be waiting for your text or call. Have a nice day, beautiful," he said as he hung up the phone before she could say a word.

When Tammy walked inside of her home, she couldn't believe how turned on she was. She quickly undressed and jumped into the shower hoping to cool herself off because she was horny as hell. But it was to no avail. Her hormones had a mind of their own and took total control over her body.

She began to rub her clit vigorously, and she added the right amount of pressure with her eyes closed. The whole time she kept thinking about Jerron's dick pumping deep in and out of her pussy. She came, and a powerful orgasm rocked her entire body and made her go slightly limp as she slid down to the tub and shivered as the hot water slid off of her body. She didn't know how long she stayed in that position because she was totally consumed with thoughts of Jerron.

What the hell am I doing? This is crazy. She got to her feet and washed herself off. She stepped out, lathered herself up with her favorite lotion, and got dressed so she could meet Debbie and Chris at Pearl's. Anything to keep her mind off of the scrumptious Texan she was obviously falling real hard for. *Damn!*

Debbie and Tammy arrived at the restaurant at the same time. They got out of their cars, gave each other a hug and air kiss, then entered and were quickly led to a table. Chris arrived a few minutes after they ordered their drinks. The ladies had to suppress their laughter when they saw the expression on Chris's face when he saw Tammy sitting at the table with Debbie. He thought he was going to have Debbie all to himself in hopes of wooing her into bed for the night.

Chris, ever the gentleman, greeted the ladies and took a seat at the table. "Since I have the pleasure of enjoying a nice meal with not one but two lovely ladies this evening, I say let's make it an unforgettable night and go back to my room after we eat. We can have some wine, enjoy the spirits, and have a monster threesome!" he said to the ladies as soon as their waiter walked off with Chris's drink order.

Tammy laughed and said, "You'll be lucky if Debbie goes home with you tonight. Don't push your luck and try to go for both of us, mister."

Debbie laughed and said, "His luck ain't looking that good, honey. It's going to take a lot for him to impress me this evening, and so far he is failing."

Chris gave the ladies his killer smile and shrugged. "Come on, ladies. You can't blame a brother for trying." They all laughed.

The waiter returned with Chris's drink; they then gave their orders to him. The ladies watched as Chris maintained his demeanor when they were ordering, but they both knew he was cringing inside at learning they were ordering the most expensive things on the menu. Again, they had to suppress their laughter.

"I see you ladies are hungry tonight. Long day at the office for you two?"

"It's always a long day for me," said Tammy.

"I concur, Your Honor," added Debbie, and they both giggled.

They proceeded to make small talk, catch up on things, and have a good evening. Tammy could tell Chris was on his best behavior saying all the right things and basically kissing Debbie's ass trying to get him some before the night ended. By the smile on Debbie's face, Tammy knew that she was going to fuck Chris. "Never turn down some good dick," was their motto. Debbie was enjoying how he was being her yes-man, so she decided to let him sweat it out some before going to his room and fucking his brains out.

Once the conversation switched to Chris and his move to Atlanta, Tammy excused herself and went to the bathroom. While there she finally gave into the desires that had been driving her crazy the entire time they were eating. She pulled out her phone and took a deep breath as she sent Jerron a text telling him that she was thinking of him and wished she was with him at that very moment. He texted right back and told her that's what he was waiting to hear. They sent texts back and forth for a few minutes; then she told him she was out and that she would call him when she made it home.

She rejoined Debbie and Chris, and they finished the evening with Debbie following Chris to his hotel downtown. Tammy went home looking forward to talking to Jerron and engaging in good conversation with him. *It will just be some long-distance flirting; what harm can that cause?* she asked herself, knowing damn well that it was much more than that. Deep down she knew she wanted that man and she wanted him bad!

CHAPTER FOUR

Three months flew by in the blink of an eye. Both Tammy and Debbie had been very busy caught up in their own lives. Debbie had been consumed by Chris. Apparently, Chris had finally realized he never stopped caring for Tammy, and he was doing his best to win her over. As for Tammy, she had been sucked in like a vacuum by Jerron. They spoke on the phone constantly and sent text messages to each other all day long. She found herself sending him texts while court was in session!

She had never felt this way for a man before. They had gotten to know one another in every way. The phone sex they had while on FaceTime was so intense she felt as if the orgasms she had were the best she ever had in her life. She craved and wanted Jerron inside of her so bad that it hurt. Her clit was so sore from rubbing it that she had to wear dresses and skirts most days because if she wore pants, it would make the soreness feel worse. She loved touching and playing with herself while she thought of or spoke to Jerron, though.

She kept telling him how much she wished he would come to see her. Her wish had been granted because Jerron was driving to the city to come spend a weekend with her. She had broken practically all of her and Debbie's rules by telling him where she lived and allowing him to get to know her so well. When he told her that he was going to Oklahoma City to see her, there was no way she would have allowed him to stay in a hotel. She gave Jerron her address, and he was coming to spend one hell of a hot, sex-filled weekend with her, and she couldn't wait. *Fuck the rules.* She had to have her young stud, and she wasn't letting him get away for nothing.

Debbie too was going through things she never thought she would, especially with Chris's pretty-boy ass. His chocolate skin and pretty smile had melted her ice-cold heart. He had been showering her with constant attention, and he was making her feel like she was the most important woman in the world to him. He was finally giving her what she had wanted from him so long ago. The way he showed his love for her made her want him in ways she never thought she would want a man again.

For so long, her and Tammy's motto had been, "Fuck love." All they needed and wanted was some good dick, but Chris was persistent, and he was winning her over. Unfortunately, Chris had just found out that his mom had been diagnosed with terminal cancer, and he really wanted Debbie to meet her before she passed. Debbie naturally wanted to go and meet his mom and make their relationship official. But everything was happening so fast, and it all felt so crazy to her. She needed to talk to Tammy about it, but she didn't want to come off as a hypocrite to her best friend since she had been so adamant about them sticking to their rules. Now, here she was breaking all of them.

Ever since Chris found out about his mother's illness, he had been staying in Oklahoma City, where his mother lived. She was hospitalized at Mercy Hospital, and Chris was making sure to visit her every day. He didn't want to stay at his mother's house because it made him feel worse about what was going on with her, so Debbie had opened up her home to him. He had been sharing her bed for the last week straight, and she hated to admit that she loved waking up with him next to her. It felt good; it felt safe; it felt right. He was going to be in the city for at least another two weeks, and she had no intention of letting him sleep anywhere else but right next to her in her California king-sized bed.

She knew she had to let Tammy know everything that was going on. She just hoped that her friend would be happy for her rekindled relationship and that she wouldn't be upset with her. *Please don't get mad at me,* she thought as she pulled out her phone and texted Tammy, telling her they needed to talk. Tammy responded that she would call her when she finished for the day, and they could meet for drinks. Debbie was meeting Chris for drinks, so she texted Tammy and told her that wasn't good for her, so Tammy called.

"What's going on, girl?" said Tammy as soon as Debbie answered.

"Way too much, for real. Girl, I've been talking with Chris a lot over the last few months. We've been fucking the shit out of each other, but it feels different with him. You remember how he did me wrong all those years ago? Well, he apologized about it, and I really think he meant it this time. I see a change in him. I'm not going to front or fake it with you because you are the only person I trust in this world. I think I'm actually falling in love. I know our rules and all, girl, but this shit feels so right and so good. I'm sitting here at the office confused as fuck about everything. I love the way he makes me feel, but I'm not sure if I'm doing the right thing."

Tammy laughed and gave a relieved sigh. "Girl, listen to me. I've been going through the exact same thing. I don't know about the love part, but me and Jerron have been talking and texting damn near all day and night every day for the last few months too. I am really feeling him, and I don't know where this is going, but I do know that I don't want it to stop. I've been meaning to call you, but so much has been going on. And it's been all about Jerron, and when we're not on the phone I'm trying to recover from the phone sex! That man makes me cum over FaceTime like he is actually touching me. It's so crazy that it feels as if I'm addicted or something. It looks as if our ways and rules are changing, girl."

"One thing is for certain: at least we're keeping it real with each other. That's most important. Oh, my goodness, I'm so glad you're not mad at me. I love you, girl, and no man will ever change that."

"Same here. I will not ever let a man or a dick, no matter how big or good, change our relationship," Tammy said sincerely.

"Well, I don't know about all of that," Debbie said, and they both laughed.

"Slut. I love you, but I gotta get back to my paperwork so I can hurry up and put this case off for a few weeks then get home and get ready."

"Get ready for what?"

"Jerron is coming to spend the weekend with me, and we will not be leaving the house until he is ready to head back to Dallas."

"Whoa. Okay, I hear you but just make sure you're still being cautious and careful with that guy. Be careful, Tammy."

"I'm gone, girl, way gone for that young man, but I haven't lost the sense God has given me nor what we learned growing up on the east side. This still Prince Hall. I ran a check on him, and he came back clean. He has no arrests or anything of the sort. That, compiled with what I've learned about him through our conversations, lets me feel comfortable about him coming to the house so we can have one hell of a weekend. So, I'm straight."

"I know you're no fool, so do what you do. Still, hit me and let me know all is well whenever y'all take a break. Hell, Chris will be over my place too, so it is what it is."

"Damn, we done finally got caught up."

"I know, right. Oh, well, let's see where it takes us, and let's enjoy the ride on the way."

"You know it. All right, I'll give you a call later, Deb. Let me get back to work. Love you to pieces, lady."

"Love you more," Debbie said as she ended the call and tried to get her mind off of Chris so she could finish up the rest of the work she had for the day.

By the time Tammy made it home, she had just enough time to prepare a nice meal of steak, green beans, and baked potatoes. Just as she got out of the shower, Jerron called her and told her that he was five minutes from her home. She told him, "Okay," then quickly got dressed. She chose a simple sundress with no undies. She figured it'd be a nice surprise for him when he ran his hands up her thighs, which she was pretty sure he'd be doing as soon as he got the chance to.

As soon as Jerron stepped through her door, he pulled her into his arms, and they shared one of the most passionate kisses she'd ever had in her life. It felt as if she were slightly delirious once he let her go. Her eyes were glazy and lustful as she stared at him totally speechless.

He smiled at her and said, "Mmm, something smells good. Did you break out your cooking skills for me?"

"Yes, I put together a little something-some-thing for us. You hungry, baby?"

"Yes, I'm starving, but not for food. For you. Now take me to your bedroom so I can give you what I've been wanting to give you since the last time I was with you. Dinner can wait. I want dessert first."

He stared at her curvy body wrapped in the sundress she had on, and he couldn't believe how horny he was for her. Even though this was all part of his plan to get his brother out of prison, he couldn't deny that deep down he was really feeling Tammy. Regardless of his feelings for her, he had to maintain his composure and stick to the script. His feelings would have to take a back seat. She had served his brother with too much time, and she was going to do what he told her to, or he was going to ruin her. It was as simple as that.

In the meantime, he was going to enjoy fuck-ing her and fucking her good because he knew once he dropped the bomb on her it would be a wrap with the sex. *Or maybe not,* he thought with a smile on his face as he let her lead him into her bedroom. Before she could make her way to the bed, he pushed her body against the wall and slid the shoulder straps off of Tammy's dress. He placed tender kisses along her neck as he tugged the dress past her breasts. He smiled as the dress slid to the floor, revealing her naked body.

"Damn, ma, you look so damn fine. Come here," he said as he pulled her to the bed and quickly started licking all over her body.

When he worked his way down to her pussy, she almost felt her legs get weak when he let his tongue swirl slowly all over her extra-wet pussy. He sucked and lightly nibbled on her clit and drove her to one hell of an orgasm so fast she couldn't believe it.

She was so turned on that she couldn't take it any longer; she had to have him inside of her. She tried to tear his clothes off. She was so hungry for the dick. Once she had him naked, she grabbed a condom, slid it on his man meat, and quickly climbed on top and put him inside of her. She rode him long and hard for ten minutes and came at least twice before he finally told her he was almost there. She slid off of him, took the condom off, and began giving him some head, sucking his dick as best she could. When he exploded, she took every drop of his semen down her throat. He held her head tightly as the last few drops escaped his body. She wiped her face with a towel and lay next to him on the bed. She nestled her head on his chest and listened to his heartbeat as their breathing slowly came back to normal.

"Damn, that was good," Jerron said as he stroked her hair.

"Yessss, it was," replied Tammy as she reached down and started stroking his semi-hard dick. "You ready for round two?"

"For sure, ma, but let me pause for a sec." They both laughed as they lay there knowing that it was definitely going to be a long and pleasurable weekend.

Debbie and Chris had been going at it like teenagers from the moment he walked into her house after visiting with his mom in the hospital. She could see the depressed look in his eyes and all she wanted to do was make him smile and feel better. So she held nothing back as they got extra freaky. She knew all of his weak spots, and she loved to tease him. She decided she'd give him a treat tonight.

She told him to shower and lie naked on the bed. She lit some candles and had Pandora playing soft R&B in the background. She began by running her hands gently all over his body. When she would reach his penis, she would make sure to let her hands stroke him gently up and down. When he was fully hard, she made her way down toward it. She started licking the tip of his dick in a circular motion, making sure her hands slid up and down his shaft as she did it. She looked up at him and saw his eyes roll to the back of his head.

"Mmmm, baby, that feels good," he whispered.

Debbie responded by taking more of his dick into her mouth. She massaged his balls as her head bobbed up and down causing him to squirm in pleasure. She picked up speed and began sucking and stroking him at the same time. When she felt him thrusting his pelvis along with her, she knew he was getting ready to cum. She made sure to let her tongue swirl on the tip of his penis when she would come all the way up. She felt his body begin to tremble and, when he told her he was about to cum, she deep-throated him and let all of his juices run down her throat. When she felt his dick stop pulsing, she released him from her mouth. She smiled at him, and she wiped at the corners of her mouth as if she had just finished a meal.

"My God, woman, what are you trying to do to me?" he groaned with a satisfied smile on his face.

"I'm trying to make your ass know to stay here and not go anywhere. I don't want you to ever leave. I want this bad," she said as she looked into his eyes to see his reaction to her words. When she saw that pretty-ass smile of his, she knew it was all good and that only made her already-wet pussy wetter. She didn't think twice as she slid on top of him and began riding him slowly without putting a condom on.

"No rubber, baby?"

She stared at him as she gyrated her hips on his hard dick and said, "Fuck a rubber. I need to feel all of this dick, raw. You don't have to come in me; just let me feel all of you."

"I want to come in you. I want you to feel all my love, baby."

His declaration sent her over the top, and she came in what felt like waves. *Damn, is this really what being in love feels like? Wow,* were her only thoughts as she continued to fuck him as good as she could.

CHAPTER FIVE

Sunday evening came entirely too fast for
both Tammy and Debbie. Tammy was saddened
that Jerron was about to leave, and Debbie was
irritated that Chris had to go spend the evening
at the hospital with his mother. Chris and Jerron
both had heavy thoughts on their mind.

Chris sighed and stared at Debbie. He wondered if what he was about to ask would destroy
what they were building. His predicament was
crazy, and he still hadn't realized how he let
things get so bad for him. With his mom being
sick, he was forced to come back to Oklahoma
City because there was no way he wouldn't be
there for his mother. What Debbie didn't know
was that he didn't leave just to open a barber
shop in Atlanta. He left because, years ago, he
had made a dumb decision that almost cost him
his life.

He had beaten some Crips out of their money.
When they found out it was Chris who had

robbed them, they threatened to kill him if he didn't pay the money back. Problem was, he had already invested that money into opening his barber shop. He dipped off to ATL and had been keeping a low profile out there. Now that he was back in Oklahoma City, he knew it was only a matter of time before they found out he was back in town and he had to pay the Crips back or they'd kill him.

Fuck! The only way he could get the money he owed them was by asking Debbie if she would loan it to him. He prayed that he had put the dick down good enough for her to want to look out and give him what he needed. He cared for her, but he knew her feelings for him were much deeper than his. He didn't love her like she loved him. He knew he was wrong for playing with her emotions but he was hoping her love for him would make her say yes to giving him some money. His life depended on it.

He sighed then smiled at Debbie. "Baby, I need to talk to you about something real serious."

Debbie stretched and said, "Can we chat after you give me a little more dick, baby? I need to have you inside of me some more since I won't be seeing you until later this evening, and by then I'll be asleep so I can be good for work in the morning."

Before he could answer her, she rolled on top of him and put his dick inside of her. She began to ride him so good that he chose to put the dreaded conversation aside while he enjoyed the early morning sex.

Jerron was staring at Tammy, wondering if he should stick to the script and follow through with his plans on blackmailing Tammy so his brother could be free from the feds. Never did he think he would catch feelings for Tammy. She was older, true, but she was classy as ever and a stone-cold freak, and that combination was deadly. He loved it! He was confused because his feelings were way too strong and that was something that was totally unexpected. He loved his brother, and there was nothing he wouldn't do for him, but now he was doubting his moves, and that was rare for him.

He tried to shake off the feelings for Tammy but, as much as he tried, he couldn't. He was falling in love with Tammy, and that wasn't cool at all. It was fucking with his head, and there could be no room for that. He took a deep breath and told himself, no matter what, he had to do what he set out to do.

He rubbed Tammy's smooth ass under the sheets and sighed. *Damn, I'm going to miss this good pussy,* he said to himself. "Wake up, ma. I need to holla at you about something important."

Tammy opened her eyes and smiled. "Do you really think I was asleep with your big man hands rubbing all over my ass like that? Look what you done to me," she said as she grabbed his right hand and placed it onto her pussy. "See how wet you got me? So before you holla at me, I need for you to cool this hot pussy off, baby."

Jerron smiled and said, "Say no more," then put his face between her legs and began sucking her pussy slowly. *Yes, might as well give her one last go at it because when I drop the bomb, it's a wrap,* he said to himself as he put his dick inside of her raw dog and began fucking her as good as he could.

Debbie came out of the bathroom and saw Chris sitting on the edge of the bed with a sad look on his face. She instantly thought something had happened with his mom and she quickly went and sat next to him on the bed. "What's wrong, baby? Is your mom okay?"

Chris stared at her for a moment in silence, then nodded. "She's fine. I got more problems than just my mother's health issue. I fucked up, baby. I fucked up real bad, and I'm in trouble."

"What do you mean, Chris? Talk to me, baby," Debbie said.

"To make a long story short, I fucked up in a major way. When I was trying to get the money to open up my shop in Atlanta, I felt as if it would take too long cutting hair and saving until I had enough to make the move. I needed a hustle to get the money and make the move. Why I was putting so much pressure on myself for that baffles me to this very day. Anyway, I was cutting the hair of this Crips guy named Cabbage, and he was telling me how he sold weed by the pound, just shooting the shit in the chair while I was cutting his hair. When he said that I thought about my cousins and some other people I knew who sold weed. So I asked him how much a pound of weed was. He told me he would give it to me for two thousand dollars. I told him I needed to make some calls and I would get back to him.

"After contacting my cousins and a few people whose hair I cut, I found out that if the weed was good, I could sell it for twenty-seven hundred, easy. So that meant I could make seven hundred dollars off every pound of weed I sold. So I got with Cabbage and bought a pound and sold it quick. Everything was going cool. I was selling like three to four pounds a week, so I was reaching my goal, so I could move way faster, and I was like, cool. Then the greed factor kicked in, and that's when I messed up bad."

Shaking her head from side to side she asked, "What did you do, Chris?"

He sighed and rubbed his bald head before speaking. "Cabbage said he needed to go out to Denver to get more weed and he needed me to do a favor for him. He had ten pounds left but had to go, so he wanted to let me handle them while he was gone and give him the money when he came back to the city. While he was gone, I sold his ten pounds in a day or so. I had his money plus I made mine, so it was all good. But like I said the greed factor kicked in, and I did something I never should have done. I took the money I made plus the money I made selling Cabbage's pounds. I left and went to Atlanta to open up my shop, figuring OKC would be forever in my rearview."

"So that's the reason why you just up and left and was like fuck me, huh? Let alone not thinking that something like what happened to your mom could happen. On top of that, you playing with a gangster's money? You don't think he was looking for you? You didn't think that you could have left your loved ones in danger because of your impulsive decision? You are a damn fool, Chris, for real. So, what are you going to do now?"

"You're right. I am a fool, and I'm worried now that I'm back in the city Cabbage will get wind of it and come get at me."

"So, that's why you been at the hospital and here only, huh? Using me to hide your scary ass. Stupid, plain stupid. I can only assume that you don't have the Crips' money now, right?"

"I used it all on getting my shop together and my place. I knew I messed up, but I figured once I got everything going out there I'd make the money back and pay Cabbage back. But it didn't work that way. Things are moving slower than I expected. Then this cancer shit hit my mother, and I had to come home."

"So, what are you going to do, Chris?"

"I have half the money. I need you to loan me the other ten thousand dollars so I can pay Cabbage back. That way I won't have to worry about him or his homeboys hurting me."

Debbie stared at him in silence for a few seconds while she processed what he had just asked of her. *So this lame tried to play me. Fuck me real good, show me all this fake-ass love and attention, all along thinking he could get*

at me for ten thousand dollars! Ain't that a
bitch! And to think I was falling in love with this
clown, she said to herself. Before she spoke, she
had another thought: *what if he's genuine and*
just needs help from me?

She battled with herself then finally asked
him, "Chris, be totally honest with me here
because right now you got me real fucked up,
and I need to be sure about you before I tell you
whether I'll loan you those crumbs you need. I
feel as if you have used me for a place to hide
while you tried to figure this mess out. Is that
true?" she asked him as she looked deep into
his eyes. "Please take your time and think about
what you're going to say before you answer that
question, because one wrong word and I'm
going to go find that Cabbage guy and tell him
exactly where your ass is at. I respect honesty,
Chris. Real recognizes real. I mean that."

"Use you? No, I got money. I could have easily
stayed at the hotel I was at. Being with you
has been a blessing, baby. I mean that. I love
you, Debbie, I really do. I can pay you back the
money. The shop is producing more and more
each month. You just have to give me some time
to get it all together. I'm asking you to loan it to
me because me being out here knowing Cabbage
may find out I'm back scares the shit out of me.

That's the only reason I asked you for the loan, and that is exactly what it will be: a loan. I will pay you back every penny. I promise."

He answered her next question without her having to ask: he loved her! Now she was really confused as she stared at him to see if her female intuition could spot some games being played. He returned her stare and looked so sincere that her heart melted, and that made her nervous. She hoped and prayed that she would make the right decision, because she knew she loved Chris. She wasn't nobody's fool, though, so she would process this and speak with Tammy about it before she made her decision.

She sighed and said, "Okay, Chris, I need time to think about this. You go on to the hospital and be with your mom, and I'll let you know when you get back what I will do. Please don't say anything else right now. I really need to thoroughly think this through."

He smiled at her and gave her a tender kiss on her lips and said, "I understand, baby." He felt as if she would loan him the money because he saw the adoration she had for him in her eyes, and he hoped and prayed he was right. All he could do now was wait and see. He just prayed that Cabbage hadn't found out he was back in OKC.

***

Jerron made sure he went all out and sexed Tammy crazy until she begged him to let her rest because she felt like she was going to pass out if she came one more time. She loved this man, and she knew she was headed for something crazy with him, but she was willing to throw all caution to the wind.

She watched as Jerron got up and went to the bathroom. When he returned he had a look of confusion on his face, so she asked him, "What's wrong, baby? You look funny. Are you okay?"

He stood in the doorway of the bathroom contemplating for a few seconds; then he decided what route to take. He decided to just keep it real with her first and see if she would be willing to help out with his brother's case off the fact that she loved him. Jerron was positive that Tammy loved him because he could see it all over her face. Now, if she straight-up said no to helping him get his brother out, then he would pull out his phone and go with his original plan to blackmail her with the video he had of her. He was hoping that she would take the easy route on this. He knew for certain that she loved him and what was even more crazy was that he knew for certain that he loved her too. But if she said no to what he was about to ask her, he would say,

"Fuck that love shit," and push the line with his blackmail move.

He took a deep breath and said, "I'm good, but I need to talk to you about something very serious. I need your help in a major way."

God, please don't let this young man screw up what we are building by asking me for money, she said to herself silently. "What is it, baby? Talk to me."

He came and sat down at the end of the bed and said, "Well, I appreciate you coming clean and telling me your real name after you gave me that fake name in the D. With you being a judge and all, I need your help to get my brother out of prison. He's been gone for seven years and still has a stretch to go."

She sighed and thought, *Thank you, Lord!* "Baby, the federal system doesn't work like that. I can't just make a call and have your brother released from prison."

"I know that, but you can help in this case because you were his sentencing judge. You have the power to grant his appeal."

"What? What is your brother's name?" Tammy wasn't expecting this at all.

"Jayson Lellis. You gave him two hundred and ten months for conspiracy to distribute seven kilos of crack cocaine. His whole case was weak, but the rats who told on him forced him to take the deal. He's a first-time, nonviolent offender so it won't look funny if you granted his appeal. You have the power, ma, and I need you to do this not only for me, but for my family. My mom is getting up there in age, and her biggest fear is that she won't get to live long enough to see her oldest child as a free man again."

Tammy sat up while Jerron was talking and the feelings that were going through her head made her feel nauseated. Never one to beat around the bush, she asked Jerron. "Is this the reason why you got with me, Jerron?"

"No way, ma. I didn't even know you were a federal judge until you told me during our marathon phone conversations. When you did, I thought about it and realized that you were my brother's sentencing judge."

His words relieved her, but she still had doubts. "How do you feel about me, Jerron? Do you see something other than just great sex happening? I don't want to get caught up playing games. I'm looking for something real. I know we have the age difference thing but, like I told you on the phone, you're very mature, and I feel like we could make it long term. If you don't feel the same way then just be honest about it, so then I'll know where we stand.

"As for me helping your brother, I will have to pull his case and see if there's some kind of loophole. If I choose to grant his appeal, I have to make sure it won't reflect negatively on my seat. If you think I will do this for you strictly on the love that I have for you, then you're wrong. If I can do something to get your brother released that is within my means, then I will. But if I have to do something shady or illegal then I won't. I cannot and will not do anything to mess up my career. I've worked too hard to let that happen to me."

"I hear you, ma, and I totally understand. I am not asking you to do anything illegal, nor would I ever ask you to do anything that will compromise your position. You have become important in my life. In reference to your question, yes, I am looking forward to a long relationship with you. Like I told you before, that age shit don't mean nothing to me. If anything, it's a plus 'cause you can teach a guy, and that's always good because I'm always eager to learn. On top of all that, your fine ass is putting women twenty years younger than you to shame, so don't ever have any doubt about how I'm feeling you. You hear me?"

His words made her blush and feel like all would be good with them. "Yes, I hear you, baby. I'll look into your brother's case and see what I can do. Now, I need to get some rest; but, first, I desperately need some more of that dick before you head back to Dallas, 'kay?"

He smiled and said, "Now you know that ain't a problem, ma."

He lay next to her as she dozed off and he smiled. *Yeah, hopefully she can find the right way to do it, then it can be all good with us. If she can't, then, fuck it. I'll make the next play where she won't have a fucking choice,* he said to himself, feeling real good knowing that, either way, his brother would be coming home soon.

CHAPTER SIX

Tammy sat in her chambers feeling sad because she had spent the better of the morning going over Jerron's brother's case, and it looked like the U.S. assistant attorney had another iron-clad plea agreement. There was no legal way she could see herself overturning the conviction. Even if she did, the U.S. attorney's office would only appeal her decision and then she would get overruled. That would then reflect negatively on her, and that would not be a good look for her career. Unfortunately, that was something she couldn't risk, not even for Jerron, the man she was falling in love with. Now she dreaded the call she was about to make, but it had to be done. She really hated the fact that she had to let Jerron down but, once again, her hands were bound by the rules of the law, the rules she swore to uphold.

When Jerron answered the phone, she wasted no time and got straight to the point. "I'm sorry to have to tell you this, baby, but I've been going through your brother's case all morning, and there is nothing I can do to help him. The U.S. assistant attorney on his case had him sign an iron-clad plea agreement, and even if I did try to wiggle in an argument in his favor, all they would do is appeal and win. Then I would be discredited. No judge can stand for that on their record. It puts on a scar that never fades. I really wish I could help you and your brother, but my hands are tied on this one, baby."

"So, there's nothing you can do to help my brother?" he asked in an icy tone.

"No, baby, there really isn't. Like I told you, even if I did rule in his favor the U.S. attorney's office would only appeal to a higher court and would win, and I'd have egg on my face."

"Well, wouldn't egg on your face be worth it for trying to do this for me?"

"Don't do that, baby. Please look at this in a broader sense of things. It would be a moot point and a temporary victory if I ruled to grant your brother some relief on his case."

"That's bullshit. I know all y'all law enforcement people are close enough where you could get at them and ask them to do you this one favor and not appeal this ruling. Y'all be having them power lunches and shit. You could make it happen if you wanted to. You just don't give enough fucks about it."

Now it was her turn to speak in an icy tone. "No, you are wrong, sir. I don't operate like that. I do what I do strictly under the federal guidelines. I don't ask for favors, and neither do any of my colleagues, so wherever you got that from you need to forget about it because nothing like that happens with me. Furthermore, I told you from the start that I would look into your brother's case and see what I could do, and the truth is there really is nothing that I can do. I hate that I can't, but that's how it is, Jerron."

"Yeah, yeah, I hear you, but now you gotta hear me, so please listen to me good, ma. You are going to rule in favor of my brother's relief, and if they appeal or do whatever bullshit you said they're gonna do, you are going to find a way to make your ruling stand. And that's that!" Jerron yelled with such attitude that Tammy pulled the phone away from her face and stared at it, shocked at what she had just been told.

"Excuse me? I don't know what you think the dick has done to me, because you are being delusional and you need to realize whom you're speaking to. As a matter of fact, I think I'll let you go. Good day, sir."

Before she could hang up Jerron laughed and said, "Look at the video I just sent to your phone and call me back when you're ready to talk some more. Good day to you, Your Honor!"

Tammy saw the text message on her phone once the call ended, and she pulled it up. What she saw made her heart skip a beat and made her feel nauseated. She couldn't believe that Jerron had taped their sexapades that night in Dallas with him and Dynasty. She flinched as she watched as he smacked her hard on her ass while she had her head stuck between Dynasty's legs eating her pussy. She continued to watch the video with the realization that she was royally fucked. And all because she had gotten fucked literally by that blackmailing asshole Jerron. *Fuck!*

When Jerron hung up the phone, he didn't expect to feel guilty for doing what he felt he had to do to get his brother out of federal prison. He didn't want to hurt Tammy's career. He realized that he did, in fact, care for her more that he thought. *Damn, this is fucked up. Come on, ma, hold me down and make this happen for me. Shit, even if she does make it happen it's not like she gon' ever fuck with me again. Damn,* he said to himself.

***

Debbie was sitting in her office, pissed off with a capital P. She couldn't believe what she was hearing as she listened as Tammy told her what Jerron was trying to do to her.

"Girl, see, this is what we get. We break our rules, and this shit comes and bites us in the ass. That fucker Chris needs me to loan him ten thousand dollars so he can pay some Crips back for taking their weed and not paying them for it. This shit is absolutely insane."

"I prayed that Jerron wasn't going to ask me for money but, after seeing this shit, I wish that prayer would have not been answered. Debbie, he has my career in his hands. He can destroy me and all I've worked for in my life with that video. What the fuck am I going to do?"

"Enough talk on this phone, girl. Meet me at the store across the street from the Temple & Sons funeral home. It's time to go back where we came from," Debbie said and hung up the phone.

Tammy knew exactly what Debbie meant. She wanted her to meet her back at the old Prince Hall Apartments where they grew up. It was a place they had been proud to get out of. Debbie wanting to meet there could only mean one thing: in order to get out of the mess they were in, they were going to have to call on some serious gangsters and, without a doubt, they both knew some men of that caliber.

Thirty minutes later, Tammy pulled into the small convenience store that was across the street from the apartment complex that was once known as the Prince Hall Apartments. The name of the large, low-income apartments had been changed after the state finally gave in and had the apartments redone. It was now called the Heritage Pointe Apartments, but it would forever be known as the Prince Hall Apartments, home of the notorious Prince Hall Villain Crips. The state did a good job making the apartment complex look more presentable, but it was still just as dangerous as it was when it was a raggedy, beat-down complex.

Tammy couldn't help feeling nostalgic as she got out of her car and entered the same store she had been to so many times as a kid growing up right across the street. She smiled as she entered and was hit with the strong aroma of fried chicken and pork chops behind the counter. She thought back to the days of those ninety-nine cent pork chops, and her stomach gave a low growl. She was hungry so, *why not?* she thought, and she ordered one large pork chop and bought a grape juice.

After paying for her pork chop and juice, she stepped outside and watched as Debbie parked her car next to hers. Debbie got out of the car and said, "Come on, girl." They started walking across the street, not toward the apartment complex they grew up in, but across Kelley Avenue toward Temple & Sons. Tammy was baffled but did as she was told and followed her friend across the street.

Once they entered the funeral home, Debbie said a few words to the receptionist and was given directions to one of the viewing rooms. They went into the viewing room and saw Debbie's cousin Crip Jack sitting down on the sofa, staring at the deceased person lying in the casket. Tammy's heart dropped when she saw the young dead man dressed in all-blue Crips attire. He couldn't have been more than seventeen years old. *Yet another young brother lost to those cold streets,* she thought.

Crip Jack stood and gave them both a warm hug and said, "Sorry to have y'all meet me here, but I had to stop in and pay my respects to my young homie here because I don't do funerals. I can't take all of that emotional shit. Especially when the preacher gets to doing his thang. You know, at gang funerals they tend to get extra long-winded, trying to reach as many souls as they can while they have us heathens in the church. Anyway, you said you needed to have a serious conversation, so I figured what better place to have that talk? In here we have all the privacy we need. On top of that, if you are calling on me I know it's serious, so we definitely need the privacy. So holla at me, cousin. Who done did you dirty enough for you to call on Crip Jack?"

"Boy, you know me too well. It's like this," Debbie said as she explained both her and Tammy's dilemmas to her cousin.

When she finished, Crip Jack shook his head and said, "Okay, is there any particular way you want me to do this? Or do I have the green light to handle it how I see fit? Because you two know how I'm going to handle it, correct?"

They both knew what he was saying, and they both knew that this had turned from a serious situation to a deadly one by calling on Crip Jack. They stared at each other briefly and then they both looked at Crip Jack and nodded in unison. They both felt they had to do what they had to do.

Debbie told her cousin, "I want you to handle it however you want to handle it, Jackson."

Crip Jack laughed and said, "Girl, if you use my government name again, I'm leaving you in here with my li'l homie who is now Crippin' in peace."

"Sorry."

"No, you ain't. You've always liked doing that shit. But, anyway, give me the info on where these weak-ass fuck boys are and let me do the rest. The Dallas dude will be touchy, but as long as you know where he rests, it should be easy. You do know I have my prices and make my dollas outta shit like this, but since you fam I ain't gonna do that to you. Never know when I may need a favor from y'all," he said, staring at Tammy, and she knew exactly what that meant. If he ever needed her, she was in his debt.

"I know that nigga Cabbage. He a good homie, so I think I can make some bread from him by handling that other clown. If he not willing to kick it in then I'll just chalk this one up. Hate fuck boys who try to take advantage of decent women. These rat hoes out here deserve what they get, but you two are the type of black women we should always look out for and be proud of for what you did to make it out this life. So, I got y'all."

Debbie and Tammy both thanked Crip Jack after giving him the information on how to get to Jerron in Dallas, and Chris, which was easy since he was staying with Debbie.

"You be careful," Debbie said to her cousin as they were leaving.

"I've been in this shit twenty-plus years, cousin. I have always been careful, but you never know how shit may fall. One thing you can be sure of is I'm gon' handle my business."

"Okay."

Tammy couldn't help herself; she had to ask Crip Jack what happened to his friend. "How did he die, Crip Jack?"

Crip Jack shook his head sadly and said, "Trying to rob some niggas and shit went wrong, and he paid for it with his life."

"That's so sad."

"This life we lead is sad, but it is what it is. I'll get at y'all when everything is everything; then you can take me to a nice, fancy dinner somewhere."

"That's a date," Tammy said and smiled.

"Stop it. You know I've been wanting a date with your cute self for decades now."

"Will you stop flirting with me in this place? Respect the dead, boy."

Crip Jack laughed and said, "Yeah, all right. I'll hit y'all up, though."

Tammy and Debbie went to their cars feeling relieved yet scared to death. They had just signed the death certificates for both Jerron and Chris.

They were relieved because they knew that this was the only solution to their problems. They were scared because, though they were both from the hood, they never had any real dealings in hood shit, and that scared the hell out of them.

CHAPTER SEVEN

It had been a week since Tammy and Debbie had met with Crip Jack and they still hadn't heard from him. Debbie knew that nothing had happened because Chris's begging ass was still at her place, so they took it as Crip Jack was taking care of Jerron first. Tammy had called Jerron a few times, and he wasn't taking her calls. After the first call, he texted her and made it clear that if she didn't do what he told her to do for his brother, then he would be forced to do what he had to do and for her not to call him unless she was informing him she would do it. He also told her that he wouldn't be waiting too long, and that made her extremely nervous. She hoped Crip Jack would hurry up and get it over with. She didn't know if she could take too much more of this. She even thought about just retiring and accepting her fate from her bad decision. Her damn hood rat ways had come back to haunt her, so maybe this was what she deserved. When she shared her thoughts with Debbie, she got cursed out in a major way.

"Are you really that lame and weak and fucking stupid? Girl, we worked too fucking hard to get where we are. That shit doesn't have anything to do with how we want to get our freak on. We just chose to break our rules with two stupid niggas who didn't deserve it! I'll tell you one thing, though: we damn sure not breaking them again! Fuck love. We don't want it or need it. We love each other and got each other. All we need from a man is some fucking dick! Period! Do you hear me?"

"Yes. I hear you loud and clear. But I'm losing my mind waiting on your cousin. This shit is driving me nuts."

"Me too, Tammy, so this is what we need to do: I'm about to book us a flight somewhere so we can go unwind and do what we do best. We'll find us some good dick and wait for this shit to be over. I'll call you back when I have everything set up and paid for, and I'm not taking no for an answer."

"You don't have to worry about a damn no from me, girl. Call me when you got it together. I need it bad," Tammy said seriously.

"'Kay, I'll call you back in a little bit," Debbie said as she ended the call.

Tammy lay down on her bed and tried her best to take her mind off the problem at hand, but she couldn't. Her thoughts were consumed by what Crip Jack was going to do to Jerron, all because of her. The law-respecting woman she was was fighting and beating herself up about this. But the hood girl who was deep inside of her was making her accept that this was how it had to be.

She didn't bring this on. Jerron did. This was the reaction to his actions, and he was going to have to pay for what he tried to do to her. If she had to suffer fighting her conscience over what was going to happen to him, then oh well. She would pray on it and hope God gave her solace over her decision.

She smiled at the thought of whatever Debbie was planning, because she needed some new dick to get her mind off of Jerron. *Fuck him.* She was moving forward, and she agreed with Debbie that there would be no more breaking the rules, and no emotions. *Men are not to be trusted, period. Fuck love. From now on it's dick only. No strings attached,* she said to herself firmly.

Debbie smiled as a plan formed in her head. She knew she was being scandalous, but what the hell? She called Chris and said, "Hey, you, looks like I've been able to save your neck with that Crip guy you owe."

"What? How? What did you do, baby?"

"We can't go into all of that over the phone. Just know everything will be taken care of this evening when I get off work. What I need you to do is get me the ten thousand that you have for him. Have that ready when I get home; then I'll go take care of everything else. And make sure that it's crystal clear that you understand fully that you will pay me back my money, Chris. I mean every penny."

"Definitely, baby. I'm going to make sure of that. I swear on my mom I will."

"No need to say all that because those are just words. I need and expect action. Speaking of action, I need some of that big dick tonight, too. Look at that as the interest on this big loan I'm giving your ass."

Laughing, Chris said, "Come on, now. You know you can have that anytime you want it, baby. But I hear you."

"'Kay. Like I said, make sure you have the money when I get home so I can go get your ass out of this mess."

"It's already at your house, babe. I'll be there when you get there to give it to you."

"All right. I'll see you later then."

"Thank you so much for doing this for me, Debbie. You really are saving my life. I love you."

Hearing those words come out of his mouth literally made her cringe with disgust for him. She was going to go on and fuck him later, but he just ruined that.

"'Kay, love you too. Bye," she lied and hung up the phone. She then went online and began looking for a place where she and Tammy could take an impromptu trip. She knew it would be expensive booking a trip on such short notice, but right now she didn't really care. The trip was going to be paid for with Chris's money. She planned on spending every dime of his $10,000.

She laughed out loud and said, "Thought you was playing me, but look who's going to get played for real! I'm from Prince Hall, fuck boy!" She was still laughing as she found the perfect place for their upcoming impromptu getaway.

Chris set his phone down after Debbie ended the call and he gave a sigh of relief. He then started laughing. "If that sex-crazed bitch really thinks I'm paying her back that loot, she's out of her damn mind. Just as soon as she tells me it's all good with Cabbage, I'm out this bitch. I'll fuck her a few more times to keep her calm then I'll tell her I'm headed back to the ATL since moms is improving. After that, she will be shook all the way back to the left. Fucking her is a plus but her pussy ain't as good as she really thinks it is."

He laughed again as he thought about how he really got down. He was into trannies, and Atlanta had some of the best ones he had ever laid eyes on. He had even taken a few to the club with him, and no one ever could tell that he was with a woman who had a dick. He couldn't help but laugh again as he wondered what Debbie would think if she ever found out that he was bisexual.

Oh, well, he thought as he grabbed his phone and pulled up some of his favorite trannie porn and began to masturbate. He was feeling extra horny knowing that Debbie was about to get him out of debt. *Oh, yeah, I'm back for good now. It's time to push on,* he said to himself as he started stroking himself.

When Tammy received the text from Debbie informing her that they were flying to Houston to take a three-day cruise to Cabo San Lucas, she smiled. She then burst into laughter when she read the rest of the text. They weren't going on just any cruise; they were going on a swingers' cruise. Nothing but a bunch of freaky couples and singles freaking like crazy while on a big-ass ship. *Perfect. Fucking perfect.*

What made it better than perfect was learning that they didn't have to spend any of their money because Debbie said the trip was being funded by Chris. After reading that part of the text, Tammy was somewhat confused, but she decided to not ask any questions. If she didn't have to spend any of her hard-earned cash, then that was fine by her.

She started to get wet just thinking about all of the dick she was going to get once they got on that ship. Though in the back of her mind, she was still worried about what was going to happen to Jerron, she knew she would be able to move forward from it simply because that was what survivors did. They survived and pushed ahead without looking back. *Fuck Jerron! Good riddance, jerk! You chose the wrong woman to fuck with. This Prince Hall, nigga!* she said to herself and laughed out loud.

CHAPTER EIGHT

Crip Jack had been a gangster for a long time now. He gave the credit to God that he was still among the living after all of the notorious things he had done in his crazy life. He thanked God on a daily basis. To his peers, though, he bragged that the reason he was still living was because he was an OG gangster and because of his no-nonsense approach when it came to handling the business. Right now was one of those moments, as he watched as Jerron eased his Buick Verano out of his driveway. Before Jerron's car could make it to the end of the driveway, Crip Jack pulled in and blocked Jerron's car.

Crip Jack hopped out of the stolen SUV he was driving and calmly walked to the driver's side of Jerron's Buick with his gun aimed at Jerron's head. "Open the door, cuzzo, or take two through this here glass. I'm just trying to handle some business. Don't make this worse when it don't have to be," Crip Jack said calmly.

It was the calm in Crip Jack's voice that let Jerron know that this man was serious about his killing, and he wasn't ready to die. So he did as he was told and opened the door. "Man, what's all this for? Who are you?"

"I'll explain all that in a minute, cuzzo. Right now, I want you to hop out your ride, and let's go inside your spot."

"If you think I got some ends in there you wasting your time, my man. I don't have any cash, and I am not on no baller status. So whoever told you that you would come up off me straight played you, my nigga. For real for real," Jerron said as he got out of the car and led the way toward his front door.

Once they were inside, Jerron turned around and faced Crip Jack. "Okay, we in here. Now what?"

"Take some of that there bass out your voice, youngsta. Like I told you outside, all I need to do is handle some business. You can make this real easy or real hard. How you answer my questions will determine that."

"Ask what you got to ask because I'm sure I don't know anything about whatever you trying to get on, my nigga," Jerron said, showing absolutely no fear of the man standing in his home with a gun in his hand.

"Oh, you know plenty, youngsta. All of this here is because of your shenanigans."

"Like I said, whoever gave you your info has played you."

Crip Jack looked at his watch, then sighed. "Whatever, cuzzo. Look here, though, I need the tape you have of you and Judge Burdine. Give that up without any issue, and all is good. Try to play me, and you die. After you give up the tape, if I find out you made a copy then I'll come back at you again, and you will die real slow. Now do you understand why I'm here, li'l nigga?" Crip Jack said in a menacing tone.

Jerron's cocky tone changed after he heard what Crip Jack told him. The cockiness was now replaced with fear. *That broad sent a killer at me. Well, I'll be damned,* he said to himself. "Look, man, I'll give up the tape with no problem. And you don't have to worry about me getting at Tammy again. It's a wrap. I was just trying to get my big brother out of jail. It's not like I was asking for money or nothing like that. I really like her, but I figured this move could help my big bro out is all," Jerron said nervously, which made Crip Jack feel real good.

"Yeah, yeah. I know the entire get-down, and I don't give a fuck what the reason is. All I want from you is the fucking tape and your word as a man that it's a wrap with you ever bringing it up or getting at Judge Burdine ever again for any reason whatsoever. You do that, then we good. If you don't, you die real slow like I told you. Now that we are clear about why I'm here, get me the tape so I can get the fuck on and you can enjoy the rest of your evening."

"My phone is in my pocket. Can I pull it out? That's where the recording is."

"Go on, but if anything other than a phone comes out your pocket, you dead," Crip Jack said as he raised his gun and aimed it at Jerron.

Jerron pulled out the phone and keyed in his security code and then said, "Here it is."

Crip Jack told him to toss him the phone. Once he had it in his hand, he started the recording and watched the freak show with Jerron, Judge Burdine, and Dynasty. He watched the recording with one eye on the screen and one eye on Jerron. After about ten minutes of the recording, Crip Jack hit the delete button and deleted the video. He then went into the deleted video setting and made sure that the video was deleted there as well.

He tossed the phone to Jerron and said, "Okay, we good. You make sure that I don't ever hear about you trying this shit again. I give you my word on Crip if she gets at me again and tells me you still have a copy, I'm going to feel like a fool for not doing you right now, and I don't take lightly to being made a fool. You feel me?"

"Yeah, I feel you. I don't have anything else. That's it right there, I swear."

"You're lying, but time will tell," Crip Jack said and started laughing as he turned and headed toward the front door, giving Jerron much relief as he realized that he wasn't about to die.

Crip Jack stopped suddenly, turned around, and asked, "Tell me one more thing before I go, cuzzo."

"What's up?"

"Did you really think that I was going to leave here with you still breathing?"

Before Jerron could answer, Crip Jack raised his gun and shot Jerron three times: once in the chest and twice in the head. He then stepped to the dead body and shot Jerron three more times because he was disgusted by how he had tried to do Tammy.

"A woman who has worked her whole life to do right and make it out the hood didn't deserve to be treating the way you did her, fuck boy. Now you dead and your brother still on lock. Stupid fuck."

Crip Jack then proceeded to search Jerron's home until he found what he was looking for.

He sat down at a desk in Jerron's den and went through all of the surveillance footage and deleted everything that was on there from the time of his arrival to him killing Jerron. He made sure everything was turned off, then calmly got up and left the house as if he didn't have a care in the world.

Once he was back inside the stolen SUV, he picked up his phone and made a call. When the other line was picked up, he said, "You got that nigga yet, cuzzo?"

"Yeah, I got this bitch nigga. Want me to do him now or wait for you, cuz?"

"Yeah, hold up for me. I got to take care of that there business. I'll be back in the city in a couple of hours. Had to come to Dallas to handle something real quick."

"No problem, cuz. I'll be here with this nigga waiting on you," the man on the other line said and then ended the call.

Crip Jack was laughing as he turned out of Jerron's neighborhood headed toward I-35 South. "One down and one more to go."

Crip Jack pulled into the driveway of a raggedy-looking house on the northeast side of Oklahoma City. He checked the time on his phone and saw that he made the three-plus-hour drive from Dallas to Oklahoma City in under three hours. He had kept his foot to the floor because he was in a hurry to get this business handled.

He knocked three times on the front door and waited as his young homeboys inside did their due diligence by making sure that it was a friend, not a foe, knocking on their door. Two minutes later the door was opened, and he was greeted by his homeboy Lowdown.

"What's up, cuz? I see you made it back from Texas real fast," Lowdown said as he stepped aside and let Crip Jack enter the house.

"Yeah, cuzzo. Had the pedal to the metal. We need to get this shit wrapped up. Where that fool at?" Crip Jack said as he gave a nod to two other Crips who were sitting on the couch in the living room.

"Got his crying ass in the back room. That's a fuck boy for real, cuz. When I took his phone, I made him give me the code to unlock it, and that bitch-ass nigga has all types of fuck boy shit in there. He be watching the he-girl fag shit."

"Huh?"

"You know, transsexual shit. That fool is either gay or bisexual. He even has flicks of him and what looks like females, but when you look closely, you can see they are men for real, cuz."

Crip Jack laughed loudly and said, "Damn, cuzzo, my li'l cousin is going to be super salty when I tell her that shit. Make sure you give me that nigga's phone so I can show her that shit."

Crip Jack then went to the back room where Chris was. It was time for him to play his hand to see if he could make a few dollars before he murdered Chris.

When Chris saw the two Crips enter the room, his heart started beating faster because he hadn't seen the other Crip before, and he could tell by his demeanor that he was the top Crip. He had his head held high with that cocky gangster swagger. Chris already knew he was a dead man simply because neither of the Crips had chosen to hide their identities. That told him out of the gate that they were going to kill him, and he was terrified. He knew it was useless, but he had to see if there was anything he could do or say to get them to spare his life.

"Say, brother, I don't know what this is about, but I can get you money if that's what you want. Please, anything, just don't kill me," Chris pleaded with tears sliding down his face.

"It's like this, cuzzo: you fucked up in a lot of ways. But, listen, I might be able to get you outta this shit; but it's definitely going to come at a price and, honestly, I don't think you can come up with enough to save yourself."

"I can, brother! Just tell me how much you want, and I can get the money from my girl. She will get you whatever you need, I swear!"

"Are you talking about Debbie? If so, then you're dead for real for real because she won't be giving me shit for your ass." Crip Jack laughed at the shocked and deflated look on Chris's face. "Yeah, Debbie is outta the country right now waiting on my text to inform her that you are no longer breathing."

Shaking his head in confusion, Chris said, "I don't understand any of what you're saying. That doesn't make any sense. Debbie loves me. She wouldn't do anything to have me hurt."

"That's where you're wrong, cuzzo. See, Debbie is from Prince Hall; and, though you can take the girl from the hood, you can't take the hood from the girl. She peeped you was trying to play her for her money to get you out that jam with Cabbage, and she decided it would be better to have your ass deleted from her life permanently. Your game wasn't as tight as you thought, cuzzo. So now it's up to me to finish this, or it can be up to you to try to convince me to let you live. If you don't want to die today, you'll have to get me at least twenty racks. Who else can you get at, cuzzo?"

Chris stared at the wall with a look of total shock on his face. He couldn't believe that Debbie did this to him. His mother told him all his life that if his heart wasn't pure with love, he would be punished by God; and now here he was about to be murdered all because he tried to trick Debbie out of some money to pay a debt that he should have never had. Greed. Greed had cost him his life.

Crip Jack sighed at Chris's silence and knew he wouldn't be getting any payday from Chris. "Okay, cuzzo, I take it you can't come up with anyone who can save your ass. I appreciate you not wasting my time by trying to play me, because that would have only made your death that more painful. I'll do you a solid and make it quick."

Crip Jacked turned to Lowdown and said, "Make it quick, cuzzo. One to the head."

Without saying a word, Lowdown pulled out his gun, stepped to Chris, and shot him point-blank in his temple. Chris had been so shocked that his brain didn't have time to register for him to scream.

Lowdown turned and walked out of the room followed by Crip Jack. Crip Jack pulled out his phone and sent a text to his cousin. Done deal! You make sure you get right at me when you get home. I have something to tell you that you need to know.

"Good looking, homies. When I get this next sack in from the West, y'all got a blessing coming for this good work."

The three Crips nodded and thanked their big homie. Crip Jack then gave them instructions on how to get rid of Chris's body, and left the house with Chris's phone in his hand, shaking his head as he looked through his photos of him and several different transsexuals.

Sad, when men don't live in their truth. If you're on some gay shit, then let it be known and do what you do. But to trick females is flat-out fucked up. That nigga deserved to die for that shit, Crip Jack said to himself as he got into his vehicle and sped away. *Two murders in less than four hours. What a day.*

CHAPTER NINE

Debbie and Tammy's trip turned out to be exactly what the doctor ordered. They were able to leave all their troubles behind and enjoyed themselves immensely. The levels of freakiness they saw and participated in blew their minds. The self-proclaimed party girls were able to take their sexcapades to a whole new level. They did things that they never thought they'd be able to do, and they even did things they swore they'd never do. Urinating on a man or having a man urinate on them seemed so disgusting to them. Yet, when they were asked to do it on the cruise, it had actually turned them on. They participated in all the orgies they could get to. They did female-only orgies as well as coed orgies. They had never had so many orgasms in their lives.

By the time the ship docked and they caught an Uber to catch their flight back to Oklahoma City, they were totally spent. They came back to learn that their man troubles had been taken care of.

The girls were both relieved and extremely grateful that their dilemmas had been taken care of by Crip Jack. Tammy had mixed emotions about the entire ordeal. She was glad to know that her career was no longer on the line and it would remain intact. On the other hand, she was sad that things turned so sour with Jerron and how it ended up costing him his life. Overall, though, she was glad it was all over and she could move on with her life.

Debbie felt no remorse whatsoever for what happened to Chris. She was happy that she had gotten rid of that bugaboo, pain-in-the-ass prick who thought he could play her. *Bye, Chris. Good riddance, nigga*. She was interested in hearing what it was that her cousin wanted to speak to her about, though. First chance she got, she called her cousin.

"What's up? You need to tell me something?" Debbie asked Crip Jack when he answered the phone.

"It's more like I need to show you something. You back?"

"Yes. I'll be home in about twenty-five minutes. Can you meet me at my house?"

"Yeah, I'll be there."

"'Kay," she said and ended the call.

After she dropped off Tammy at her home, she went to her house and saw that her cousin was right on time pulling into her driveway right behind her. She got out of the car, gave him a hug, and let him carry her luggage inside. After pouring some drinks, she said, "I'm going to have to take you on a cruise like I just went on and watch you lose your mind." She told him about some of their sexual exploits, and Crip Jack couldn't stop laughing.

"Oh, you definitely going to have to do that for me and with the fucking quickness. Let a nigga enjoy some freaky shit like that before I leave this world."

"Stop that. You ain't going nowhere, boy, so don't even speak on shit like that," she said seriously.

"You never know. I've had God on my side a long time, but this life is a mothafucka. But, anyway, I got that fuck boy Chris's phone, and there's some shit I'm positive you wasn't up on. That nigga was on some foul shit, for real."

"For real? What was he up to?"

Crip Jack gave her Chris's cell phone and watched as she scrolled through some of the many pictures and videos he had saved of him and several different transsexuals. There were explicit pictures and videos of Chris giving and receiving oral sex to different trannies, as well as Chris being fucked and him doing the fucking.

When Crip Jack saw tears start to fall from his cousin's eyes, he took the phone from her and said, "You need to go get yourself checked out, li'l cousin. That nigga was foul and not living in his truth. Now, I don't give a damn about what type of freaky shit people are into. A man has the right to live his life the way he chooses to, but to hide that type of shit ain't right."

"Fuck that bitch-ass nigga! I'm so glad his ass is dead! I fucking hate him! Burn in hell, bitch nigga, burn in hell!"

Crip Jack hugged his cousin as she cried her heart out, terrified that she may have some type of disease from having unprotected sex with Chris.

Tammy unpacked as soon as she got home. Once everything was back in its place, she decided to take a long, hot bath. When she finished, she made herself some tea and pulled out a few motions she had to go over for the upcoming workweek.

Her phone rang with a Dallas area code, and she instantly felt panicky. She was about to send the call to voice mail, but something told her she needed to answer it. "Hello."

"Hi, Tennelle, this is Dynasty. Do you remember me?"

"Now, how could I ever forget you, girl? You gave me a very memorable time in Texas. How are you doing?" Tammy was nervous and shaking but did her best to sound nonchalant over the phone.

"Not too well."

"What's wrong?"

"Everything is going wrong right now," Dynasty said as she held back tears. "I'm out here in Oklahoma City. Jerron told me once that you live out here. Can we meet somewhere? I really don't want to talk over the phone."

"Well, to be honest, I just got back in town and I'm very tired. Could we meet tomorrow?"

"No. I'm going back to Dallas tonight. I don't really want to, but I need to get everything in order for Jerron. I just left his mom's home. I really need to speak with you."

"Get things in order for Jerron? What's going on with Jerron?" Tammy pretended to act as if she had no idea what was going on.

"Tennelle, can you meet me? Please, this is important!"

"I can't meet you, but you are welcome to come to my house. I'll text you the address."

"Thank you. I'll be there just as soon as I can," Dynasty said and ended the call.

Tammy slipped on a pair of jeans and waited for Dynasty to come over. She figured Dynasty was distraught over the news of Jerron's death. She figured she could have Dynasty over and let the girl get it all out. She would have to put on the best acting job of her life to make sure Dynasty didn't suspect her of having anything to do with Jerron's demise. *All right, Tammy. Time to put on the waterworks,* she said to herself as she went into her living room to wait for Dynasty.

Twenty minutes later, Dynasty was at her front door. Tammy let her in, and the ladies took a seat in the living room.

"Do you want anything to drink? I have water and orange juice." Tammy smiled at Dynasty. "Other than that, I have vodka and Southern Comfort. Unfortunately, I'm all out of wine."

"I'm not thirsty. Thank you," Dynasty politely declined. The girls looked at each other, and an awkward silence filled the room.

"Okay, now, tell me what has you so terrified, girl," Tammy said. She made sure to sound concerned.

"Let's not play any games, because I don't have time for them and neither do you," Dynasty said with attitude and certainty. "Jerron is dead, and I know you know it. I can't prove that you had something to do with it, so you don't have to worry about me going to the cops about it."

"Look, I don't know where all of this is coming from but—"

"You know exactly where all of this is coming from, *Tammy,* or as some call you, Judge Burdine." Dynasty crossed her legs and smirked. "Now, here's what you're going to do. You're going to pay for Jerron's funeral expenses, and you're going to give me twenty thousand dollars cash on top of that."

"And what makes you think I'm just going to pay for that nigga's burial and just give you my hard-earned money? Like you said, you have no way of proving anything," Tammy said calmly. Inside, her blood was boiling. She couldn't believe she had fallen for the girl's trick. Just twenty minutes ago she sounded like a sad woman over the phone, and now here she was sitting in her living room, trying to extort her for money.

"Because if you don't do as I ask, I'll follow through with what Jerron was going to do to your ass. And I wouldn't play games if I were you because I have the recording of our freaky night and I will sell it to the highest bidder asap. I'll have your ass all over the news stations before you can even book a flight out of town."

Tammy instantly went from being angry to feeling scared about Dynasty's threats, but she refused to let Dynasty see her sweat. "Okay. Like you said, let's not play any games. As far as me paying for Jerron's funeral expenses, that's out of the question. I do not want any ties to that. Regarding the video, though, what assurances are you going to give me that you won't try to come back at me again for more money after you spend what I give you?"

"I hear you about Jerron's stuff, and it's all good. About the video, though, I will give you what Jerron gave me. He gave me the video on a USB drive because he thought you would put the law on him and try to get it back when he realized you weren't going to help get his brother out. Never did he once think you would have him killed. But you don't know nothing about that, right?" Dynasty winked at Tammy.

"Anyway, I'll tell you what: give me twenty-eight thousand and I'm out of your life. I will give eight grand to Jerron's mother so she can pay for the arrangements and I will give you the USB that has the video. Simple as that. I swear, I won't come back at you because I'm going to use that money to get my life right and take care of my daughter. I'm tired of dancing and shit. I want to turn my life around, and your money will definitely help."

Tammy's first mind was to slap the shit out of Dynasty and then have Debbie's cousin come and take care of her ass too. But she wasn't about to go down that route again. *Just pay this bitch and let it all end. This is my punishment for what happened to Jerron. Hell, just consider it a charity donation. Call me Captain Save a Ho.* All she could do was pray that Dynasty was being honest and she'd never come back to her again.

"Okay. I will need a day to get that kind of money out of my account to avoid any penalties."

"That's fine. I'll get a room and wait for your call. Just know that I'm going to make sure the USB is somewhere secure until we get together so if you have the law get at me, then it will still come back and bite you in the ass. I have my peoples waiting on special instructions, especially if something happens to me. I know you're not to be fucked with so I am going to be prepared. So as long as you stay straight up and down, so will I."

"Agreed." Tammy stood and walked her to the door. Once Dynasty was on the other side of the door, Tammy said, "I'm glad you do know I'm not to be fucked with. I will keep it real straight. If you fuck me over, I have my people too."

Dynasty laughed and said, "I hear you. See you soon."

Tammy closed the door, walked over to her liquor cabinet, and drank vodka straight from the bottle. She thought about calling Debbie but decided against it. She would handle this situation like she said she would and see how it would fall.

CHAPTER TEN

One thing Tammy had learned the hard way was that everything happened for a reason. That lesson was so true in her life, and that was what gave her solace after she left the bank with $28,000 of her hard-earned money. She didn't need a full day to get the money out of her account. She told Dynasty that to buy herself a little time to make sure she was making the right decision. She had to sleep on this decision and, after sleeping peacefully, she felt she was doing the right thing. If it came back and bit her in the ass, then she would deal with it just as she had dealt with every other turmoil she'd had in her crazy life. As she got in her car, she thought about calling Debbie, but again chose not to involve her in her mess.

Debbie gave a huge sigh of relief when she got the results back from the quickie HIV test she paid sixty dollars for. *Okay, cool. No HIV from that nasty-ass freak nigga.* She couldn't believe that Chris was like that. What was even more crazy about it was that if he had been open with her about his bisexuality, she may have been willing to roll with it. *Guess it's just the freak in me,* she thought as she went into her office to start her day, feeling good that now things could go back to normal in her life.

Tammy chose to take the rest of the day off so she could handle her business with Dynasty and then have a good massage to help ease the stress from her body. She called Dynasty and told her to meet her at Bedlam Bar-B-Q restaurant. She intentionally arrived fifteen minutes late just to make sure everything was kosher. She felt like she was acting a bit paranoid, but she had twenty-eight large on her, so she wasn't taking any chances.

She went inside the restaurant and saw Dynasty sitting at a table, sipping a drink. She ordered a rib dinner, paid for her food, and went and sat down across from Dynasty.

"I got the money for you, but before I give it to you I want to make sure that everything is crystal clear," Tammy said. "I want you to understand that I know absolutely nothing about what happened to Jerron and I don't give a damn what you think on that topic. If you ever try to associate my name with whatever happened to Jerron, I swear that you will regret it. And that is not a threat. That's a promise. I also don't plan to ever see or hear from you again on that matter or with regard to the video. If you think I will be your cash cow later in the game, you are dead wrong, and I mean that. I'm doing this only because I want closure to all of this bullshit. I will not be blackmailed again. Is everything clear to you?"

"Crystal clear, hon. You won't ever hear from me after today. Like I said to you before, I am moving on with my life and my daughter's life. I'm leaving Texas for the West Coast so I can start fresh. I won't ever come at you again. You have my word."

"Yeah, okay. Here is the money," Tammy said as she slid over an envelope with the $28,000 inside of it.

Dynasty smiled as she reached for the envelope full of money. She checked the contents, and her face lit up like a Christmas tree. *This bitch is stupid as fuck if she really believes I'm not coming back for more money. As long as I have this video, bitch, I own you.*

"All right, we're all good. Thank you for doing this and, don't worry, you won't ever hear from me again. Best wishes to you in the future, Your Honor." Dynasty stood and reached out her hand toward Tammy.

"Same to you," Tammy said as she shook hands with the stripper. "You be careful out there." Tammy smiled and winked.

"Yeah, you too." Dynasty smiled back and left.

Tammy took a deep breath, sat back in her chair, and waited for the waitress to bring her the rib dinner she ordered. She watched as Dynasty left the restaurant and got inside of her car. As soon as Dynasty backed her car out of the restaurant parking lot and onto Fiftieth Street, a car came flying across Lincoln Boulevard and slammed right into her. Dynasty's car spun out. Tammy saw a look of shock and fear on the stripper's face as she struggled to turn the steering wheel in an attempt to regain control of her car. The car flipped over on its side and smashed into a pole.

Tammy took a sip of her drink as she watched the events unfold. She looked on as Crip Jack got out of the SUV that hit Dynasty's car. He ran toward the car with a pistol in his hand. Tammy watched casually as she saw Crip Jack reach into the car and shoot Dynasty twice in the head. He reached past the body, pulled out her purse, and grabbed the envelope with the $28,000 in it. He then ran toward another car that was parked at the street corner and sped away.

All of this lasted no more than two minutes but, to Tammy, it seemed like a movie in slow motion. Everyone inside the restaurant was screaming for someone to call 911. Tammy sat at her booth and felt numb. It was a shame that it had to be this way, but she knew in her heart that this was her only way out of her nightmare. She had no doubt in her mind that Dynasty was going to continue to blackmail her whenever she needed money, and that was something she was not willing to get caught up in. She was from Prince Hall, and Prince Hall didn't raise no fools. She'd rather let Crip Jack have that money and wish him the best in his crazy life. That way, she could kill two birds with one stone. She'd never have to worry about Dynasty again, and she wouldn't owe Crip Jack any favors later on down the line.

The waitress brought her food to the table. She ate and watched on as the police and paramedics arrived on the scene. A large crowd was beginning to form around all of the commotion. She got a text from her best friend asking her what she was doing. She responded by informing

Debbie that she was eating. She had no intention of telling her friend about what she had done. This was something she planned on taking to the grave with her. She felt relieved that it was over and she could move on with her life.

Tammy texted her friend. I had a ball on that swingers' cruise. Let's do it again next month.

Debbie responded right back, You know I'm with that. Party girls all the way!

Tammy smiled and replied. That's right, bitch. Party girls forever!

The End

Do or Die

India Johnson-Williams

CHAPTER ONE

KALI

"Do you love me, baby?" Bernard "Bird" Harris asked while sitting on the edge of his king-sized bed. He was topless; therefore, his huge, tattoo-covered belly was exposed. His head hung toward the ground, and his eyes were closed.

"Bird, what's wrong?" His girlfriend, Kali, sat up from her position on the navy blue sheets. At five foot five, the caramel-colored girl with slanted hazel eyes and deep dimples looked flawless as she sat there naked on the sheets. She was gorgeous. "What happened?" she asked softly while kissing his shoulder where her name was tattooed. He'd been sulking for the past few days, and it worried her. In the entire four years the couple had been together, she had never seen him like this.

"Do you love me, Kali? I mean, really love me?" This time he turned to look at her.

"Of course I do." Her hazel eyes met his, and they both smiled. "Do you love me, Bernard?"

"I love you more than anything in the world," Bird replied before leaning in to kiss his princess on her full, pouty lips.

Some days it was hard for him to believe such a beautiful girl could be with someone like him. His skin was the color of rich, dark oil, his teeth were slightly crooked, and one of his eyes wandered from time to time. Back before he had money, girls called him ugly and treated him like shit; but not Kali. From day one, on the playground of Schultz Elementary School, she told him he was a king, and she treated him as such. Although they didn't start a relationship until much later down the line, she was always his best friend.

"So, you love me more than money?" Kali teased, and Bird nodded. "How about more than your Jordan collection?" she continued and, again, he nodded. "What about more than your momma?"

"Kali, I trust you with my life, and I love you more than anything in this world," he repeated for clarification.

"Do you really mean that?" Kali's smile grew wide, exposing her deep dimples.

"You know I do, baby." Bird lay down across the bed and put his head in Kali's lap. "If something were to happen to you, I don't know what I would do."

"Well, if something were to happen to you, I would die," Kali admitted. Although she and Bird were from two completely different worlds, she loved him immensely and could never picture life without him. He was her protector.

"Nah, man, if something happens to me you just go on and keep it pushing." Bird looked up at her to let her know he was serious. "You got too much to offer this world."

"Bernard."

"Kali!" Bird mimicked. "If anything happens to me, promise me that you will keep on pushing."

"Do you think something is going to happen to you?" Kali was good at reading between the lines. It was something she'd learned to do in her law classes.

"Nobody plans for shit to happen to them; it just does. You just got to be prepared, that's all." Bird sighed.

"Baby, is there something you're not telling me?" Kali knew her man was heavy in the streets. If anything was going on, she wanted to know.

"Nah, man. We're just having a conversation, that's all," he lied. In all honesty, Bird could feel something bad brewing; he just didn't know what it was. After putting nearly a decade into the dope game, he was beginning to get uncomfortable. He was tired of looking over his shoulder and having sleepless nights. Sure, the money was good, but was it worth his sanity? He knew it was time to change up his routine and get the fuck out of dodge, but without a high school diploma, he didn't know where to start.

Buzzzzzzzz. The pink cell phone on the night-stand vibrated. One quick glance at the screen and Kali decided to let the call go to voice mail. "Babe, you got to stop ignoring the first lady." Bird laughed. "How many times has she called you?"

"You already know that woman has called too many times to count." Kali grabbed the phone just in time to see the voice mail notification pop up.

She played the message aloud: "Kali Ann Franklin, this is your mother calling again! I understand that you are an adult, and I'm trying to give you space, but you've missed Bible Study, choir rehearsal, Sunday School, and church for the last three months. Enough is enough! You bring your tail home or I will come down there with my law enforcement friends." Click.

"Can you believe her?" Kali tossed the phone down.

"Look, I know the first lady be tripping, but you need to call her. The last thing I need is for her to send five-o this way." Bird knew Kali's mother wasn't tossing idle threats. As the pastor and first lady of a very prominent church in Royal Oak, Kali's parents were well-connected. One call from them could send him upstate for a long time.

"Let's not forget the bitch was the one who put me out of the house and cut me off in the first place," Kali reminded him. "Plus, I'm not calling her until she apologizes for how she treated you that night."

After nearly four years of her parents begging to meet Bird, Kali finally went against her better judgment and agreed to take him to dinner at her family's house. Although her mother promised to be on her best behavior, she cut right into him the minute he walked through the door. She started with jabs about his weight and the way he was dressed, which was nice according to most people's standards, and then she went in about his upbringing and lack of education. By the end of the night, she'd basically called him everything but a child of God.

Kali was pissed to the max and mad at herself for bringing him to dinner. Her father, who was usually vocal about everything, was strangely silent on the matter. Yet and still, Kali knew he didn't care for Bird either by the way he avoided making eye contact and conversation. She just wished her parents could see him the way she did; instead, all they saw was a street thug.

By the end of the night, her mother gave her an ultimatum: she could either be with Bird or be cut off. Needless to say, Kali chose the latter, and the rest was history. From the moment she left her family, Bird stepped up and took care of all her needs, even her education, which was putting a pretty good hole in his profits.

"It's all good, ma. My mother and sister don't like you either, so we're even." Bird chuckled.

"I guess you're right." Kali couldn't help but laugh too as she recalled the first time she'd met his family. It was at his nephew's first birthday party a few years ago. Bird warned Kali that his mother and sister were protective of him and could be very nasty to the women he brought around, but she ignored him. Kali was a girl who always saw the best in people until they showed her otherwise. Her mother used to say she walked around the world with blinders on. During the introductions, Kali greeted his mom, Lisa, with a hug and she immediately tensed up.

"Girl, I don't know you like that to be touching all up on me." Lisa pretended to wipe the cooties off her body.

"I'm sorry. I didn't mean any harm. I'm a hugger." Kali smiled nervously.

"Who is this?" Rochelle, Bird's sister, walked up to the group with an attitude.

"This is my girlfriend, Kali. Kali, this is my sister." Bird tried to give Rochelle a look that said, "Be nice," but she wasn't having it.

"I bought Joseph a gift." Kali handed over the perfectly wrapped gift. "I hope you like it."

"This is a private event for family, but you can put it on the gift table with the other gifts before you leave." Rochelle rolled her eyes. "Thanks for stopping by." She waved in a sarcastic manner.

"She ain't going anywhere," Bird stated as a matter of fact.

"Bernard, this is not the time or place for a date, especially when you'll have a new girlfriend next week," Rochelle replied, and Lisa laughed.

"First of all, you can kill that noise." Bird was irritated. "Don't act like I use the word 'girlfriend' loosely. Second of all, if she leaves I'm leaving and so is the money in my pocket that's supposed to pay for this."

Naturally, Rochelle changed her tune that day, but it was four years later, and the hate between them was still real!

"Anyway, baby, enough with all that. I think it's time to make a change." Bird sat up and stood from the bed.

"What do you mean, a change?"

"I'm ready to walk away from the streets and settle down." Bird opened the dresser drawer and pulled out a black bag.

"Let me check your temperature." Kali stood and placed the back of her hand to his forehead. "Boy, as long as I've known you, you've been in love with the streets."

"I'm serious, Kali." Bird sighed. "I've been thinking long and hard about this. I'm going to keep hustling until I finish paying for your law degree, but the day you walk across that stage, I'm out. Then, while you're at work becoming the best lawyer in the state, I'll be working on my GED. When that's done, I may just enroll in college my damn self." Bird had been thinking of a master plan since he began getting bad vibes last month.

"Oh my God, are you serious?" Kali smiled from ear to ear. "I'm so proud of you." She wrapped her arms around his neck and kissed his lips passionately. "Look at my man growing up."

"I'm ready to get married and have some babies, ya feel me?" Bird admitted.

"I can't wait to become Mrs. Kali Harris!" she squealed.

"Why wait, baby?" In one swift motion Bird dropped down to one knee and pulled a box from the bag he was holding. "Will you marry me, and be mines forever and a day?" He flashed a simple yet beautiful oval-shaped diamond engagement ring. A few days ago, he'd gotten the ring from a dopefiend who needed to settle her debt. He'd taken it to the jewelry store to get it appraised. When the jeweler said the ring was worth $3,000, he had it cleaned up and boxed.

"Yes, baby, I will be yours forever and a day." Kali extended her hand then watched him slide the ring on her finger. It was a size seven and fit perfectly.

"Baby, I know it's not much, but I promise when I stack a little more money I'll get you the biggest diamond you've ever seen."

"Bird, it's not about the ring. Never was. I love you for you." Kali wiped the tears that dropped down the side of her face.

"What's wrong?" Using the back of his hand, Bird wiped her face.

"Nothing's wrong. I just wish I could share this moment with my family, that's all."

"I know your parents don't think much of me, but I swear I'll prove them wrong." Bird always felt he had something to prove to people like the Franklins. He knew all the upper-class people looked down on niggas from the ghetto like him, but he was a diamond in the rough. He had big dreams of being the CEO of his own company one day. Until then, though, he had to beat the block and get paid by any means necessary.

"Bird, don't worry about them, or anyone else for that matter." Kali placed her head on his chest. "I know what kind of man you are, and I believe in the man you're destined to be." Kali had seen Bird's potential from day one. He was a good guy, just born into a bad situation.

"That's why I love you, baby." Bird kissed her forehead and thanked God one more time for placing her in his life. He didn't know what he'd done to receive such a special blessing, but he was so glad she was his.

"Can we go out and celebrate tonight?" Kali pulled back from him and jumped up and down. "Please!"

"You need to study," he reminded her.

"Baby, please, it's one night." Kali knew the exam coming up was worth 40 percent of her grade, but she needed a break.

"All right, shorty, tonight is your night." He knew she couldn't wait to show off her ring and tell her friends she was engaged. "We'll hit the

town for a few hours, but then it's back to study-
ing for you," Bird said before pointing down at
the law book resting on the dresser.

"Thank you, baby!" Kali kissed Bird one more
time then grabbed her phone and sent a text to
all her best friends. Tonight was going to be lit!

CHAPTER TWO

FLY GIRL

"So, are you going to let a nigga take you out or
what?" some guy standing in front of the liquor
store wearing a dingy white T-shirt and ripped
jeans asked Hope Felicia "Fly" McDonald as
soon as she stepped outside.

"I told you I got a man." Felicia smiled while
bypassing the familiar stranger who harassed
her every time she shopped there. The tall yellow
girl with red hair made all the niggas go crazy.
She was a cute hood chick with crazy style.

"What your man got to do with me, redbone?"
He laughed before taking a sip from the bottle
he concealed with a brown paper bag.

"Is this nigga bothering you, baby?" a tall,
caramel-skinned brother with chiseled features
asked after stepping from a red Cadillac with
dark-tinted windows.

"Who, him?" Fly asked while looking back at the wino. "No, he's harmless." She smiled, trying hard not to stare this fine-ass man up and down. Little did she know he was checking out her five foot eight inch frame too.

"Okay, just making sure. I told your brother I'd look after you and I'm a man of my word," the guy explained.

"Forgive me, but what's your name?" Fly knew all of her brother's friends and this guy was not one of them.

"My name is Eric, but most people call me Chicago." He extended his hand and shook hers. "I was your brother's bunkie. Just got released two weeks ago. My grandmother lives around here so I told Q I would keep my eyes and ears open with regard to you. You're Hope, right?"

"Oh, yeah. Chicago. Now I remember." Fly smiled after recalling her brother having lots of good things to say in his letter about Chicago being a stand-up guy. "Everybody calls me Fly Girl or Fly for short." She hated anyone other than her mother or big brother calling her by her first name.

"Can I ask a question?" The stranger smiled.

"You just did." She smiled back while opening the bag of Better Made potato chips she'd just purchased. "Nah, I'm just playing. What's up?"

"How did the name Hope turn into the nickname Fly Girl or Fly for short?" he mocked her.

"Because I'm fly as hell. Don't act like you don't see me shining." Fly pointed from the crispy sew-in in her head down to the Jordans on her feet. She even pretended to brush dirt off her shoulders.

"Oh, please believe me, I see you." Chicago smirked.

"Anyway." Fly blushed. "I was named after my grandmother, who lived with us until she died. Whenever someone called one of us, we both answered. After a while that got old, so I started telling everyone to call me by my middle name, Felicia, and somehow that turned into Fly."

"Fly-ass Felicia." Eric laughed. "Q said you were something else."

"Nah. But, for real on a serious note, how was Q when you last saw him? Did he look good?" She only heard from her brother when he sent letters and called home. He didn't want her to see him behind bars, so he didn't add her name to his visitors list. She hadn't been able to lay eyes on him for nearly eight years.

"He looked as good as anyone can look behind bars, I guess." Chicago shrugged. "Prison is a tough place, but Q is a soldier. He'll be all right."

"He should be home soon," Fly said excitedly.

"Twenty-four months and twelve days," Eric added, and then felt the need to explain why he knew so much. "See, we were supposed to get out on the same day, but I got approved for early release due to good behavior. Hopefully the same will happen to Q."

"Yeah, I hope so too." She nodded. "I miss my brother."

"He misses you too. Believe it or not, you are all he talks about."

"His big-head butt don't miss me too much. He still didn't add me to his list." Fly was in her feelings. Before her brother left, they were extremely close.

"It's pretty dark out here. Can I give you a ride somewhere?" Eric asked.

"I'm good. My house is right around the corner." She pointed.

"Nah, ma, stay put. I'll give you a ride." Eric wasn't taking no for answer. "Let me go play my grandmother's number first," he said before unlocking his car then heading into the store.

Fly wasn't one to complain, especially when a fine-ass nigga was involved. Therefore, she politely got into the passenger seat of the Cadillac and waited patiently for him to return.

Buzzzzzzz. Her cell phone vibrated, indicating she had received a text. She looked down to see a message from her on-again, off-again boyfriend, Syris Washington aka Synful. She smacked her lips and rolled her eyes, already knowing it was an apology for him cheating on her with yet another bitch.

Can we talk? he asked.

Talk to that bitch, Fly replied.

Don't be like that. I'm sorry, he texted back.

Yes, you are sorry!

Fly hit send, and another message came through. This time, it was her best friend Kali asking to meet at a college icebreaker going on tonight at the Underworld, a popular club on the east side.

Hell yeah, I'll be there! After sending her reply to Kali, she forwarded the invite to her friend Jamaica. Fly then slid the phone into her purse and waited for Eric. He was back within minutes.

"Sorry about that, baby girl. I seen my mans in the store." He put the car in gear and reversed from his parking spot.

"It's all good. Make a left up here, then turn at the light and my house is four doors down on the right." Fly pointed as they pulled from the lot.

"So, what do you got planned this weekend?" Chicago made small talk.

"My girl just invited me to this party tonight. What about you?"

"I'm just kicking it with my grandma, that's all."

"Stop lying! Your ass is too fine to be that lame. I know you got some pussy lined up." Fly laughed. She always said whatever was on her mind. It was a gift and a curse.

"I wish I were lying. A nigga dick been dry since I hit the bricks." Chicago usually didn't talk like that to females he just met, but since she came on him like that first, it was what it was.

"Whatever, nigga."

"I'm for real. Aside from checking in with the probation officer, looking for a job, and taking care of my grandmother, I don't have nothing else going on."

Fly reached into her purse and pulled out a pen. "Look, if your grandma lets you out tonight, call me. I might find somebody willing to get rid of that dry desert dick for you." She scribbled her number on a piece of paper she pulled from his cup holder.

"Is that right?" Eric smirked while bringing the car to a stop.

"Bye, Chicago." Fly stepped from the car then tossed up the deuces. "Call me."

With a laugh, Eric drove off just as a money green Dodge Charger pulled up taking his parking spot.

"Damn, Syn, I told you don't be pulling up on me like that," Fly said while rolling her eyes.

"Who was that nigga?" With much attitude, Synful stepped from the car. His hair was an unbraided mess, but even still the boy was handsome. Standing at six feet even, weighing a solid 175, Syris pulled all the hoes with his dark caramel complexion, Colgate smile, and charming personality. His long, thick hair and eyelashes didn't hurt either.

"That was my brother's friend. Why the fuck are you over here unannounced anyway?" Fly folded her arms. "I told you we're done."

"As long as you live you will never be done with me," Syn stated as a matter of fact.

"Don't count on it, nigga." Fly started to walk away, but Synful pulled her back.

"Come on, ma, don't walk away when I'm talking to you." He licked his lips, something he knew drove Fly crazy.

"Go talk to Precious. That was her name, wasn't it?"

"Look, my nigga, that shit you seen in my phone the other day was nothing. I love you, and that's all that matters. These hoes know who's got my heart, baby." He pulled her closer. "I even got that shit inked on my arm, so you know it's real." He extended his arm to show her the tattoo with her name making a heart as if she didn't already know it was there.

"Instead of having the tattoo on your arm it should be on your dick, so every time you pull it out, you're reminded." Fly shook her head. "Look, I love you, but this time I'm done for real." She tried to walk away and again he pulled her close.

"Fly, baby, don't do this to me." Although Synful was a player, he loved Fly with all his heart. He knew from the moment he met her at a dice game six years ago she would be his wife one day.

"You did this to us." Fly hit his chest. "How would you feel if I went out and did what you did? How would you feel if niggas came up to you telling you how good my pussy was? How would you feel if a nigga you knew slid up in this?" Fly paused and watched Syn get uncomfortable. "I'm done being disrespected."

"Can I make it up to you?"

"I think we're past that point." Fly patted his shoulder. "I've got to go, but you stay safe out here. I'll see you around." Fly walked away just as Syn got a call from his boy Nutt, which he'd been waiting for all day.

"Look, ma, I gotta take this so I can't chase you right now, but you already know what it is. Syn and Fly forever!" Synful hollered before answering the phone and heading back to his vehicle.

"Fuck you, Syn!" Fly hollered before jogging up the stairs to her dilapidated two-bedroom house.

Although the house was clean as a whistle on the inside, the outside definitely needed some work. Most of the paneling was missing, the roof had a few holes, and the steps to the porch had seen better days. Fly's mother hadn't had a real man at the house to do the outdoor work since Q went up top to do his bid. After paying for lawyers and putting money on Q's books, there wasn't much left for her to hire anyone to do the work either.

"Hey, Momma, I grabbed your Newports from the store." Fly placed the bag down on the table. Her mother was sitting in the dark living room, crying softly. "What's up? Did they cut the lights out again?" Fly hit the switch, and the lights came on.

"No." Jackie sniffed.

"Thank God! I sure didn't want to call Syn back over here to ask for money, but I would've." Fly removed her jacket. "What's wrong then?"

"Nothing, baby." Jackie lifted her head, and that's when Fly saw the bruises covering her beautiful face.

"Where is the muthafucka at?" There was no need to ask who'd done this, because it was the same lame-ass nigga who'd been doing it for the past five years.

"He's asleep, Hope. Don't go in there starting nothing. Please just leave him alone." Jackie had already gone one round with Holyfield; she didn't have enough strength to do it again.

"Fuck him!" On impulse, Fly stormed into the bedroom and punched her stepfather square in the dick.

"What in the hell is wrong with you?" Ray's bald-headed ass jumped up from his sleep.

"Nigga, I swear to God if you put your hands on my momma one more time I will shoot your bitch ass!" Fly screamed at the top of her lungs. She was so angry that her usual yellow complexion was now fire engine red.

"Fuck you and your momma," Ray hollered, trying his best to stand from the bed.

"Get the fuck out!" Fly pointed at the door.

"You know what? That sounds like a good idea." Ray began grabbing items from here and there to make a show. "I'm leaving and I ain't ever coming back!"

"There is the door, my nigga!" Fly pointed again. "Get to steppin'," she said in her Martin voice.

"Ray, baby, don't leave," Jackie spoke through her swollen lips.

"What do you mean, don't leave?" Fly was bewildered. "This nigga just gave you lumps, bruises, busted lips, and two black eyes, and you got the nerve to say don't leave?" She was hot. How could her mother be so stupid?

"Baby doll, you wouldn't understand." Jackie shook her head before getting off the couch and walking over to Ray.

"I understand completely. You're just a weak-ass bitch!" Fly spat. "You're just a weak bitch, plain and simple." She really didn't mean to disrespect her mother like that, but the truth was the truth. Over the years, she'd watched Jackie be the punching bag for many men. The only difference was she married Ray and had a baby by him.

"Fuck you, Felicia!" Jackie spat. "You don't know shit!"

"I know if Quincy were out, this nigga would've been dead by now." Fly's big brother Q was legend on the streets of Detroit. He was already serving the last part of his ten-year bid for armed robbery, and assault and battery. She knew bodying this bastard was nothing to him.

"Get out, Felicia," Jackie screamed.

"You got me fucked up, momma." Felicia shook her head. "As long as I pay most of the bills around this muthafucka, I ain't going anywhere," she stated as a matter of fact. More times than not she used the money she'd earned from her job at the nail salon and the money Syn gave her to keep the lights and gas on around this bitch. Therefore, she wasn't going anywhere.

"We don't need you or your money making trouble around here anyway." Jackie pulled Ray over to the couch. "Get your shit and leave us alone."

"Are you serious?" This time Fly asked the question with a lump in her throat. She and her mother always had a rocky relationship, but never had Jackie told her to leave the house.

"Felicia, please just go, all right?" Jackie used the back of her hand to wipe the blood drying on her chin.

"All right, I'll leave, but I'm taking Braxton with me." Without waiting for a response Fly walked over to the bedroom she shared with Braxton and opened the door. He was asleep in her bed.

"You ain't taking my son nowhere!" Ray and Jackie said in unison.

"Get up, Brax." In one swift motion, she leaned down and picked him up.

"Put him down!" Ray ordered.

With her eyes fixed on him, Fly reached between her mattress and box spring to grab her .22 handgun. It was given to her as a gift one year by Syn.

"Try me if you want to, and the coroner will be around shortly to get both of y'all." Fly wasn't one to be fucked with, especially with regard to her baby brother. She cared for and protected him the way she wished someone cared for and protected her. Back in the day, Q was that person, but then he got too busy in the streets, and before she knew it he was gone to do his bid.

"Hope, put the gun down," Jackie said from behind Ray.

"Momma, you've stated your piece, and I respect your decision. You can sit around here and get your ass beat all day long if you choose to, but Braxton will not be a part of this. Call me when you get some common sense."

With her gun pointed at the couple, she slowly backed out of the house. Once she was outside, she walked with Braxton over her shoulders as fast as she could. Fly didn't know what she was doing or where they were going, but it didn't matter as long as they were together.

CHAPTER THREE

JAMAICA

"Aww, shit, that pussy is wetter than a mutha-fucka!" Halo moaned as Jamaica Jackson rode him like her life depended on it.

"If you think the pussy feel good wait until you feel this ass." She stood up from his dick and watched it pulsate.

"Don't stop." Halo slapped her chocolate thigh. "Ohhhh, shit," he hollered as she dropped her juicy ass down onto his dick. She was not new to anal sex; therefore, his large dick slid up in her with ease. "Gotdamn!"

"You like that?" she asked while throwing that ass back with aggression.

"Hell, yeah. I'm about to nut." Halo gripped the sheets like a bitch. Her ass muscles were tight, wet, and warm. Although he'd done a few girls in the ass, it never felt like this. With them, he had to go slow and be gentle, but Jamaica was completely different. The shit blew his mind on so many levels.

"Come all in me, baby." Jamaica rubbed her erect nipples. "I want to feel you explode."

"Oh, shitttt!" Just like that Halo came all inside of Jamaica's asshole. Once his dick stopped jerking, Jamaica slid off of him and sucked him dry.

"You are a bad bitch in every sense of the word." Halo had to give props when they were due.

"I know." With a smile, J slid from the bed and found her panties.

"I mean, damn." Halo continued singing her praises while lying across the bed with a limp dick. "You make a nigga wanna wife you, girl."

"I ain't the marrying kind, but you can pay me." Jamaica was flattered by the compliment, but she was all about the coins.

"I'm a little short tonight, but I got you next time." Halo reached down and grabbed some money from his jeans and handed it to her.

"Don't play with me, nigga," Jamaica said while counting the money. "You are a Benjamin short."

"I had to give my baby mother some money for my daughter's milk." Halo stood from the bed then quickly slipped into his jeans. He'd gotten what he wanted; now it was time to go.

"Not trying to sound rude but what the fuck that got to do with me?" Jamaica stood from the bed still wearing nothing but a pair of blue lace panties. Her body was the picture of perfection, not an ounce of fat or cellulite in sight.

"Come on, J, I have never been short before. Can't you let it slide this one time?"

"Nigga, please!" Jamaica smacked her lips. "If you knew you were short you should've never slid up in the pussy," she said while going over to her nightstand.

"It's so fucking good, though," Halo admitted. He was addicted to that pretty thing between Jamaica's milk chocolate thighs. Never in a million years did he think he'd be paying for pussy, but here he was every week getting his fix like a dopefiend.

"Run my bread!" In an instant, Jamaica pulled out a silver revolver and pointed it at her john.

"What the fuck is this?" he asked, astounded.

"Son, you know what this is." She bucked. "Hate that it had to come down to this but you know I don't play about my bread, B." Her New York accent was out, and she was ready for action.

"So you gon' draw down on me and then what?" Halo grabbed his shirt from the floor and slid it over his head.

"Son, you got three seconds to find my money in your pockets or I will shoot you," Jamaica said with a grimace that told him she wasn't playing.

Halo knew she was crazy, but he didn't know exactly how deep crazy ran in her blood. At one point her father, Jasper, was the head of the Jamaican mafia. He ruled with an iron fist for nearly three decades, until he and several of his goons went to prison for the murder of one very influential Jamaican official and his wife. Somehow the man had gotten mixed up with the mafia and ended owing Jasper a ton of money. When the guy didn't pay up, Jasper personally set the couple on fire and watched them burn. He tried to flee to America, where he'd sent his wife and daughter to live in New York years prior; but the police captured him before he had the chance to go. After his arrest, Jamaica and her mother, Margaret, moved to Detroit where they struggled to make ends meet. Jamaica learned early on that pussy could pay the bills. Therefore, from the age of twelve, she'd been using what she had to get what she needed.

"J, are you really drawing down on me like this?" Halo asked again, trying to buy himself some time.

"Three!" Jamaica let a shot off. It hit Halo in the left arm.

"What the fuck is wrong with you?" he screamed in pain as his flesh separated and blood oozed out. "Take the fucking money." With his left hand, he reached into his pocket and produced a pile of crumbled twenties and fifties.

"I should shoot you again for trying to play me." Jamaica grabbed the money and counted. The nigga had $270 in total. "Get the fuck out and don't come back!"

"You crazy bitch!" Halo grabbed his arm. "I'ma see you," he warned before opening the bedroom door and walking out.

"Not if I see you first!" She laughed then slid the pistol back into her dresser.

Buzzzzzz. The phone on the bed vibrated, and Jamaica went to see who it was. The message on the screen was from Fly inviting her out tonight with Kali. Instantly Jamaica smacked her lips. Although she tolerated Kali on the strength of Fly, she really didn't care too much for the bougie bitch. She'd met her on a few occasions but they never really vibed.

"Maybe. Maybe not!" Jamaica said aloud while texting back. She had no intention of going, though. She had other plans.

"J," Margie called from the living room of their townhouse.

"Ma'am," Jamaica hollered from her bedroom.

"Come out here at once." Margie was standing in front of the window watching Halo walk to his car.

"Yes, ma'am," Jamaica said as she approached her mother, still topless and in nothing but her panties.

"What was that shot I heard and why was that man bleeding when he left here?" Although Margie had been a U.S. citizen for quite some time her Jamaican accent was still heavy.

"The nigga tried to play me for Benjamin, so I shot him," J stated as a matter of fact. She didn't keep secrets from her mother because she didn't have to. Margie knew what her daughter did to pay the bills. Although she didn't like it, she understood it was done as a means of survival. Being from Kingston, Jamaica, Margie knew about survival all too well.

"Did you at least get the money?" Margie asked after watching Halo drive off.

"I got what he owed me and then some." J smiled before handing her mother the extra $170. "You should call your girls and go shopping or something."

"I'm going to take thirty dollars and head to MGM. The rest I'll save." Margie smiled. She loved when her daughter broke her off a little extra.

"Well, I'm going out tonight, but I'll be home by two."

"Be careful out there, me daughta." Margie slipped the money into her back pocket then went to retrieve the mop to clean up the trail of blood Halo had left in her hallway.

CHAPTER FOUR

KALI

Boom. Boom. Boom. The loud knocking at the door caused Bird to reach between the sofa cushions and pull out his pistol. "Who the fuck is that knocking on the door like the gotdamn police?" he cursed while creeping up to the peephole.

"It's me, Bird."

"Girl, don't you know better?" He opened the door then tucked his weapon into the waist of his jeans.

"I'm sorry."

"What's wrong?" he asked after noticing the makeup running down her face. "What happened? Did somebody hurt you?" Bird was ready to go. All Fly had to do was give the word.

"I'm sorry to show up unannounced like this, but I didn't know where else to go." Fly sniffed. She'd walked almost ten miles from her mother's house to Bird's apartment. Her feet were hurting tremendously but not more than her heart.

"Chill with all that noise. You are welcome here anytime." Bird grabbed Braxton from her. "Make yourself comfortable. I'll get Kali; she's in the bathroom curling her hair."

A few minutes later Kali entered the living room with her hair half done. "Fly, what's wrong?"

"Girl, my mom put me out." Wiping her eyes Fly tried her best to look presentable, but it was no use.

"She put Braxton out too?" Kali had known Fly's mom to do some crazy stuff, but this was by far the worst.

"Nah." Fly shook her head. "I took him." She sniffed. "You know if I ain't there then he can't be either."

"I'm hungry, Fly." Braxton was still in Bird's arms with his head buried in Bird's chest.

"Okay, Brax. Give me a few minutes, okay?" Fly sniffed.

"Hey, little man, do you want to ride with me to McDonald's?" Bird didn't wait for an answer before grabbing his car keys. "I'll be back. Text me if you want something."

"Thanks, Bird." Fly sighed.

"No problem," he said then closed the door.

"What am I going to do now, K?" During the entire walk to Bird's apartment, Fly pondered over her next move. She wasn't making enough money to care for Braxton alone.

"Have you talked to Syn?" Kali knew Syris was an asshole for cheating on Fly the way he did, but she also knew he loved her tremendously and would never see her out in the cold world hurting for paper.

"I called him, but it went to voice mail. He's probably with some skank bitch!" She smacked her lips.

"Look, you can stay with us as long as you like." Kali placed a hand on her girl's knee. "We got you and Brax."

Fly was Kali's best friend, and they were as close as sisters. They were there for each other through thick and thin. The ladies had been best friends since they met in Mrs. Wilson's third-grade homeroom almost two decades ago. Although the bond they created back then was nothing more than a playground pact, today that same bond was stronger than ever.

"Bitch, do you have something to tell me?" Fly pointed to the ring on Kali's finger, completely putting her own dilemma on the back burner.

"I do, but that can wait." Kali didn't want to brag while her friend was going through something.

"Bullshit!" Fly smiled. "Is this what tonight's celebration is all about?" Almost immediately she forgot about her problems and hugged her girl tight. "I'm so happy for you, girl." Fly knew Kali and Bird belonged together before they did. In fact, she was the one who finally forced them out on a date. In her eyes, they were the Obamas of the ghetto.

"Bird wants to settle down once I finish law school." Kali smiled while adoring her ring.

"I told you he was going to be your husband." Fly laughed. "I wish he could talk some sense into Syn." Although she loved Syn, she didn't see a future with him the way she saw Bird and Kali leaving the hood, having babies, and growing old together.

"Quiet as it's kept, y'all might get married before we do." Kali laughed.

"Girl, bye." Fly smacked her lips.

"Do you want a drink?" Kali stood from the sofa and walked into the small galley kitchen.

"Henny on the rocks, please."

"Any Coke?" Kali grabbed a glass from the cupboard and poured a double shot.

"Have I ever liked Coke with my Henny?" Fly hissed. Just then her phone rang. It was Syn. "Hello?" she answered with an attitude.

"What's up, ma? I just got your calls."

"I needed a ride but don't worry about it. I'm good now."

"Where you at?" Syn knew his lady was feeling some type of way. He needed to pull up on her and show her some love.

"Why, Syris? It's not like you care anyway."

"Felicia, stop fucking playing with me. I ain't in the mood for the games. Where the fuck you at?"

"I'm at Bird's." Fly reached for the drink Kali had brought her, then took a sip.

"I'll be there in ten," he said before ending the call.

Twenty minutes later Bird and Braxton walked through the door with Syris right behind them. "The little man fell asleep eating on a fry," Bird said to the women while carrying the boy back to lay him down across the bed.

"Thanks for taking him, Bird." Fly downed her second drink then wiped her mouth.

"What's up, Kali?" Syn walked over to the sofa and gave his homegirl a hug before sitting down between them and repeating the gesture with Fly. "You good, ma? What the fuck happened?"

"Nah, I'm not good, but I will be," Fly said while inhaling his Versace cologne. The shit always got her juices flowing. Already feeling the effects from the Henny and now smelling the cologne, Fly was ready to fuck her pain away. "Long story short, I came home and found my momma all bleeding and shit. I jumped on Ray and told him to go. My momma started to defend him and ended up putting my black ass out."

"That's fucked up, but don't even trip." Without a second thought, he pulled a key off his key ring and handed it to Fly.

"What's this?" She already knew what it was, but she needed clarification.

"The key to *our* place," Syn said with a smirk. Fly had been on his head about getting her own key to his apartment for quite some time. Today was a better time than any.

"Thank you, Syn. I appreciate it." Fly took the key and tucked it into her bra for safe keeping.

"Did you tell my sis the good news yet?" Bird asked Kali when he stepped back into the living room.

"Are you pregnant?" On instinct, Syn looked at Kali's midsection.

"Boy, stop! If I were pregnant would I be sipping this yac?" Kali laughed while raising her cup full of Hennessy. Simultaneously she raised her left hand and wiggled her ring finger to show off her rock.

"Oh, shit! Congratulations, fam." He stood from the couch and gave a pound to his nigga. "Damn, I gotta get my suit together. I already know you want your boy to be the best man." Syris and Bernard had been boys since practically forever. Their mothers went to high school together and became pregnant in tenth grade. By the time their mothers entered eleventh grade, he and Syris were day care buddies.

"You already know your crazy ass is going to be right beside me." Bird went to the kitchen to grab some glasses and poured drinks for himself and Syn.

"Your boy said he's leaving the game when I graduate," Kali announced.

"Nigga, please!" Syn smacked his lips, but when Bird confirmed it with a nod it was official. "Damn, boy, I never thought I would see the day."

"Hell yeah, my G. Ya boy is out." Bird was proud of the man he was becoming. He couldn't wait to have a house full of kids, a dog, and the white picket fence niggas in the movies had.

"The game has been good to us, bro. Why you want to change up on me?" Syn was in his feelings a little.

"No doubt, the game has been good to us, but you know like I do all good things must come to an end at some point." Bird took a swallow from his glass. "We've been speeding through life since we was fifteen. It's time to slow it down, my nigga."

"Nigga, you only twenty-four." Syn laughed. "You got the rest of your life to slow down, but for now I say let's get this paper." Syn downed his drink. "YF 'til the day we die, remember?" Syn reminded his boy about their pact then grabbed the bottle of Hennessy and poured another drink.

"Young and flashy 'til the day we die, I remember; but most niggas like us don't make it to see twenty-five," Bird added. "Now do you see where I'm going with this?"

"I feel you, my G. But, me, I'm going to ball 'til I fall!" Syn lived to hustle, simple as that. "As a matter of fact, I got this one thing I need to holla at you about ASAP."

"Come on, let's go outside then." Bird walked over to the door. "We'll be right back, ladies."

"Don't miss me too much, baby." Syn winked at Fly, and she blushed.

"What's up, fam?" Bird asked once they were outside on the patio.

"Earlier I ran into my nigga Li'l Nut at the barber shop."

"Are you talking about Li'l Nut from the east side?" Bird asked, immediately on the defensive.

"I know you don't like the nigga but just hear me out." Syn laughed.

"It's not that I don't like him, he's just a sucka-ass nigga, and you know I try to stay sucka free." Bird shook his head. He and Li'l Nut ran in some of the same circles back in the day. Whenever a situation came up that required the nigga to boss up, he usually bitched up, and Bird despised him.

Syn knew his boy was telling the truth, but still he continued with the story. "Li'l Nut told me he been talking with this nigga from the A named Dre, Kay, Tay, or some shit like that." Syn shrugged. "His team is moving hella weight and they ready to expand. They got a big shipment they need help moving, and he asked Li'l Nut to put him on with us."

"Wait!" Bird was alarmed. "The out-of-state nigga asked for us by name?"

"Not necessarily. He told Nut he'd heard that he was cool with some YF niggas who had the west side on lock and he wanted to arrange a sit-down with them. He asked Nut if he knew how to make it happen. Nut said he might be able to help but to give him a few hours."

"First off, the nigga is not cool with us; he's cool with you. Second, I'm still trying to figure how these out-of-state niggas even know us." Bird looked puzzled.

Syn laughed lightly. His boy was always reading too much into shit. "Look, nigga, you know we get it popping. There ain't a nigga in the D who don't know about us."

"That's true, but I ain't with no sit-downs, especially with some out-of-town niggas." Bird deaded the deal before it even started.

"I ain't about no sit-downs either," Syn added.

"So what the fuck are we talking about then?" Bird was getting frustrated.

"If you keep your big mouth closed for just a second you'll see where I'm going with this." Syn took a sip from his glass. "Like I said, Nut said these niggas got a big shipment coming in tonight." He took another sip just as his phone started to vibrate.

"What type of big shipment?" Bird knew from previous experiences that his definition of big and Syn's definition could definitely differ.

"These niggas got five pounds of dog food," Syn whispered. He didn't need the neighbors overhearing their conversation about heroin.

Again his phone vibrated. He looked down at the screen then rejected the call.

"Whew!" Bird blew out an audible breath. "Them Atlanta niggas moving weight like that?" He felt borderline disrespected that niggas from out of town could come to his city and get that type of money.

"You heard what I said, didn't you?" On cue, his cell phone vibrated again. This time he answered. "What the fuck is the emergency?" While awaiting the reply, he downed the rest of the drink. "Listen, bitch, and I'm going to need you to listen well. Don't call my fucking phone no more." Click!

"You just need to get a new phone altogether." Bird laughed. His boy had too much drama.

"I know I do, especially if Fly moving in." Syn shook his head. "Anyway, I told Nut I wasn't down for no meet and greets, and that's when he suggested we rob their ass and steal the shipment," Syn whispered. "He gave me the lay of the land and told me the house will be empty tonight. Supposedly these niggas hit the strip club every Friday like clockwork."

"I don't know about this." Bird sighed. "Did your man do his homework? I mean, did he really look into these cats?" He had been in the game long enough to know if some shit looked too good to be true then it probably was.

"He's been on these niggas since last year, my dog! The time to move is now!" Syn smacked the banister for emphases. "Opportunities like this don't come that often."

"That is a lot of money." Bird rubbed a hand down his face. "But I still don't know; let me think on it for a minute."

"Time's up, my dog. The shit has to go down tonight, remember? Their whole crew will be at the titty bar," Syn reminded Bird. "You're either in or you out."

"Why are you just now coming to me with this shit?" Bird hated making split-second decisions. He was more of a calculated move maker. That was probably the reason they'd been in the game so long without taking any major losses.

"Li'l Nut just gave me the info today." Syn shrugged, and his phone vibrated again. Without even looking at the caller ID he tossed the phone up in the air then watched it come down and crack all over the pavement.

"What's in it for your man?" Nothing in the game was free; everything and everybody had a price.

"All the nigga asked for was a pound to keep for himself." Syn paused to let his words sink in. "Do you know how much we can make from the other four pounds?"

"Yeah, I do." Bird did a quick calculation and, if everything went according to plan, the men would stand to make nearly a quarter of a million dollars. "Fuck it, nigga, let's do it," he finally agreed. "This shit has to be airtight, though."

"Trust and believe it's going to be tight like virgin pussy." Syn smiled and dapped his friend while dollar signs danced in his mind.

CHAPTER FIVE

JAMAICA

After pulling up to the large one-level brick building, Jamaica parked her champagne-colored 2009 Nissan Altima. She took one last puff of what was left of her kush blunt then put it out in the ashtray. "Not bad," she said, then took a sip of the vodka she'd poured in the Everfresh juice bottle before leaving the house.

"Jamaica, what the hell are you doing up in here on your day off?" Dejuan, the bouncer, asked after tapping on her car window.

"I heard the money calling." Jamaica laughed before exiting the car and giving the tall, muscular bouncer a tight hug. He had been her protector ever since she started dancing at the Upper Room two years ago.

"You came right on time. The place just got packed." Dejuan licked his lips as Jamaica bent down to grab her purse off the tan passenger's seat.

"Good! Have any of the good tippers gotten here yet?" She glanced around the parking lot trying to see what the niggas inside were driving.

"Now you know I don't know shit about that." Dejuan shook his head.

"Well, can you at least tell me if they are regs or newbies?" Jamaica pulled down the tight pink mini that was damn near cutting off her circulation.

"Nah, I ain't ever seen these cats before. They sound like they're from down South or something." Dejuan yawned.

"Rappers?" Jamaica smiled widely.

"Maybe." Dejuan shrugged. "Before I walked out I did see them throwing mad money. You know when Mr. Harry seen that shit he sent them niggas straight into the velvet room."

"Who's in there dancing?" Jamaica's eyes lit up like a kid on Christmas. Whenever Mr. Harry, the club owner, allowed customers to use the velvet room it meant money was flowing like a waterfall. "Anything goes," was the motto when you worked in the special VIP room, and the two dancers who had the privilege to host were practically guaranteed to walk away with garbage bags full of money.

"Britain and Rayne," Dejuan replied while shaking his head. He already knew what was about to happen. The strip club was a jungle; everybody was out for themselves. Over the years he'd broken up many fights, and the fighting came more often from the strippers and not the customers.

"Thanks, D. I'll catch ya later." With a smile, Jamaica sashayed through the parking lot and waltzed into the newly renovated club like she owned the joint.

For it to be a Thursday night the place was packed just like Dejuan said. Every seat in the club was taken, just the way Jamaica liked it.

"Hey, stranger. I thought you only worked weekends, superstar," Kat hollered from her position behind the bar. She was a feisty, tattoo-covered redhead working to pay her way through veterinary school. "What the hell are you doing up in here, boo?"

"I'm about to fuck this club up! This shit is packed out tonight!" Jamaica laughed before walking over and giving her girl a hug. "How is school going?" Although she wasn't into animals, Jamaica was happy to see a girl from the hood following her dream.

"I have one more semester, and then I can start my clinical rotations." Kat smiled.

"That's awesome. Keep up the good work." Jamaica stepped away from the bar and headed down the stairs.

She entered the red dressing room, and several faces stared up at her and then the whispers started. Not one to beat around the bush, Jamaica cut right to the chase. "Yes, bitches, I'm here on my day off, and there is nothing y'all can do about it!" she stated with much attitude while walking over to her locker in the back of the room.

For a second the room fell silent, but then one ballsy bitch named Leesha spoke up. "I thought it was mentioned at the last meeting that we would respect each other's shifts."

"What are you saying?" Jamaica asked while rummaging through her locker.

"We don't come in on your days and work, so why come in on ours?" Leesha continued.

"Exactly!" Tera added.

"Because I fucking can!" With that, Jamaica began to change into a see-through bodysuit trimmed with rhinestones.

She knew half of the girls she danced with were jealous of her. Although she wasn't the prettiest girl in the group, nor did she have the best body, Jamaica made more money than all of them put together. Maybe it was her swag, the way she danced while she worked the pole, or her freaky reputation, but niggas stayed making it rain on her.

"Does anybody else got something to say, or can we move on so I can get to making some money?" she asked.

Although a few eyes rolled, and some lips smacked, everyone seemingly went on about their business. However, before she could throw some baby oil on her ass and lace up her heels, Mr. Harry was standing behind her.

"I know one of you childish bitches didn't go snitch on me, B." Jamaica laughed, knowing good and well why Harry was there to see her.

"Nobody told me anything, sweetie." He laughed, completely oblivious to the tension in the dressing room. "I saw you and that big ass come through the front door." Harry was a sixty-something white man with gray hair and yellow teeth. He dressed like he was an extra in an old movie, and his body always smelled like mints. "What are you doing here, Jamaica?"

Harry really liked the young girl, especially because she was a moneymaker; but he couldn't show favoritism in front of the other dancers. He knew a few of them despised her so much that they had threatened to quit. Although they had yet to actually do so, he couldn't afford to lose employees on account of one dancer.

"I came to dance." Jamaica finished lacing up her shoe with a smirk. "If you need me, Harry,

I'll be in the velvet room." Without another word, she sashayed through the dressing room like she was that bitch and no one said a word because, in all honesty, she was!

"Kat, I need a bottle of Hennessy," Jamaica hollered over the music as she walked behind the bar. "Put it on my tab."

"Coming right up." Kat grabbed the bottle, filled a bucket with ice, and put a few cups in it.

"Thanks, girl." Jamaica took her purchase and headed to the velvet room. This was her game. She often treated her customers to a bottle of alcohol to get them drunk and loosen the grip on their wallets. While other dancers kept their hands out, Jamaica understood that sometimes you had to give a little to get a lot.

"Somebody told me to come in here and turn this party up," she said upon entering the small room covered wall to wall with mirrors.

"This here ain't for you." Britain bucked. She was standing barefoot, giving one of the four customers a lap dance on a leather recliner.

"Bitch, you better stay in your lane. I'm not playing with you tonight," Rayne hollered while holding steady her position on the burgundy metallic pole. Her legs were wide open, giving everyone in the room the money shot. Jamaica wanted to tell that bitch to get her pussy a face-lift because it looked nasty the way it hung out, but instead, she ignored her.

"Who's the boss?" she asked the men, turning away from Britain and Rayne.

"Who wants to know?" a yellow dude with deep brown waves replied. He was sitting in the chair closest to the small stage. A bag full of money rested at his feet.

"This is for you." Jamaica extended the bottle she'd placed in the ice bucket. "I'm Jamaica, and you are?"

"You can call me Dre." He took the bottle and wasted no time pouring a drink.

"Well, Dre, Harry sent me up here to take care of you personally." She casually straddled his lap and started grinding. Jamaica knew Rayne and Britain were pissed, but she didn't give a fuck. She was leaving with Dre's bag.

"Take care of me how, baby girl?" he said while licking his pink lips. He'd seen a lot of ass tonight, but shorty definitely had his full attention.

"I can take care of you however you like." She unzipped his distressed Robin jeans and watched as his erect dick popped out of his boxers on demand. Silently she wondered why most light-skinned men had dark penises. "You want some pussy now, or would you like some head first to get you in the mood?" She cut right to the chase.

"Damn, baby girl, it's like that?" Dre heard how dancers got down at the Upper Room but seeing it in person made him a believer.

"Let's start with some head." In one swift motion, Jamaica flipped her body upside down until they were in a sixty-nine position.

"Damn, you got a pretty pussy," Dre whispered before placing his tongue right on her clitoris.

Jamaica didn't expect to get a little mouth service in return, but she dared not complain. Dre went to work nibbling on her vagina through the sheer lining in her body suit, and she loved every minute. "Ohh," she moaned while forcing his dick into her wet mouth. It smelled like a combination of must and cologne, but still, Jamaica sucked and licked that shit like it was fresh out of the shower.

"Shit!" Dre squirmed. He'd received head from plenty of bitches in his day, but the tricks this girl was doing made him lose his mind.

"Yo, Dre, it's almost midnight, man. We need to bounce," Scooter said while shooing the dancer off his lap.

"Nah, man, I need this." Dre's eyes were rolled in the back of his head.

"The sergeant is going to call us in the next thirty minutes," Scooter reminded him. "If we aren't at the trap house where we should be, that's our ass, man."

"Fuck Sergeant Boyd!" Dre spat. "This has been my case for the last twelve months, and it's going to stay my case until it's over. Just relax. We'll make it on time."

"Man, Dre, if we aren't there when the YF boys come through for the stick-up then the whole operation is a failure." Scooter stood from his chair, and the other two men followed suit. "Come on, nigga," he barked.

Yet and still, Dre remained seated. "Relax, we got time." He was on the verge of coming and just needed a few more minutes.

"I didn't leave my wife and two-year-old daughter back in Atlanta to come all the way to the cold-ass D for nothing," said Scooter. Until now their mission to apprehend the YF boys had been nothing but a clusterfuck of failure.

"I'm trying to figure out why we got sent on this dummy mission to begin with," Ken added with disdain.

After a murderous strain of heroin hit the streets of Georgia, people began dying and over-dosing left and right. The news channels had a field day with the story and, before long, the

mayor personally challenged his old colleague
Sergeant Boyd and his intelligence department
to get to the bottom of the deadly source. On
cue, they hit the ground running and reexam-
ined every statement, crime scene, and piece of
evidence.

Upon further investigation, they found the
common thread among all the ODs was empty
Baggies stamped YF. Their team spent weeks
on the streets until they eventually appre-
hended the guy they believed to be behind the
deadly doses of heroin. However, after hours
of interrogation, they quickly learned he was
merely a midlevel dealer. The mayor wasn't
satisfied, and he offered the man full immu-
nity in exchange for the head of YF on a platter.
Without hesitation, the dealer led the intelligence team to Detroit. Needless to say, Sergeant
Boyd sent Dre and his team to the murder city!

Immediately they went hard to build their
street reputation enough to play in the big-boy
league. Month after month they worked their
way up the chain, until they had finally reached
the top. Initially, the plan was to meet the YF
boys, build their trust, and create a business
relationship that would provide airtight evidence of their street dealings. However, time
was almost up, and the APD was out of options.

As a last-ditch effort, they devised a plan with the informant to make the YF rob their spot. Once they were in possession of the heroin, they would be arrested and be put away for a very long time.

"Come on, man! This is our last opportunity to fix this shit." Scooter was getting more irritated by the second.

"Yeah, man, let's get this shit over with," Dewayne added. "We need to put these little niggas in jail so I can get back to the A." They'd been away from home for way too long. Although he'd come to love Detroit, Atlanta was home.

"Just ten more minutes, man," Dre almost begged. "Let shorty top me off, and then we'll head back over to the spot. Sergeant Boyd will call at midnight, and the rest is history." He spoke while jerking his pelvis up and down. The men were finding it hard to take him seriously as he sat there talking to them while getting his dick sucked. "We will have Bernard and Syris in handcuffs before breakfast, believe me."

At the mention of familiar names, Jamaica sucked Dre's dick so hard he climaxed all over her face within seconds. Without even bothering to wipe the white cream off her face she flew from the velvet room, through the club, and down into the dressing room without so much as a second thought. Hell, she didn't even stay long enough to get her money.

"Hello," Fly answered on the second ring.

"Fly, where is Syn and Bird?" Jamaica's heart raced while waiting impatiently for the answer.

"They went to make a run. Why? What's up?" Fly liked Jamaica, but she didn't like the way she was asking about her man.

"Girl, get them niggas on the horn and tell them to cancel that shit pronto! They've been set up!"

CHAPTER SIX

FLY

"What's wrong? Why is your face all twisted up?" Kali asked when she returned from the bathroom.

"Jamaica just called and told me to call Syn and Bird."

"For what?" Kali smacked her lips, instantly on the defensive.

"She told me to tell them they've been set up." Fly tried to dial Syn, but there was no answer.

"Are you serious?" Simultaneously, Kali grabbed the cordless phone off the arm of the couch and called Bird.

"Hello," he answered on the second ring.

"Baby, come home now." She exhaled.

"I'll be back shortly."

"It's a setup," she mumbled.

For a moment Bird was silent. "What you mean?"

"Fly's friend just called and told her to let y'all know it was a setup." Kali looked nervously at Fly, who was still trying to get Syn on the phone.

"All right, we're headed home now." Bird paused. "Tell Fly to call her girl back and have her meet us at the crib." Without another word, he ended the call.

"What he say?" Fly was on the edge of her seat.

"He said call Jamaica and tell her to come over." Kali didn't know how she felt about Jamaica being at her house, but she wanted to know what was up, so she obliged.

"Oh my God, girl! Do you think everything is okay?" Fly asked before dialing J.

"I don't know, but I hope so." Kali stood from the sofa and began to pace the living room floor. "Where were they supposed to be going anyway?"

"Who knows, but Jamaica sounded serious. Wherever they went, I hope like hell they get back home soon."

"Hello. Did you catch them in time?" Jamaica answered abruptly.

"Yes, thank God." Fly blew out an audible breath. "But can you get over to Bird's crib as soon as you can? We need to know what the fuck is up."

"All right. I'll be over shortly." Click.

"I wonder what the hell they have gotten into now." Fly placed her cell phone back on the table and refreshed her drink.

"Your girl didn't need the address?" Kali's bullshit detector was on twenty.

"I guess not, since she didn't ask for it," Fly replied then smirked because she knew exactly where Kali's mind was. "Relax. She dropped me off over here a few times, remember?"

"Don't let me catch a body fucking with your friend." Kali busted out laughing, and Fly did the same. They both were serious when it came to their men. Jamaica was known to get around; therefore, they always kept an extra eye out with Jamaica.

"You know I would beat her and Bird's asses for you if I ever got wind of some foul shit."

"No need for all that. Just put money on my books because I would kill them both and go to jail for a double homicide," Kali joked.

"Bitch, I would call Annalise Keating before I let that happen."

"You better." She laughed.

A little less than twenty minutes later they heard a noise outside. It was Bird and Syn. "Where did y'all go?" Fly started just as soon as they opened the door of the townhouse.

"Where is your girl?" Syn asked with a scowl on his face.

Fly ignored his question. "Why haven't you answered my calls?"

"I broke my phone." He paused. "Where the fuck is Jamaica?" On cue, there was a knock on the door. It was the lady of the hour.

"Come on in, Jamaica." Kali opened the door then stepped aside and let her enter. She was still wearing the sheer outfit from the club, which made everyone in the room uncomfortable.

"Where did you get your information from?" Bird grabbed the bottle of Henny and took a drink straight from the neck. His nerves were on edge like a muthafucka.

"Tonight at the club, one of my customers had loose lips," Jamaica explained. "He started talking about sergeants and shit and working a case for the past year. It didn't take a genius to realize he and his boys were the hook." She paused. "Anyway, the nigga slipped up and said that Bernard and Syris would be in handcuffs before it was over. Y'all the only niggas I know named Bernard and Syris who hang together, so I called Fly and gave her the word. Shit, I left outta there so fast, I didn't even get paid for my services."

"Damn." Syn reached for the bottle and took it to the head. "We appreciate you, shorty, for real. And, don't worry, I'ma get you paid for tonight."

"Okay, that's what's up." Jamaica smiled. "Fly is my girl. I know you her boo, so I had to look out." Jamaica felt good that she had been able to help her friend. She was proud of herself.

"Your boy is a dead nigga." Bird slammed his big fist into the wall, causing everyone except Syn to jump. "I knew that story sounded shaky! I swear if we go down for some shit I will kill the nigga myself!" Bird's rage had him acting completely out of character. Never in a million years would he have said that shit in a room full of people if he were in his right mind. Bird always kept his thoughts and plans to himself.

"I'm going to run down on the nigga, don't worry." Syn killed the rest of the contents in the Hennessy bottle. He couldn't believe Nut would play him like that. "My bad, bro. I'm going to handle this and find out what the fuck is going on." Syn felt bad for even bringing Bird in the mix.

"I mean, ain't no need to go crazy. We Gucci, right, baby?" Kali walked up to Bird. "We called y'all in time, so it ain't nothing, right?"

"It's the principle of the shit, though." Bird was steaming but, as always, Kali found a way to calm his nerves.

"Well, since everything turned out all right, and we're all here, we might as well still follow through on our plans to go out tonight." Kali flashed her ring.

"Yeah, it's still y'all night, so let's turn the fuck up," Fly added, and just like that the tension disappeared.

"Who's going to watch Braxton?" Bird asked, remembering the boy lying across the foot of his bed.

"I'll take him with me so y'all can have a good time," Jamaica spoke up, still not wanting to go.

"No, shorty, you gotta come with us." Kali smiled. "After saving my man's ass, the least I can do is buy you a drink or two." She still wasn't a Jamaica fan, but the girl had proved herself to be valuable. For that reason alone, Kali decided to keep her close.

"Are you sure? I don't want to crash your shit."

"Look, I ain't asking again." Kali smirked, and Jamaica relented.

"Okay, I'm down."

"What about Braxton?" Bird asked again.

"I have to go home and get out of these clothes so I'll take him with me to my mother's. She'll watch him for the night," Jamaica offered. Her mother had watched Braxton on more than a few occasions.

"Ms. Margie is the best." Fly headed to the bedroom to wake up her brother. She hated taking him from place to place, but tonight she needed to step out and clear her head.

"Well, it's a little after one in the morning. The club is about to close so let's just get changed and head over to Janet's." Syn looked down at his chrome Gucci watch.

"Sounds good to me," Jamaica chimed in. "Janet's is always poppin'."

"What's Janet's?" In all the years Kali had been clubbing in Detroit, she'd never heard of it.

"It's an after-hours joint that everybody hangs out at," Bird replied then dapped Syn. "Let's meet in about an hour." He needed to shower and get right before stepping out.

"Bet, my nigga. And, again, my bad about earlier." Syn headed toward the front door. "I'll get that one thing in the morning." He spoke in code.

"For sho."

Minutes after Jamaica, Syn, Fly, and Braxton made their exit, Bird went outside to his car and was back within a few seconds.

"What's that?" Kali pointed to the five black garbage bags in Bird's hands.

"Remember when I told you never to ask questions that you really didn't want the answer to?" Bird carried the bags to the bedroom.

"And remember I told you that I got your back, regardless of how bad it may seem?" Kali slipped her top off and then stepped from her jeans. Bird peered at her for a second, trying to decide if he should talk or keep his mouth closed.

"Each bag contains a pound of heroin and about five thousand dollars in loose cash." He dumped the contents on the bed and watched Kali's eyes explode.

"Bird, what did you do?" She walked over to one of the bricks of heroin and picked it up.

"We robbed them niggas," Bird replied smoothly while undressing for his shower.

"But I thought we called y'all in time." Kali's heart rate began to speed up.

"Nah, we was already on the way home by then." After walking into the bathroom, Bird turned on the water. He could see the worry in Kali's eyes, so he went ahead and put her at rest. "Look, when we got to the spot nobody was there. These dumb niggas had the work and the money on a table in the dining room. We took that shit and got the fuck out. That's when y'all called." He grabbed his face towel and stepped into the warm water.

"What if the house had cameras?"

"We wore masks." Bird looked at Kali like she should've known him better than that.

"So, what do we do now?" Kali had never been in this situation before.

"We don't do shit."

"What do you mean? We can't just sit back and pretend nothing happened." Kali grabbed her towel and jumped in the shower too. It was too cold for her, so she turned the hot water up a notch, damn near scalding Bird. He quickly pushed her to the front and took cover in the back of the bathtub.

"All we can do is lie low and wait. Now that we know we're on the police's radar, we know how to move." He leaned in and kissed Kali's neck.

She wasn't done with the conversation, but the circles he was making on her body with his tongue had her out of whack. For now, she decided to let the issue rest, and she hoped like hell her man's trail of kisses would lead him straight between her thighs.

CHAPTER SEVEN

FLY

"What's wrong? Why are you so quiet?" Syn glanced over at Fly, who hadn't uttered a sound the entire ride.

"Did you really break your phone or were you just fucking with me?"

"Is that what this is about?" Syn laughed.

"Answer the question."

"I swear on a stack of Bibles I broke my phone in Bird's parking lot before we left."

"I've never even seen you pick up a Bible. Swear on something else." Fly wasn't letting up; she was tired of being lied to and fucked over.

"I swear on my brother's grave." Syn sat up in his seat. His little brother, Keith, who was killed in a house fire a few years ago, was always a sensitive subject. "Is that enough for you, or do I have to cut off my dick for you to believe me?"

"Boy, stop being dramatic."

"Fly, I'm for real, ain't nothing I do is ever good enough for you," Syn barked. "I get tired of jumping through hoops for you just to prove my love."

"Your love was never the problem," Fly shouted. "It's your fucking loyalty that's the issue."

Syn didn't know what to say at that moment because he knew she was telling the truth. Over the years he'd had some not-so-proud moments during his relationship with Fly, and some were worse than others. He wished like hell he could take some of it back.

"Look, I'm sorry for all the bullshit I put you through, okay?" He hit the steering wheel. "But you can't keep bringing up the past and expect us to have a bright future. I want you and only you. I swear on everything that I will do right from this point forward." Syn placed his hand on Fly's thigh. "Can we please start over for the last time?"

"This is the last time." Fly held out her pinky finger, and they shook on it.

All was well in their world for a good, solid twenty minutes until Syn pulled in front of his apartment building and Shamika jumped from the passenger seat of a blue Toyota parked a few spots down. "Syris, I've been calling you all night. Where have you been?" She didn't give him a chance to fully get out of the car before starting with all the questions.

"Why the fuck are you here?" Syn was completely irritated because he knew how shit was about to go down. He'd just made a truce with Fly and now here came Shamika fucking it up.

"Who the fuck is that?" Both Fly and Shamika asked at the same time.

"Don't worry about who the fuck I am." Fly bucked.

"Girl, bye!" Shamika smacked her purple-painted lips. The lipstick matched her hair weave, which was strategically braided into a Mohawk. "Syn, we need to talk." She tried to pull Syris away from the car, but he didn't budge.

"Look, shorty, I don't know what you was thinking when you showed up here unannounced, but you need to go."

"We need to talk in private." Again Shamika tried to pull at the pocket of Syn's jeans, but he wasn't having it.

"Whatever you got to say to me you can say it in front of my girl." This was his only opportunity to score some brownie points with Fly before things went south for good.

"Your girl?" Shamika rolled her eyes and folded her arms.

"My girl," Syn repeated louder, just to make sure she heard him. From the corner of his eye, he could see Fly smiling.

"This bitch wasn't your girl last month when you ran up in me raw, was she?"

"Bitch!" Within the blink of an eye, Fly made a dash for the dark-skinned girl, and Syn didn't bother breaking it up. Whap! Fly smacked Shamika so hard she left a purple mark on her face. "I got yo' bitch!" She balled up her fist and prepared to strike.

"I'm pregnant!" Shamika hollered.

Fly stopped with her arm in midair when she heard those words.

"Pregnant?" Syn asked in disbelief.

"Are you lying?" Fly asked with her arm still in midair and her fist balled up. She wasn't sure if the bitch was telling the truth or just trying to buy time.

"The pregnancy test is in my back pocket." She reached back and pulled it out. "That's what I came here to tell you."

"Girl, that pregnancy test don't mean shit!" Syn was furious. "Bitches in the hood be selling them shits all day, every day. Come on, Fly, let's go."

"Really, Syris?" Shamika began to cry. "Just last month you was hitting my phone with all types of sweet messages, and now you want to dog me like an average bitch out in the street?"

"You are an average bitch on the street." This time he pulled Fly by the arm toward his building. "You're a delusional bitch in the street at that!" he added once they made it to the door. "Come on, baby." Syn held the door open then followed Fly to his apartment, which was on the first floor.

Once inside, he began doing damage control. "Baby, I swear on my brother I didn't fuck her raw."

"But you admit that you fucked her, right?" Fly glared at him, and he nodded.

"I told you in the car I was done with my past bullshit, and I am. Shorty was in the past. Yes, I did fuck her twice, but I ain't ever took the jimmy off. I wouldn't do that to you, me, or us." Syn wrapped his arms around Fly's waist. "Believe this or not, but you are the only person I ever had unprotected sex with because you're the only person I want to have my seed."

"You can still make a baby even when you wear a rubber. You realize that, right?" Fly sighed. It was like she was on a never-ending rollercoaster with Syn. Sometimes she enjoyed the thrill, and sometimes she just wanted to get the fuck off.

"This might be too much detail," Syn said hesitantly, "but on top of using a rubber I pulled out before I came."

"You're right; that's too much detail." Fly tried to push away, but Syn reaffirmed his grip.

"I love you." He rested his head on her chest and inhaled her scent. When she didn't respond, he looked up at her.

"I guess I can't be too mad because I fucked someone too," she blurted out.

Immediately, Syn tensed up. "What's the nigga's name, when did it happen, and were we together?"

"The past is the past, right?" Fly backed away.

"Yeah." Syn grimaced.

"Then you don't need to know all of that." She headed into the bathroom, which was located off the living room, and she closed the door.

"Fly, that's bullshit and you know it. I need a name, and I need it now." He hit the door and Fly giggled silently. "I ain't fucking playing!" he barked.

"Calm down, killer." With a smile, she opened the door. "I have never fucked anybody besides you and my first, but do you see how tight you just got?"

"Swear on Braxton's life." Syn was visibly relieved but still needed to be sure.

"I swear on Braxton's life." She raised her right hand as if she were about to take the stand and testify.

"Why would you play like that?" He smacked her ass. He was so happy that he would've given her the world right then if it were his to give.

"I had to teach you a lesson." Fly began to undress. "You damn near had a heart attack the entire minute I was joking, yet you cheat for real and expect me to forgive you time after time. The shit takes a toll on you."

"Are we back on this again?"

"Nope, just showing you how it feels so you think before you act next time." After slipping off her clothes, Fly tested the water then stepped in.

Syn loved the way her slim, thick body was shaped and he instantly had an erection. While unfastening the button on his jeans, he slid the red shower curtain back and admired the way her D-cup titties looked all suds up. Her freshly trimmed pussy was nice too!

"Stalk much?" Fly laughed while trying to pull the curtain closed, but Syn wasn't having it. "Stop it or your floor is going to be drenched with water."

"Fuck the floor." Stepping from his jeans and boxers, Syn hopped into the shower still wearing his undershirt and Polo V-neck.

"What are you doing?" Fly asked when she saw him get down on both knees. The water had completely soaked him from head to toe.

"Put your leg up here." He pointed to the corner of the tub, and she did as she was told. Without another word between them, Syn began to explore every inch of her womanhood with his tongue.

"Oh, shit," she moaned and gripped the ceramic wall tile for dear life. Syn had never gone down on her without her asking, and even still it only happened once a year on her birthday. She wanted to ask him what had gotten into him, but instead, she remained silent, enjoyed the moment, and prayed for many more just like it.

CHAPTER EIGHT

JAMAICA

"Where the fuck is you at, girl? Call me back when you get this." With frustration, Jamaica ended the voice mail she was leaving on Fly's phone and glanced down at her silver Coach watch sparkling beneath the club lights. Fly and her crew were almost twenty minutes late. Although she was a big girl and could hold her own, Jamaica never visited Janet's alone. From time to time some wild shit went on there. In fact, someone had torched the place three years ago after a bar fight. Thankfully, Ms. Janet had good insurance and was able to rebuild quickly.

"Let me get a Long Island and a pink pussy for the lady," said a voice behind her.

"Boy, what are you doing up in here? I thought your celebrity status prevented you from hanging out with us common folks." Jamaica stood from her barstool and hugged as tight as she could the super producer, who stood at six feet four inches. "I haven't seen you in forever."

"I've been on tour with some dudes making moves." T-Tone slapped a twenty-dollar bill on the bar. "We just flew back this morning."

"Okay. I see you doing big things."

"I'm trying." He was a well-known street dealer turned super producer on the music scene in Detroit. He used his drug money to buy a studio and started making hits for some of the best artists in and around the city. After he produced a track featuring a few go-getters, the music industry took notice, and T-Tone blew up.

"Enough about that, though. What have you been up to, Ms. Jamaica?" T-Tone licked his lips. He'd been around the world and could've had a slew of models and industry chicks at the drop of a dime, but he was only interested in Jamaica. It had been that way ever since they met at the Upper Room a year ago. Although he'd heard the rumors about how she got down, he never pursued her in that way.

"I'm good over here, big shot. Just maintaining like everybody else, I guess."

The bartender placed the drinks before them, and Jamaica grabbed hers. "Let's make a toast." She raised her glass.

"Here's to old friendships and new beginnings." T-Tone raised his glass then took a drink.

"Look at this nigga here." Bird walked up to the couple with a smirk.

"Oh, shit. If it isn't my niggas Bird and Syn." T-Tone placed his glass down and dapped up his boys.

"What's popping, family?" Syn and T-Tone went all the way back to fourth grade, but T-Tone and Bird went as far back as kindergarten.

"I see you been eating good." Bird pointed to the diamonds dripping from T-Tone's neck and ears. The boy was very frosty.

"Don't let my new music shit fool you. Y'all know better than anybody that I been eating good since before I started that up," T-Tone reminded his boys. All three men had been on the same moneymaking squad from day one. The money, power, and respect kept them beating the block from sunup to sundown. The only thing that separated T-Tone from Syn and Bird was his musical talent. Had it not been for one of his songs going viral on YouTube, he would've still been a major player in the dope game.

"Where are the ladies?" Jamaica scanned the club with her eyes.

"They made a stop at the bathroom." Bird shook his head, never understanding why they didn't use the bathroom before they left home or why they always had to make a trip to the ladies' room a team sport.

"What are y'all drinking?" T-Tone waved the bartender over.

"Are you buying?" Syn asked, and T-Tone nodded. "Then, in that case, I'll take a double shot of Don Julio."

"Make that two double shots, my brother," Bird added.

"Watch my drink. I'm going to find the girls." Jamaica made her way across the floor. Janet's was beginning to fill up; she knew it was only a matter of time before they wouldn't be able to find a seat.

"Hey, Jamaica." A redhead waved as Jamaica passed the girl and a few of her friends on the dance floor. She didn't know anyone in the crowd, but that didn't stop her from waving back. Ever since she became one of the main attractions at the Upper Room, people knew her wherever she went. She relished the attention.

"Panda panda panda."

"That's my shit!" Kali emerged from the bathroom with her hands in the air. Fly was right behind her rapping along to the song blasting over the loud speakers.

"About time you bitches acted like you came to party." Jamaica gave them both a smile and then pulled Fly toward the dance floor. Fly pulled Kali and, seconds later, the three of them were turning up in the middle of the dance floor like they owned the joint. The only reason they decided to take a break was because the DJ started spinning some bullshit.

"I saw you over there working it, shorty." Bird handed Kali a bottle of water.

"I hope you liked what you saw." Kali untwisted the cap and took a sip.

"What are y'all drinking?" T-Tone asked, prepared to order another round of drinks.

"I know you're feeling generous, my nigga, but your money is no good when it comes to my lady." Bird appreciated the gesture, but he wasn't the type to let another nigga pay for his girl's shit. In his mind, it was an open invitation for some underhanded shit to occur. He liked T-Tone and loved Kali; therefore, he didn't want any reason to fuck either of them up.

"Damn, dog, since when it got like that?" T-Tone began stuffing the money in his hand back into his pocket. He was lightweight offended.

"No disrespect, my G, but that's just how I operate." Without another word on the matter, Bird waved the waitress over and placed orders of vodka and cranberry for Kali, Fly, and Jamaica.

"Where is my drink at?" a voice hollered from the other end of the bar. Only Bird and Kali heard it. Everyone else was engaged in conversation.

"Rochelle, what the fuck are you doing up in here?" Bird wrapped his arms around the big, tall black girl who looked almost identical to him. In fact, the only reason you would be able to tell them apart was because one had breasts and a lip ring.

"Bro, you know I be dangling." Rochelle smiled. "Question is, what the fuck are you doing in here?" Lately, she hadn't seen her big brother as often as she used to. "I'm surprised your owner let you off the leash tonight."

"Don't start that shit." Bird knew damn well his sister saw Kali standing there. He didn't want any drama on their night of celebrating.

"Hello, Rochelle." Kali gave a halfhearted smile.

"I didn't even see you, girl," Rochelle lied. "So, what brings you two lovebirds out?"

"Well, I was going to come by Mom's tomorrow and share the news, but since you're here, I might as well tell you." Bird grabbed Kali's hand and held it up. "We're engaged."

"Engaged? As in getting married? As in you're giving this bitch your last name?" Rochelle couldn't hide her annoyance.

"Who are you calling a bitch?" Instantly Kali was ready for war.

"If the shoe fits." Rochelle smirked.

"Ro, are you fucking serious right now?" Bird frowned. "Even if you don't like the situation, at least show some fucking respect to me." The way his sister and mother felt about Kali was not a secret, but Bird never tolerated them disrespecting her in his presence.

"All right, bro, you got it. My bad." Rochelle hated to argue with her brother, especially over someone as unimportant as Kali, so she let it go. "Congrats." She forced a smile at Kali. "Now, where is my drink?" She turned back to Bird.

"Tell me where you're sitting, and I'll have the waitress bring it over." Bird rubbed his temples.

"I'm right over there by the pool table with Melinda." Rochelle pointed to her childhood friend. "Hey, bro, my ends is a little tight this month. Can I borrow a few dollars to pay my cell phone and get my nails done?"

"Didn't I just pay your fucking phone bill the other day?" Bird raised a brow.

"That was the house phone. This time it's my cell phone." Rochelle held out her hand, already knowing her brother was going to lace her as usual.

"Ro, you need a job."

"I have one. It just don't pay much." Rochelle looked past her brother at Kali who was shaking her head. It took everything in her not to snatch little Miss Perfect up by the collar of her dress, but she decided to let it go.

"This is the last time." Bird reached into his pocket and retrieved a wad that totaled $423. Bird never liked to carry around too much cash. "You better make this three hundred dollars work." He handed his sister the money then put the rest back into his pocket.

"Thanks, bro." Rochelle kissed her brother's cheek then headed back to her friend.

When Bird turned around, he could see the disappointment on Kali's face. "What?"

"She got you again, that's what."

"She ain't get nobody." Bird tried to walk past her, but she stopped him.

"Baby, why do you let Rochelle and your mother treat you like a one-way ATM?" Kali hated to see anyone take advantage of her man, especially his own family.

"What is a one-way ATM?" Bird sighed.

"Them bitches always make withdrawals but don't ever make any deposits."

"You better watch who you call a bitch!" The same way Bird demanded respect from his mother and sister with regard to Kali, he demanded the same from Kali in return.

"I didn't mean it like that, but it's the truth, baby." Kali wrapped her arms around Bird and pulled him close. "When I become Mrs. Harris I will be putting an end to that, just so you know." She kissed his lips, and he smirked.

"I already know you'll be watching the bag close." Bird laughed before returning Kali's kiss with one of his own.

"Look who the fuck just walked in the mutha-fucking door." Breaking up their moment, Syris tapped Bird then pointed at the front of the building. Li'l Nut was strutting through the joint like he didn't have a care in the world.

"Ain't this a bitch!" Bird pushed Kali away and instantly went into beast mode. "Baby, give me a second." Without another word, he and Syris walked away.

"What the fuck is going on?" Fly asked her girl.

"I don't know, but I think that's the nigga who set them up," Kali whispered. Instantly her head was on the swivel. Although she was a good girl at heart, she was trap queen by nature. Her hood instincts were on a thousand right now.

The conversation among the three men appeared to have taken a turn for the worse. They were now in a heated debate. Kali knew things would only escalate from here. "Go get the car, now!" she hollered.

"Oh, shit, he has a gun!" some girl screamed just before three flashes of light covered the dance floor. Pop! Pop! Pop!

Kali watched in slow motion as people began to scatter like roaches, nearly knocking her over. "Go get the car!" she screamed again.

"Where is Syn?" Fly scanned the chaotic club. Her heart damn near jumped from her chest. She was petrified.

"I'll find him. Just go get the fucking car!" Kali repeated for the third time.

"He has the keys." Fly shook her head nervously.

"My car is down the block," Jamaica told the girls. "I'll grab it and meet y'all at the front door in five minutes." She took off running toward the back exit.

"Kali, get the fuck out of here," Bird hollered over the commotion. He was sitting on the floor with blood covering his shirt.

"Oh my God!" she screamed and ran toward him. "Baby, are you okay?"

"It's not my blood," Bird admitted.

"Where is Syn?" Fly began to fear the worst.

"He went to get the car." Bird pointed to the door.

"Whose blood is that?" Kali was now crying. Although Bird told her it wasn't his, she had trouble believing him because there was just so much on him.

"Look, y'all got to get the fuck out of here." He pulled the girls toward the door, and that's when they saw Li'l Nut lying dead in the middle of the floor, surrounded by a puddle of blood.

"I'm not leaving without you," Kali cried.

"I'll be right behind you," Bird tried to reassure Kali, but she wasn't having it.

"I'm not fucking leaving you here!" she barked just as Jamaica ran through the front door.

"Come on, y'all."

"I got to get Rochelle out of here." Bird backed away. "I'll be home soon." No sooner than he said the words, he was lost in the sea of faces still making a run for the door. Kali wanted to go find him, but she knew it wasn't the best thing to do.

"Come on, Kali, he'll be all right." Jamaica could see the pain in Kali's eyes. For the first time, she saw the girl in a new light. She admired the love she had for Bird and respected that she wasn't willing to leave him at the first sign of trouble. Maybe she'd underestimated the spoiled church brat. "He'll be okay," Jamaica repeated and finally convinced her and Fly to leave the club.

As soon as they were outside, police sirens could be heard in the distance. Kali didn't have a good feeling, but what could she do?

"I'll get Bird. Y'all go home!" Syn ran past the ladies and reentered the bar.

"Be careful," Fly hollered with a shaky voice and a heavy heart. She too had a bad feeling about the events to come, but she held it in and hurried to Jamaica's car.

CHAPTER NINE

JAMAICA

"Yo, son, that shit was bananas!" Jamaica peeled down the block trying to get as far from the bar as she could. Within minutes several police cars passed them. "That shit is going to make the news, just watch what I tell you."

"I hope Syn and Bird are all right," Fly mumbled.

Kali didn't respond. She was too busy scrolling down the contacts in her phone. Seconds later, she stumbled upon the name she was looking for and pressed SEND. Immediately the voice mail came on, and Kali remembered it was almost 4:00 a.m.

"Hey, Desmond, this is Kali Franklin." She paused. "I'm sorry to call you so late, but I might need a favor. Please call me as soon as you can. Thanks, and God bless." Kali slid the phone back into her purse and sat back on the seat.

"Who was that?" Jamaica looked at Kali through the rearview mirror.

"He's an attorney who belongs to my daddy's church." Kali really hated asking anyone for help, especially church folks, but this was an emergency. Although she didn't see anyone pull the trigger, deep down in her heart, she knew Bird was the guilty party.

"Desmond Waters, the fine-ass lawyer your parents wanted to hook you up with?" Fly turned around to face her girl as a sly grin swept across her face.

"Yes, that's the one," Kali admitted with disdain.

She and Desmond were raised in the church together and at one point were great friends. Time and circumstances had changed all of that, though. He was four years her senior, but it didn't matter because Kali had always been mature for her age. They shared a lot of the same interests, as well as an unborn child.

His parents were longtime members at Higher Ground Ministries and best friends with her parents. Sometime after Kali's fifteenth birthday, they began concocting an arranged marriage type of deal. The only problem was Desmond and Kali had already gotten to know each other personally and physically. After just their third time having sex, she ended up pregnant. Desmond urged her to keep the child, and he offered to take the heat from their parents, but Kali refused. She was wise enough to know she was too young to be anyone's mother.

After days of praying and pondering, she decided to cop a fake ID and have an abortion. Kali never told anybody but Desmond what she'd done, and she begged him to keep their secret. He was furious to say the least, but he agreed to take it to the grave. Both the friendship and their relationship were strained from that point forward. Although their parents kept urging them to date and get to know each other, Desmond eventually went off to law school in California and Kali met and fell in love with Bird.

Nearly twenty minutes after leaving the bar, Jamaica pulled up to Bird's townhouse and cut the engine. Everyone in the car was quiet.

Jamaica decided to break the silence. "Ladies, everything will be okay. Niggas like Syn and Bird know what they're doing. Trust me." She reached into her glove box and produced a tightly rolled kush blunt. "Anybody want to hit this?" she asked after lighting the brown paper and taking a hard pull.

"Hell, yeah." Kali extended her hand and Jamaica almost choked. She couldn't believe

Miss Bougie was a weed smoker. "Don't look so surprised." Kali put the blunt between her lips and inhaled softly. With a smirk, she blew out smoke rings.

"I'll be damned!" Jamaica busted out laughing.

"I told you this bitch wasn't no Goody Two-shoes." Fly held her hand out indicating it was her turn to puff on the magic dragon. "Don't let the innocent look fool you. This bitch probably been in more shit than me and you combined." Fly retrieved the blunt and took two short puffs.

"Damn, I had you all wrong." Jamaica was totally impressed.

"That's why they say never judge a book by its cover," Kali stated as a matter of fact. She was so used to people judging her based on her looks and religious background that it didn't even faze her. She decided a long time ago to let people believe whatever they wanted. As long as she knew who she was, it didn't matter.

"Here come the guys," Fly said when she saw them pull up. She took one more puff and put the blunt out in the ashtray container Jamaica had in her cup holder.

"Come on, y'all." Kali opened the car's back door.

"Nah, I think this is personal. I'll get up with y'all tomorrow." Jamaica started the car.

"Girl, after what you did for Syn and Bird today we are family, so come on in the fucking house." Fly wasn't taking no for an answer. Her friend had proved her loyalty in more ways than one and for that Fly was grateful.

"Well, if you insist." Without argument, Jamaica stepped from her car and followed everyone into the house.

"What the fuck was that?" Kali hollered as soon as they were safely behind closed doors.

"All I know is shit went sideways tonight." Bird pulled off his bloody shirt and tossed it in the garbage can sitting beside the refrigerator in the kitchen. "That wasn't supposed to happen."

"Well, tell me what exactly was supposed to happen." Kali folded her arms.

"We went to talk to the nigga, and we asked him about the cops." Syn spoke while pacing the floor nervously.

"What did he say?" Fly asked nervously.

Syn gave her a look that meant not to interrupt him again, and then he continued. "Nut starts back peddling his story, just trying to buy time and shit. Then out of nowhere, this nigga pulls something black out of his pocket." Syn stopped pacing and looked at Bird.

"Long story short, it wasn't a gun that he pulled, but we thought it was, so we both pulled ours." With a deep sigh, Bird continued. "I put two shots in his torso, and Syn clipped his neck."

"If it wasn't a gun in his pocket, then what was it?" Kali asked the million-dollar question.

"It was a motherfucking recording device!" Bird hit the arm of the couch. "He had on a fucking wire the whole time!"

"The nigga probably been wearing it all day!" Syn thought about the conversation they'd had earlier.

Instantly the room got deathly silent as the severity of the situation kicked in. Not only had Syn and Bird committed the murder of an unarmed man in a club full of witnesses, but the police were listening to the entire thing. In fact, they were probably waking some judge up from his comfy bed right now to sign the fucking warrant they needed for Syn and Bird.

"Did he die?" Although Kali had seen the man on the floor with her own eyes, she was now hoping that she'd been wrong. She prayed for a miracle.

"The nigga probably died instantly," Syn replied.

"So, what do we do now?" Fly asked. Dreadfully she began to remember the night her brother Quincy came home and told her he'd done something bad, and that he would be gone for a while.

"Did you know that your boy was a criminal informant?" Kali asked Syn.

"Nah, man. You think if I knew that shit I would've merked that nigga tonight?" Syn was insulted that Kali would ask him that, but he knew her question was legit. After all, he was the one who'd orchestrated the whole thing.

"Yo. Everybody in the room just shut the fuck up!" Bird rubbed his face. "Syn, let's take a walk!" Without another word, he opened the door, and the men walked out.

The cold wind hit the men's faces. It felt refreshing as the men walked. Moments of eerie silence passed before Syn finally spoke up. "Bird, I swear on my grandmother and my brother I didn't know about none of that CI shit."

"We're about to go up top for murder, you do realize that, right?" Bird kicked at a rock resting on the sidewalk. Just like that, he saw the rest of his life flashing before his eyes. Not only was his freedom in jeopardy, but he knew his relationship with Kali was over. "You fucked up this time."

"Fuck! Fuck!" Syn cursed. He was mad at himself but even madder at Bird right now.

"Just like that, you took away your life and mines." Bird was so angry that he reached out and swung. His fist caught Syn in the jaw. "I

asked if you'd done your fucking homework!"
He swung again and hit Syn in the stomach.

"Bird, chill the fuck out, man!" Syn wanted to
swing back, but he knew it wouldn't end up good
for either of them. They both could lay those
hands. The last thing they needed to do was
start brawling in the street and wake up some
neighbors.

"You want me to chill, really? After the shit you
just got us caught up in you want me to chill?"
Bird wanted to hit Syn a few more times, but
instead, he walked away.

"Bernard, come back in the house, baby," Kali
called from the doorway. Although the night had
gone awry, she hated to see such close friends
fighting.

"Kali, I need a minute." Bird continued walking
down the street. Steam was practically exploding
from his head.

"Baby, come back in so we can figure this out."
Kali stepped outside with Fly on her heels.

Jamaica stayed in the house. Although she
was nosey, she definitely didn't want to hear
anything that could implicate her in any way,
shape, or form. It was already bad enough that
she could possibly be interrogated as a potential
witness to what happened in the club. A lot of
people had seen her tonight and could easily
drop her name to the cops.

"Kali, you need to go back to your parents' house until I call you." Bird didn't mean to be rude, but he needed some space.

"Baby, stop playing with me." Kali smacked her lips. "You know I'm not leaving you."

"Kali, I wish I was playing right now." Bird sighed. "You need to leave and never look back. I can't let you get caught up in any of this shit."

"Man, damn!" Syn hollered. He wished like hell he'd never even heard about the lick.

"Syris, is this fixable?" Fly asked with a cool head. She usually stayed calm in the midst of all hell breaking loose. It was one of her stronger qualities.

"It might've been fixable if the police weren't called before we were able to move the body," Syn replied honestly.

"What about cameras? Did y'all pull the tapes?" Fly continued.

"Janet's don't have cameras," Syn told her.

"What are we going to do?" Kali ran up to Bird, completely ignoring the other couple.

"I don't know about Syn, but the best thing for me to do is turn myself in before they send the tactical team out."

"What's a tactical team?" Kali asked.

"They are basically a SWAT team. They will find names and witnesses and kick in everybody's door until we're in custody." Bird envisioned the chaos in his head. "The last thing I need is for you to get dragged into some shit behind this." Bird never wanted to put his family in harm's way. "You need to go home."

"This is my home!" Kali grabbed his hand. "We will get through this together. Now let's go back." Gently she turned around and ushered Bird back toward his townhouse. As they walked away, they could hear Fly and Syn having a similar conversation.

"I'm not going to jail!" Syn stated as a matter of fact. "I'll go on the run before I turn myself in."

"How long do you think that's going to last?" Fly shook her head.

"I don't know, but I ain't going down without a fight."

"What if they kill you out there?" Fly quizzed. Although Syn worked her last nerve, she loved him and didn't want to see anything bad happen to him. "With all this mess of police killing blacks, the last thing you need is a run-in with the cops."

"Look, it is what it is! I'd rather die on the streets than behind bars." Synful was as serious as a heart attack. Reaching into his pocket, he pulled out a small wad of money. "Fly, this ain't much, but it's all I got right now. I want you to take this and buy some food and shit for you and Braxton. I'll hit you up as soon as I can, okay, baby?" He pulled Fly in close and inhaled her scent one last time.

"Syris, don't leave me." She wrapped her arms around him.

"I have to, baby, but I'll be back." He kissed her cheek. "I'll hit you up as soon as I can, believe that. If the police try to question you, ask for a lawyer!" Syn scrolled down the contacts in his phone, then texted a number to Fly. "His name is Kenneth Lorton. He owes me one and will take care of anything you need. Same goes for you, Kali."

"Okay, I'll call him." Fly squeezed her man one last time.

"Syn and Fly forever, remember that," he whispered and she nodded. "I love you, girl."

"I love you too." She sniffed.

"Big boy." Syn turned to Bird. "Word to God, I'm sorry about all this," he said as sincerely as he could. "I'll see you on the other side, my brother." He dapped his man up, bid Kali farewell, and hopped into his whip, disappearing into the night.

As soon as he was out of sight, Fly finally lost it and cried like a baby. She knew she would never see Syn again, at least not as a free man. She prayed to God she'd never have to see him as a dead man, either.

CHAPTER TEN

KALI

For nearly two hours Kali and Jamaica consoled their friend until she practically cried herself to sleep on the sofa. "Tell Fly I'll hit her line tomorrow," Jamaica said while grabbing her belongings.

"Will do," Kali replied as she walked over to the door and held it open.

Without another word between them, Jamaica left the townhouse and Kali closed the door. With a deep sigh, Kali pulled herself together and walked into Bird's bedroom. He was sitting at the foot of the bed and had the television on. "Thank you, baby, for being patient and letting me be there for my friend."

"It ain't no thang." Bird looked up at his beautiful woman. "I hope she'll be there for you too when I leave."

"Please don't leave me just yet." Kali took a seat beside him and placed her head on his chest.

"Kali," Bird groaned. He wasn't in a rush to go to jail, but he knew the longer he remained a fugitive, the search for him would intensify. "I'll stay until morning, but then I got to go turn myself in," he relented.

"How do you know they're even looking for you?" Kali remained hopeful until Bird pointed at the television screen. It was on Fox 2 News.

"As we reported earlier, police are still on the hunt for these two men." A picture of Bird and Syn appeared on the screen. "Bernard Harris and Syris Washington are wanted in connection with the shooting tonight at a popular after-hours nightclub on Plymouth Road. It has been reported that at least one man was killed. The victim's name is being withheld, but we have reason to believe that the victim is a criminal informant. Gus, what can you tell us about what took place tonight?" the news reporter asked the on-scene reporter who was now on screen.

"Right now, all we know is that members of the Atlanta police department have been working an undercover case here in Detroit for the past year. Harris and Washington were at the center of this investigation," the reporter read from his notes. "Witnesses here at Janet's Place say the suspects approached the victim and began having a heated exchange on the dance floor. Seconds later, shots were fired. At this time, it is not clear if both suspects fired or just one." The reporter adjusted his glasses. "By the time police and paramedics arrived on scene, it was too late, and the shooting victim was declared dead at the scene." The on-scene reporter looked down at the ground before peering back into the camera.

"Thank you, Gus. If you have any information on the men pictured here, please call the crime stoppers division at 1-800-CRM-STPR."

"This shit is crazy! You should've never gone and done any of this with that fool Syris. None of this would've happened." Kali was pissed.

"I did, and we're here now. Life is about choices, Kali, and I made mine." Bird had been raised by his grandfather to be a man of honor. He stood tall even when he was in the wrong. As much as Kali hated it, she loved him for never running like a coward no matter how bad things looked.

Buzzzzzzz. Bird grabbed the phone resting in his lap. It was his mother, Lisa. "Hey, Ma. I know, I saw it. Did they? I know. All right. Come and get me. I'm ready." With a grimace, he ended the call.

"What did she say?" Kali searched his face for signs.

"Baby, there has been a change of plans. Mom is on the way to come and scoop me. I'm turning myself in tonight."

"Bird, you said tomorrow." Kali smacked her lips.

"They just kicked in her door since that's my last known address. I got to go before they come here." He stood from the bed. "Take these bags and hide them, baby. Can you do that for me?" Bird handed Kali all of the garbage bags he'd gotten earlier from the robbery.

"Of course I will." Kali took the bags without hesitation.

"Hide this shit as soon as possible!" Bird instructed. "They may come and interrogate you. If they do—"

"I won't tell them shit." Kali cut him off mid-sentence.

"That's my baby." Bird leaned down and kissed her forehead.

"I love you, Bird." After seconds of silence passed, Kali looked up to see a single tear fall down Bird's face.

"I love you more," he mumbled. His heart was completely broken. Just yesterday afternoon they stood in this very spot and got engaged. Now, less than twenty-four hours later, here they were saying goodbye.

***

An hour later, Lisa was using her spare key to enter Bird's condo. "Son, I'm here," she called from the living room.

"Hey, Lisa. He's in the bathroom." Kali stepped from the bedroom with swollen eyes from crying. "I think his stomach is upset."

"We can't blame him for that, now, can we?" Lisa snapped. She was a full-sized woman in every sense of the word. Not only did she weigh about 375 pounds, but she stood tall at five feet ten inches. Her large attitude matched her size, and Kali couldn't stand her.

"Was the door unlocked?" Kali asked as an afterthought.

"I used my key." Lisa waved her key from side to side.

"What's up, Momma?" Bird walked into the living room with his shoes in hand. He sat down on the sofa to put them on.

"Negro, don't 'what's up, Momma' me." Lisa smacked her lips. "What the fuck is going on with you and Syris?"

"I don't feel like talking about it right now. Can you just take me to the police station without all the questions, please?" Bernard loved his mother, but sometimes she got on his last nerves.

"Negro, if I can't ask no questions then you shouldn't have asked me to come and get your black ass!" Lisa flopped down so hard on the sofa there was a cracking sound in the wooden frame. "I don't see why Ms. Thang ain't taking you to the police station." She pointed back at Kali.

"Ma, please chill." Bird stood.

"Chill my ass, boy," Lisa hissed. "I guess she too bougie to be seen there, huh? Her parents would probably die at the first sign of bad publicity, right?"

"Ma, you need to cut this out. Kali is my fiancée, and I need for you to treat her as such until I get back." Bird knew he had to put an end to the drama before he left or things would only escalate.

"Did you say fiancée?"

"Yes. I proposed yesterday afternoon." Bird sighed. "I was going to tell you this morning but then this crazy shit popped off."

"Are you pregnant?" Lisa blatantly asked. "You did put on a little weight."

"No, I'm not pregnant." Kali shook her head and sucked in her stomach.

"Um-hm." Lisa rolled her eyes. "Well, come on, son. Let's go." She made a show of trying to get off the sofa. Both Kali and Bird watched her struggle until he finally helped her up on her feet. Her ankles were so swollen that her shoes leaned sideways.

"Kali, don't forget what I told you this morning. Please take care of that for me." He walked over and gave her one last hug. "If something happens to me, move on. I love you, baby," he whispered in her ear.

"I love you too. I'll have an attorney for you as soon as possible, baby." Kali squeezed him tight.

"Fa'sho." With a nod, Bird pressed his lips against hers then pulled away. "If I have to do a bid behind this, move on." Those were his last words before he and Lisa walked out of the townhouse.

Kali wanted to run behind them and beg him to stay, but she knew it would've only made things worse. Instead, she watched from the window as the love of her life left her twisting in the wind.

CHAPTER ELEVEN

JAMAICA

"I'm hungry." Braxton stood at the foot of Jamaica's bed poking her through the covers.

"Huh?" Jamaica groaned. She was in the middle of a good dream with Rick Ross.

"I'm hungry," Braxton repeated. He was an early riser and was used to eating first thing in the morning.

"Go and watch cartoons or something." Jamaica wasn't the most pleasant person in the morning. Therefore, she gently kicked at him and turned back over.

"Do you have some Froot Loops?" Braxton wasn't letting up. He'd already been up for two hours. His little stomach was growling. "Where is my sister?" he whined. Braxton had searched the whole house for Fly and couldn't find her.

"I'll take you to her later. Let me at least get one more hour of sleep." With one eye open Jamaica peeped the alarm clock on her nightstand and winced. It was only 9:03 a.m.

"But I'm hungry!" Braxton slapped the bed. "I need you to call Fly, now!" he demanded with his arms folded.

With a smile and a chuckle, Jamaica sat up and yawned. "Okay, killer, don't hurt me." She laughed. "What do you want to eat? Besides some damn Froot Loops. I'll cook you something." Jamaica had never tasted cereal as a child because her mother made breakfast every morning without fail.

"Can I have pancakes?" Braxton asked after pondering for a minute.

"You can only have pancakes if you promise to help me make them."

"Deal." With all of his teeth exposed Braxton held out his hand, and Jamaica shook it.

Together they headed down the hallway to the kitchen. "Do you like chocolate chips in your pancakes?" She hit the switch on the wall and turned on the light.

"Yes, I think so." Truth was Braxton had never had chocolate chips in his pancakes, but he loved the way it sounded.

"What about whipped cream?" Jamaica asked. Braxton smiled and gave her two thumbs-up. "Okay, well, you sit here and I'll grab the stuff."

"Okay." With a big grin, he flopped down on the bench at the breakfast nook and waited patiently.

Jamaica began pulling all the ingredients out and placing them on the laminate countertop. Although she was sleepy as hell, she enjoyed moments like this. It always made her reminisce about her childhood. After Margaret fled Jamaica, they didn't have much, but the love and care she provided her daughter was priceless.

"Okay, Brax, can you crack eggs?" She slid a bowl and two eggs his way.

"Of course I can. I'm not a baby!"

"Well, excuse me." Jamaica busted out laughing just as the doorbell rang. "Okay, sir, you handle that, and I'll be right back." She patted Braxton on the head before going to the door.

A quick glance through the peephole indicated that no one was there. Jamaica headed back to the kitchen.

Ding dong!

This time she ran to the door and snatched it open. "Who the fuck is out here playing at the door?" she said, hoping to bust the ding-dong ditcher. However, no one was there. In fact, the only evidence that someone had been there was the brown paper bag on her porch that was on fire. Quickly Jamaica ran up to the bag and stomped it out using her house shoe. "Oh, hell no!" she screamed loud enough to wake the dead.

"What's wrong? What is it?" Margaret asked from the doorway. Braxton was at her side.

"Some jackass decided to burn a bag of dog shit on our porch." Seething mad, Jamaica turned around and showed her mother her shoe and foot covered in shit.

"Oh my God." Margaret tried hard to suppress her laughter, but it was no use. Within seconds she was riddled with giggles. Jamaica wanted to be upset, but she had to admit the shit was kind of funny. "I wonder who would pull such a prank."

"Who knows?" Jamaica stepped out of the house shoes she had on and hopped into the house. She had so many enemies that the prankster could've been anyone.

After breakfast, Jamaica and Braxton got dressed. She called Fly but still got no answer. "Your sister isn't answering. Do you want to roll with me or do you want to stay here?"

"I want to go with you." Braxton didn't want to spend his day watching old movies with Ms. Margaret like he usually did whenever she'd watch him.

"Okay, little man, let's roll." Jamaica grabbed her keys, and they headed out. "I need to get my hair done, but first I need some money."

With a devious smile, she backed her car out of its parking spot and headed to Jay's car wash on Greenfield. He was one of her special friends who laced her from time to time. Jay was married to a woman who'd lost her mobility in a car accident a few years ago. He loved his wife to death but needed wild sex from time to time. Jamaica provided that for him and more. She agreed to keep his secret, and he agreed to look out for her every now and then.

During the ride to the car wash, Jamaica unwillingly played a game of twenty questions with Braxton. "Why is your name Jamaica?" he asked two seconds into their journey.

"That's what my mother named me," Jamaica replied.

"Why did she name you that?"

"She named me after the place I was born."

"Why were you born there?"

"That's where my mom and dad are from. We lived there when they had me," Jamaica answered.

"Where is your dad? I never seen'd him."

"He's in jail."

"My teacher said that's where bad people go." Braxton paused. "Is your dad a bad guy?"

"I don't think so, but it depends on who you ask." Jamaica looked back at him through the rearview. "Not all bad people are in jail, and not all free people are good."

"Yeah." Brax nodded. "My dad is a bad guy, and he's not in jail," he said calmly.

"What makes you think your dad is a bad guy?" At first, she was annoyed by the multitude of questions and wanted to drown him out with her gangster rap music; but now she was glad they were talking.

"He did some bad things, but I'm not supposed to tell anybody." Braxton began to look uncomfortable.

"We're friends, aren't we, Brax?" Jamaica wanted more information but didn't want to alarm him.

"Yeah, I guess so." He shrugged.

"Friends should be able to share anything." Jamaica peered at him again through the mirror. "What bad things did your dad do?"

"I'm not supposed to tell anybody, not even Fly." Braxton shifted in his seat.

"I promise I won't tell." There was a brief silence. "Brax, I cross my heart and hope to die."

"Okay." Braxton's eyes met hers through the mirror. "My dad makes me take off my clothes and take pictures for him."

"What?" Jamaica screamed then regained her composure. "Has your dad ever touched you?" She swallowed hard.

"No, but he did make me touch his thing a few times. And he'll hit me if I don't do what he asks me to do." Braxton was now looking at the floor trying to decide if he should've told her.

"You're right. Your dad is a bad man." As soon as Jamaica stopped her car at the red light, she turned to face the little boy. "I promise I will never let that happen again. Does your mommy know?"

"I told her once, and we both got in trouble real bad." Braxton's eyes started to water. "He told her I was lying and whooped both of us, but my mommy was bleeding." He wiped his little eyes, and Jamaica wiped hers. "That night he came into my room and told me that he would kill Fly if I told her what happened." He looked up at Jamaica in sheer panic. "Please don't tell her 'cause I don't want my big sister to die."

"Your dad is not going to kill Fly, I promise." She held out a pinky, and he locked his with it. Car horns started blowing because the light was green, but she didn't care. "He won't be taking any more pictures of you, either." She turned back around and pulled off.

"How do you know?" Braxton looked skeptical.
"Because I won't allow it." With a heavy heart,
her mind went into overdrive thinking about
when and how to tell Fly her little brother's
secret.

CHAPTER TWELVE

KALI

After checking in on Fly, who was still snoring in the guest bedroom, Kali grabbed Bird's garbage bags and headed to the car.

"Good morning, Mrs. White." She waved at her neighbor while placing the bags into the trunk. Every time they saw each other, Mrs. White made it a point to start a long conversation about this or that. Surprisingly, today she didn't even make eye contact with her. Paying the minor detail no attention, Kali got into the burgundy Jeep Cherokee and pulled off.

Seconds later, the phone rang. It was Desmond. Her heart skipped two beats before she answered. "Hey, Desmond, thanks for calling me back."

"Good morning, Kali." Desmond's voice was still as confident and smooth as Kali remembered. "I got your voicemail. What's up?"

"Desmond, I need you to take on my fiancé's case."

"Oh, man, I wish I could be of assistance," he said, "but my caseload is overflowing. I'll call a few colleagues and see if I can find Mr. Harris representation."

"No, Desmond, it has to be you," Kali snapped. "You are the number three criminal defense attorney in the state of Michigan. Your record stands at fifty to seven. Please, Desmond, I need you."

"I see someone has done her homework." Desmond was elated that she knew his stats. He was flattered.

"We may not talk, Des, but I've studied your career ever since your first case." She smiled. "You are a damn good lawyer. I aspire to be just like you, if not better one day." Truth be told, Kali's interest in becoming a lawyer only stemmed from watching Desmond be so damn good at it. She saw him making a difference in the community and wanted to do the same.

"While that's flattering and all that, you should know with stats like mine, a lot of zeros come with my fee." Desmond wasn't one to mince words, especially not about money. "Can you afford my services?"

"No! Well, not yet anyway. But I promise I will pay you every penny," Kali replied honestly.

"Kali, I don't know too much about your boy-friend but, from what I do know, he is somewhat of a street businessman, isn't he?" Desmond paused and was a bit hesitant in what he was going to say next. He didn't want to offend Kali but, by the same token, he wanted to say what was on his mind. "Tell me how these thugs make all this money in the street and don't think enough of their freedom to save a dime for lawyer fees? We all know when you live that life, you will eventually need a lawyer. I mean, that's Street Knowledge 101. Even I know that."

"Desmond, Bird is not who you think he is. Please don't refer to him in that manner!" Kali was beginning to lose her cool. "He does what he has to do to help his family, and he could've saved money if he weren't paying off my tuition. You and I both know how expensive law school can be."

"Bird? Is that what his mother named him?" Desmond laughed. He couldn't believe the woman he would have once died for had left his Ivy League ass for a nigga named Bird. "And, furthermore, I know you didn't just tell me your law degree is being funded by drug money! Who are you, Kali?"

"Oh my God, are you serious right now? You're going to pick a time like this to come riding on your high horse?" Kali snapped. "People like you kill me talking about somebody living a lifestyle you don't approve of; but how quick you are to forget the skeletons in your own damn closet. I'm sure the others partners at your firm would love to know about how you got a fifteen-year-old minor pregnant when you were twenty years old!"

"Oh, please, Kali! I was nineteen."

"The point being, you were an adult, and I was a minor! In this state, that is statutory rape. And you knew what you were doing was wrong, but you kept fucking me anyway. In fact, if memory serves, you didn't stop fucking me until you were twenty-two and I seventeen." She was beyond pissed. "Anyway, I really don't know what I was thinking calling you for help. I appreciate you taking the time to hear me out. I hope you have a good day."

Without another word, she ended the call. Desmond called her phone three times after that, but she didn't answer. She wished she hadn't even called him in the first place.

Ten minutes later, Kali pulled her Jeep into a parking spot at her father's church then got out and grabbed the garbage bags. The only other cars in the lot belonged to her father and Deacon Mason. She straightened her cream-colored dress then gave herself a once-over before heading into the two-story brick building that had over two dozen stained-glass windows. A gold statue of Christ met her at the door, and she took a minute to bow her head in prayer.

"Kali Ann?" He father, Bishop Thomas Franklin, smiled as he and Deacon Mason exited the church. "You see how fast the Lord works, Deac? We just prayed for her in my office."

"Amen, Bishop." Deacon Mason leaned back with his hands resting on his big belly.

"Hello, Deac. Hey, Daddy." Kali wrapped her arms around her father, and he squeezed her back.

"What brings you by?" Bishop Franklin pointed at the garbage bags. "What do you have there?"

"These are some items I wanted to donate to the church store," she lied quickly. "A few tops and jeans, that's all."

"Okay, baby. You know we appreciate all you're willing to give." He reached for the bags. "I'll take them inside for you."

"No, I'll take them to the mission room, Daddy." She tightened her grasp on the bags. Her stomach was doing backflips, and her palms were clammy. "Besides, it gives me a reason to wander around the old place and reminisce. I've really been missing the church lately." Quickly she kissed her father's cheek and went inside before he could dig any deeper.

"Well, look at God!" Bishop hollered as the door closed.

Kali smiled from cheek to cheek. She loved to see her father happy. Ever since she could remember she was always a daddy's girl. Sometimes, she felt that her mother hated their bond and tried to force a wedge between them. Of course, if anyone ever asked First Lady Ilene if that was her intention, she would politely deny it.

Hastily, Kali flew through the vestibule, knocking down a stack of programs on her way. When she reached the end of the hallway, she opened the second door on the left and poked her head in. The coast was clear. She slipped inside and began searching for a place to stash the garbage bags. It didn't dawn on her until that very moment that she was actually storing bricks of heroin inside the church: a sacred, holy place.

"I can't do this," she said aloud as her conscience kicked in. "I've got to find somewhere else." Just as she put her hand on the doorknob to exit, she heard her mother's voice in the hallway.

"Damn!" she cursed. "Oops, excuse me, Lord." Frantically her eyes roamed the room trying to find somewhere to quickly stash the bags.

"Francine, the bishop said that child of mine was in the mission room. Can I call you back, girl?" Ilene Franklin stood at the door and opened it slightly.

Kali's heart skipped two beats until her eyes stumbled on the vent. With ease, she pried the cover off then threw the bags inside. After putting the cover back on, she tossed a few boxes in front of it, then dropped down to her knees just as the door opened all the way.

"Kali Ann, what are you doing over there?" Ilene waltzed into the room wearing a pastel pink suit with matching shoes and purse. The silver LV scarf around her neck complemented the diamonds in her ears beautifully.

"Amen." Kali stood from the floor then dusted her knees off. "Sorry, Momma, I was praying."

"Um-hm. I'm sure you were." Ilene rolled her eyes, already knowing better. "I'll ask you again: what are you doing here, child?" Although she was happy to see her one and only daughter, she was feeling some type of way toward her at this time. Kali had been ignoring her phone calls for days, and she was not happy about it.

"You've been blowing up my phone about missing church, then I show up, and now you got an attitude." Kali shook her head. "I can't win for losing with you."

"Excuse me, young lady, but you will not have that kind of attitude with me!" Ilene snapped. "Your father and I did not raise you to be this way, so please talk like you have some sense and manners."

"As always, it's nice to see you, Momma." Irritated, Kali bypassed her mother and headed for the door.

"No, ma'am, you won't be leaving here that easy." Ilene turned on the balls of her pink suede Louboutin heels. "What is going on with that boy and his friend? Did they really commit murder?"

"I don't know what happened. I haven't seen or spoken to him, so I have no idea what is going on with all of that." As Kali spoke, she could feel her cell phone vibrating in her pocket. She ignored the first call but then it started over.

"I warned you about being careful with who you spend your time with. And I know I told you not to go messing with people like that boy. They are nothing but trouble!" Ilene pushed open the mission room door and called for her husband. "Thomas, I'm going to need you to get in here and talk to Miss Thang over here before I hurt her."

"Daddy, she's asking me questions about what's going on with Bird. I already told her I don't know what happened. As soon as I know something I will let you know," she said as she stood between both of her parents. "I don't need a sermon right now, please." Kali was beginning to feel emotionally drained. She took a deep breath and hoped to get out of there soon. Again, Kali's phone started vibrating in her pocket.

"All of this happened for a reason, Kali. God is trying to get your attention!" Bishop Franklin started anyway. "See, we serve a jealous God! You been making that boy so much a priority that you forgot about your commitments. You forgot about the church. You forgot about God!" He raised his hand toward heaven. "But God said, 'No, sir, not my child.'" He took a long, dramatic breath in true preaching fashion. "He had to remove the distraction so that He could regain your attention. Let that boy deal with the mess he made and come on home where you belong."

"Daddy!" Kali snapped. "Please, not right now."

"Kali, nobody like you should ever end up with a man like that! The life he lives ends in only one of two ways." Bishop Franklin put his arm around his daughter. "Nothing good will ever come from selling dope! He's poisoning our people, God's people, and profiting from the blood money. Do you know how many families I've had to counsel about drug abuse?"

"Daddy, Bernard is not like that. He's not like the rest of them. He has plans for his life. He had plans for *our* life." Kali blinked back a few tears. "He proposed last night. He loves me." She held up her hand to them.

"Baby, I love you, your mother loves you, and God loves you!" Bishop Franklin pulled his daughter in close. "If this man loves you so much, why on God's green earth would he do something to jeopardize his freedom?" Bishop pulled back from his daughter. "Kali, I know you don't want to hear this, but I'm glad it happened. Now we can get you back on a spiritual track."

"How can you say that?" Kali wiped her eyes. Once again, her phone started vibrating. "Never mind. You don't have to answer that. I have to go. I'll talk to you later." Without so much as a glance their way, Kali left her parents standing there.

"So we're just going to let her leave, just like that?" Ilene hissed.

"She will be back, my dear. Don't worry." Bishop Franklin kissed his wife and retreated to his office.

Once outside, Kali answered the twelfth call with a little bit of an attitude. "Fly, what's the emergency?"

"Bitch, these people are over here trying to put me out. I need you to come home quick!"

"What people?" Kali had delivered this month's rent check personally five days ago.

"Your mother-in-law and her offspring." Fly smacked her lips.

"Oh, shit. All right. I'm on my way."

"Yes, you need to hurry before I go to jail for fucking a bitch up!" Click!

CHAPTER THIRTEEN

FLY

"Why are you still standing there? I told you to leave!" Rochelle hollered. She was rummaging through the drawers in the kitchen while her mother went through the couch.

"And I told your fat ass I wasn't moving until Kali got home." Fly bucked. She wasn't sure what ugly and uglier were looking for, but Fly wished they'd find it and get the fuck on.

"This is my son's home, sweetie," Lisa corrected her.

"I'm sure your son wouldn't be too pleased with the way y'all going through his shit like you're the fucking police." Fly was irritated to the max. Not only had Lisa and Rochelle let themselves inside the apartment without knocking first, but they'd searched through every inch of the guest room where she was staying, including the mattress. They started searching it while she was sleeping on it.

"Ma, please put this bitch out." Rochelle slammed a kitchen drawer then went for a cabinet.

"I'll be back, Ro." Wobbling and breathing heavy, Lisa walked out of the townhouse.

Fly stood guard at the window to make sure her crazy ass didn't have a gun in the car. That's when she saw Jamaica pull up to the place.

"You good, ma?" she asked after stepping from her whip with her beloved 9 mm gripped for dear life.

"Yeah, I'm good. I don't know what these goofy bitches are up to, but I don't like it." Fly hugged Jamaica while watching Lisa walk toward the rental office. "Where is Brax?"

"When you called and said you needed backup I told my homeboy to watch him," Jamaica explained. "I didn't want him to see nothing; he's already been through enough."

"Did something happen?" Fly was concerned. "What has he been through?"

"I think we need to take care of what's going on right now. I'll talk to you about what's going on with Brax later." Jamaica knew this wasn't the time or the place.

"J, you got five seconds to tell me what is up with my brother, or me and you will have issues." Fly didn't care where they were or what was going on. Her number one concern was always her baby brother.

"Look, Fly, I really don't think it's the right time to talk about it."

"Any time is the right time to talk about anything that has to do with my brother. C'mon, bitch, get it out."

"All right. I'ma talk, but don't say I didn't warn you. We really should have left this conversation for later." Jamaica took a deep breath, knowing that what she was about to reveal to her friend was going to devastate her. "Today he told me that Ray made him pose for nude pictures and touch his dick." Jamaica's stomach flipped just thinking about it.

"What?" Fly gasped.

"He said he told your mom about it before and Ray beat both of their asses."

"Why didn't he tell me?" Fly didn't know how to feel. Her body felt as if someone had just poured a bucket of cold water on her.

"Ray told him that he would kill you if he said something to you about it."

"I'm going to kill his ass!" Fly had put up with a lot of shit from Ray and her mother, but this was the last straw. She wanted Ray's head on a platter.

"I told you that shit could've waited. But, look, there is Kali. Let's handle this first, and then we'll handle Ray." Jamaica moved aside just as Kali pulled into her neighbor's parking spot.

Fly looked over at Kali and decided to put the Ray and Braxton situation on the back burner for now.

"What the fuck is going on?" Kali noticed the gun in Jamaica's hand and immediately feared the worst. "Did someone get hurt?"

"Not yet," Jamaica replied.

Fly ran everything down. "All I know is Lisa and Rochelle been going through your crib like detectives with warrants. These bitches even lifted the bed while I was lying on it. When I woke up, they told me I had to rise and fly. Naturally, I called you. Ro in there now. Lisa just went to the rental office."

"Thanks! Y'all stay out here in case Lisa comes back with some bullshit. I'll handle Rochelle." Seeing red and seething mad, Kali burst in the townhouse. "What are you looking for?"

"None of your business, bitch!" Rochelle replied from the kitchen.

"Everything in here is my business, bitch!" Kali entered the kitchen prepared for a fight. That's when she saw Ro looking in the freezer, and it dawned on her. Back in the day when she and Bird got together, he told her that he kept most of his savings hidden in the house. He stored money is odd places like the freezer, inside cereal boxes, in the water tank above the toilet, and under the mattress. Kali told him how stupid that was, but he insisted on being able to put his hands on his cash at a moment's notice if need be.

"Your brother would give you the world and here you are trying to rob him!" Kali yelled, "I can't believe you two right now. Bird hasn't been behind bars a solid ten hours and his own mother and sister are already here to collect on whatever it is y'all think he has. Do you two even care about what's about to happen to him right now?"

"Bitch, you don't know shit about me or my mother. This don't even concern you so mind your business."

"Bird is my business." On impulse, Kali charged at her full speed. Rochelle saw her coming and tried to get out of the way, but her weight wouldn't allow her to move fast enough. Within seconds, Kali was all over her like a fly on shit. Fly and Jamaica heard the commotion and rushed into the house. They thought Kali needed help but, by the look of things, it was the other way around.

"You're lucky I love Bird or I would kill your trifling ass." With one more punch to her jaw, Kali got off of Ro. "They're in here tearing shit up trying to find Bird's money," she told her girls.

Before anyone could respond, the front door opened. Everyone turned around to see Lisa and a middle-aged white man. "Sorry to barge in, Mrs. Harris." Dexter, the property manager, fixed his glasses and shifted nervously. There was a stupid look on his face. It was almost as stupid as the grin on Lisa's face. She was cheesing like a fat rat in a cheese factory.

"Go ahead, boy, tell her!" Lisa pointed. "And her last name ain't Harris!"

"Tell me what?" Kali sighed. She didn't have time for games.

"Unfortunately, you have to get your things and leave." Dexter loved Kali; she had been one of his most pleasant tenants these past few years. He hated what Lisa was forcing him to do, but the rental agreement was set in stone.

"What do you mean, leave?" Kali wasn't sure she'd heard him right.

"Since the lease is in Ms. Harris's name and she no longer wants you staying here while her son is away, you must vacate the premises." Dexter looked down at his clipboard. "Do you receive mail here?"

"No," Kali blurted before she realized he was mouthing for her to say yes.

"Oh, that's unfortunate. If you were receiving mail here, by law Ms. Harris would have to give you thirty days to vacate the premises."

"But the bitch said she don't get no mail here, so end of story!" Lisa butted in. "Grab your shit and go."

"I'm sorry, Kali, I really wish there were something I could do. I'll give you 'til the end of the day to get your belongings. After that, if you're still here, Ms. Harris has the right to call for the police to come and remove you." Deflated and feeling helpless, Dexter walked back out of the townhouse.

"Why are you doing this, Lisa?" Kali wanted to cry, but she was too proud and strong to show these bitches any sign of weakness. "Isn't it bad enough I may have lost my fiancé, and now I'm losing our home?" Truth be told, Kali expected some drama between her and Bird's family, but nothing like this, and not so soon.

"Little girl, do you really think I care about you losing your fiancé when I just lost my son?" Lisa rolled her eyes and gritted her teeth. "And this ain't your home; it's my son's house, bitch!" Although she'd never really had a good reason, she hated the little bitch standing before her.

Maybe it was because Kali came across like she was better than everybody, or maybe because it seemed like Bird loved her more. Whatever it was, Lisa couldn't stand Kali. Lisa was clicking her heels just knowing she didn't have to see or hear about his son's perfect little girlfriend anymore. "Now grab your shit and go!"

"Fuck them, B. Just grab your shit and let's ride." Jamaica felt bad for Kali, but she knew her friend was better off just cutting her losses and leaving. It would make no sense for them to stay there and continue to argue.

"Yeah, fuck them," Fly added.

In silence, Kali grabbed her text books off of the dining room table and a photo of her and Bird off the wall. "Come on, let's go," she mumbled.

"That's all you taking?" Fly said, following her outside. "I know there's way more valuable shit in the townhouse besides a picture and some books."

"Yeah? They can have that shit." Kali unlocked her car and got inside. She didn't want the money, clothes, or jewelry. If they wanted it that bad, they could have it.

"Where are you going to go?" Jamaica leaned into the window.

"I could always go home, I guess." In all honesty, that was the last place she wanted to go, but her options were slim.

"I still have the keys to Syn's place. We can crash over there until we figure this out."

"Okay, cool. Let's go." Kali desperately needed to smoke a blunt and chill before deciding on the next move.

"Jamaica, can you pick up Braxton so I can take Kali straight to Syn's?" Fly asked her friend.

"Yeah, I'll go scoop him up. Y'all go ahead." Jamaica got inside of her car. "I'll be over in about an hour. Call me if you need me, though!" With that, she pulled off the same way she'd pulled in: like a bat out of hell.

CHAPTER FOURTEEN

JAMAICA

"Thanks, Jay. I appreciate you watching my friend's brother." Jamaica was leaning up against her car.

"It ain't no thang. I enjoyed the little dude. He's been out here helping me dry cars since you left." Jay removed the Detroit baseball cap from his head and wiped the sweat off his forehead. "The little nigga done made about twenty dollars in tips."

"Aww, thank you." She wanted to give Jay's fine ass a hug but knew better than to do so in public. Although Jay fucked her every which way but loose behind closed doors, he always remained professional in public. The last thing he wanted was someone riding by the car wash and telling his wife what they saw. "Did you still need me to look at the books in your office?" she asked with a wink.

He played along. "Yeah, I do. Hey, Tyrone, keep an eye on little man for me," he called over to one of his employees.

"Got you, boss," Tyrone called back.

Jay led Jamaica inside the small building attached to the car wash. "I like the new paint," she complimented him on her walk through the lobby, which also served as a break room for the employees to get out of the sun on hot days.

"Yeah, I'm trying to spruce up the joint a bit. I even put in some vending machines and a few tables." Jay locked the door behind them as soon as he and Jamaica got into his office. It was small, with nothing but a desk in the corner and a television mounted to the wall.

"How do you want this pussy, baby?" Jamaica wasted no time pulling her jean dress over her head.

"Can I get in through the back door today?" Jay unbuttoned his navy blue Dickie shorts, and his curved dick damn near jumped from the hole in his boxers.

"Ooh, daddy, fucking me in the ass is going to cost you." Jamaica reached into her bra and retrieved a condom. After removing her panties, she slid to her knees and put the rubber baby-catcher onto his dick with her mouth.

"Mmm," he moaned before lifting her up and bending her over the desk. Without saying another word, he forced himself inside of Jamaica's asshole and began to stroke her deep and hard. She screamed out in both pain and pleasure. Although she'd had plenty of dick in her ass, Jay's was by far the biggest. Yet and still, she threw her body back against his until her nipples were as hard as bullets and her pussy was soaking wet.

Jay climaxed inside the condom within twenty minutes, which was fast for him. He hadn't seen Jamaica in a while; therefore, his stamina wasn't up to par. "Did you cum?" he asked after pulling his manhood out of her.

"Nah, but it's cool. I'm glad you did." With a genuine smile, she reached down and grabbed her clothes. She couldn't care less about a nut; all she wanted was the almighty dollar.

"I needed that." After removing the condom and wiping himself with some napkins from his desk, Jay reached into his pocket and handed Jamaica three crisp Benjamins.

Buzzzz. The cell phone in his pocket vibrated. "What up, doe?" he answered while zipping his shorts. "Are you outside? Cool. Here I come." He ended the call then went behind the desk and grabbed a duffle bag. "I gotta handle this real quick, but you can chill in here as long as you need to."

"Go handle your business. I'll catch you later." Jamaica slid the dress over her head as Jay walked out. She watched from behind the window in his office as he walked outside and greeted a man she knew in the hood as Yayo. He was big coke player in Detroit. She watched in silence as they exchanged duffle bags. Either he was copping from Jay or Jay was copping from him. Either way, never in a million years did she imagine that her side piece was in the dope game. Obviously, their sexcapades wasn't the only secret he was keeping.

CHAPTER FIFTEEN

KALI

"Are you fucking serious?" Kali sat up on the couch where she was sitting Indian style. Fly and Jamaica had just broken the news to her about Braxton and Ray.

"I'm going to kill him." Fly didn't even bat an eyelash.

"I'm going to kill him for you." Kali was irate.

"I got the gun right here." Jamaica reached into her purse and placed the 9 mm down on the glass coffee table.

"Shit, I got one too. We about to be on some *Set It Off* type shit. I'll be Latifah. Who's gonna be Jada?" Fly reached into her purse and pulled hers out.

On cue, all the women busted out laughing. For the past two hours they'd been smoking kush blunts and drinking some leftover Cîroc that Syn had in his refrigerator; they were all drunk and high. Fly was glad that Jamaica had suggested that Braxton stay with her mom again so they could talk about everything without him being around to hear any of it.

"Seriously, y'all, I don't know what I'm going to do." Fly put the gun back into her purse. Hurting people really wasn't her thing, but she wasn't about to let Ray get away with that shit. And she wasn't a cop caller so turning him in was not an option. She believed in street justice wholeheartedly, but usually Syn or her brother Q fought her battles. With both of them gone, she didn't have anyone she could call on.

"I don't know where or when, but Ray will get what's coming to him, believe me." Kali stood from the couch and tried to get her bearings. The alcohol had her dizzy.

"There is the story on Syn and Bird. Turn the volume up." Jamaica pointed. They had been watching the television on silent waiting for the news to come on.

"Good afternoon." The blond reporter in a red dress sternly looked at the camera. "Yesterday we reported the shooting death of one man inside of Janet's Place in the early morning hours. Today, the victim's name has been released as Perry 'Li'l Nut' Johnson. Today, Detroit Police Chief Harry Calloway confirmed Johnson's role as a criminal informant in an ongoing Atlanta heroin investigation. He said although the murder occurred in Detroit, Atlanta will take the lead on prosecution. We have this clip from earlier."

Her male coanchor was replaced with a video clip of the police chief addressing the media. "Earlier today, Bernard Harris turned himself over to police custody where he was interrogated and subsequently charged with first-degree murder. The second suspect, Syris Washington, is still on the run. He is considered armed and dangerous. Due to the circumstances surrounding this shooting, both the Detroit and Atlanta PDs will participate in the manhunt for Mr. Washington. Once we apprehend him, Atlanta's prosecution team will take over. We will provide them with all the resources needed to put these men behind bars."

Fly grabbed the remote and muted the television. She wished like hell she could call Syn right now.

Boom! Boom! The knock on the door startled the women. They all looked at each other silently. Jamaica picked up her gun.

Boom! Boom! Crash! This time the knocking was accompanied by the door being knocked off its hinges. Swiftly Jamaica tucked her gun into her panties as at least ten police officers raided the apartment with their guns out.

"Get down on the ground!" one officer hollered. Without hesitation, the women did as they were told.

"Where is Syris Washington?" Another officer asked while walking into the bedroom.

"I swear we don't where he is. We have nothing to do with any of this. Please don't shoot us!" Fly screamed. She'd read news stories and seen way too many videos about police raids going wrong and innocent people getting hurt.

"Bedroom clear!"

"Kitchen clear!"

"All clear!" Several officers hollered as they came back to the living room and stood over the women.

"You all can get up." The officer who'd ordered them to the ground tucked his weapon into his holster. "Where is your boyfriend?"

"I haven't seen him," Fly admitted.

"Bullshit!" the cocky officer snapped. "We know you were with him last night. In fact, witnesses put all of you at the scene." He stared at each woman. "Now, we can play nice, or we can play dirty down at the station. If we go down to the station, I will charge you as being an accessory to murder."

"Don't believe him, Fly. He's just trying to scare you," Kali spoke up. "Is she under arrest?" Kali asked.

"Not yet!" the officer replied.

"Then she doesn't have anything to say, especially without her attorney present." Kali knew civilian rights like the back of her hand. In fact, she'd just taken an exam on it last week.

"I see we got a smart ass in the bunch, huh?"

"No, sir, I'm not a smart ass. I just know the law."

"Let's wrap it up, boys." After a brief stare down with Kali, he gathered his troops. Within minutes they'd left just as fast as they came.

"Whew!" Fly exhaled. "That went a lot smoother than I imagined."

"I know, right! Usually they come through tearing the house up." Jamaica untucked the pistol from her underwear and placed it into her purse.

"They were probably exercising an arrest warrant or a fugitive warrant," Kali explained. "That's when they come looking for a person, not an object, which is considered a search warrant."

"See, it pays to have a lawyer friend." Fly laughed. "Speaking of lawyers, I need to call the guy Syn told me about." After rummaging through her purse, she found the card and called the number. The secretary told her that Mr. Lorton was in a meeting but that she could make an appointment for first thing tomorrow morning.

CHAPTER SIXTEEN

FLY

All night Fly tossed and turned in her sleep thinking about what Jamaica had shared with her. The news bothered her so much that when she finally woke up at 8:00 a.m., her stomach was in knots. When she couldn't get back to sleep, she decided to grab her gun and catch the bus over to her mother's house.

Upon her entrance, the place was dark and silent. The only evidence that someone was home was the sound of the television coming from the living room. She peeked inside and saw Jackie asleep on the couch. Fly closed the front door and walked across the hall and into her mother's bedroom. Ray was asleep on the chair in the corner with two beer bottles resting at his feet.

She closed her eyes and pulled the pistol from the pocket of Syn's hoodie she borrowed. She aimed the gun squarely at Ray's dome and prayed hard about pulling the trigger. The only thing stopping her was Braxton. She knew if she went to prison he wouldn't have anybody.

"Hope!" When she entered the kitchen, Jackie was startled to see her daughter sitting on the laminate countertop. "You scared me, girl."

"Why didn't you tell me, Momma?"

"Tell you what?" Jackie walked over to the coffeepot and started it up. "Where is Braxton? It's about time for you to bring him home."

"Why didn't you tell me he was making my brother do that nasty shit?" Fly used the back of her hands to wipe the tears from her eyes. She'd been crying in the dark while she contemplated what to do.

Jackie tried to play it off. "You know how children and their imaginations get."

"Bitch!" Fly hopped down from the counter. "He is your son!" Within an instant, she pulled her gun out and pressed it up against her mother's head.

"Oh my God!" she screamed. "What are you doing?"

"You love this nigga that much?" Fly hit her mother with the handle.

"Hope, stop it!" Jackie wanted to catch the blood dripping down her forehead, but she was too afraid to make a move. She'd never seen this look in her baby girl's eyes before, and it petrified her.

"What the fuck is going on in here?" Ray barged into the kitchen with the Louisville Slugger bat he kept near the front door.

"You fucking disgust me!" Fly turned the gun on Ray. "Of all the muthafuckas in the world why did you fuck with my baby brother?" She sniffed. "It's plenty of men out here willing to give you what you want. Why are you fucking with children?" With each word, she walked closer.

"What I do is none of your gotdamn business!" Ray bucked.

"Anything that involves Braxton is my gotdamn business." Fly forced the tip of the gun into Ray's mouth. "I should kill your black ass right now."

"Please, Hope, cut this mess out," Jackie begged. "Don't do something you'll regret."

"At least I'll be doing something instead of sitting back and letting this sick bastard hurt somebody else." Fly cocked the pistol just as her phone started ringing. She tried to ignore it, but the caller started calling back to back. "Hello?"

she asked, still holding the gun between Ray's fat lips.

"Fly, the police just picked up Syn." Jamaica had been lying across the couch reading a novel called *The Real Hoodwives of Detroit* while simultaneously watching television when the story came on.

"Is he okay?"

"Yeah, he's cool. There was a standoff in front of the Coney Island on Six Mile for a few minutes, but he gave in. They got him in the back of a police car now." Jamaica gave the play-by-play so good Fly didn't miss a beat. "This is going to be a big deal when it goes to trial. You better make sure you secure that lawyer ASAP!"

"I'm headed there now."

After placing the phone back into her pocket, Fly uncocked the pistol. "Look, I don't care what the fuck y'all got going on around here. Leave my brother alone, and we won't have any problems. I'm going to get some paperwork for you to sign, Mom. You're going to sign your rights over and give me full custody. Don't try to fight or play with me on it or, I swear to God, you're going to regret it."

With a quick glance at both Ray and her mother, Fly backed into the living room with the gun still pointed. "He's dead to y'all and y'all are dead to him!" With that final warning, she left just as quietly as she'd come. Deep down she was mad at herself for letting Ray off so easy but, in her heart of hearts, she knew she'd figure out a way to make sure he got what was coming to him.

As soon as she stepped outside, a car zoomed down the street then slammed on the brakes. After a second passed, the car reversed toward Fly. "What's up, Fly?" Eric called from the driver side window.

"What up, doe Chicago?" Fly wasn't in the mood to converse, but she didn't want to be rude.

"Where are you headed this early?"

"I'm headed to the bus stop. What about you?"

"I was headed to grab something to eat. Do you need a lift?"

She shook her head. "I'm headed out of the way, but thanks anyway."

"Hop in. I ain't got nothing but time."

Fly leaned into the window. "I need to go out to Ten Mile and Evergreen, though."

"Don't trip. I'll take you." He hit the lock on the door and Fly got in.

"Thanks for the ride. I have gas money." She began reaching into her pocket.

"Nah, your money is no good here; but can I ask a question?"

"What?" She looked at him with a raised brow.

"What you got the heat for?" He pointed to the exposed handle in the pocket of her jacket.

She shrugged. "It ain't nothing to concern yourself with."

"I mean, if we got beef just let a nigga know." Eric raised the bottom of his shirt. Although he was only trying to show her that he was packing too, he wound up exposing a tattoo that read LOYALTY with a question mark. Beneath the ink was a mess of scars. For some reason, Fly was instantly drawn to them.

"What up with your stomach?" she asked after he'd caught her staring. "Why the question mark?"

"On my eighteenth birthday, I was shot nine times and left for dead by someone I would've once died for." Eric dropped his shirt. "The funny thing is we got our loyalty tattoos together. Our motto back then was L.O.E. It stood for Loyalty Over Everything." He looked at Fly then back at the road.

"Damn, I'm sorry that happened to you. I guess it's a thin line between loyalty and hate."

"Yeah, I guess you could say that." Eric nodded. "Me and him used to hit licks back in the day. One night we hit this house that was supposed to be loaded, but all we found was five hundred dollars in a sock drawer. We laughed about that shit and said, 'Fuck it.' At least we would smoke good for the next few days. Well, on our way out the door the nigga turns and fires nine shots my way. Of course, I'm stunned, but still trying my best to beg him not to leave me there. He reached down and took the money from my pocket, then left me dying in the hallway. When I woke up, I was in the hospital, handcuffed to the bed."

"Damn." Fly shook her head.

"The shit is deep, right?" Eric peered out the window. "I spent six months in the hospital, and then I went to the county jail for two months. When I was released, the first thing I did was go back to the tattoo shop and have the question mark added to my tattoo."

"I wonder what ended up happening to your boy. You know they say karma is a bitch."

"I sent that nigga on a permanent vacation." Eric usually didn't open up to people that easily but, for some reason, he felt comfortable talking to Fly.

The remainder of the ride went just as smoothly as the beginning. Eric and Fly spent most of the drive comparing Detroit to Chicago and arguing about which city was better.

"This ain't over." Fly grabbed her purse. "Thanks for bringing me and being willing to wait for me, too. Hopefully, I won't be long." On the way over to the office, Eric had offered to wait for her while she went in to speak with the lawyer, on the condition that they grab something to eat afterward.

"Take as much time as you need." Eric cut the engine.

Before exiting the car, Fly put her gun in the glove box then checked the mirror to make sure she was on point. Eric wanted to tell her she looked flawless but he grabbed his cell phone instead. Being fresh out of prison, he didn't want to come off like he was just trying to get at her. Besides, he was best buds with her brother, and he wanted to get Q's approval before trying to make any moves on her.

With confidence, Fly walked into the small, single-dwelling law office. The place was bare, except for a receptionist desk and two chairs in the lobby.

"Hey, sweetie, can I help you?" Taylor looked up from her magazine.

"I have an appointment with Mr. Lorton."

"You're Ms. McDonald, right?" Taylor stood from her desk. Fly was surprised to see the lady dressed in a pair of spandex yoga pants and flip-flops.

"Yeah." She nodded.

"Follow me." Taylor knocked on the door behind her desk then led Fly inside. "Your morning appointment is here, Ken."

"Fly, nice to finally meet you." Kenneth Lorton stood from his chair, wearing a white T-shirt and blue jeans. "Syn has told me so much about you." Kenneth gestured for her to take a seat.

"Unfortunately, I can't say the same about you." Fly sat down in the worn faux-leather chair that had seen better days. She glanced around the room at the sports posters taped on the walls and felt more uneasy by the second. "Excuse me, Mr. Lorton, but before we start, I have two questions for you."

"Go ahead, shoot." Ken smiled.

"Where did you meet Syn, and are you really a lawyer?" Fly found it hard to believe this clown had any type of law degree.

"Of course I'm a lawyer." Kenneth looked offended. "Just because I don't wear a suit and tie or work out of a fancy office, you don't think I'm legit?" He laughed. "Oddly enough, it's for those same reasons that people like your boyfriend can even afford my services!" Kenneth learned a long time ago that most inner-city street thugs had caviar dreams on a tuna-fish budget.

"I can respect that." Fly nodded. "Now, back to my first question. How did you meet him?" She wanted to know every aspect of what she was dealing with.

"The only thing I'm allowed to say is that he handled some things for me." Kenneth leaned back in his seat.

"Speaking of which, he told me that you owed him one." Fly didn't mince words. "I'm sure you saw the trouble he got into all over the news. He needs representation."

"Lucky for him my roster is open, but I need twenty-five hundred dollars to get started."

"What part of 'owe him one' did you miss?"

"Doing someone a favor and doing something for free are two different things in my book," Kenneth scoffed. "None of the shit he gave me is worth free representation, trust me."

"So he was your dealer?" Fly frowned.

"What? No!" Ken tried to clean up the mess he'd made. "Listen, I think we got off on the wrong foot." He sighed. "Syn is my man, so I will cut you a deal."

"What are we talking?" Fly was ready for some bargaining and negotiating.

"I'll take two thousand to get started."

"Fifteen hundred and we're in business," Fly countered.

"Deal, but tell no one of the discount I am giving you."

"Sounds good." With a smile, Fly stood from the seat.

"I'll start the process, but I will need half by the weekend."

"No problem." Fly held out her hand, and Ken shook it. Although she didn't know where the hell $1,500 was going to come from, she made the deal anyway.

CHAPTER SEVENTEEN

KALI

"Welcome to Criminal Justice 201." The new, young, tattooed law professor with slicked-down hair stood in the lecture hall addressing the students in his first class at Wayne State University. "My name is Mr. Bridges, but you can call me Matt."

With everything going on, Kali had almost forgotten about her classes starting this week. When her phone buzzed to remind her, she contemplated going to the registrar's office and dropping her classes for this semester. If she took the semester off, she'd be able to put all her time and energy into what was going on with Bird's case. The more she thought about it, though, the more she came to the conclusion that it made no sense for her to skip the semester. Aside from getting Bird a lawyer, there wasn't much else she could do. She decided going to her classes would actually be a good distraction for her.

"I'd like to call you Zaddy!" a student named Theresa said with a laugh.

"Zaddy is fine too, but I don't think my girlfriend would like that," Matt replied, and the whole lecture hall erupted into laughter.

"In this class, you will learn about the art of an argument." He wrote the word "argument" on the board then underlined it. "By learning the art of an argument, you will learn how to reason with purpose, present logical information, and elucidate your evidence in such a way that your opponent's debate doesn't have a leg to stand on."

As Matt spoke, Kali's eyes rolled back into her head, and she struggled to keep them open.

"Here, take this." Ahmad leaned over and nudged Kali.

Immediately her eyes popped open. "Huh?" She yawned.

"It's Adderall. It'll help you stay awake." Ahmad Ali was known as the university's pusher. With all the college students looking to stay awake for all-night cram sessions, begging to fall asleep because the dorms were always loud, or just trying to party, his business was booming. The Arab dealer sold everything you could think of.

"No, thanks. I'm good." No matter how sleepy she was, she didn't want to develop a bad habit of taking pills. Becoming an addict was never going to be an option.

"Suit yourself." Ahmad shrugged. "But if you ever find yourself in a jam, hit me up. I deliver." He proudly produced his card. Reluctantly, Kali took it and slipped it into her pocket.

Buzzzzz. Her phone vibrated in her purse. There was no number on the caller ID, so she ignored the call. Seconds later her phone began to vibrate again. Quickly, she grabbed her stuff and headed into the hallway.

"Hello."

"You have a collect call from Bird. Press one to accept."

"Baby, are you all right?" Kali asked after pressing one.

"I could be better, but I won't complain. How are you holding up?" Bird was putting on his strongest voice, but deep down he was breaking.

"I'm okay." Kali sighed.

"Were you able to secure a lawyer?"

"Not yet but, I promise on everything, you will have one shortly." Kali had put out calls to two law offices and was waiting to hear back. Although she was discouraged, she remained hopeful that everything would pan out.

"I got some money stashed at the house. It ain't much, but it should be enough for a retainer. I'll work on getting the rest somehow. A few niggas owe me."

"Baby, we can't count on the money at the house. Whatever you had in there is gone." Kali hated to be the bearer of bad news, but she wanted Bird to know exactly what was going on in his absence.

"What do you mean, gone?" he snapped. "I had over forty thousand dollars in that bitch!"

"The same day you turned yourself in, your mother and sister came in and started ransacking the place while I was gone. When I got home, Lisa had the rental manager evict me."

"Are you sure?" Bird knew his mother and sister were capable of a lot of things, but being this underhanded was not one of them. They knew how much he needed his money, especially at a time like this.

"Would I lie about something so serious?" Kali smacked her lips, completely offended. "Anyway, I'll probably have to take a loan from somewhere, but I will figure this out."

"Just sit tight for a day or two. I'll see what's up on my end and hit you back with the plan." Bird sounded as if the weight of the world were resting on his shoulders.

"All right. I love you." Kali closed her eyes.

"I love you too!"

"Ms. Franklin, right?" Matt stepped into the hallway just as the call ended. "I don't usually come looking for students but, to my understanding, you're one of the special ones, and I need to keep my eyes on you." He made air quotes.

"Did my parents contact you?" Kali frowned. "If so, I'm not special, and I don't need supervision." Her parents had been known to contact her teachers since grade school and throw their status around so that she received special attention.

"Whoa!" Matt raised his hands in surrender. "I didn't mean anything by that. I just reviewed the grades, and you're one of the top students in my class this semester." He laughed lightly. "I like to keep an eye on the special ones because I know you will make an awesome attorney one day." He held a hand out and shook hers.

"I'm sorry; it's just been one of those days. I didn't mean to snap at you like that." Kali was embarrassed. "I have a lot going on that you wouldn't understand." She sighed.

"Try me." Matt leaned up against the wall and peered at Kali intently. Part of his teaching style was to connect with his students on a personal level.

"Have you seen the story on the news about the shooting the other night?" Kali usually didn't share her problems with strangers, but something about Matt felt comfortable.

"This is Detroit; you've got to be more specific." He laughed.

"A criminal informant was murdered," she spat.

"Oh, yeah, I caught that one." He nodded. "Did you know the guy?"

"No, but I know the person being accused of the murder. He's my boyfriend."

"No shit!" With a smirk, Matt stood up straight and folded his arms. "That's going to be a big trial. Does your boyfriend have representation?"

"Not yet. That's what I've been trying to work on, but it seems like the odds are stacked against me right now. I have no money and, without that, I'm not getting very far."

"What if I told you I would represent your boyfriend pro bono?"

Over a decade ago, Matt was the top criminal lawyer in Chicago. He'd provided services for several members of the drug cartel, as well as for plenty of crooked politicians. His name was notorious on the streets as the man who always had a plan to get his clients out of trouble. However, three years ago Matt's reign came to an abrupt end when his alcohol addiction sent him on a downward spiral. He lost his firm, his

6,000-square-foot home, and his family all at damn near the same time. The only thing Matt had left to his name was his law degree.

He checked into rehab and relocated to Michigan in a desperate attempt to start his life over. For the past year, he'd been filling in at Michigan State for a law professor who was on maternity leave. When she came back, he got the boot and ended up at Wayne State University. The local school wasn't his favorite choice; in fact, Matt had given himself a semester before quitting. He saw Kali's boyfriend's case as a great opportunity to get his name circulating in a positive light again. Like in *Charlie and the Chocolate Factory*, he felt like he had just found his golden ticket.

"Do you mean that? You would really work for free?" Kali asked cautiously.

"Yes." Matt couldn't help but chuckle to himself. Back in the day, he could name any price in the world for his services and now here he was doing charity work.

"Well, you're hired." Kali was so excited. She wasn't too sure about Matt's skill set, but he couldn't be that bad if he was qualified to teach law.

"Let's get back to class for now, but we can set aside some time this evening for a consultation." Matt walked over to the lecture hall door.

"Wait." Kali stopped. "Off the record, um, he . . ." She fumbled over her words. She wanted to be honest with him and tell him to be prepared for a fight because Bird really was guilty, but she wouldn't dare let those words leave her lips for fear that he would change his mind about taking on the case.

"Is there any evidence?" Matt knew exactly why she was stumbling over her words.

"No tape and no weapon that I know of." Kali exhaled, glad that she didn't have to verbally spill the beans.

"Then don't worry." With a smile, Matt held the door open. "It's never about what really happened. It's about who can tell the best version of it. Trust me, I'm a great storyteller." Matt winked at his new client before they reentered the classroom.

CHAPTER EIGHTEEN

JAMAICA

"One, two, three . . ." Jamaica began counting to ten. She and Braxton were playing their third round of hide-and-seek. She was the seeker. "Four, five—"

Buzzzzz. Buzzzz.

"Six. Hello?" Jamaica flopped down on the couch, grateful for the interruption. It was a much-needed break.

"Jamaica! We're not done playing hide-and-seek!" Braxton whined.

"Hi, Ma. Hold on a second." Jamaica turned her attention to Braxton. "I'm sorry, little man, but I have to take this call. I'll tell you what: you count to twenty, and then you go hide so I can look for you."

"Okay. So you still gonna play with me then?"

"Of course I am. Go in the other room and count to twenty like I said. When you get to twenty go and find the best place to hide, so it's really hard for me to find you. One, two, three, go!"

With that, Braxton took off running into the other room.

"Hello? Sorry about that, Mom."

"Where have you been? I've been calling you all day," Ms. Margie asked, sounding very agitated.

"My bad. I've been at Fly's boyfriend's house playing with Braxton. What's wrong?"

"There has been a strange black car sitting across the street off and on all day," she said as she peered through the blinds in her living room. She closed the blinds when she got paranoid that they would see her looking.

"Maybe the car is there for one of the neighbors." Jamaica knew her mother could be very paranoid at times.

"Maybe, but I get a bad feeling every time I see dat thing."

"Do you want me to come home and check it out?"

"No, you don't have to do dat. Just be careful out there and watch your back." Margie sat down on the couch and put her feet up. "Love you, Jamaica. I'll talk to you later."

"Love you too, Ma." Jamaica ended the call just as Fly walked into the apartment with Kali on her heels. Both women looked exhausted. "How did it go with the lawyer?"

"This Lorton guy is a clown, but I don't have much of a choice, so I have to use him." Fly kicked off her black and pink Nikes and sat down on the sofa beside Jamaica. "He's charging me fifteen hundred dollars to start." She sighed. "I don't know where I'm going to come up with that money, but I'll figure something out." She knew the money she made as a part-time hair salon receptionist wasn't going to cut it.

"Damn, Fly. Don't worry. We'll figure it all out," Jamaica said, trying to sound positive. "And how was your first day of classes?" Jamaica asked Kali.

"It was good. The strangest thing happened. My professor offered to represent Bird pro bono. I don't know his stats or why he agreed to do it, but I'll take whatever I can get."

"What the fuck does pro bono mean?" Jamaica hated when people used words she wasn't familiar with.

"It means he'll do the work for free," Kali explained.

Boom! Boom! The knocking on the door grabbed everyone's attention. They thought there was about to be another raid. Instead, a slip of paper was slid under the door. Kali walked over and grabbed it.

"What does it say?" Fly sat up in her seat.

"It's an eviction notice." Kali scanned through the words. "It's saying that Syn's involvement in criminal misconduct violates the lease agreement and we need to vacate the premises immediately." She handed the paper to Fly.

"Damn, y'all bitches done been kicked out twice in less than a week." Jamaica reached behind her ear and grabbed a freshly rolled blunt.

"Now what the fuck are we going to do?" Fly set the letter down on the table and picked up the lighter.

"Y'all can always stay with me and my mom." Jamaica grabbed the lighter from Fly and sparked the blunt.

"That's cool and all, but we need to be thinking long term." Kali took a seat on the thinking chair. "Now that Bird and Syn are gone we need to learn how to secure our own bag." Kali was regretting not being more independent. She had grown used to Bird always taking care of things. Now, she wanted to make her own money, so if shit ever went sideways like this again, she wasn't left twisting in the wind.

"You could always sell some ass like Jamaica." With a giggle, Fly snatched the blunt and took a hard pull.

"Fuck selling ass; we need to sell that work!" Jamaica stated as a matter of fact. "Now don't get me wrong, selling pussy pays the bill, but selling dope elevates you to a whole other level!"

"I hate to say it, but I definitely agree with what you're saying." Kali nodded. All summer she'd watched Bird make money hand over fist. Although she knew the risk that came with his profession was huge, she felt the reward was so worth it.

"Even if that were the case, we don't have no drugs to sell." Fly shook her head while passing the blunt to Kali.

"All we need to do is come up on a few dollars and buy a pack," Jamaica said, serious as a heart attack.

"Bitch, if I don't have money for a lawyer, where do you think I'm going to find money to buy some dope?" Fly rolled her eyes.

That's when it hit Kali. "Before Bird turned himself in he gave me the garbage bags they took from the undercover stash house. He said there were five pounds of heroin and five thousand dollars in cash in them. Oh my God, I can't believe I forgot about it so quickly."

"Bitch, you been sitting on all that this whole time?" Jamaica jumped to her feet. "We could've been hood rich by now," she joked.

"With so much going on I completely forgot. My bad, y'all." Kali's mind began racing.

"Let's go get the work and put that shit on the streets," Fly joined in. She was chomping at the bit to make some fast cash.

"Nah." Kali shook her head. "We can't use their drugs. That shit is probably hot or fake. But we can use their money to buy more drugs."

"The money is probably more traceable than the dope. I say we go get that shit and get it popping," Jamaica added.

"Who is going to buy from us?" Fly quizzed. "We need a team."

"Shit, with all the street hustlers we know I'm sure that won't be a problem." Dollar signs began to dance in Jamaica's eyes.

"What happened to you?" Braxton charged into the living room. He was pissed off. "I've been hiding for five hours." On cue, Jamaica, Kali, and Fly busted out laughing at his overdramatic antics.

"It was more like five minutes, but I'm sorry, little man." Jamaica tried to hug Brax, but he wasn't having it. Instead, he went and sat on Kali's lap.

"Hey, little man. Don't be so upset!" She shook him up and tickled his stomach.

"Stop!" he said through giggles and chuckling.

"Hey, Braxton. You want to watch *The Lego Batman Movie* in the other room?"

"Yeah, yeah, I wanna see it!" Braxton said as he leaped off of Kali and started jumping up and down.

"Okay, c'mon. I'll order it on the TV. Let's go," she said as she led him into the other room. She disappeared for all of thirty seconds and came back to join her friends so they could continue with their game plan.

"Is it raw or cut?" Although Fly had never dealt directly with heroin, she knew there was a significant difference between the two.

"I never even looked in the bag," Kali admitted.

"If it's raw we're screwed, unless either of you knows how to cut that shit." Jamaica looked from Fly to Kali.

"I think I got a guy who can help us," Kali said deep in thought. "Jamaica, we'll take you up on your offer to stay with you and your mom but, first, I need to go do something. In the meantime, y'all grab whatever we need from this place, and I'll meet y'all at Ms. Margie's house in a few."

"Where are you going?" Both Jamaica and Fly asked in unison.

"Church!" With a smirk, Kali tossed up the deuces and walked out. It was time to get the dope and call Ahmad.

CHAPTER NINETEEN

KALI

Just after 7:00 p.m., Kali pulled up to the church. "Fuck!" She hit the steering wheel. The entire parking lot was full, which meant there was some kind of event going on inside. She pondered coming back another time but remembered how important getting those bags was, so she parked.

Stepping from the car, Kali swung the book bag she'd brought with her over her shoulders and headed toward the door. Once inside, she walked through the church like she belonged there. Her father's voice could be heard from the sanctuary. He was talking about marriage being a sacred institution ordained by God between one man and one woman. Kali peered into the window on the door of the sanctuary and saw several couples sitting in pews and listening to the Word.

"I didn't expect to see you here tonight," a voice called from down the hall.

Kali turned to see Desmond. "And why is that?"

He was dressed to the nines in a tailored gray Italian linen suit. "Because it's couples' night, and we both know your man ain't here." He smirked.

"I'm glad you find that funny." Kali tried to bypass her old lover, but he gently grabbed her arm.

"I'm sorry. I shouldn't have said that," he mumbled. "How are you holding up?"

"I'm fine."

"That's good." Desmond nodded. "You're looking good, too." Silently he roamed every inch of her body and wished like hell she was still his.

"Thanks, Desmond, so do you." Kali glanced at him with a smile. She had no hard feelings toward her ex, really. She'd cooled off since their last conversation. In fact, she still cared for him tremendously, but she knew just as he did that they would never be together; at least, not in this lifetime.

"Maybe one day we can grab lunch or something." Right in the middle of his invitation the door to the sanctuary opened.

"There you are." A beautiful dark-skinned woman with sister locks stopped in the doorway.

"Nicole, this is Kali. Kali, this is Nicole, my fiancée." Desmond let Kali's arm go.

"It's nice to meet you, Nicole." Kali extended her hand.

"Same here." Nicole purposely avoided Kali's hand and grabbed her man's arm instead. "Come on, baby. The pastor is on fire in here."

"See you later, Kali." Desmond followed his woman back inside.

"Later." Kali laughed all the way into the mission room. Like a thief in the night, she grabbed the bags and stuffed them into her book bag. After everything was secure, she fled the church like a fugitive on the run. The last thing she needed was another run-in with her parents.

Quickly she opened the book bag and tossed the bags into her trunk. She ripped one open. "Damn!" Just like she suspected, the heroin was raw. Kali closed the trunk and got in the car. Before starting the engine, she reached into her purse and retrieved Ahmad's number.

"Hello," he answered on the third ring.

"Hey, it's Kali."

"I knew you'd be calling sooner or later." He laughed. "Just tell me what you need, and I got it."

"I need a favor. Can we meet somewhere private?"

"I'm at my family's store on the corner of Livernois and Eight Mile. Come through; I'll be waiting for you."

"See you in about twenty minutes." Kali tossed the phone onto the passenger seat then took off toward her destination.

Exactly nineteen minutes later she pulled up to the corner store and parked. She grabbed the trash bags then walked up to the store. The sign on the door said CLOSED, but Ahmad buzzed her in.

"Are we alone?" she asked.

"Yeah." He nodded. "Follow me." He walked toward the back of the store, past the chips and popcorn, and then made a left past the beer and wine. Ahmad pressed his thumb on the door panel, and it opened up. Kali wasn't sure why the corner store had a thumbprint reader, but she was sure she'd find out shortly.

"Welcome to the candy shop!" Ahmad turned on the light, and Kali gasped. The room was filled with weed plants, tables of Baggies and pills, as well as various store merchandise.

"Damn, this is impressive." Kali was used to only seeing shit like this on television.

"So, what can I do for you?"

"Are you familiar with heroin?" Kali tossed her bags at Ahmad's feet. "I need this cut."

"Holy shit!" He reached into a bag and pulled a few bricks out. "Where did you get this?"

"That's not important," Kali snapped. "Can you show me how to cut this or not?"

"Yeah, I got you, but I can't do it for free. This is going to take a few hours."

"Of course. I got you." Truth was Kali had no money to pay him, but she'd figure something out by the time he was finished.

"Okay, let's do this." Ahmad walked over to one of the empty tables and put on a pair of rubber gloves. He unwrapped the first package of heroin and grabbed a few items from another table. "I'm going to mix this with quinine and dormin," he said before putting on a pair of safety goggles.

"What is that?" Kali stood a safe enough distance from the product.

"The quinine is used for the initial rush it gives the person injecting or inhaling the blow to enhance their experience. The dormin is like a sleeping pill. The reason this was added is self-explanatory." As Ahmad worked he went on to explain that cutting heroin was a very delicate process; one small mistake could potentially destroy the entire bag. He recommended that they only mix a little bit at a time, but she told him to whip it all.

Kali watched closely and even got hands-on with the second batch. She wanted to get the formula down pat so she wouldn't need a third party next time.

Two hours later and all the work had been whipped and bagged for distribution. "Now all you have to do is put it out there." Ahmad snatched off his gloves and threw them in the trash.

"Can you help me with that? Since you showed me how to cut it and all, I'll sell it to you for a good price." Kali smiled. "I usually don't fuck with the hard stuff."

Ahmad started to say something but then thought about it for a second. "I have had a lot of requests lately; so, how much of a good price are we talking?" He knew a pound of good snow powder could go for around $15,000. He needed Kali's number to come in under that before he took the bait.

"I'll sell it to you for twelve thousand dollars a pound. If you buy two, I'll sell them for eleven thousand dollars each." The last few months Kali spent with Bird she paid a lot of attention to detail, especially when it came to money. She knew what the going rate was;

therefore, she knew Ahmad wouldn't dare turn down her offer.

Ahmad blew out a whistle. Although he wasn't prepared to drop twenty bands, he knew he couldn't afford to pass up a deal with so much profit potential. "Wait here." He walked over to the safe on the wall, used his thumbprint again, and retrieved a few stacks of money. "You know we can't both sell this at the university." Ahmad liked Kali immediately, but he wanted her to know the school was his turf.

"It's all yours." She raised her hands in surrender. In all honesty, she didn't want any part of selling heroin on campus.

"Cool." With that, Ahmad handed over the money.

Hurriedly Kali put the cash in her book bag along with the other two pounds of heroin, and she got the fuck out of dodge. She couldn't wait to tell her girls they were already $20,000 richer.

Almost as soon as she stepped outside, her phone rang. She glanced down at the screen and saw that it was Matt. "Hello."

"Hey, Kali, it's Matt. I just wanted you to know that I made a few calls and, unfortunately, I won't be able to represent your boyfriend."

"Why not?" Kali bucked.

"It's too late. He already took a plea deal."

"A what?" Kali had trouble comprehending that. "Bird would never do that."

"Well, he did." Matt sighed. "He was facing life without parole, Kali. The deal he took is for a twenty-five-year sentence."

Kali felt as if the wind had been knocked right out of her. She couldn't believe what she was hearing. "I need to see him. Can you make that happen?"

"I'll see what I can do, but no promises."

"Thank you." She dropped the phone and laid her head on the steering wheel. Her day had taken so many turns that she was beginning to feel nauseous. Just when she thought she had everything figured out, here came another curveball.

CHAPTER TWENTY

FLY

"I wonder what's going on." Fly peered out through the window as Jamaica drove down her block. There were about ten police cars and two ambulances on the block.

"Girl, anything could've happened. Just last week two guys attempted a home invasion on the neighbors down the street." Jamaica didn't live in the safest neighborhood; therefore, she wasn't too concerned with the scene. Things like this unfolded all the time.

"Girl, I think they are at your house." Fly squinted down the block. "Yeah, your door is open." She pointed.

"Shit!" Jamaica slammed on the brakes and parked the car right in the middle of the block. Without a word to Fly she jumped from the car and ran toward her house. "What happened?" she screamed. "Where is my mother?" Panic set in as Jamaica roamed the sea of faces standing on her lawn.

"Do you live here?" a female officer asked.

"Yes, I live here with my mother. Where is she?" Jamaica ducked under the crime tape and started toward the house.

"Ma'am, you can't go in there." The officer tried to stop her, but Jamaica forced her way up the stairs and toward the doorway.

"Sorry, but you can't come in here." Another officer blocked Jamaica from entering the house.

"Oh my God!" she screamed. "Momma, get up. Please get up." Jamaica went into a fit when she saw her mother lying in the entryway to the kitchen. Ms. Margie was riddled with bullet holes and covered in blood. "Is she dead?" Although she already knew the answer, she still needed someone to confirm it.

"Yes, ma'am. I'm sorry for your loss." The officer wrapped his arms around Jamaica and cradled her as best he could.

"I can't believe this," she screamed.

"That's my friend. Can I go up there?" Fly tried to catch her breath as she spoke to a female officer. Braxton was breathing heavy too. They had both run up toward the house.

"I'm sorry. I can't let you in."

"I understand." With tears, Fly watched from behind the yellow tape as her friend's world changed forever.

Shortly after the coroner came to remove the body, Kali pulled up. She stood with Fly and Brax on the lawn until the police cleared the scene and allowed them to enter the house. The hallway was covered in blood.

Jamaica was sitting on the sofa with her arms wrapped around her knees. "They said it was a drive-by."

"Do they know who did it?" Kali sat down beside her.

"Not yet, but the next-door neighbor was outside when it happened." Jamaica sniffed. "He got hit in the head with a stray, but if he makes it hopefully he'll have some information."

"I'm so sorry this happened to your mother." Fly couldn't even begin to imagine her pain.

"She called me earlier to tell me that someone in a black car had been sitting across the street all day." Jamaica looked at her friends. "Do you think they did it?"

"Maybe, but then again maybe not." Kali shrugged. "Let's let the police have a crack at it before we start jumping to conclusions."

"You're right." Jamaica wiped her face. "I need to get out of here."

"Grab some things, and we'll all go stay at a hotel." Kali knew the last place they needed to be was Jamaica's house, especially now.

"Kali, we don't have any money right now," Fly reminded her.

"Yes, we do." Kali tossed her book bag on the coffee table. "I already sold two pounds."

"How much money is this?" Fly couldn't believe her eyes.

"Twenty thousand dollars!" Kali stated as a matter of fact. "That's about $6,660 apiece." She was happy to have at least a little bit of good news on such a tragic day. "There are three pounds left. We can divvy that shit up tomorrow, but tonight let's just get a room and get some rest."

"Thank you." Jamaica sniffed. In that moment she was beyond grateful to be included in their friendship.

The next morning Fly hit the ground running. She called Eric and asked him to pick her up. Next, she kissed Braxton, who was still asleep in her hotel bed; then she peeked in on Jamaica and Kali. They were both fast asleep too. She took a shower, dressed in a red BCBG maxi dress and put her hair up in a bun. After slipping on her gold Coach sandals, she grabbed her MK bag and slipped out of the penthouse suite. Their room was at the Marriott in Southfield. The penthouse cost a pretty penny, but with their newfound wealth, none of them had an issue dropping the money.

"Good morning, gorgeous." Eric was waiting outside the door at 9:00 a.m. sharp just like he promised.

"Good morning." Fly smiled.

"Where are we headed to first?"

"I need a ride to the attorney we went to the other day, and then you can drop me off at a Buy Here Pay Here car dealership if you don't mind."

"You know I don't mind." Eric started the car, and they pulled off. "I'm actually glad you called me this morning."

"Why is that?" Fly blushed.

"Because I have a surprise for you."

"What could you possibly have for me?"

"Just wait for it." Eric looked at the time on dashboard.

"What is it?" The anticipation was killing her. At 9:15 a.m. on the nose Eric's cell rang.

"Answer that for me."

"Are you sure?" Fly hesitated.

"Yeah, hurry up," Eric urged.

"Hello."

"You have a collect call from Q. Press one to accept the call."

The minute Quinton's voice hit Fly's ears she burst into tears. He sounded so different than she remembered, but she still knew it was him.

"Q!" she screamed.

"Hope, is that you, sis?" Q smiled.

"Yeah, it's me. How have you been? I can't believe I'm talking to you," she rambled.

"I know it's been awhile, and my bad about that. I'll make sure we fix that from today on. How are Momma and Braxton?"

"Everybody is good." Fly was bursting at the seams to tell her big brother everything that was going on, but she knew better. It made no sense to give him all the bad news knowing there was nothing he could from the inside. She knew not being able to do shit about it would only torment him.

"That's good. I heard about your boy Syn. Tell that nigga to hold his head up." Q only knew about Syn through his sister's letters, but he still felt like he knew him.

"I will. Love you, bro."

"I love you too. I'll get your digits from Chicago. When I call you better pick up."

"I will, so you better call." Fly handed the phone to Eric, and they conversed for a few minutes.

"How did you know he was going to call?" she asked when their conversation was over.

"He calls me every morning at nine-fifteen a.m. That's when they let us out of lockdown." Eric saw the way she was looking at him, and he felt the need to explain further. "Behind the wall, Q became my best friend. We got each other through some very rough days. I promised that nigga I wouldn't change up when I got released. I also promised to put money on his books and accept all his calls. Real niggas do real things."

"I feel you." Fly was satisfied with the answer, so she left well enough alone. "I would do the same for my girls if I had to."

The remainder of the day went smoothly. Fly dropped the money off to Kenneth, and then Eric took her to a small dealership near the hotel. She walked the lot for probably an hour before she settled on a 1998 candy-apple red Lexus RX 350. The old car cost exactly $4,900, which was almost all she had to her name. However, she was just happy to be pushing a luxury vehicle.

After calling and getting no-fault insurance, her money dwindled to seventy-eight dollars, but she was still smiling. Fly told Eric goodbye and thanked him for the ride. She took her last bit of pocket change and stopped by one of her favorite boutiques. She wasn't able to buy anything but a fifty-dollar bodycon dress, but she didn't complain.

"What up, doe Fly!" Smoke walked into the boutique with his girlfriend as Fly was walking out. He worked for Syn and Bird.

"What up, doe my nigga." She gave her boy a hug. "Long time no see."

"How are you holding up?"

"It's rough, but I know this too shall pass." Fly shifted. "How is the crew?"

"Man, you already know it's a dog-eat-dog world out here." Smoke laughed. "Some of them niggas jumped ship the minute them cats were arrested, but it's a few of us still holding on to see what happens."

"I'm sure both Syn and Bird would appreciate the loyalty. They worked hard to assemble the team."

"I know, but niggas gotta eat, so once this last pack run out I don't know how much longer we can hold on. They was the plug, ya feel me?"

"Take my number and put yours in my phone. Syn left me with a contingency plan," Fly lied; but Smoke's team needed product, and she, Kali, and Jamaica needed a team. The only problem was she knew those guys would never willingly hustle for women. Therefore, they had to believe the product was still coming from Syn and Bird.

"All right, for sho." Smoke locked his number into Fly's phone. "Call me asap, and we can get down to business!"

CHAPTER TWENTY-ONE

JAMAICA

It took almost three weeks after Ms. Margie's private memorial service before Jamaica began to feel like her old self. In that time, she'd missed several calls from her regulars and even some of the dancers at the club. Everyone had heard about what happened to her mother and wanted to pay their respects. They still hadn't caught her mother's killer, but Jamaica knew it was only a matter of time.

"I'm glad you came out with me tonight. We had a fucking ball." She looked over at Fly, who was proudly pushing her new whip. Although Kali had given their girl a hard time about the way she spent money, Jamaica could see that Fly was unbothered. If nothing else it made her hustle harder to make sure her cash flow stayed plentiful. In fact, everyone's pockets were thicker these days.

In such a short time the heroin business was proving to be very lucrative for the women. Fly had picked up a mass clientele at the beauty shop she worked in, and Kali worked her hand through Ahmad. Jamaica, on the other hand, was slacking; but her girls understood. Therefore, they split their profits with her.

"I'm just glad to see you're feeling better, boo." Fly knew nothing could ease the hurt Jamaica was feeling, but she tried her hardest to make sure her friend had a good time.

"I wish Kali could've come out." Without Ms. Margie, the trio would no longer be able to party together because someone had to watch Braxton.

"She had to study for an exam anyway." Quickly, Fly deaded that conversation before it had Jamaica in her feelings. "I'm mad you didn't dance tonight, though."

"You weren't the only one who was mad." She laughed thinking about all the regular tippers she disappointed tonight. "At least I still worked the room and got us some new customers, though." She slapped high fives with Fly. Although this evening was more of a social occasion, Jamaica used her time out to give away sample packs of heroin to some of the dancers and regulars who, she knew, used the potent drug. Before the night was over, she had people practically begging to cop. The rapid response was so impressive that she could just about see the money rolling in.

As they came to a red light in front of a liquor store both Fly and Jamaica gasped when they saw Ray. He was just getting into his car, about to pull off. "Where is my gun?" Fly hollered.

"Fly, let's think about this for a second. We've been drinking. We don't want to do anything crazy, do we?" Jamaica immediately sobered up. She knew something big was about to go down.

"Where is the fucking gun?" This was the perfect opportunity to serve Ray the street justice they both knew he had coming.

Without another word Jamaica reached into the glove box and handed the gun to her friend. Fly stalled the car long enough for Ray to pull out in front of her and then it was on.

"What are you going to do?"

"You'll see." Fly waited for Ray to turn onto a side street and that's when she bumped the back of his car. Naturally, he pulled over and got out of the car fussing and cussing. Fly cut her engine and cocked the pistol.

"Get out of the car!" Ray slapped the hood of her car. "Are you drunk or something?"

Silently Fly opened her car door and lit Ray up like a firecracker on the Fourth of July. Pow! Pow! Pow! Both she and Jamaica watched him fall to the ground.

"I told you, you never should've fucked with my brother," she said walking closer to him. "It doesn't feel good when you're scared and helpless, does it?" Fly squatted down in front of Ray to look him in the eyes.

He began to gag and choke on his own blood. "I'm sorry." He gasped for air.

"It's too late for apologies, Ray." With no remorse, Fly pushed the gun to the side of Ray's head and pulled the trigger. Blood and brain matter exploded in her face, but it didn't bother her one bit. In that moment she felt good enough to do it again; but, as soon as she heard the police sirens blaring in the distance, reality hit her like a ton of bricks.

"Come on, we have to get out of here!" Jamaica called from the car.

Nervously, Fly ran back just as two police cars whizzed down the main street. Once the coast was clear Fly popped her trunk and grabbed the gas can she'd just bought and filled up. Her fuel gauge was broken; therefore, the indicator stayed on E. The sales rep told her to keep a gas can on deck, just in case she needed it. Little did she know she'd be needing it this soon.

"Give me a lighter." Fly stuck her head in the window, and Jamaica passed one to her. She ran back up to Ray and covered him in gas. Once the can was empty, she took the lighter and lit his shirt. Within seconds his body burst into flames. Once Fly was satisfied that she'd seen enough she sashayed back to the car feeling like Angela Bassett in the movie *Waiting to Exhale*.

CHAPTER TWENTY-TWO

KALI

It took no time at all before Ahmad was pressing Kali about getting some more heroin. She sold him the little bit she had left, but she knew that wasn't going to hold him for even a week. Between him and Smoke's crew, the product had been depleted. Kali knew what she had to do, although she damn sure didn't want to do it.

"Have a seat and keep your hands to yourself," the CO informed the group of visitors waiting to see inmates.

Kali shifted nervously in her seat. She'd never gone to jail to visit anybody, so she was a little uncomfortable.

After a few minutes of silence, a metal door in the corner opened up, and men in orange jumpsuits filed out. About fifteen men came out before Bird, who lagged behind. His hair was an uncut mess, his eyes were a mixture of yellowish red, and his belly had gone down an inch or two. He'd definitely seen better days.

"Hey, baby." Kali smiled while forcing herself to remain seated. She was so happy to see him, but the feeling didn't appear to be mutual. "What's wrong with you?" she asked after noticing the scowl on his face.

"Kali, what the fuck is going on with you?"

"Excuse me?" She was taken aback.

"You heard what the fuck I said. What the fuck is going on with you? What's this shit I'm hearing about you hustling?" Word had gotten back to him almost immediately after Fly met with Smoke. For some reason news traveled faster behind bars than it did on the street.

"What's this shit I'm hearing about you taking deals?" Kali snapped back to let him know he wasn't the only one with questions.

"That's beside the point." Bird shrugged.

"No, it's not!" Kali hit the table. A CO glanced her way but didn't say anything. "Tell me why, Bird! I think I deserve that fucking much."

"The state's attorney's office told me they were only offering a plea deal to one person." Bird peered at Kali. "It was me or Syn."

"Bird, I had found you a good lawyer. We could've fought this." Kali understood why he did what he did, but she would've preferred he take his chances.

"*We* wasn't going to fight anything." Bird shook his head. "This is my life, Kali, not yours. I had already told you what to do."

"What kind of woman would I be if I just forgot about you at the first sign of trouble?"

"A smart one," he scoffed.

"Why are you being mean?" Kali wanted to cry, but she dared not let a tear fall.

"I'm not being mean, baby. I'm being real." Bird sat up in his seat. "You're a rider now, but I'm wise enough to know that you ain't gon' stick this twenty-five-year bid out with me, baby."

"Bird—"

"Stop it, Kali. You and I both know how this is going to play out, so it's better to cut the ties now. The last thing I need to do in here is go crazy wondering why your visits and letters stop or why you quit answering my calls after a while." Bird cleared his throat. "Eventually, you're going to want to get married, have kids, and build a life with somebody, and twenty-five years is an awfully long time to wait to do it."

"So what now?" Kali used the back of her hand to wipe at her eyes. She knew Bird was telling the truth, but she couldn't imagine being out of his life for good. She knew that, although he talked that big-boy talk, he would need her now more than ever, especially since his mother and sister weren't dependable.

"Can we at least be friends?" She looked up to see Bird's eyes water.

"I'd love that."

"Me too." Kali gave a halfhearted smile. "Well, as your friend, I'll make sure money stays on your books. I'll write letters as often as I can, and I'll answer every collect call."

"They'll be moving me in a week or so to Jackson State Prison. I'll hit you up when I get where I am going and give you the info."

"Cool." She nodded.

"So, back to what I was saying earlier: is any of what I'm hearing true? Are you out there hustling?" Bird whispered.

"I am." Kali shook her head and watched Bird's expression change.

"Kali—"

"Bird, you are not my daddy, or my man any-more for that matter. I respect your opinion, but I no longer have to listen to it. I'm doing what I have to do to get on my feet. This whole situation taught me to stop depending on people for everything. For once in my life, I need to be my own lifeline."

"I understand," Bird relented. Although he didn't like it one bit, he knew there was not a damn thing he could do about it. "I hear y'all doing pretty good for yourselves. Who's the plug?" Bird needed to be sure she wasn't working with any snakes.

"That's the thing I came to talk to you about." Kali paused. "We sold everything that was in the bags you left me. We have run out. We need to re-up, so I came to ask who your connect was." She knew she was asking for a lot, but she prayed Bird wouldn't give her a hard time about giving her the information.

"I can't give you that, Kali." He shook his head adamantly.

"Why not?" Kali smacked her lips just as the guard hollered that time was almost up for visiting.

"Because you're not ready for that information."

"Bird, I will make sure we break you off a percent of every dollar we make," Kali tried to bargain.

"It's not about the money."

"Then what is it?" Kali was growing more irritated by the second.

"Time's up," the CO yelled, and Bird stood.

"Who is it, Bird?" Kali stood up with him, insistent on getting an answer.

"I can't." He tried to back away, but Kali grabbed his sleeve. "You don't really want to know."

"Please," she begged.

Seconds felt like hours as he stared into her eyes, and then he gave in. "Kali, it's your father," he whispered.

"What?" she hissed. "Have you lost your fucking mind? Please tell me you're kidding."

"Your pops has been my connect for years. He and I always talked, but we didn't know each other personally until you introduced us. I swear." Bird knew the bomb he'd just dropped was heavy. He felt bad for keeping such a secret and for dropping it on her like that.

"Not my daddy. You can't be fucking serious!"

"I told you, you weren't ready for that kind of information." With those words, he walked away, and Kali fell back into her chair completely flabbergasted.

How could the good bishop also be the drug connect? She felt like she had no idea who her father was. She couldn't believe that he had been leading a double life like that. And, all this time, he would speak to her with such disdain for and disapproval of her drug-dealing boyfriend, when he was the one supplying him. The hypocrisy of it all made her blood boil. She had a lot of questions for her father, and Kali was now hell-bent on getting them.

***

Kali looked for parking in her father's church parking lot. It was a beautiful Sunday morning, and church was in service. She decided to park in an empty handicapped spot in the front. She could hear the church choir singing their hearts out as she walked toward the sanctuary. She let herself in through the double doors and proceeded to walk down the aisle and straight to where her father was seated at the pulpit.

He stood up when he saw her walking. "Praise Jesus! My daughter has returned home!" he exclaimed as he raised his arms and looked up. "I tell you, church, God is good!"

The entire church erupted in praise. All through the sanctuary, you could hear "amens" and "hallelujahs" from the congregation.

Bishop Franklin walked toward his daughter and embraced her. "I'm glad you are here, child. I've been waiting on God's promises to bring you back." He leaned in and tenderly kissed his daughter on the forehead.

"Oh, yeah? Did God also promise to never let you get caught supplying drugs to your people?" Kali got straight to the point. She saw her father's face turn pale, and the smile he was proudly wearing quickly disappeared.

He looked around to see if anyone had been within earshot of what she had just asked him. "Let's talk about this after service," he said to his daughter as he looked into her eyes.

"No, we're gonna talk about this now, or I will expose you in front of everyone, Father. For years, I have had to deal with your and Mom's constant judgment of my life. You have made me feel so guilty about who my heart chose to love and, all this time, you were no better than him."

"Kali, let me explain. Let's go back to my office, and we will talk right now." Bishop tried to usher his daughter so they could exit through the back of the stage. He hurriedly asked one of the leaders to take over the service for him.

When the father and daughter were finally in the office, the tension could be cut with a knife. Bishop Franklin was the first to break the ice. "I'm sorry."

"Sorry about what exactly? Sorry for lying to me all of these years? Sorry for making me feel guilty about my life choices? Sorry for you and Mom always judging me? I'm going to need you to be a little more specific."

"I'm sorry about everything." Bishop took a deep breath and sat in his chair. "I never thought you'd find out. I never wanted you to find out."

"Well, I did, Dad. I know all about you being Bird's supplier. He told me how you've been his supplier for years."

"Yes, I am his supplier. I got into the business long before you were born. I made good connections with some people in Colombia, and I have been working with them ever since. Somewhere along the line, I found God; and, although I changed a lot of things in my life, I never was able to walk away from the drug game. I decided I'd just be a silent supplier. I met Bird's mentor and began selling to him. When he was killed, Bird took over his position, and that's when I became his supplier."

Kali was listening to everything her father was saying, but she still didn't understand why her father had been so mean about her relationship with Bird. He had been against them from the very beginning. "Okay, I get all that, Daddy, but why have you always been so cold about me being with him?"

"Because I never wanted my baby girl to end up with a drug dealer. Your mother and I gave you a good life. You had a great upbringing and never needed for anything. For you to end up with a drug dealer was a slap in the face."

"But I fell in love with him! You can't help who you love. I know you know that, Daddy," Kali tried reasoning with her father.

"Yes, I understand that now," Bishop Franklin said as he lovingly looked at his daughter.

"I'm glad you do. And I also need you to understand that I will now be taking over Bird's position."

"Absolutely not! No daughter of mine is going to be a drug dealer hustling on the streets." Bishop Franklin practically jumped out of his chair and slammed his hands on the desk.

"This is not up for negotiation. I am taking over Bird's position, and you are going to be my supplier, or I will expose you to your congregation," Kali said as she took out her cell phone, to show her father that she had been recording their entire conversation. "I'm sorry, but a girl's got to do what a girl's got to do and, right now, I need to make sure I get my money up so I can figure out my next moves."

"Kali, I don't think you know what you're getting yourself into," Bishop tried to school his daughter. "When you get into this business, you will be stabbed and double-crossed. You have to be on the constant lookout because you never know when someone will come after you. People you think you can trust will turn their backs on you. Friends will become enemies."

"Oh, I'm good on that. My friends would never turn against me. Me and my girls are in this together," Kali assured her father.

"For your sake, I hope to God you are right," was all Bishop Franklin could say.

"Trust me, Daddy, I'll be fine. I'll let you know when I need to place an order." With that said, Kali stopped recording and walked out of her father's office.

EPILOGUE

KALI

Five Years Later

"Are you sure you're ready to leave the game, sis?" Jamaica's soft, sensual voice asked on the other end of the phone. She was smacking hard on a piece of Winterfresh gum. Although it was an old classic, it was still her favorite.

"Yeah, I'm done. So much shit has happened in so little time that my head is spinning!" Kali looked at her reflection in the rearview mirror. She still looked good, but she'd aged tremendously in the past few years. At twenty-six years old, she shouldn't have had wrinkles in her forehead, or gray strands of hair. Yet there they were. "This shit ain't for me, Jamaica. It never was." She sighed hard thinking about how she'd gone from being an innocent church girl to the cocaine and heroin queen.

"What about the money?" Jamaica pressed.

"What about it?" As much as she enjoyed the financial stability, she hated all the bullshit that came with every dirty fucking dollar.

"Whatever!" Jamaica smacked her MAC-glossed lips.

"For real, J. Fuck the money, fuck the fame, and fuck the haters. I told you I'm done with that shit." Kali laughed.

"But you're so fucking good at hustling!" Jamaica paused. "Besides, Kali, we're a team. What about me and Fly? Are you really going to leave us twisting in the wind like that?"

"It ain't about leaving you twisting in the wind," Kali said. "I need to do this for me. It's time to move on, J. I can't stay young and dumb forever. Let me grow up."

"I feel all of that, believe me, I do, but what about us?" Jamaica continued as if she hadn't heard a thing Kali was saying.

"Y'all bitches need to grow up too."

"I don't know if you noticed, sis, but I'm grown as hell." Jamaica laughed to lighten the mood, but she was dead-ass serious. She didn't need another bitch to validate her level of maturity, not even her girl Kali.

"Bitch, I know you're grown, but growing up is something different." Kali rolled her cat-shaped eyes as if Jamaica could see them. "You need to stop worrying about your hair, getting your nails done, buying new bags, and clothes, and start worrying about shit like real estate, retirement plans, stocks, and bonds." For the last couple of years, Kali had been investing her street dividends wisely, and she'd encouraged her girls to do the same. She doubted they were listening, though. All they cared about was staying fly and flashy.

"Look, Kali, I ain't really in the mood for the speeches and shit. All I need to know is can me and Fly at least get the plug's info?"

"J, I already told you my connect doesn't want to deal with anybody but me. If I'm out, then my plug is too." Kali was getting frustrated with having to go into this much detail on the phone, especially because she knew Jamaica knew better.

"I understand that's your plug, but we are supposed to be a team; or, at least, that's what I thought." Jamaica paused then tried to redirect the conversation. The last thing she wanted to do was piss Kali off when so much was at stake. "Look, sis, just hear me out. I've been in the fucking game way too long to be starting back at square one. This thing we got going is too smooth to stop now. I don't want to get in bed with nobody else."

"J, I'm out," Kali repeated.

"Sis, you don't even have to get your hands dirty, I promise. Just keep hooking me and Fly up and you can keep like ten percent of the profit." Jamaica wasn't taking no for an answer. "Think about it, Kali, you'll be making money without having to do anything."

"J, I appreciate what you're saying, but I'm done. End of story!"

Jamaica was pissed. After everything they'd been through, she felt it was messed up of Kali to just walk away and not even be willing to let her and Fly keep the business going. "Well, can you at least get one more order to hold us over until we find someone else?" she asked grudgingly.

"Hold on, girl, let me get this call." Kali put Jamaica on hold then clicked over. The call was just in the nick of time.

"Hello? Hello?" she repeated in an aggravated tone when there was no answer. Someone had been calling her private phone for the past two weeks, and it was starting to get on her last nerve. "Stop playing on the gotdamn phone!" she hollered before clicking back over to Jamaica. "Sorry about that, girl."

"Still getting them prank calls, huh?" Jamaica said after noticing the irritation in Kali's voice.

"Hell, yeah, and the shit is annoying." Kali smacked her nude matte-painted lips before pulling up in front of a two-story brick home resting in the center of a cul-de-sac.

"I would've been changed the fucking number if I were you," Jamaica stated as a matter of fact.

"I ain't got time for all that shit." Just as Kali started her sentence the phone beeped again. This time Kali clicked over without a word to Jamaica. "Stop playing on this muthafucking phone before I find your ass and make you regret it." Lately, she'd been trying to turn over a new leaf, but every now and again the hood side of her came out to play.

"You're a dead bitch!" The computerized voice sounded like one from a scary movie.

"What?" Kali was alarmed. Within the past two weeks the caller had never uttered a word, and now the motherfucker was bold enough to toss threats.

"Count your days, bitch! Your time is coming!" Click!

For a second, Kali held the phone in silence until it rang again. "Hello." This time she answered cautiously.

"Why did you hang up on me?" Jamaica asked.

"Some crazy shit just popped off, J, but I'm good. Let me hit you right back." Kali needed to get her bearings before she got out of the simple but clean 2017 burgundy Lincoln MKX.

"You don't sound good, sis. Do you need me to draw down on a bitch or something?" Jamaica was always down for whatever, which often proved to be a gift and a curse.

"Nah, sis. I'm good. Let me go in here and holler at Fly real quick. I'll hit you back later."

"I've been calling that bitch all day, and she ain't answered none of my calls. I see how it is." Jamaica was in her feelings. "Anyway, I'm one call away, B. Hit my line if you need me." She was using her New York accent, and Kali laughed. Although her friend had lived in Detroit for the past fifteen years, her New York swag sometimes came out. Lately, she'd been

consistently wearing Tims, saying things like
"dead ass," and calling niggas "son." It amused
Kali for the most part, but sometimes Jamaica
was too much.

"Thanks, J. I'll holla back shortly." Kali placed
the phone into her purse, grabbed the navy blue
duffle off the passenger seat, and got out of the
car.

"Are you coming in or what? I can't keep
standing here all night, Kali. I have to get back
to the phone," Fly hollered, anxious, from the
porch of her four-bedroom house. She saw
when Kali pulled up and had been waiting on
the porch for her to come in. She was pacing
back and forth like a crackhead and puffing on
a Newport cigarette like it was going out of style.

"You look like a fiend," Kali joked, trying to
lighten Fly's spirits.

"Bet I'm the freshest fiend you know, though,"
Fly said halfheartedly. As usual, she was dressed
to the nines in the latest Victoria's Secret Pink
spandex outfit. Diamonds were dripping from
her ears, neck, and wrist, and her hair was spiral
curled to death! Even on her worst day, like
today, Fly somehow managed to look good.

"Shut up," Kali said. "When did you start doing
that shit again?" She pointed at the cancer stick

before giving her friend a much-needed tight hug.

"I started back today. This bullshit got me stressing, girl." Fly flicked the butt of her cigarette into the flower bed filled with pink daylilies. Together she and Kali headed inside the house. "I can't believe these niggas violated me like this."

"What time did it happen?" Kali asked while closing and locking the wooden door with colored stained-glass panes.

Fly's house was hooked all the way up. In addition to the stylish brown, cream, and gold décor, there was a movie theater in her basement and a large fish tank in the wall separating the kitchen from the dining room. Although she wasn't much of a chef, she loved to entertain her friends with lavish dinner parties, card parties, movie nights, and karaoke.

"It had to have happened sometime between last night and this morning." Fly walked across the large living room toward the brown oversized leather sectional, and she took a seat. Kali followed, inhaling the scent of jasmine and vanilla that filled the air from the incense burning on the table.

"Did you notice anything strange before you went to bed? Was anybody parked on the block?"

"No." Fly shook her head while replaying last night's events. "I picked Braxton up from school around four thirty, and I took him out for dinner. When we got home, he did his homework and showered, and we decided to watch an episode of *Nightwatch*. As soon as it went off, he said he was tired, so we said good night. He went into his room, and I went into mine. When I got up this morning, I made breakfast like I always do on Saturday. I never have to call Braxton because he always smells the bacon." She laughed with watery eyes.

"After I fixed our plates, I went to see why he hadn't gotten up, but he was gone." Fly blinked back a few tears. "They left this shit on his bed." She handed Kali the handwritten note that she'd found on her little brother's bed.

Although Fly had already told her about the ransom note over the phone, Kali still read the message aloud with tears in her eyes. "'One hundred thousand dollars or he's dead!'" Ten-year-old Braxton was like her brother too. She couldn't believe someone had kidnapped him. "Were any of the doors or windows unlocked?" Kali went into detective mode.

"No. The alarm was set, too!" Fly had been racking her brain for the past few hours thinking about how the fuck someone could do her like this. Anybody who knew her knew how much she loved her little brother. He was more of a son than a brother; she had practically raised him. "I swear to God whoever did this is dead!" She hit the couch.

"Did they leave a number?" Kali studied the paper to see if there was anything familiar about the writing that stood out.

"Nah." Fly shook her head, causing her mess of curls to shake wildly. "I've been by the house phone and my cell phone all day." She paused briefly then began to cry uncontrollably. "Man, they better not hurt him, Kali. They better not touch a fucking hair on his head!"

"We will get him back, I swear." Kali nodded. "I'll be right here with you until they call," she assured her bestie.

"Even when they call, I ain't got the money. You know I don't be saving my shit like that." As the severity of the situation set in, Fly began to get more anxious and nervous. Although she'd made good money in the streets the last five years, she wasn't as smart as she should've been with her finances. Fly spent money just as fast as she got it. Her vices were name-brand clothes, designer shoes and bags, and expensive cars, all of which were the reason her nickname was Fly; baby girl stayed fly.

"I got you, sis." Kali slid the duffle bag she was carrying across the couch and watched her friend open it.

"I can't take your money." Fly was amazed by the amount of dollar bills neatly stacked in the bag, but she was even more amazed that her friend would so easily share her earnings. In the ghetto, where they'd come from, a dollar was hard to come by and even harder to part with.

"Braxton belongs to both of us. I got you." Kali put the bag on the table next to the incense that was beginning to burn out, and she moved closer to her friend. "I got you," she repeated.

"I know you do, K, and I really appreciate you but—"

"No buts. I got you."

"When I get this situation taken care of I'll get this back to you, I swear." Fly wiped her runny nose with the back of her hand.

"We'll discuss that later but, for now, let's wait on this call." As Kali spoke, both women looked down at the two phones resting on the gold coffee table in front of them.

Seconds turned into minutes and, before either of them knew it, three hours had passed.

"What's next for you, Kali?" Fly asked.

"What do you mean?" Kali was in the kitchen raiding the refrigerator. So far, her search had turned up nothing but a bottle of vodka, a few bottles of water, a half-eaten sub, and a few condiment containers.

"I mean, since you're retiring and all, what's the plan? Are you going to travel? Are you going to finish working on your law degree? Are you going to get married and have babies?"

"Girl, you know I'm not getting married or having babies until my man gets out." Kali closed the refrigerator and returned to the couch. "Five more years and I will be married, barefoot, and pregnant, which is why I need to get out of the game now. I don't want to be caught up in nothing illegal by the time Bird gets out."

Just the thought of Bird getting out and them being able to get married made Kali's heart skip a beat. She was so glad that she had decided to stay in school that semester and met Matt. With his help, they had been able to appeal his case and get his sentence reduced to ten years. Now, five years into his bid, Bird was at the halfway point. He had been doing very well on the inside. He'd been taking business courses and had plans to start his own construction business when he got out.

"Yeah, yeah, I know you want to be on the straight and narrow with your Goody Two-shoes behind." Fly rolled her eyes. "But that still doesn't answer my question. What are you gonna do in the five years until he gets out?"

"I'm going to get the hell out of Detroit, go back to school, and get my law degree," Kali answered in a matter-of-fact tone.

"Okay, good. Just in case me or Jamaica get caught up in some shit, it's good to know we will have you to save our asses!" The two girls busted out laughing.

"Once we get Braxton back, y'all could come with me. We can just pick a city and start over." Kali's eyes lit up at the thought.

"Detroit is home. There ain't no other place for me." With a smirk, Fly lifted up her shirt to expose the tattoo of the city on her side.

"What has Detroit brought us besides pain, tears, and heartache?"

"Money, power, and respect!" With a yawn, Fly closed her eyes.

Kali wanted to rebut that, but she decided to remain silent. She knew her girl hadn't slept much the night before and needed to get some rest. She grabbed her phone and started surfing the Web. Before she knew it, sleep had found her too.

Boom! Boom! Boom!

The banging noise snapped Kali from her slumber. She looked at the time on her phone and yawned. "Damn, it's almost midnight."

Boom! Boom! The knocking started again. Kali jumped up and wiped her eyes. Fly was on the other end of the sofa, snoring. Boom! Boom! As the banging continued, Kali ran to the door and opened it without so much as peering through the peephole. She never did anything that stupid, but she thought it could've been Braxton.

"Hit the safe, bitch, and nobody gets hurt!" a masked man said with his gun pointed at Kali's chest as another masked person in oversized pants and a hoodie followed him.

"What the fuck is this?" she screamed as the man pushed her back into the house. The second gunman followed silently.

"You already know what it is!" the boy yelled. "Like I said, hit the safe and nobody gets hurt."

"You got the wrong house. Ain't no safe in here, man." Kali shook her head.

"Stop fucking playing!" he shouted before sending a jab at Kali's face. She winced in pain but continued trying to deter him.

"Don't do this. This ain't what you want," she mumbled before spitting blood onto the floor. Her lip was busted from the hit.

"Wake that bitch up," the man directed his accomplice. Without a word, the other person shook Fly violently until she opened her eyes.

"What the fuck is going on?" she asked, trying to fully assess the situation.

"We came for the money and the dope. Crack the safe!" he demanded.

"There is no money, no safe, and no dope!" Fly declared. "You got the wrong house, my nigga."

"I see now y'all bitches like to play games."

"I swear to God there ain't no dope or money in here." Fly raised her right hand toward the sky. She never kept dope in the house, and her money was gone just as fast as she received it; therefore, she was 100 percent sure they wouldn't find any money.

"Shut the fuck up!" the gunman hollered at Fly. "Go check the crib." He pointed at the other gunman. "Turn over every mattress and pull everything out of all the closets."

The room remained silent as the second intruder rummaged through the house for nearly twenty minutes.

"Did you find anything?" the gunman asked his flunky, who had returned to the living room. When the person shook their head, both Kali and Fly felt a sense of relief. However, the feeling was short-lived when the gunman noticed the duffle bag on the coffee table. After a quick glance inside he smiled widely. "Thought there was no money in here," he said to Fly.

"That's for—" she tried to explain but, before she could finish her sentence, the gunman hit her repeatedly on the head with the butt of his gun. Kali screamed in utter shock as she watched the man hit her friend like that. She heard a cracking sound as the metal connected with the side of her friend's head. She felt helpless as she watched her best friend fall from the couch onto the floor. Within seconds blood was staining the entire area rug beneath the coffee table.

"Please, just take the money and run!" Kali screamed. "I need to call an ambulance. She is badly hurt!" she cried.

"Where is the rest of it? I know there is plenty more where this came from."

"Please, just take that money and get the fuck on. She needs help!" Kali couldn't believe what was going on. "Please, please, just leave!" she screamed again and made a move toward Fly.

"Leave her be or I will pump you with bullet holes, bitch!"

"Do what you have to do then. It is what it is." Kali tried to sniff the snot running down her face. "I won't just sit here and watch her bleed out!" The way she saw it, she was damned if she listened to the gunman or damned if she didn't, so fuck it; she was going to try to help her friend.

She knelt at her friend's side. "Come on, Fly, don't do this to me." She turned her best friend over in the hope of getting her to regain consciousness. Her head and face had been hit pretty hard, though. She had swelling, and she was bleeding profusely.

"I said leave her be!" the gunman yelled, but Kali had no fucks to give.

"And I said it is what it is!" she spat. "We're here now; there ain't no turning back, so do what you have to do!"

"Where is the rest of the money? Where is the dope?" the gunman asked.

"Nigga, there's a hundred thousand dollars in that bag! Just take it and get the fuck on," Kali cried.

"A hundred thousand is cool but I know there is more and I ain't leaving until I get it." The gunman laughed.

"I don't have anything else to give you," Kali mumbled with tears rolling down her face. "Just kill me, nigga!" Kali stood up to get in the gunman's face. At this point, she felt she had nothing else to lose.

"You sure you ready to die just like that, Kali?" She heard a familiar voice come from the other gunman, causing the hairs on the back of Kali's neck to stand straight up. She turned to face the direction the voice came from.

"Really?" Kali said while gasping for air. "It's been you this whole time?

"Yup. I told you your time was coming."

"Oh my God." Kali was still in disbelief of who was behind all of this. "That was you calling me all those times? Why are you doing this?"

"Because you're a selfish-ass bitch, that's why!" Jamaica screamed as she took off her mask.

"Selfish? What the hell are you talking about? I been there for you through everything since we became friends. I've shared the business with you. I've laughed and I've cried with you. I thought we were like sisters." Kalie couldn't believe what she was hearing. She felt angry, hurt, and confused all at the same time.

"See, and that's exactly what I'm talking about. It's always 'I, I, I' with you." Jamaica started pacing back and forth while aiming her gun at Kali. "'I want to get out of the business. I want to move on with my life. I want to do better.'" Jamaica twirled her hair with her free hand and tried to sound like a spoiled valley girl.

"So, all this time, you were just pretending to be my friend? What about Fly? Were you pretending to be her friend too? You just stood there and watched this other nigga bash her head in like that."

"Let's get shit straight here. I never pretended to be nothing. I always keep it real. I was a ride or die for you and Fly but I got tired of always being the third wheel around y'all two. I got tired of you walking around like you're so much better and smarter than everybody and Fly walking around like she's the hottest bitch in Detroit."

"Jamaica, I wish I knew what the hell you were talking about because we never left you out of anything. We do everything together. It's been just the three of us for years."

"Yeah, okay. That's why you two have been hanging out all day today, and she hasn't been taking my calls, right? For all I know you two are making plans on having her get in touch with the connect and cutting me out, and that ain't gonna happen on my watch. I ain't going back to stripping and selling pussy to survive and pay for my shit."

"Jamaica, it's not like that at all, though. It's never been like that," Kali tried hard to convince her so-called friend.

Just then, Fly seemed to be waking up and began moaning. "We need to get her some help." Kali looked over at Jamaica and over at the first gunman, who had taken a seat in the living room and was watching the conversation unfold.

"No, you ain't gonna sit here and bark out orders at me! I'm in charge here."

"Okay, so what are you going to do, let our friend just lie here and bleed out? That's messed up, Jamaica."

"You know what? Fuck you, Kali! Fuck you and fuck Fly! I'm done with this shit." Jamaica raised the 9 mm handgun and pointed it right at Kali. She pulled the trigger, and two bullets ripped through Kali's shoulder and hand like hot shards of glass. Kali screamed out in pain while falling down to the floor beside her friend. She watched as Jamaica stepped over Fly and aimed the gun right at Fly's stomach.

"Please don't do this," Kali begged for her friend's life.

"It's too late, Kali. You can't save her now," Jamaica said before firing.

Bop! Bop! Bop! Three shots rang out and then the house went silent. Jamaica instructed the gunman to grab the duffle bag and wait for her outside. Then she walked over to where Fly kept her liquor bottles. She threw a bottle to the floor, pulled out a pack of matches, and struck two of them.

Jamaica leaned over Kali. "Don't worry, I'll take care of Braxton. Both of you bitches can burn in hell!" With those final words, she tossed the matches onto the puddle of liquor and set it ablaze. She ran out of there as fast as she could.

Kali blinked rapidly, trying to get her bearings. She grabbed on to her friend's body and tried to muster all the strength she needed to pull herself up. However, the more she tried, the more her body seemed not to cooperate.

"Fuck!" she spat, not wanting to believe her story would end here, especially like this. She began coughing as the room filled with smoke.

She wasn't ready to die, but God must've had other planso.

She prayed that God would watch over Braxton and Bird. She asked God to make sure they would both move on with their lives and be happy. She closed her eyes and felt the heat from the flames take over her body just as everything faded to black.

The End